THE WEAVER AND THE WITCH QUEEN

"Intimate and sweeping, richly detailed and propulsive, tragic and uplifting, *The Weaver and the Witch Queen* proves Genevieve Gornichec really can do it all."

—Vaishnavi Patel, *New York Times* bestselling author of *Kaikeyi*

"Gornichec is a masterful storyteller, crafting remarkable characters full of bravery and heart, a rich world, and the intimate and unbreakable bonds of sisterhood and love."

—Sue Lynn Tan, bestselling author of *Daughter of the Moon Goddess*.

"The women will do everything in their power to find their blood-sworn sister, and Gornichec carefully weaves multiple storylines full of political upheaval, romance, and self-discovery into their quest.... There's plenty to enjoy in this lush, Norse mythology–infused world. Fans of *Circe* and *The Book of Gothel* will be especially enchanted."   —*Publishers Weekly*

"Gornichec showcases her knowledge of Icelandic folklore and history, while her storytelling reveals the complex and engrossing lives and emotions of her characters."   —*Library Journal*

"From the moment I picked up *The Weaver and the Witch Queen*, I was enthralled. This is a rich, magical reimagining of Viking history, with all the bloodshed, tragedy, and tangled webs of fate required of any great epic—but it is above all a gloriously woven tapestry of love, loyalty, and the extraordinary bonds of sisterhood."

—Sangu Mandanna, national bestselling
author of *The Very Secret Society of Irregular Witches*

"Gornichec presents a page-turner that gives readers a look into prejudices and what one can see when looking past them. It's a lesson in knowing someone truly to the core, creating bonds that cannot be broken. Friendship, love, power, and resilience reign in this historical fantasy full of witches, Vikings, raids, and braids."   —*Booklist*

"Entwines impeccable storytelling, fascinating historical detail, and characters so nuanced and mercilessly human that I fell for every one of them and still can't let them go. Give me everything Gornichec writes—I will devour it."   —H.M. Long, author of *Hall of Smoke*

"A saga of blood and magic and hardship that explores what we owe to those we love—and what it costs to actually pay that debt."   —*BookPage*

"Beautifully woven and achingly human . . . a masterful tale about sisterhood, destiny, and what we're willing to do for the people we love. Gunnhild['s] and Oddny's journeys cut to the heart of what it feels like to be right and wrong, together and alone, bold and afraid, all at once. I loved it."   —Allison Epstein, author of *Let the Dead Bury the Dead*

"They say your second book is the hardest one to write, but Genevieve Gornichec—leaning on her Norse mythology love yet again, as with debut *The Witch's Heart*—performs a magic hat trick with her sophomore novel. . . . The ingredients are there for a heroine's journey, and the result is a delicious Christmas pudding—crunchy, sweet, rich, and a little bit hot once you set it on fire."   —The Associated Press

"Gornichec's book takes the scant details about the historical Gunnhild's life—her author's note has some helpful details about which specific sagas her story draws from—and spins them into a rich and magical tale of sisterhood and survival, revenge and sacrifice, with a satisfying dollop of enemies-to-lovers romance and trans representation on top. The historical world she constructs is rich and vivid, full of the sort of lived-in, careful details that make the setting come alive on the page."   —Paste

"A breathtaking saga of a novel that brims with page-turning tension and wit, impeccable historical and cultural detail, and heroines [who] are at once fierce and complex but also full of true heart and soul."
—Olesya Salnikova Gilmore, author of *The Witch and the Tsar*

"Filled with sea voyages, political intrigue, surprise betrayals, and tender love, this historical fantasy will thrill readers and capture their hearts."
—Shelf Awareness

ALSO BY GENEVIEVE GORNICHEC

The Witch's Heart

The
WEAVER
and the
WITCH
QUEEN

GENEVIEVE GORNICHEC

Ace
New York

ACE
Published by Berkley
An imprint of Penguin Random House LLC
penguinrandomhouse.com

ISBN: 9780593438251

The Library of Congress has cataloged the Ace hardcover edition of this book as follows:

Names: Gornichec, Genevieve, author.
Title: The weaver and the witch queen / Genevieve Gornichec.
Description: New York : Ace, 2023.
Identifiers: LCCN 2023016607 (print) | LCCN 2023016608 (ebook) |
ISBN 9780593438244 (hardcover) | ISBN 9780593438268 (ebook)
Subjects: LCSH: Norway—History—1030-1397—Fiction. |
Prophecies—Fiction. | Magic—Fiction. | LCGFT: Novels.
Classification: LCC PS3607.O5979 W43 2023 (print) | LCC PS3607.O5979 (ebook) |
DDC 813/.6—dc23/eng/20230410
LC record available at https://lccn.loc.gov/2023016607
LC ebook record available at https://lccn.loc.gov/2023016608

Ace hardcover edition / July 2023
Ace trade paperback edition / June 2024

Printed in the United States of America
1st Printing

Interior art: Textured borders © cepera / Shutterstock
Book design by Alison Cnockaert

For the friends who walk beside us,
and the ones who take another path

The
WEAVER
and the
WITCH
QUEEN

PART I

EARLY 900s CE, NORWAY

1

A HORN SOUNDED ACROSS the water in two short bursts.

Upon hearing it, Gunnhild Ozurardottir dropped her spindle and distaff and ran, ignoring the admonishments of the serving women she'd been spinning with under the awning. They would scold her later, but she cared little.

Her friends were about to arrive. And at such times she found it hard to care about anything else.

Gunnhild rounded the corner of the longhouse and sprinted up the hill, making for her father's watchman on the eastern side of the island. He was stationed on a small platform overlooking the water and always had a blowing horn on hand.

"One ship!" he called over his shoulder at the other men milling about, not noticing as Gunnhild hiked up her dress and scrambled up the platform's short ladder. "It's Ketil's!"

Before he could protest, Gunnhild grabbed the horn off its peg and blew it twice. As she lowered it she heard noises of disappointment coming from the children on the incoming ship, and she pumped a fist in victory. "Yes!"

"Oi!" the man said, snatching the horn from her. "That's only for emergencies!"

"This *is* an emergency," Gunnhild replied with gravity. She pointed to a dark shape in the water. "As soon as they pass that big rock in the bay, they blow the horn. And if I don't respond before they dock, I owe them a trinket. Two blasts for 'hello,' three for 'goodbye.'"

"Aren't you a little old for games, girl?"

"Not when I know I can win!" With that, Gunnhild scampered back down the ladder and ran for the shore, leaving the watchman shaking his head.

As she approached, Gunnhild could see Ketil and his son, Vestein, tying up their ship at the rickety wooden dock. Three other people disembarked: Ketil's wife, Yrsa, and their daughters, Oddny and Signy, whom Gunnhild practically tackled in a hug. Sighing and shifting the bedroll in her arms, Signy rummaged in her rucksack and handed over a single glass bead, which Gunnhild snatched up with an air of triumph and stuffed into the pouch at her belt.

At twelve years old, Gunnhild was exactly between the sisters in age— Signy a winter older, Oddny a winter younger—and the girls rarely got to see one another except at gatherings, which made this day even sweeter.

"You're too fast," Signy complained as Gunnhild threw an arm around each of her friends and herded them up the hill toward her father's hall.

"Or maybe you're not fast *enough*," Gunnhild said, "because when I visit *you* I still win. I have a collection to prove it."

Oddny sniffed and picked at one of the furs in her bedroll, her thin shoulders hunched, her pinched face looking more so than usual. "Maybe we'd win every once in a while if Signy ever stopped daydreaming and paid attention."

"Hush, you. I pay attention," Signy said lightly, but her green eyes were brimming with mischief. Gunnhild appreciated that about her: Whether it was stealing oatcakes from the cookhouse or pulling a well-timed prank on the farmhands, Signy was always up for a little fun, whereas Oddny was more likely to sit back from whichever of her chores she was dutifully performing and give them a disapproving look. Oddny wasn't much fun, but at least she never tattled on them.

As they entered the longhouse, Gunnhild saw that preparations were well underway for the ritual and feast taking place that evening. Near her father's high seat at the far end of the hall, a small square platform had been raised for the visiting seeress to sit on, so she could look out over the crowd as she revealed their futures. It sat just under the wooden statues of the gods Odin, Thor, and Frey, which loomed beneath the jutting lintel above the entrance to the antechamber where Gunnhild's family slept.

Gunnhild had never seen her father's hall looking quite like this: buzzing with activity, the air charged with excitement. The seeress's impending arrival had turned the entire household upside down, and Gunnhild considered herself lucky to have escaped from her spinning in the chaos.

A knee-high platform ran the length of the hall on each side, where guests would feast and then sleep. By day, light streamed in through the holes in the roof above the two center hearths; by night, the longhouse would be dim and smoky, lit only by the hearth fires and by the lines of oil braziers hanging from the posts that ran down either side of the hall and divided the seating areas into sections.

"Where is our family sitting?" Oddny asked her as they neared the center of the hall.

"My mother assigned the seats," Gunnhild said. "We can ask—"

As if on cue the woman in question came out of the antechamber, already dressed to welcome the guests in her finest brooches and beads, and with a gauzy linen head scarf knotted at the nape of her neck. Before Gunnhild could so much as speak, her mother was upon them.

"What mischief have you been up to, Gunnhild?" Solveig demanded. "Why aren't you spinning with Ulfrun and the others? They're supposed to be keeping you out of the way."

They didn't tell on me, Gunnhild thought with short-lived relief, for the look on her mother's face was nothing short of hostile.

Oddny and Signy moved in fractionally closer on either side of Gunnhild, Signy's arm tightening around her friend's back, and even Oddny—a paragon of submitting to parental authority—stiffened as if bracing for an attack. Solveig would never dare strike her daughter in front of guests, but that didn't mean she hadn't done so in private, and both Ketilsdottirs knew this. They had seen the proof more than once.

"I—I heard the horns," Gunnhild said at last, her friends' presence giving her strength, helping her find her voice. "I had to win."

"Not this silly game again," Solveig said scathingly, and she echoed the watchman's earlier sentiment: "Aren't you girls a little old for this?"

"It's only a game." Gunnhild raised her chin. As she stared her mother down, Oddny and Signy held their ground beside her until their own mother entered the hall.

"Hello, Solveig," said Yrsa with forced politeness. "Are my daughters causing trouble already? We've only just arrived."

Solveig plastered a look of equally strained courtesy onto her face. "Not so. I only suspect that mine is, as always, up to no good."

Yrsa's voice turned cold. "Gunnhild just came down to the dock to escort us to the hall. Why does this offend you?"

"I feel compelled to remind you, Yrsa, that you are a guest in my home," Solveig said stiffly. "I don't recall asking for your opinion on the way I choose to deal with my own daughter."

"Of course." Yrsa's eyes narrowed, but she gave her host an insipid smile. "Before we get settled in, is there anyone in need of my services?" There was usually no shortage of sick or injured people on any given farm, and Yrsa was a skilled healer.

"Not that I know of. Please, make yourselves comfortable." Solveig gestured to the section of the platform two spaces down from the high seat, then looked to Gunnhild. "Clean yourself up and get ready at once." She made to breeze past them but stopped to hiss in her daughter's ear, "And do not embarrass me tonight."

Then she was gone, and Gunnhild could breathe again.

Yrsa's keen eyes followed Solveig as the woman went to greet the next guests. "Oddny, Signy—why don't you help Gunnhild get ready?"

The sisters dumped their bedrolls and scurried off with Gunnhild to the antechamber. Her parents slept on the right side, and behind a curtain on the left side were two wooden bunks with thin straw mattresses atop them.

Gunnhild had once shared this room with her sisters, but as they were much older and had long since been married off, she now bunked with Solveig's most trusted serving women, and she was glad to see that none of her aged roommates were present. Besides the bunks, the only other fixtures were a few small chests, one of which was Gunnhild's. She opened it and added the bead Signy had given her to the little pouch full of smooth skipping stones, seashells, and other baubles she'd won over time from the Ketilsdottirs. Then she took out a bone comb and began to assault her thick dark red hair.

Gunnhild's feast clothing was already spread out on her bunk: a linen dress soft from years of use; a woolen apron-dress, faded and threadbare but woven in a fine diamond pattern; and a pair of tarnished oval brooches with a simple string of beads. All had been handed down to Gunnhild from her older sisters.

"Mother asked to foster you again at the midsummer feast, last time we were all together," Signy said as she sat down on the bunk with the clothing on it, the beads clinking together at the movement. "Your mother refused."

"She said you were too old now." Oddny sat down on the opposite bunk. "As if she hasn't been asking forever."

Gunnhild grimaced, but this came as no surprise; she knew there was no escape for her. She'd tried to run away once or twice, slipping out during the commotion of a feast after stealing some finery from her parents' chests to pay her way to . . . Where? If not to Ketil's farm—the first place they would look for her—where could she possibly go? Each time, she'd ended up returning in the dead of night, putting her parents' things back where she'd found them, unpacking her bag, and slipping into bed.

She had thought that nothing would frighten her more than Solveig, but it turned out that the unknown was more terrifying still.

"Of course she refused," Gunnhild said hollowly. *She loves to deny me anything I could possibly want.* "And on top of everything else, I'm not allowed to have my fate told tonight."

Signy had been running her hand enviously over the diamond twill of the apron dress on the bed, but her head snapped up at this. "What do you mean, you're not *allowed* to have your fate told?"

"My mother decided it." And, as usual, she hadn't offered an explanation besides *because I said so*. Her father, however, had been a bit more willing to talk after a few drinks and a prolonged exposure to Gunnhild's whining. "But Papa said it's because I had my fate told when the last seeress came through."

"But you were *three* when the last one was here," Oddny said with a frown. "That's not fair. You can't possibly remember what she said."

"Of course I don't." Gunnhild crossed her arms. "And no one will tell me!"

"For once, I agree with Oddny Coal-brow," Signy said, and her sister *hmph*ed at the nickname, earned because Oddny's thin eyebrows were a much darker brown than her fine, mousy hair. "What if you just came with us when our mother calls us forward? Solveig can't make you sit back down without embarrassing you both. People would want an explanation."

"She'll make my life even more miserable this winter if I disobey her," Gunnhild said glumly, and neither of her friends disagreed.

Gunnhild braided her hair into a thick plait, donned her dresses, and pinned her beads and brooches in place. When she was done, Signy gave a sigh of admiration and Oddny gave a nod of approval. Neither of the sisters owned a set of brooches. The two wore faded woolen gowns—red for Signy and dull yellow for Oddny—and Gunnhild knew Oddny's was a hand-me-down, for the younger girl had it tightly cinched at the waist with a thin overlong leather belt.

Nevertheless, their dresses were free of stains and didn't show any obvious signs of mending or patching, so Gunnhild knew that these were likely the best garments her friends had; even their mother's weren't much better. And yet, though the family had so little to their name, Yrsa was still adamant about bringing their neighbor's mistreated daughter into their home.

Gunnhild swallowed the lump in her throat and sat down beside Oddny. "Let's stay out of the way until the ritual starts."

"Otherwise Mother might put us to work," Signy said, disgusted, as she flopped onto her back on the bed. "I want to go one single day without picking up a spindle. Is that too much to ask?"

"Just because you pick up a spindle doesn't mean that you get anything accomplished with it," Oddny said under her breath, and Signy stuck out her tongue.

To keep themselves busy, they decided to rebraid Oddny's and Signy's hair, which had become windswept during the crossing. By the time Gunnhild had fixed Oddny's twin plaits and Oddny had done the same to Signy's, they could hear more and more voices coming from the main hall.

"I suppose we should go before our mothers come looking for us," Gunnhild said at last, standing. The ritual would begin at dusk, and by now the sunlight outside was spent; the start of winter was almost upon them, and the days were getting shorter. Soon the sun would barely rise at all, and she'd be trapped inside this hall, weaving and sewing by firelight, completely under her mother's thumb.

But not yet. Tonight, she had her friends by her side, and the future awaited.

THE HALL WAS FULL and the braziers had been lit, and the seeress herself was the last to arrive, borne north by King Harald's tax collector and his retinue.

Along with the neighboring farmers, Gunnhild's father's friends among the Sámi had been invited to attend. They clustered together at the back of the hall, although Gunnhild saw that a few of the women had wandered over to chat with Yrsa in Norse. Ketil and Ozur had stopped to talk with the Sámi in their language, and Gunnhild heard Ketil's roaring laugh from across the room as the largest of the men clapped him on the back with a grin.

Gunnhild would have to go sit with her parents once the feast began, but for now she sat with Signy and Oddny, content to watch their fathers conversing in a tongue the girls didn't understand.

"I wonder what they're talking about," Signy said.

"*I* wonder what the Sámi will think of the seeress," Oddny replied. "Did you know Papa said their men are more likely to be seers instead of the other way around? I'll bet their rituals are much different, too—"

Signy batted her sister's arm. "Shh. It's starting!"

A hush came over the hall as the seeress finally appeared. The old woman was frail and peculiar, from her lambskin cap and gloves to the multitude of mysterious pouches at her belt. But what drew Gunnhild's eye most of all was her iron staff, twisted at the top, its brass fittings gleaming in the firelight.

The girls couldn't help but stare. Gunnhild's hands clenched into fists on her lap, and her heart felt ready to beat out of her chest.

While the rest of the people in the hall watched with a mixture of fear and respect as two of the tax collector's men helped the hobbling old woman to the platform, the Sámi looked on with unveiled curiosity. The seeress's stool—a plain piece of wood with three short legs, topped with a feather-stuffed cushion—had been assembled atop the small platform. The room quieted as she broke away from her escorts and straightened her spine, then ascended the steps and took her seat.

"Will those willing to sing the warding songs come forward?" she said. Her voice was surprisingly commanding, booming from her small body like a thunderclap.

Yrsa, Solveig, and the rest of the women stood and formed a circle around the platform.

Signy grabbed both Gunnhild and Oddny by the arm and whispered, "One day, that'll be us up there." Oddny shushed her, but Gunnhild nodded. Yes, their mothers had taught them the songs, and it was likely that one day when they were older, the girls would be called upon to assist in rituals just like this one.

But Gunnhild could not imagine herself as one of the singing women. The power the seeress commanded by her mere presence—as if she could change their fates on a whim instead of simply being the messenger of what was to come—was more appealing to her. It was downright intoxicating.

The seeress looked out over the women. "Your agreement to assist me must be given freely, so I ask you again: Are you willing to help me summon the spirits tonight? Will you raise your voices together to call them here, and to keep out any who mean us harm?" They expressed their agreement, and the seeress said, "Then let us begin."

When the women began to sing, the sound sent a thrill through Gunnhild's bones. There were no words to these songs, but the melodies made the hair on her arms rise. After a few moments, the seeress closed her eyes and, tucking her iron staff under her arm like a distaff, began to mime spinning.

Gunnhild let out a small gasp. As one of the old woman's hands pinched and pulled invisible wool from her staff, the other hand flicked an imaginary spindle, and Gunnhild saw that a thin thread was forming between her fingers, pulsing with a strange white light.

No one else seemed to be reacting to this impossible sight.

"Do you see that?" she whispered to Signy and Oddny.

"See what?" Signy whispered back.

"The thread," Oddny breathed. "I see it, too."

"What thread? I don't see anything," Signy said, raising her voice, which caused her to be shushed again, this time by several nearby adults.

The girls turned their attention back to the ritual. The seeress suddenly dropped hold of the invisible spindle, the other hand clenching her staff tightly and pulling it from beneath her arm. The end of the glowing thread reached from her chest to twirl around the staff, then dropped down into the floor; and now it was taut, as if something pulled it from below.

Gunnhild's stomach twisted.

The seeress opened her eyes—which had rolled back into her head to reveal only the whites—and intoned in a voice that was much like her own but not quite: "Would those who wish to know their fates come forward? Be warned: We'll say only what we wish, to whom we wish."

"That's a spirit talking through her?" Signy said in a loud whisper, and Oddny shoved her and said, *"Hush."* Gunnhild ignored them both; she was transfixed by the spectacle, the warding songs humming in her bones as the women continued singing, more quietly now so the seeress's words could be heard.

One by one, people approached—some on their own, others ushering their entire families toward the platform, and the circle of women parted to receive them. The seeress, keeping her chin raised and her unseeing gaze distant, told them that their harvests would be good, that their children would be healthy, that the livestock they didn't cull would make it through the winter.

For some, the seeress hesitated a few moments, white eyes flicking around as if searching. For others, the spirits seemed to come more readily. The Sámi murmured among themselves, but none of them came forward to hear their fates.

"Is there anyone else?" the seeress asked the assembly when it seemed as though most in the hall had had their turn, including each of the singing women.

Yrsa turned and looked at her daughters, her eyebrows raised as she subtly jerked her head to beckon them, and Signy and Oddny stood and went to the center of the room. Signy cast a look at Gunnhild over her shoulder as if to say *Come on* before she and Oddny took their places in front of the seeress, and the circle of women closed around them.

Gunnhild's eyes bored into the back of her mother's head, anger rising in her. *It's not fair that I can't hear my fate when no one will even tell me what the last seeress said about me.*

But maybe this one knows, too. Her outrage gave her a sudden burst of courage. *So I guess I'll have to find out for myself.*

She hesitated a moment longer before she stood and bolted after her friends, pushing through the circle until she was standing next to Oddny and Signy. She could feel her mother's eyes on her, could feel the rage coming off her in waves, but Gunnhild didn't turn to look at her.

Up close, the fires of the center hearths and the braziers gave the seeress a haunting look, the dancing orange light intensifying the deep wrinkles in her skin and glinting off the brass casings on her staff. She seemed to have been about to speak—until the moment Gunnhild stepped up to join Oddny and Signy. Then the old woman faltered, scowled, sucked her teeth.

Oddny was shaking. Gunnhild took her hand and gave it a reassuring squeeze. Beside them, Signy bounced on the balls of her feet.

Then the seeress finally spoke: "One of you clouds the futures of the others. For better or worse, your fates are intertwined." Her features contorted again, this time in fear and confusion. "I dare not say more."

Gunnhild heard a collective intake of breath around them, followed by shocked whispers, but she could scarcely hear them over the blood roaring in her ears. Oddny seemed equally distressed, her fingernails digging half-moon ridges into Gunnhild's skin; but Signy, undaunted as ever, was the one to finally say: "What do you mean?"

But the seeress offered nothing further. She seemed suddenly tired, and much older than she had a moment before. "I have said enough tonight, and now I shall be silent."

She slumped forward on her stool, her chin falling down to her chest, and Gunnhild watched as she yanked up the glowing thread as if it were a fishing line. As soon as she did, her body jerked, her eyes opened, and her pupils and irises returned. The tax collector's men stepped up to help her down from the platform.

And Oddny, Signy, and Gunnhild stood perfectly still, all eyes on them, until Solveig stepped out from her place among the women, whose singing had halted the moment the seeress had awoken. With a thin smile, she announced that the feast would now begin, and the hall filled with hesitant chatter, soft at first before growing in volume.

Then Solveig turned back to her daughter.

And Gunnhild would never forget the way her mother looked at her then, as though she were sorry that Gunnhild had ever been born.

2

GUNNHILD AVOIDED SOLVEIG AS best she could after the ritual, though she still had to sit by her family during the feast, dread simmering in the pit of her stomach all the while. Luckily, Ozur and Solveig soon became too busy playing host and hostess to take notice of her. The servants and thralls gave her pitying looks every time they passed with pitchers of ale and trays piled high with smoked meats and flatbreads. The only other person who dared look her way was her father's friend, an ancient farmer whom the children called Old Man Skuli, who sat with his bickering wives and unruly children one section over.

Gunnhild pointedly did not acknowledge him. She'd caught him leering at her before the ritual, but now he stole fearful glances at her, as though she were a snake about to bite. She didn't know which looks should worry her more.

Her older brothers, on the other hand—swaggering young men, red-haired as herself and their mother—had either missed the implications of the seeress's prophecy or were ignorant of her troubles as always, for they came to bother her as if nothing at all had changed.

"Why do you look so sad, Little Gunna?" Alf asked as he plopped down on one side of Gunnhild, a full horn of ale in hand.

Eyvind took his place on her other side, his own cup overflowing. "Yes, you *do* realize this is a party, don't you, little sister?"

"What are we celebrating?" Gunnhild asked as she picked at her stew, which now looked more like porridge. She hadn't eaten a bite of it and

had started taking out her nervousness on its overcooked root vegetables. "The joyful fates of everyone here except for me?"

"Oh, you know how seeresses can be." Eyvind waved his cup. "So
vague."

"I'm sure no one thinks anything of it," said Alf.

Eyvind took a long swig of ale. "Cheer up. It's not so bad."

"Yes, it is. Mother is furious with me," Gunnhild said sullenly.

The twins exchanged a look over her head as she mashed up another turnip in silence. They could never understand. The youngest of
Gunnhild's older siblings at ten winters her senior, Alf and Eyvind had
been largely absent from her life. They'd left to go make names for themselves as raiders the moment they were old enough. Gunnhild had hoped
that the arrival of her only brothers and their summer's worth of plunder
several days before would soften their mother, but she'd been sorely mis-
taken.

"Oh, come, now," Alf said. "Do you really think she's so cross about
you jumping in during the ritual? We disobeyed her all the time when we
were your age."

Gunnhild eyed him. "She told you she was forbidding me from having my fate told?"

"We assumed," said Alf with a shrug. "Especially after last time."

Gunnhild sat up straighter and gave Eyvind—who seemed to be the
drunker and therefore the more pliable of the brothers—a look. "What
does he mean, 'last time'?"

"Last time a seeress came through," Eyvind slurred. "Do you not remember?"

"I was three winters old," Gunnhild said, whirling back to face Alf.
"What did the last one say about me?"

The twins looked at each other again, and Eyvind shook his head and
made a show of draining his cup, hopping to his feet, and declaring,
"More ale!"

"Never mind, Gunna," Alf said hastily. "We shouldn't have said anything."

Gunnhild seethed as they went to seek out the nearest servant girl for a refill. As she stood to follow in hopes of wheedling more information from them, Oddny came up beside her, clutching a thick shawl about her shoulders, and whispered, "Come—the boys started a fire outside."

The girls slipped out of the noisy hall and made their way toward a small bonfire surrounded by dark shapes. As they got closer, Gunnhild recognized the girls' brother, Vestein, and a few other local children sitting on blankets and pelts.

Gunnhild and Oddny hunkered down next to Signy and listened as one of the boys, who fancied himself a skald, recited a poem about Valhalla: where those who were slain in battle would fight and feast until Ragnarok, the final confrontation between the gods and their enemies. The other children listened intently, though they'd surely heard the poem many times before. Soon they'd be old enough to go on the raids themselves and seek their own fame. Many of them wouldn't return; Gunnhild's brothers were some of the lucky few, well on their way to becoming career raiders, which made them akin to legends among the children of Halogaland—most of whom would go on a handful of raids and, if they lived, settle down on a farm to live a peaceful life unless a local hersir, like Gunnhild's father, called them to muster on the king's behalf.

Gunnhild found her mind wandering during the poem. Ragnarok—as well as her own destiny and that of her friends, according to the seeress—was an abstract problem. A future problem. Her mother's punishment was going to be more immediate and more tangible. What would Solveig do to her once she didn't have to behave like a decent person in front of guests?

The winter was long and the possibilities were endless.

Feeling the sudden urge to vomit, Gunnhild stood and stalked away from the fire. Once she was far enough from the other children, she plopped down on the rocky strand, drew her legs up to her chest, and folded her arms atop her knees. She kept her eyes closed until the wave of nausea passed, then took in the scene before her: Moonlight glimmered on the dark water of the strait, and beyond it, the northern lights danced against the jagged mountain peaks of the mainland. It was a dazzling sight, but the beauty of her home did nothing to soothe her, so she buried her face in her arms.

The crunch of pebbles behind her told her she wasn't alone. Moments later, she felt a blanket drop over her shoulders as Oddny and Signy settled in on either side of her.

"My mother is going to kill me." Gunnhild raised her head. "And there's something my family is keeping from me. My brothers told me it had something to do with what the last seeress said. It makes me think that I—that *I'm* the one clouding all our futures. I shouldn't have disobeyed my mother. I've ruined everything."

"People are already starting to whisper about us. And no one came over to speak with us during the feast," Oddny said. "Mama already overheard people saying we'll never get married now."

Gunnhild put her head back down and groaned into her arms. "See?"

Signy scoffed. "People talk all the time. It hardly means that Gunnhild is some harbinger of doom. And besides, is 'not getting married' the worst thing that could possibly happen to us? You've seen your sisters' husbands, Gunna—old goats, the lot of them."

"Maybe we should ask the seeress to tell our futures again?" Oddny suggested, wringing her hands.

"You saw her," Signy shot back. "She wouldn't say what she was so frightened about then, so why would she say now?"

Oddny glared at her. "But our reputations—"

"Are now one and the same, thanks to that old lady." Signy brightened. "We should take a blood oath!"

"We're already blood sisters, you fool."

"I meant we should take one with Gunnhild. Why not fulfill the prophecy right here by binding ourselves together?"

"Even though one of us has an ominous destiny that's going to ruin things for the other two?" said Gunnhild, again with an awful certainty that she was speaking of herself.

"But one of us could also be the next Queen Asa, for all we know.

Whatever happens, we'll face it together," said Signy with feeling. "What do you say?"

Gunnhild supposed she could play along. She affected an overly regal bearing and said in her most dramatic voice, "If I didn't know better, troublemaker, I'd say you were trying to make the future most powerful woman in all of Norway beholden to you."

"I mean . . ." Signy raised her hands as in praise as she turned to Gunnhild and intoned, "O Future Most Powerful Woman in All of Norway! Please take a blood oath with us, and make yourself obligated to us forever!"

Gunnhild snorted, but Oddny said, "No blood oaths."

Signy dropped her hands with a flourish. "Why not?"

"I don't see a problem with it," Gunnhild found herself saying. The sisters fell silent and turned to her: Oddny blinking furiously, Signy's mouth widening into a grin as she drew her small utility knife from the sheath at her belt.

"Then let's do it," Signy said. "Let's promise that we'll always be there for each other, even if we don't walk the same path."

"Signy, no," Oddny said crossly, and made a face as her sister sliced a shallow cut across her palm, then passed the knife to Gunnhild. "That's going to be such a pain to heal."

Gunnhild imitated Signy, flinching as the blade bit into her skin. Then she handed the knife over to Oddny, who eyed it and said, "You're really going along with Signy's foolishness?"

"Be careful," Gunnhild warned her. "You could be talking to the future most powerful woman in all of Norway."

Oddny pursed her lips and snatched the knife away. "Fine. But I'm already obligated by blood to clean up Signy's messes. I'll swear myself only to you."

It was Signy's turn to roll her eyes, but Gunnhild said, "All right." And once Oddny had cut her hand, they pressed their palms together.

"We'll always be there for each other," said Gunnhild quietly.

"Even if we don't walk the same path," Oddny finished.

Gunnhild clasped bloodied palms with Signy next.

"There," said Signy when they broke apart. "Now we're all sworn sisters."

Something nagged at Gunnhild then—something she'd noticed during the ritual and had subsequently forgotten in the wake of the troubling prophecy. Once they'd bound their cuts with scraps cut from the blanket, it came to her and she said, "Signy—is it true that you really couldn't see the seeress's thread?"

"There wasn't any thread," Signy said stubbornly. "You two must've been imagining it. Don't you think people would have reacted if there had been? Mother, Papa, and Vestein didn't see it—I asked, and they looked at me like I was mad. But still, the fact that you both had the same hallucination . . ." She feigned astonishment. "Oddny, I can't believe *you* have an *imagination*."

"I've had enough silliness for one night," Oddny said, standing. "I'm going to bed." She headed back to the longhouse, clasping her bound hand against her chest and looking thoughtful.

Signy turned to Gunnhild. "I'm going back, too. Are you coming?"

"I'll stay up awhile longer." Gunnhild drew her knees to her chest once more, wrapping her arms around her legs and tilting her head back to look at the aurora dancing in greens and purples above. She lost track of how long she sat there, alone, contemplating.

By the time she slipped back inside, the hall had quieted and most of the guests were snoring. She tiptoed by the tax collector and his men, past the Sámi, past where Signy and Oddny and their family slept. As she went, she scanned the sectioned platforms for signs of the old seeress, but the braziers had been put out and the fires were burning low, so she had no luck.

As she approached the antechamber, she looked up at the wooden statues of Thor, Odin, and Frey and sent up a silent prayer that her parents were also asleep so she wouldn't have to face her mother's wrath tonight.

Her plea was granted: When she slunk through the door, Solveig and

Ozur were sleeping soundly, and she mouthed *Thank you* to the gods as she crept to her own bed—only to find it occupied by none other than the seeress.

Behind her, the old servant Ulfrun rolled over and whispered, "You're to share with me, lamb. Your mother's orders."

Gunnhild made a quiet noise of acquiescence and undressed in the flickering light of the soapstone lamp that sat atop one of the chests. She kept her woolen dress on over her linen shift for extra warmth, then crawled into bed with Ulfrun, who rolled over to face the wall.

She waited until her bunkmate had dozed off again before she crept out of bed and across the narrow chamber to the seeress, whose slack, wrinkled face was cast in sharp relief by the lantern light. Although her eyes were closed, she wasn't taking the slow, deep breaths of one asleep.

As Gunnhild crouched beside her, the woman cracked open one eye.

"I saw your thread," Gunnhild said in a low whisper.

The seeress opened both eyes now. "Oh, did you?"

"Yes. And please—which one of us is it, from your prophecy? The one who will spoil things for the others?"

The old woman remained silent.

Gunnhild thought again of the power the seeress had demonstrated during the ritual, the honor she'd been shown, and the silver she'd received as payment for her services. The only way Gunnhild could ever expect to gain such wealth was if her father and future husband both paid an exorbitant dowry and bride-price, respectively. Her value would depend on what others deemed her to be worth.

I wonder what it's like, Gunnhild thought, *not to have a mother or a husband telling you what to do all the time. I wonder what it's like to be a woman respected on her own, for her own skills, and not who she's related to.*

And then it occurred to her: a way to find all this out on her own, escape her mother's wrath, *and* distance herself from Oddny and Signy, who had already been tarnished by her stepping into the circle with them.

"Will you teach me to be a seeress?" Gunnhild asked.

The woman squinted at her. "And why would you wish to be a seeress?"

"I wish to be feared and respected. I wish to be *seen*."

"I would put this from your mind if I were you." The seeress sounded agitated, and Gunnhild heard a hint of fear in her voice, just as during the ritual.

Gunnhild balled her fists. There was still something she was not being told. "But I want to be like you. I want my life to be my own."

The seeress stared at her a moment longer, then sighed and rolled over to face the wall.

"Will you teach me?" Gunnhild said to the woman's back. "Please?"

The seeress did not stir at her words. Gunnhild made a defeated noise and crawled back into bed with Ulfrun.

Sleep did not come easily, but when it did come, Gunnhild dreamed that she was the one atop that platform with an iron staff clutched in her hand, gazing out over an enraptured crowd.

In her dreams, her fate was hers and hers alone.

3

GUNNHILD AWOKE WITH THE knowledge that the punishment for her behavior the night before was drawing nearer with each guest's departure from the island.

Ketil's family was among the first to leave, claiming a long day of farmwork ahead. Gunnhild kept her head down except to bid Signy and Oddny farewell. She didn't respond when they blew the horn three times for goodbye; she'd owe them each a prize later, but that was the least of her worries.

Finally, at around midday, the king's tax collector and his men were the last ones left, as they were staying an extra night—more time for Gunnhild to agonize over what her mother was going to do with her. Her only spot of hope was that the old seeress had disappeared from her bed. There were whispers that she was sitting out on the far side of the island. Nobody knew what she was up to, but Gunnhild listened to the servants' speculations as she hid in the cookhouse and helped prepare supper, thus managing to avoid her mother's wrath for a second night.

The seeress reappeared the next morning as the family and their guests were settling in for breakfast, after which the tax collector and his crew would ferry her along to their next destination. The old woman entered the hall silently and hobbled over to the high seat to look upon the heads of household, who were seated on their elaborately carved bench atop the platform.

"Ozur Eyvindsson and Solveig Alfsdottir," the seeress said, shoulders squared as she planted both hands firmly upon her walking stick, "your daughter Gunnhild expressed to me her wish to learn the ways of a seeress from me, and after thinking upon it, I wish to take her under my tutelage."

Gunnhild spat a mouthful of porridge back into her bowl.

Her parents did not speak, and the light chatter around the hall ceased as all heads turned to the hersir and his wife: Ozur seemed flabbergasted, but Solveig looked murderous. Gunnhild, sitting across the hall from them, swallowed heavily.

"I . . . am not sure what to make of this," said Ozur as he looked to his wife. "Solveig?"

"We already have an arrangement for Gunnhild." Solveig's eyes flicked over to where her daughter sat. "As of yesterday, in fact."

An arrangement?! Gunnhild set her porridge aside, her appetite suddenly lost. Whatever her mother had in store for her—had she been sold as a servant? Betrothed to a man so old he'd probably die before she came of age?—it wouldn't be something Gunnhild wanted for herself. That much was clear from the smug look on Solveig's face.

"May I inquire as to the nature of this arrangement?" the seeress asked.

Ozur said, "I talked to my old friend Skuli just before your ritual, and we've come to an agreement that we think will be beneficial to all of us. In three winters' time, Gunnhild is to marry him."

Old Man Skuli?! Gunnhild thought, horrified. *But he's—he's—no, this can't be—*

"But he's *old*," she blurted before she could stop herself. "He's got three wives already and twelve sons between them, and they're already fighting over their inheritance—"

"Skuli is extremely wealthy, Gunna," said Ozur. "You'll be well taken care of. It's no less than we've done for any of your sisters."

I don't want to be taken care of, Gunnhild wanted to scream. *I want to be free.*

"Would that we could be rid of her sooner, useless daughter that she is," Solveig added. "Trust us, Heid—you don't want this girl. She's been trouble since the moment she was born."

The old woman raised her sparse eyebrows. "Oh? How so?"

Solveig's lip curled. "Her brothers were to be my last children, but this body of mine had other plans. I hadn't even known I could still conceive, and her birth nearly killed me. Yet she's an ungrateful little whelp. She's stubborn and insubordinate and balks at the auspicious marriage we've secured for her. She should be ashamed of herself."

"Solveig," Ozur said sharply.

Gunnhild felt Heid's eyes upon her, studying her. *Heid*: so common a name for a seeress that it seemed more of a title. She wondered what the old woman's true name was.

"So this is my punishment, Mother?" Gunnhild asked through clenched teeth. "For my behavior at the ritual?"

Solveig's eyes flashed with anger. "You deliberately disobeyed me. You should be grateful we're not selling you into servitude instead of marrying you off."

"What's the difference?" Gunnhild fired back. "And why didn't you want me to hear my fate in the first place? Alf and Eyvind said it was because of something the last seeress told you."

Solveig cut a withering look to her only sons, who suddenly became very interested in the floor.

"I have a right to know, Mother," Gunnhild said.

"Is that so?" Solveig whirled back to face her. "You are twelve winters old. You have a right to nothing at all save what your father and I deem fit to give you, which is already more than you deserve." And then, sensing an opportunity for cruelty, she smiled. "But since you're so intent upon it—when you were small, yes, another seeress passed through here during a storm, so only our household heard what she had to say: that a terrible future awaited you. We would've never been able to get rid of you if anyone else knew, so we swore everyone to secrecy."

Gunnhild's breath caught. *A terrible future?*

"I'm only thankful that you decided to run into the circle with your little friends," Solveig went on, "so it wasn't clear who the prophecy concerned. Now you've doomed Yrsa's girls, but at least you already have a match—you're lucky your father shook on it with witnesses before the ritual even began, so Skuli can't back out."

"I'm *lucky*?" Gunnhild echoed.

Solveig continued as if she hadn't spoken. "Nothing will save your friends' reputations now, for the seed of suspicion has already been planted. We've spared you that pain. You should be thanking us."

Gunnhild's vision blurred with tears. She hated to admit it, but Solveig was right about what would become of Signy and Oddny. Even at her age, she knew that once people got a superstitious idea into their heads, it was hard to shake even when presented with evidence to the contrary.

"You truly are a vile woman," Heid cut in, her dark eyes fixed on Solveig. She ignored the subsequent noise of outrage from the lady of the house and turned her attention to Ozur. "Whatever Skuli is paying for her bride-price in three winters, I'll pay double right now, provided you also give her a dowry to take with her on our journey."

Gunnhild could not believe her ears.

As Solveig sat seething, Ozur looked to his youngest daughter. "I'm sorry, Gunna. As your mother said, Skuli and I have already shaken on it. The deal has been made."

"Then the matter is settled," Solveig said, smiling, showing too many teeth.

Heid inclined her head and said coldly, "Then I respect your decision, and your unwillingness to break the oath you've sworn your friend."

No. She'd been *so close.* Horror welled up from the pit of Gunnhild's belly, but as she turned to run from the hall, she caught the twinkle in Heid's eye.

A twinkle that clearly said, as if the seeress were speaking in her own mind: *This is not over.*

Gunnhild pretended not to notice. She shot her mother a doleful look—Solveig smirked back at her, satisfied—and fled to the bunk room instead.

The chest that the seeress had brought with her sat open in the middle of the room, empty save for her deconstructed stool and some spare clothing. Gunnhild was peering at it, considering whether she was small enough to fit inside, when the woman herself parted the curtain and swept into the room.

"I see now why you wish to leave this place," Heid said after a moment. "I'd forgotten what it was like to be a young girl with few prospects, forced into a marriage she doesn't want."

Gunnhild hung her head.

"And worse yet," Heid went on, "was to see how you're treated here, not because of anything you've done but because of the prophecies of one of my sisters. For that, I apologize." She reached over and put a shaky hand on the girl's shoulder. "You are not a bad child. You are not a burden. I'm sorry that you've been made to feel that way."

Gunnhild had never thought that anyone would say those words to her. It took everything in her power not to cry as she looked up at the old woman.

"I understand now, too, why you wish so badly to become a seeress," Heid added. "No matter what your parents say, I wish for you to leave here with me today."

"Really?" Gunnhild's dark blue eyes were huge and pleading. "But my father would be furious. You'd be making an enemy of a hersir. You would really do that for me?"

"I fear no man," said the seeress. "And as for your mother, she didn't tell you the whole truth." A sigh. "But then again, neither did I. There are things I held back last night."

Gunnhild felt cold as she waited for Heid to continue.

"Your fate is intertwined with that of your friends; that much was true. As for you, Gunnhild Ozurardottir—I see blood in your future. Blood and terror," Heid told her. "But I also see greatness. These things are, in many ways, inseparable from one another."

Gunnhild committed her words to memory.

"And my friends?" she whispered. "Will this—will the blood and terror—will I hurt my friends?"

"That, I don't know," Heid said sadly. "That's why I refused to say more when you stepped into the circle. Sometimes saying nothing at all is better than speaking without seeing the entire picture, and I hadn't seen enough to rule one way or another. I didn't wish to curse you, and yet it seems I've done so anyway."

Heid considered her for a moment. "Gunnhild Ozurardottir, if you come with me, I can teach you not only how to gain the knowledge of the spirits as a seeress does but all manner of witchcraft I know: how to curse and to heal, to conjure storms and befuddle enemies, to cast charms to protect and destroy, to use the runes for magic, and to travel out of body. But I won't lie to you: It'll be difficult. Nothing in this life worth having comes easily. You'll spend many years with me in isolation, but at the end, you'll be a seeress and a sorceress both. You shall be a witch. Do you understand and consent to this?"

The shallow slice on her palm started to burn a little as if in warning, and Gunnhild winced. How could she leave Oddny and Signy behind after they'd vowed to always be there for one another? But her mother had been right—their prospects were ruined now, thanks to her. Perhaps the best thing she could do for her friends was disappear.

The seeress—the *witch*—was still staring at her.

"Yes, I consent," Gunnhild said fervently. "Take me with you. I wish to learn."

Heid gestured to her chest. "Then pack only what you need, and we'll hide you away in here."

Gunnhild made to do so, but then hesitated. "But, Heid, if my future is to be terrible, why take a chance on teaching me? Aren't you afraid that I'll—that I'll harm you?"

"If I thought I had anything to fear from you, child, I wouldn't be making this offer. Only time will tell how your story goes. There's nothing that will cause you greater grief than trying to fulfill or avoid a prophecy."

"I don't understand," Gunnhild said weakly.

The old witch bared her yellow teeth in a wide grin.

"Oh, my girl," she said. "You will."

PART II

TWELVE YEARS LATER

4

ON THE EARLY-AUTUMN MORNING that her life changed forever, Oddny Ketilsdottir woke up with a stabbing pain in her lower abdomen and a curse on her lips. She curled up into a ball, gritted her teeth, and braced herself to begin another day.

"Ah. Mother figured that was why you slept in," came Signy's voice from above her. "She told me to let you sleep, but how could I let you miss such a delicious breakfast?"

Oddny took a deep breath and tried to muster the will to sit up. "Give me a moment."

"All right, but guess what we're having," Signy said. "Ah, I'll spoil it for you—it's curds."

"What's spoiled is you, sneaking cheese all summer at the dairy," Oddny grumbled.

Signy put her hands on her hips. "Well, with Mother about to preserve the vegetables and Vestein about to cull the herd, you'd think we'd be able to eat something fresh. But no, it's curds. It's always curds for breakfast and fish for dinner. You know I actually start missing pickled turnips at this time of year? And porridge. Gods, I wish I could have some porridge right now."

"You'll be glad of it when we have enough food to eat come winter." Oddny heaved herself to a sitting position and doubled over. The pain was worse today than it was yesterday—her blood would be upon her soon.

Signy sat down beside her on the bench where she'd slept. "Do you want me to ask Mother to make your tea?"

Oddny shook her head. "I've been making it myself." *But I need to go foraging for some of the ingredients. Get them dried to last the winter, too, along with the last of the herbs from Mother's garden.*

"Look at you. Mother's little prodigy." Signy nudged her sister playfully with her elbow. But then she sobered. "And speaking of which, before you ask, we haven't heard news of Solveig."

Oddny grimaced. She'd been learning the art of healing from Yrsa since her early teens, and the two of them had been monitoring Gunnhild's mother's illness all summer. When they'd last visited Solveig a few weeks ago, Oddny had been stunned at the sight of their patient: cheekbones jutting, eyes sunken, red-streaked silver hair falling out in chunks.

Though Oddny had little love for the woman, she remembered the pall that had fallen over the room when they'd entered and seen Solveig's state, remembered the lantern burning low, remembered an unseen bird tittering away in the rafters. Most of all, she remembered the shock she'd felt when Yrsa had withdrawn a smooth, flat stick of wood from her pack in lieu of her usual supplies.

"Runes?" Oddny had asked. She'd seen her mother use them only a few times. Yrsa was more likely to employ physical implements when healing: potions, salves, teas. Magic was a last resort, because it didn't always work.

Then again, nothing else had improved Solveig's condition so far. Yrsa had been desperate.

"Watch me closely, Oddny," she'd said. "Anyone can carve runes, but not everyone has a strong enough will to make them do what you want them to do."

Oddny said, "So why not just use them for everything? Isn't that what Odin got them for when he sacrificed himself to himself?"

"Because there's too much room for error. They must be carved precisely and with specific intent so they can work on your behalf while you're not present. If they're wrong, at best they'll have no effect, but at worst they'll kill the person you're using them on, even if their illness or injury wasn't life-threatening to begin with."

Then Yrsa had sung the runes under her breath as she carved them into the wood, and stuck the stick under the sick woman's pillow.

Oddny knew there was more at stake here than just Solveig's life: Her mother's reputation as a respectable healer was on the line. Yrsa and Solveig had despised each other privately for years, but the enmity between them had become public knowledge after Gunnhild vanished. Whenever Yrsa heard people whispering that the disappearance of the hersir's daughter was a result of the prophecy dooming the three girls, she was quick to correct anyone who would listen—and not just for the sake of her daughters' prospects—by offering that the child most likely ran away because of her mother. And Solveig took any opportunity to slander Yrsa in return, right up until she'd fallen ill and suddenly had need of a healer.

Regardless, Oddny knew that if Solveig died, her mother would take it as a personal failing. And worse—others might think Yrsa killed her.

"Vestein is going to row over there later to ask after her. He planned to fish today anyway," Signy said, snapping Oddny out of her reverie. "I may have also bullied him into taking me with him and letting me stay until the king's retinue passes through again."

Oddny gave her a sidelong look. "Mother couldn't possibly have agreed to that."

"Mother doesn't have to know."

"Signy, you have no idea when they're coming back—"

"It can't be long. Winter will be upon us before we know it."

Oddny raked her fingers through her long thin hair and started to braid it over her shoulder. Her pain had dulled for now, but another wave could hit her at any moment. She would need her tea soon and she didn't have the patience for her sister's fantasies.

At the beginning of summer, King Eirik, chosen successor of King Harald, the ruler of all of Norway, had passed through Halogaland on his way to raid along the Dvina River in Bjarmaland, to the north and east, with his hird—his retinue of sworn men—and they'd stopped at Ozur's for a night. With Solveig's illness in its early stages, Ozur had summoned his neighbors to welcome his distinguished guests, with Yrsa helping the cook to organize the feast and enlisting her daughters to serve the men.

While Signy had made heads turn, few of the hirdsmen had spared Oddny more than a passing glance, likely taking her for a servant girl. Oddny had gotten used to this, given how many feasts she and Signy had helped serve at the hersir's. Her eyes were a brownish version of Signy's bright green, her fine hair teetering between brown and blond, whereas her sister's was thick and glossy, the rich brown of freshly tilled earth. They had the same heart-shaped face, but Oddny's was thinner. She was half a head shorter than Signy and had no curves to speak of, and her dark, thin, straight brows gave her a perpetually severe look.

So while Oddny had haunted the feast like a small shadow wielding a pitcher of ale, Signy had been in her element, flirting shamelessly with the hird, fighting to catch King Eirik's eye for some time before finally disappearing with him at the end of the night. Oddny had to suffer through her sister's ensuing bragging all summer at the dairy as Signy told the younger girls of her conquest in great detail. Their father, Ketil, had enjoyed telling tall tales of his adventures on the raids and of his encounters with trolls and wights and all other manner of creatures, and Signy took after him in more ways than one; Oddny knew her sister's story was full of embellishments, for it changed a bit every time.

But at the dairy, where girls from the surrounding farms herded the livestock inland to the lush mountain valleys each summer, Signy had a captive audience of bright-eyed, eager teens who didn't necessarily care how much of what she told them was true. Signy and Oddny were the oldest of the lot besides the mothers who had come along, who overheard Signy's story with a more critical ear and shook their heads. Signy, twenty-five winters old and unmarried, was not the woman they wanted their daughters to emulate. Signy knew this, and it only emboldened her in the telling of her tale, which became raunchier each time she told it.

"Nothing happened, actually," Signy had confessed to Oddny in private on their final night at the dairy, as they curled up together in one of the shacks. "We were both very drunk and passed out fully clothed in the hay."

"If that's the case, I suspect Papa would be proud of how much you've managed to exaggerate such a mundane experience," Oddny had replied, earning a smack on the arm from her sister.

Presently, Oddny stood and said, "You can't think King Eirik will come back here and decide to make you one of his wives, or whisk you away and take you on all his adventures?"

Signy stuck out her lower lip and stood as well. "And why not?"

"You know exactly why." Oddny gave her a flat look as she finished her braid. "We're poor. We're cursed. Need I go on?"

Nobodies at best, social pariahs at worst, despite Mother's best efforts. Ever since the night of the seeress's prophecy.

Ever since Gunnhild disappeared into thin air.

Oddny looked down at the silvery scar on her palm and squeezed her hand into a fist. She hoped, as she often did, that wherever Gunnhild had gone was a far cry better than her mother's clutches.

"Well, King Eirik isn't exactly popular himself," Signy pointed out, "having killed two of his brothers—"

"Right. One of the worst crimes a person can commit, and he's done it twice."

"But I heard the one was on his father's orders—"

"Don't defend a kinslayer, Signy." Oddny wrinkled her nose in distaste. "I'd take a decent man over one like him any day, king or no."

"Well, maybe our prospects would be better than crotchety old men and brother-murderers if Vestein had gone raiding more than once," Signy said as they headed to the door. "You know, made the necessary connections. Plundered some gold from unsuspecting monks. Actually attempted to find us husbands . . ."

This particular complaint was the one Signy most often voiced, so Oddny rolled her eyes and offered her usual response: "And if you'd been the one to see Papa take an axe to the head on your very first raid, I doubt you'd be keen to go again. But, you know, I think if you asked

Mother one more time if you could replace him, she might actually let you, just to be free of your whining."

Signy pitched her voice high. "'Signy, you shirked your father's fighting lessons as a child just as often as you shirk your chores. You can barely chop firewood and you haven't practiced with a weapon since before he died.'"

Their mother sounded nothing like that, so Oddny added, in a disturbingly accurate imitation of Yrsa: "'Signy Ketilsdottir, you'd be killed the moment you stepped off a ship. Go finish your chores and do not speak of this again.'"

"Yes, yes, we all know you're the best mimic in Halogaland. It's not polite to brag." Signy opened the door of the modest hall and a crisp breeze blew in. Outside, Vestein, their mother's servant Lif, and a half dozen farmhands were sitting on stools and eating their curds in silence. The farm's two dogs lazed in the sunlight near the door; they had kept the girls company at the dairy all summer, helping to herd the livestock and providing protection. Oddny gave one of them a scratch behind the ears as she passed.

"Signy Ketilsdottir." Yrsa stormed up to them the moment her daughters appeared. "You're not going anywhere today. Is that clear?"

Signy shot Vestein a murderous look. "You told her?"

"How long did you think you could get away with hiding out at Ozur's?" Yrsa demanded. "Don't think I haven't heard the nonsense you've been spouting all summer about bedding a king."

Now Signy turned to glare at Oddny, who pointedly looked away. She might have mentioned it to Yrsa out of frustration as they'd unloaded the dairy cart upon their return yesterday, but she hadn't thought her mother would ever bring it up.

"Well, if you'd heard *anything*, you'd know there was no bed involved," Signy said, and Vestein made a choking sound and spat out some of his breakfast. The older farmhands rolled their eyes, but the younger two—who Oddny knew for a fact her sister had lain with—looked slightly miffed. "I don't understand why you're shaming me for—"

"You may do as you wish where men are concerned," Yrsa snapped, "as up until now you've been discreet about it." And that was the case: One of the first things she'd taught Oddny was how to brew a contraceptive. "But now that you've made a spectacle of yourself, the other mothers are going to give me an earful at the next feast."

Signy threw her hands up. "I don't understand why you wouldn't want this for me. You act like me marrying a king wouldn't be good for our family."

"If this king is anything like his father," said Yrsa with icy disapproval, "you're more likely to end up as his concubine than his wife."

"And are concubines not well taken care of?" Signy pressed. "Would the sons I'd give him not stand to inherit the title of king should he choose to legitimize them?"

Oddny rubbed her temples. The way Signy vacillated between her two opposing life goals—of fighting and raiding and adventure, and of attaching herself to a rich man with whom she'd want for nothing—would never cease to amaze her.

"My sister wishes to marry the most hated man in Norway." Vestein glanced upward as though directing his words at the gods. "Our family truly is cursed."

"Being a king's concubine would be better than this." Signy gestured around them, the color rising in her cheeks. "This—this simple little life."

For a moment Oddny thought her mother was going to argue, but instead Yrsa deflated, shook her head, and sat down heavily on her stool.

"Don't be so ungrateful, Signy. We're alive, aren't we? No thanks to your laziness," Vestein growled. He had grown into a quiet, gangly man with prematurely thinning hair and no beard. That raid—and their father's death—had changed him. While many other men his age were off making names for themselves, Vestein worked hard but was unambitious beyond completing the day's farmwork. Legally the farm was his, but everyone knew Yrsa was in charge.

"Don't you dare start," Signy said, turning on him. "It's at least partially your fault that we have no prospects. You, and that thrice-damned old seeress."

Vestein countered, "You know very well that the only men who haven't cared about the prophecy hanging over your heads are old goats desperate enough to take cursed women as second or third wives. And all of them offered a bride-price far less than either of you is worth. Was I wrong to refuse them? Is this life truly so bad by comparison?"

Signy dug her fingers into her hair and gestured wildly at the fjord, at Ozur's hall on its distant island across the strait. "You think so small, brother! There's a *king* coming through here again, and I—"

"Enough, Signy," Yrsa said softly. "Eat your breakfast. Don't speak of this again."

Maybe it was because of the resignation in her mother's voice, and the way that none of the rest of them—including Oddny—would look at her, but something in Signy seemed to break.

"Fine," she said, and then, more forcefully, *"Fine,"* before she turned and stormed off in the direction of the woods. This in itself was nothing new—and in truth was how most arguments between Signy and Yrsa ended—but the fact that she'd gone without having breakfast was worrisome, though Oddny didn't follow her. Signy always needed time to cool off before anyone, usually Oddny, attempted to soothe her.

Deep down, Oddny knew that Signy's fears were not unfounded: One day Vestein would marry and have children, and his sisters would become two extra mouths to feed. Oddny stole a few glances at the faces around her before landing on Lif, her mother's age, the last daughter of a poor family who could afford no dowry; she'd had few other options than to become a servant. At this point, Oddny had to wonder if her future would end up looking similar, and she told herself it wouldn't be so bad. Lif seemed content enough.

Once they'd finished breakfast, Yrsa handed Oddny a basket. "For your ingredients. And find your sister and make sure she's all right. I fear I pushed her too far today, and I regret it."

"I don't think you did," Oddny said. "I think it was kinder of you to disabuse her of her fantasy than to indulge it."

Yrsa put a hand to Oddny's cheek. "Sometimes I think I've made you too much like me, dear one. Often the stories we tell ourselves are all we have to hold on to. Perhaps I should've let her go on dreaming."

"It wouldn't do her any good," said Oddny bitterly. "She's right about one thing. Our prospects are limited."

"You can't lose hope." Yrsa tilted Oddny's chin up. "You're diligent, a hard worker, and a fine spinner and weaver, and a healer on top of it. You'll be a wonderful wife one day, Oddny. Your prospects aren't as bad as you think."

The words almost escaped her then, her deepest, darkest fear: *Maybe I'm more like Signy than you think, but I'm good at hiding it.*

When Oddny's blood first came in her early teens there had always been at least one full day during her cycle when she was completely bedridden, feeling guilty and useless, and Yrsa had known her daughter well enough to know that she wasn't simply trying to get out of doing chores. Eventually she'd managed to concoct the tea that would ease Oddny's pain, but those first few moons of trial and error had been the worst.

"Does having a child hurt this badly?" Oddny had asked once in the throes of agony.

"Oh, my dear," Yrsa had said, wiping the sweat from Oddny's brow. "I won't lie to you. It's much, much worse."

Oddny didn't doubt this. Of the seven children Yrsa had borne, two had been stillborn, and two had died before their first winter. Vestein, Signy, and Oddny were the only three to live past infancy. And while Oddny and Signy had always been good with children and were often the ones to mind a small horde of youngsters at local gatherings—Signy's stories and boundless energy keeping them entertained, and Oddny's patience and no-nonsense attitude keeping them in line—the thought of birthing a baby herself made Oddny feel ill.

But she would endure, just as her mother had. Yrsa could never know what was truly in her heart. Oddny would not disappoint her.

"Thank you, Mother," she whispered, and went off to find Signy.

THE FARM WAS BORDERED on one side by the deep, dark waters of the fjord, and on three other sides by scant pastureland, which sloped upward into forested foothills and eventually mountains. The foothills were where Ketil's burial mound lay, and a massive pine tree loomed over it, causing a gap in the foliage that gave the clearing a view of the farm, the fjord, and Ozur's island in the distance.

In death, Ketil was always watching over them, and his grave was Signy's favorite spot to brood. So after filling her basket with plants for the tea, Oddny knew exactly where to find her sister.

As she made her way through the woods, she saw a swallow watching her from its perch on a tree branch, and she smiled as she passed it and said, "Hello, little friend." The bird cocked its head and disappeared into the pines just as Oddny reached her father's grave.

"Signy?" she said. "Are you all right?"

Signy sat on the mound with her knees to her chest, her arms folded atop them and her chin resting on her forearms. "Leave me alone."

Oddny clambered up and sat down beside her, mimicking her pose. She could make out Vestein and one of the farmhands in the rowboat, fishing in the fjord.

"I'm so tired of this," Signy said when it was clear her sister wasn't leaving.

"I know," Oddny said.

"Oh, do you?" Signy returned. "I find that hard to believe. Honestly, Oddny. You're just like Mother."

Oddny bristled. "Is that such a bad thing?"

"Isn't it? You've always looked down on me. You and her both. You never take my side. I'm tired of it."

Here we go. "You always do this. Don't take your anger out on me—"

"Oh, *you*. Perfect little *you*. Let me tell you something about *you*, Oddny, you plain-faced little twig," Signy sneered. Whatever had broken in her earlier that morning, it now seemed to have given way to something desperate, something cruel. "You've only resigned yourself to the fate Mother's set out for you because in your heart you know you're not exciting enough for anything else. The only thing that makes you special is how perfectly you fit the mold of what a woman is *supposed* to be, so you're threatened by others who want to break out of it and be something more."

Oddny reddened, all attempts at calm forgotten.

"People say things they don't mean when they're hurt and wish to make others hurt with them," her mother had said once when Oddny was younger and had come crying to her after an argument with Signy. *"You're sisters. When two people know each other as well as you girls do, you know the exact things to say that will cause each other the most pain."*

Never had Yrsa's words seemed more true—but even if Signy didn't mean what she'd said, Oddny was sick of being the target of her sister's ire, born from bitterness at their lot. This had been the way of things ever since they'd become ostracized the night of the prophecy: Oddny remaining silent while Signy carried on as though she were the only one suffering, as though their situations weren't exactly the same. And Oddny was through.

"And you think your looks will disguise how fickle and rotten you are on the inside," Oddny snarled, "but the truth is that any man worth having as a husband would know better than to take someone as flighty as you for a wife. You'll get bored with him in no time and find some other lover, and run all your reputations into the ground."

"Who says a woman has to be defined by her men? By her male kin, and then by her husband and sons? Who *says*? Who says a woman can't stand for herself and make her own way?"

"She can, Signy! But she has to *do* something about it! What have you done to change your lot? Nothing, besides dallying with every man you think will be able to take you away from here. You could disobey Mother and go on the raids if you really wanted to, but you don't even practice fighting. You're too much of a coward."

The barb struck true. Signy turned away from her and said coldly, "Leave."

Oddny stood. "I only came here to comfort you—"

"Go."

"Fine." Oddny huffed and slid off the mound, then made her way back to the deer trail, holding on to trees to support her as she descended the slope. The pain in her belly pulsed down her legs. Up until a certain point she could force herself to push through it, but her limit was rapidly approaching.

As she headed home, she heard a startled cry as Signy burst from the trees and came up behind her. Oddny turned.

"Do you see that?" Signy pointed.

A thick fog was rolling through the mouth of the fjord, creeping toward the farm in long tendrils, skimming like fingers across the water's eerily still surface as though seeking something just out of reach. Fog in itself was not unusual—but appearing so suddenly on an otherwise clear, cloudless day, it seemed downright sinister.

"What . . ." Oddny said, bewildered.

Signy gasped. "Is that—?"

Suddenly a ship barreled forward out of the fog, its sail full as it sliced across the water as cleanly as a blade through butter. It was coming in fast—unnaturally fast. Oddny felt the scar on her palm prickle as if in warning.

"Vestein!" Signy shouted. "Mother!"

"Signy, hold on—"

But Signy was gone in a flash, sprinting across the pasture, dodging cows and sheep and goats and their young as she went. Oddny followed, and when she looked at the water again, she saw Vestein and the farmhand rowing hastily to shore—but the ship was overtaking them.

At the same moment Oddny realized that the crew of the incoming ship had not removed the dragon head at its prow, she saw a tall, helmeted person come to stand beside the carved beast. Saw them hold up a bow, nock an arrow, and draw.

"No!" Oddny cried as she saw her brother crumple, and then there was another arrow and the farmhand collapsed as well, falling over the side of the boat and causing it to capsize with Vestein still in it. Only the farmhand resurfaced, facedown in the water, the arrow's fletching sticking out of his back. On shore, the farm dogs bayed, frightened into a frenzy.

Oddny's instinct was to run back to the trees and hide, but Signy was ahead of her and running straight into danger, and what about Yrsa and

Lif and the rest of the people on the farm? She continued forward on wobbling legs, her breath coming in gasps, her feet moving of their own accord.

"Arms! To arms!" she heard Yrsa shout in the distance. She could picture her mother snatching her father's sword from where it hung on the wall, and could see the farmhands grabbing axes and pitchforks to defend themselves.

Every child in the north knew their way around a weapon, regardless of gender, even if that weapon was a farm tool. And this was exactly the reason why.

The raiders disembarked before the ship was fully beached. They carried axes, spears, short swords. None but the archer wore helmets or much armor. They didn't look too different from the men her father had raided with every summer, but they shouted words Oddny understood in a dialect that sounded strange to her ears.

Signy had stopped, frozen with fear, just before the earthen wall of the hayfield.

Oddny finally reached her, tackling her from behind just as one of the men turned in their direction. The sisters didn't move a muscle, and the raider's eyes passed over their hiding spot. Oddny stifled a sob as the barking, snarling farm dogs that had run up to defend their home were quickly dispatched, and she and Signy watched as one of the oldest farm-hands was slain mercilessly before he could so much as swing his fell-ing axe.

She didn't know what came over her in that moment, the horrible calm that descended on her as she realized exactly what was going on. The only farmhands still alive, their hands and feet wrestled into ropes, were the two youngest: those who would fetch a good price.

Beneath her, Signy began to weep, and Oddny clamped a hand over her sister's mouth, the other still clutching her basket.

Slavers, Oddny mouthed to her. Signy's teary eyes widened and the look that passed between them was one of mutual understanding, of the knowledge of exactly the purpose two young women might be sold for if they allowed themselves to be captured.

They heard screaming from inside the house, heard the wet, muffled sounds of weapons finding their targets. Oddny tried not to picture her mother and Lif bloody and splayed across the floor.

Men exited the hall carrying what little finery the family possessed: Yrsa's chest, containing what was left of the spoils from Ketil's raids; the good pottery; the cauldron; Ketil's heirloom sword. Oddny saw other raiders assessing the livestock, leading the best-looking animals to their ship, scattering or slaying the rest. Her entire body felt cold as she watched.

And then a man sporting a nasty gash in his upper arm dragged Yrsa from the house and threw her onto the dirt, where she fell on all fours, a bloody axe clutched in her hand.

Every bone in Oddny's body screamed at her to *help her mother or she would die or worse*, but she found that she couldn't move.

The biggest raider—the only one in a helmet, the leader, the one who'd shot Vestein—kicked the axe away and said, "Is there nothing else, you sorry old bitch?"

Oddny jolted at the sound of the voice—a *woman's* voice—and when Yrsa offered no reply, the big warrior took off her helmet, revealing a brass-colored braid and eyes hard as steel. The man who'd dragged Yrsa out of the house now grabbed her by the hair and forced her to her knees.

"Don't make me ask again," the woman said.

Yrsa hissed, "You raid my farm, murder my son, and steal my people, and act as if I've cheated *you* by not being rich enough to make it worth your while?"

The woman slapped her across the face. Yrsa did not make a sound, but with her head now turned to the side, she caught a glimpse of Oddny and Signy peering at her over the hayfield wall. Her eyes widened briefly in surprise before sharpening into a look that commanded the same respect she'd demanded of the girls since they were very small.

It said, *Stay right there. Do not help me.*

It said, *Save yourselves.*

"There's no sign of them, Kolfinna," one of the raiders said to the tall woman. "We've searched the outbuildings—"

"They must be here somewhere." Kolfinna turned back to Yrsa. "You and your *people* are a sorry lot. Where are the rest of them?"

"There's no one else," said Yrsa, tearing her gaze from her daughters and staring hard at the ground.

"You're lying," said Kolfinna with a hint of desperation. "There are others here. Where are they?"

Yrsa lunged faster than Oddny had ever seen her move, picked up the axe from where Kolfinna had kicked it, and swung it clumsily at the larger woman. Kolfinna managed to dodge in time to protect her flank, but the axe was sharp and Yrsa landed a shallow slice on her thigh.

"Bitch!" Kolfinna howled. She clutched her leg with one hand, and with the other she punched Yrsa in the jaw, causing her to drop the axe. The man who'd been holding Yrsa grabbed her by the hair again and forced her back to her knees.

Kolfinna straightened, scowling down at her torn pants and bleeding wound. In one slow, menacing movement, she picked up the axe, leveled it at Yrsa, and said, "I'll give you one last chance, woman. Where are the others?"

Yrsa looked up at Kolfinna, bared bloodied teeth, and spat at her feet. "May the dragon devour you slowly in Hel."

Kolfinna raised the axe and brought it down.

Oddny's hand slipped from Signy's mouth in shock.

Yrsa fell forward in a heap, unmoving.

Signy screamed.

And silence followed as every one of the raiders turned to look in the direction of the two women hiding beyond the hayfield. With a sudden lurch in her stomach, Oddny realized just how visible they were if one knew exactly where to look.

"Bring them to me," said Kolfinna, and pointed the axe—still dripping with Yrsa's blood—at the sisters. "Intact."

Oddny dropped her basket and was on her feet in an instant, dragging

Signy with her, holding on to her hand for dear life as they sprinted into the pasture, toward the trees. She heard the heavy footfalls of the men behind them, and her blood pounded in her ears, her legs burned, and they were almost there, if they could just get to the woods—

Someone grabbed her arm and jerked her to a stop, and she went flailing off to the side, letting go of Signy's hand—

The man holding her did not yield as Oddny struggled in his grasp. Behind her, Signy screamed as a larger man threw her over his shoulder and began to carry her off toward the ship.

Someone had set fire to the hall.

"Oddny!" Signy shrieked. *"Mother!"* And then, when she saw Yrsa's cooling body tossed unceremoniously into the burning building, her screams became wordless, horrified.

Oddny felt her strength draining as the man who'd grabbed her dragged her toward the ship. This was it, then. This was how her world ended; this, to Oddny, was Ragnarok: Signy screeching, reaching for her over her captor's shoulder—the burning hall with the bodies of her mother and Lif inside—Vestein's body, somewhere at the bottom of the fjord—

A shrill, inhuman cry split the air.

Oddny's would-be kidnapper released her suddenly, and before she knew it she was sprinting for the trees again as fast as her legs could carry her, sparing only one look behind her to see that there was a swallow—the one from earlier?—attacking the man who'd been holding her, its tiny talons wicked sharp, its chirping growing angrier. A whisper-thin thread extended from its breast into the sky, into nowhere.

The man tried to bat the bird away, and Oddny saw his face—he had no beard and his wide eyes were a strange pale green—and the swallow must've gotten in a good scratch, because he yelped and fell back, covering his eye with both hands.

"What are you doing, Halldor?" Kolfinna bellowed. "She's getting away!"

By then Oddny was well into the pines and she did not stop. Her thighs screamed from the incline as she headed up the slope.

"Run, Oddny!" Signy shouted, her voice hoarse and pained. *"Run—"*

Her cries stopped abruptly, as if she'd been gagged or worse, and gods, *how could Oddny have left her behind?*

Oddny didn't stop running until she reached her father's burial mound, where she climbed into the old pine tree, found a sturdy branch, and sat on it as she clung to the trunk, chest heaving, eyes squeezed shut. Judging from the silence around her, no one had followed. She didn't know how long she stayed there before she summoned the courage to look back toward her home.

Her father's hall was still burning, and the fog was gone, the ship a smudge in the distance, veering south into the strait, heading for the open sea. She wondered if the raiders would raze Ozur's farm as well, wondered if they knew how rich he was compared with the humble family whose lives they had destroyed in the blink of an eye.

Oddny climbed down from the tree, hands and feet unsteady. Then she collapsed on her father's grave and sobbed until the world went dark around her and she could feel nothing at all.

5

THE SWALLOW FLEW ABOVE the din.

After ensuring nobody had followed Oddny into the woods, she made for Signy, who thrashed and screeched through her gag as the raiders bound her hands and feet and tossed her into the ship with the two young farmhands. The swallow followed.

It's going to be all right, the swallow said, despite knowing Signy couldn't hear her. She dove down and started nipping and clawing at Signy's restraints, but she quickly learned that it was a futile endeavor: The ropes were thick and heavy, and she was very small—and even if she managed to free Signy, her friend would never escape the raiders. There were too many of them.

So she flitted onto the gunnel and willed Signy to *see.*

Signy finally stilled when she saw the bird and met its human eyes— and her own eyes widened in recognition, even after all these years. Her voice was muffled through the gag, but the swallow made out her own name, a whisper, Signy's voice rough from screaming: "Gunn . . . hild?"

Heid is trying to clear the fog so my father's men can come to rescue you. Everything will be fine.

Oh, none of that, now, said another voice—a woman's voice, high-pitched and smug—and the swallow took to the air to avoid being tackled by a white fox that leapt at her. Its eyes were amber, and as human as her own.

Another witch.

Who are you? Gunnhild demanded. *What's the meaning of this?*

None of your concern, the fox replied. *We have nothing against you, sister. Go now, and speak of this to no one.*

The fog over the water was beginning to clear, which meant Heid must have succeeded, but Gunnhild couldn't spot her in the air.

"Where is that blasted witch?" said the raiders' leader, squinting at the sky as the others pushed the ship off the rocky beach and climbed aboard. She turned to the fox. "Where did your eagle friend go? Isn't she in charge of the fog?"

"There's no time," said one of the raiders. "It's clearing. The hersir's men will spot us any moment."

"There's the other one," said a second, pointing to something that Gunnhild could not see in the water. "Kolfinna, we must go."

The eagle will catch up, said the fox.

Kolfinna could clearly hear her—how the fox accomplished this, Gunnhild didn't know—for she said, "She'd better, because we're not waiting for her."

The fox jerked her head at Signy. *Do what you will with this one, so long as she can never return to Norway.*

"And the other half of our payment?"

I told you to get rid of them both by any means necessary. But since you let one escape, I'm not paying the rest.

Kolfinna balked. Signy seemed as confused as the other captives—and indeed, as the other crew members—at what was going on, and Gunnhild realized that none but Kolfinna could hear the animal's responses. To them, it must look like their leader was inexplicably talking to a fox.

"You double-crossing little bitch," Kolfinna said.

You did only half the job, said the fox. *But at least you've captured the more comely of the two—she'll sell for a better price than the other, no?*

Shaking with fury, Kolfinna turned away from the fox and started ordering her people about the ship, which began to gain speed. Then she stopped in front of the man who'd nearly captured Oddny. Blood dripped down the side of his face from where Gunnhild's claws had put three slashes through his thick eyebrow.

After taking in his wounds, Kolfinna growled, "You let her go for a few scratches? You've cost us half our pay!"

Gunnhild did not hear his muttered response, but it caused Kolfinna to take a swing at him, which he easily ducked before tackling her to the ground. Several other crew members tried to break them apart, and the fox turned to the swallow.

Why aren't you gone? the other witch asked, eyes moving to her tiny talons. *Don't tell me* you're *the reason the other escaped? Who are these women to you?*

You'll never make it past my father's men, and I intend to stay and watch them capture you, Gunnhild said, more confidently than she felt. There were no warships coming from across the strait, not yet, though she did see some movement. *Whatever you hoped to accomplish here—*

The fox stilled, then bared her teeth in a horrible mockery of a grin. *I see. So you're Gunnhild Ozurardottir? How fortuitous.*

Before Gunnhild could ask how in the Nine Worlds this witch knew her name, the fox leapt high and snatched one of her legs between sharp teeth—an action that would have snapped a normal bird's leg clean off—and dragged her down to the deck to pin her with both paws.

I should've guessed you'd taken to spying on your little friends. Pity it'll be the last thing you ever do, said the fox, jaws opening wide—

But Signy, who had been watching all this unfold in stunned silence, without hearing any of the words passing between the two witches, raised her bound feet and brought both heels down upon the fox's head as hard as she could. Gunnhild saw it coming just in time to dodge before the animal's chin hit the deck with a thunk, and she took to the air well out of the fox's reach.

Damn you, said the fox, and sank her teeth into Signy's calf, and Signy screamed through her gag and tried to shake her off. Kolfinna, who had been dragged off her companion, kicked the fox away.

"If you're going to damage the goods, witch," she spat, "then you can get off my ship."

With pleasure. We're through here, the fox snarled, teeth and maw bloodied, before leaping over the gunnel and into the sea.

"And *you*," Kolfinna said to Signy, whose leg was bleeding freely onto the deck. "Mind yourself, or I may deem you more trouble than you're worth. Is that clear?"

Signy gave her a baleful look, but didn't argue.

Gunnhild soared upward and beat her wings to hold a safe position above the ship. *Come on, Father. The fog is gone. Come and help your neighbors—*

But a flurry of activity caught her attention: Two birds were fighting in the air above them. Like Gunnhild—and the fox—each had a gossamer thread extending from its chest. One was a massive brown eagle Gunnhild had never seen before, but the other was a crow she knew well.

Heid! she cried, hurtling toward her mentor.

Save yourself, child, said the old witch with a calm belied by the frantic beating of her wings, the patches of feathers missing, the scratches and blood visible on her exposed skin. *Go!*

Gunnhild had never been particularly good at following orders.

She whooshed past Heid and slammed into the eagle with the full force of her small body, channeling every bit of her power and will into knocking the other witch out of the sky. The impact sent both birds spiraling before they stopped midair and righted themselves.

Heid hovered nearby, panting. Gunnhild could tell that they needed to get home and soon, but it was safer for them to stay together. She stole a last glance over her wing as the ship passed into the strait. More movement from her father's island, but still no ships. They'd be too late.

I'm sorry, Signy, Gunnhild thought to herself. *I'll find you. I promise.*

She turned her attention back to the fight.

How dare you interfere in our business? said the eagle, whose human eyes were a flat, pale gray, her voice gravelly. *Who do you think you are?*

It's her. Gunnhild. The fox was below them, paddling through the water, her little white head bobbing up and down. *Kill her.*

The eagle rocketed forward and had the swallow in her talons before Gunnhild could react. But then Heid dove—not for the eagle but for its thread, which she clutched in her beak and yanked. The eagle squawked, thrown off balance, and released Gunnhild. And before the larger bird could regain herself, Heid took off toward land, dragging the eagle behind her.

Gunnhild darted after them. *Heid! What are you doing?!*

Katla! the fox cried.

The eagle screeched as she was hauled along, flapping uselessly; she might have been bigger, but Heid was clearly the more powerful witch of the two. *Truce, you old hag! I yield!*

But Heid didn't stop until she reached the woods, where she wove her way purposefully between trunks and limbs. By the time Gunnhild arrived, the old witch had managed to subdue her opponent: The eagle was suspended between two trees, hopelessly tangled in her own thread.

Gunnhild found the crow resting on a branch. When Heid saw her, she said weakly, *That should keep them busy for a while.*

Will you be all right? Gunnhild asked, landing beside her teacher.

Thorbjorg! Help me! the eagle cried as she struggled.

We must go. Heid took to the air again.

Gunnhild looked back toward the water one last time: The ship was nowhere in sight, and the fox had dragged its sopping body to shore. She met Gunnhild's eyes and bared her little teeth in a snarl that gave Gunnhild the visceral impression that this was not the last time their paths would cross.

Then Gunnhild tore her gaze away and flew upward, and as the crow and swallow cleared the treetops, the fox and eagle were lost to view.

THEY FLEW FOR QUITE some time, mountains and valleys and forests passing below them, for they were a very long way from home.

Around nightfall, Heid suddenly listed sideways and began to fall. Panicked, Gunnhild followed her, grabbing her teacher's thread in her talons and hauling her along as best she could.

But Gunnhild was mentally exhausted, and it was beginning to manifest in her swallow.

Leave me, girl, Heid croaked.

I won't, Gunnhild said. *We're so close.*

They managed to make it to the edge of the clearing where the cottage lay before Gunnhild's strength gave out and the swallow and crow crashed to the underbrush. Heid did not move after they hit the ground.

The swallow skittered forward across the clearing and slipped through the cracked door of the cottage before flying up and into the back of a young woman with auburn hair, who sat very still atop a stool in front of a dying hearth fire, a wooden distaff in one hand—the staff that had, until that moment, anchored her thread, keeping her body and her bird-self joined—and an earthenware cup on the floor at her feet.

Gunnhild's eyes snapped open the moment her mind rejoined her shape. She dropped the distaff and scrambled around to the other side of the fire, where Heid had tipped off her stool and lay as still as the crow outside, her own staff clutched tightly in her hand. The witch had become even smaller over the past twelve winters, her frame thinner and her teeth fewer in number, with only a few wisps of white hair remaining on her head.

But the old woman was still breathing, and Gunnhild noted with relief that Heid's iron staff still had its thread attached, extending out through the door and into the crow in the clearing. It shimmered like a spiderweb catching the sunlight.

Gunnhild staggered into the clearing and scooped up the crow, then went back inside and put it atop Heid's chest. Once the bird had been reabsorbed into the witch, Gunnhild picked her up as carefully as she would an infant and slid her onto the rickety bed pallet to examine her. Heid's wounds reflected those inflicted upon her in her crow form and they were much deeper than Gunnhild had thought, though not deep enough for stitches. But Heid was already so fragile.

Gunnhild grabbed a healing salve from their stores, smeared the green paste onto Heid's wounds, and arranged the musty furs around her. Then Gunnhild crouched on the packed-earth floor of the cottage and grabbed her mentor's gnarled, knobby hand.

"Heid, say something. Please."

The old woman's lips moved, but only a whisper of air came out. Gunnhild leaned in close to try to decipher her words, to no avail.

Then Heid let out a rattling breath as her chest fell, and it did not rise again.

"Heid?" Gunnhild said feebly. "*No.* No, no . . ."

This can't be. I'm not ready. I'm not established.

I can't be alone. Not yet.

A dangerous thought occurred to Gunnhild then, and she took up her wooden distaff once more, along with her cup, which contained the remains of the henbane tea she'd consumed in order to loosen her mind from her body. She dragged her stool over to Heid's bedside and sat, then drank the dregs of the tea, which made her stomach twist; she had been fasting since the day before in preparation for this journey, which she made periodically to check on her friends and family.

Then she began to mime spinning as she sang the warding songs. She would have to leave part of herself behind to keep her body singing while she went under, and she'd never attempted such a thing alone. She wasn't supposed to. It was dangerous. It was something Heid had always warned her about in the direst terms: *"Travel with a companion always, or have another woman sing for you, for there are witches who know the charms that can sever your mind from your body—and that, dear child, will lead to a slow and painful death. It's a fate I wouldn't wish on my worst enemies."*

Recalling those words filled Gunnhild with an icy terror. Cold sweat dripped down her back despite the heat from the fire. Her hands shook on her distaff.

"Feel your fear," Heid had told her the first time she'd gone into trance. "You never know who you'll meet where you're going, never know who your song will summon. It could be Odin himself for all we know."

That had not comforted Gunnhild one bit. "Will it get easier with time? I've been frightened my entire life. I came with you to *escape* my fears. I loathe being scared."

"Of course you do. And it doesn't get easier with time, but you'll become more courageous," Heid had replied. "You'll get used to being afraid. If you don't feel fear, why would you need to be brave?"

Many winters later, Gunnhild still didn't understand what she'd meant. All she knew was that this couldn't be the end—she needed her teacher back.

This time, instead of sending her mind out into the world as the swallow, she forced it to sink down, and down, and down.

She opened her eyes to the utter blackness of the void, the place between worlds. Her form was illuminated by an inner light, a thin wisp of thread reaching from the center of her chest and upward into nothingness, where her own song echoed above her from very far away.

But no spirits had come, as they usually did when Heid sang for her—why?

Suddenly Gunnhild felt a tingle, as though she were being watched: Something was circling her out there in the dark, and it wasn't Heid.

But where *was* Heid? Where were the spirits?

"Heid? Heid, please!" she called. Then she paused, felt the prickling again. *Someone is here.* "Heid, you must come back. I'll find a way to heal you. I'll find a way—"

"You're bolder than I thought if you think you can raise the dead," said a familiar, gravelly voice. The voice of the eagle. Katla.

This was wrong. This was all wrong. This was not how it was supposed to be.

A woman's chuckle resounded through the deep darkness, and Gunnhild felt someone reach out and grab her from behind—but at that exact moment she willed herself up, following her thread back to her body.

When she opened her eyes, she was back in the cottage, throat raw from singing. She threw down the distaff and reached for Heid's body, taking the old woman's bony hands in her own, and cried as she never had before.

"I'm sorry, Heid," she whispered. "I've failed you . . ."

But once her tears subsided, a fire began to burn within her. All was quiet so deep in the woods—a glaring contrast to the chaos she'd so narrowly escaped—but her blood pounded in her ears as she released Heid's hands and stood, fists balled at her sides.

As she stared down at the body of her mentor—her surrogate mother for these past twelve winters, her teacher, her entire world—her mind reeled with all that had transpired that day, tried to make sense of it. Who were these witches, this Katla and Thorbjorg, the eagle and the fox—and their unknown companion, whom one of the raiders had pointed out in the water? How had Katla followed Gunnhild to the dark place? What did they have against Oddny and Signy and their family? What would've happened to Oddny if Gunnhild hadn't decided to spy on her friends that morning? And what would've happened to *Gunnhild* had Heid opted to stay behind and sing for her instead of joining her as a crow?

And, perhaps most important—how had these witches known her name? How had they known *anything* about her? And why?

She needed a plan. She needed answers. She needed to find Signy, who was being taken farther away with each passing moment. The encounter with Katla in the dark place must have been a fluke. Gunnhild would find Oddny, make sure she was unharmed, and have her sing the warding songs so Gunnhild could ask the spirits where Signy had been taken. And there was only one place Oddny could have gone once the coast was clear: to her closest neighbor, Ozur.

Gunnhild needed to get home.

She had friends at the Sámi encampment nearby, and they would be heading west soon to meet with King Harald's men as they did each autumn. If she caught them, she could go with them. She would close up the cottage and leave first thing in the morning.

But first she needed to bury Heid.

6

ODDNY AWOKE IN THE empty bunk room in Ozur's hall.

She didn't fully remember how she'd gotten there. She'd been flickering in and out of consciousness for . . . she didn't know how long. For all she knew, she'd been in a state of grief-induced catatonia for days or even weeks—no, it must have been only a day or two, for her blood hadn't yet come. Her stomach should have been roaring with hunger, but the pain in her womb overshadowed it.

She had only snippets of memory, brief flashes of staggering toward Ozur's approaching warriors, being guided onto the ship. A rowboat had washed to shore, and there'd been a corpse underneath with an arrow sticking out of its neck. She hadn't looked, hadn't dared. The boat and her brother's body, along with those of her beloved farm dogs and the slain farmhands, had been somberly laid out atop the charred ruins after Oddny had told the men—*Had* she told them? Had that been her own voice? It'd sounded so far away—that her mother and Lif were already buried beneath the pile of blackened beams that had once been her father's hall.

She'd watched without seeing as Ozur's men had torn down the earthen hayfield wall and used it to build a mound over the remains of her home and the people who had lived there. No fine grave goods to take to the afterlife, not for her family: They'd be destitute in Hel's realm, even more so than they'd been in life.

And now she was alone. For those precious few moments upon waking, she almost forgot what she was doing there. But then the raid came flooding back, her mother's last moments repeating over and over in her mind's eye:

Yrsa on her knees in front of the axe-wielding leader of the raiders.

Yrsa, eyes locked on Oddny and Signy, bidding them to stay quiet, stay hidden.

Yrsa, stone-faced and fearless as the axe came down.

Oddny took a breath and tried to hold back her tears. Her mother wouldn't want her to cry.

This can't be real.

Signy . . .

Signy, reaching for her over the shoulder of her captor, calling her name, then begging her to run, her voice cut off midscream.

Oddny wanted more than anything to go back to sleep again, to forget that any of this had ever happened. But now she was wide-awake and the pain in her mind and body was overwhelming. It took every ounce of her strength to sit up, swing her legs over the side of the bed, and stand.

She heard the rap of Ulfrun's cane moments before the thick curtain separating the bunk room and the anteroom parted and the woman herself tottered in.

"Oh, Oddny! Goodness, I'm glad to see you awake. You've been lying there for two days," said Ulfrun. She pointed with a knobby finger to something behind Oddny. "They found your basket in the field at your farm. They thought it might be important, seeing as you're a healer."

"Thank you." Oddny picked up the basket, relieved: Her plants were wilted, but they would do, and she would scavenge from the kitchen's garden for the rest. She needed her tea badly. Pain rippled down her legs, making her knees threaten to give out. "Is there news of my sister?"

Please, tell me that Ozur's men tracked the raiders down. Tell me that she's all right. That she was rescued.

"None," Ulfrun said sorrowfully. "The first sign of trouble we saw when the fog cleared was the smoke, and by then—oh, by then, it was too late. I'm so sorry, lamb."

Oddny's chest felt tight. She spent a few moments getting her bearings after Ulfrun left. Every step was agony, but Oddny managed to make her way out of the bunk room, parting the curtain to reveal—

Solveig, propped up in bed, color in her cheeks, unsteady hands attempting to mend a dress in her lap. And as much as Oddny resented the woman who'd caused her best friend so much pain, it was a relief to see her alive. To know that Yrsa's last act as a healer had succeeded.

"Oh," said Oddny. "Solveig. You look—"

"Better, thanks to your mother. At least for now. It comes and goes," Solveig said. Her expression softened as she took in the young woman in the doorway. "I'm sorry for your loss, Oddny Ketilsdottir. It was unjust and undeserved. I'm certain my husband will make arrangements for you. Go to him when you can."

"Does Ozur mean to let me stay here?"

"He does. You've no kinsmen to look after you, so I trust he'll allow you to work toward a dowry and help you find a husband." Solveig gestured to a haversack sitting on a chest nearby. "And that's for you."

Oddny picked up the bag and recognized the weight and shape of the object inside without opening it: her mother's statue of Eir, the gods' physician. She knew every carved groove that made up the goddess's likeness, every drop of blood that had ever blessed the statue during sacrifices and festivals. Eir had always been Yrsa's patron, and Oddny's own as well.

"The skalds say the gods don't favor the weak," Oddny had said to her mother once when she was twelve winters old, the third or fourth time her blood had come. It was before she'd begun to learn the healing arts and sworn herself to Eir, before Yrsa had come up with the perfect recipe for Oddny's moon tea. The pain had rendered Oddny prone on her bedroll. She'd never felt so betrayed; her own body had turned on her and would do so every moon until she was her mother's age. She'd felt utterly hopeless. "Will any of them favor me?"

Yrsa had sat down beside her and said with conviction, "Of course they will."

"I suppose enduring this will make me stronger, then," Oddny had said bitterly.

"If it comforts you to think so," Yrsa had replied. "But it's all right to feel weak, Oddny. Sometimes our bodies give us more pain than we can bear. But any gods worth worshipping know that not every person can give the same effort." She'd nodded to where Ketil's statue of Thor was lofted upon the lintel—later, it would be buried with him in his mound—and then to her own statue of Eir on the trestle table where she mixed her tinctures. "Do you think they resent that we sacrifice one sheep where Ozur could afford to sacrifice five bulls if he so chose? They know how little we have to give—that we give at all is what matters to them. Do you understand? When your patron calls you, they'll judge your strengths and weaknesses against yourself, not against others."

Presently, Oddny clutched the bag to her chest, and she did not move to wipe the tears running down her face.

"Our men found it in the ruins before they built the mound. They tried to give it to you as you waited on the ship but said you couldn't seem to see or hear them," Solveig said quietly. "You may keep the bag as well. But first, open it, child. You should see for yourself the miracle it holds."

Oddny pulled out the statue and was unable to stifle a gasp: There was not a single scorch mark on it. Eir was as whole as she'd been the morning of the attack, her round, carved face warm and reassuring. Swallowing a sob, Oddny stuffed it back inside the bag, closed the flap, and looked back to Solveig. "Thank you."

Solveig nodded. Oddny ducked out of the anteroom and into the main hall, then out into the open air toward the cookhouse—it still boggled her mind that Ozur had a separate hall just for *cooking*—where she hoped to be allowed to brew her tea.

The mistress of the cookhouse was a prickly woman named Vigdis, who grudgingly let her take from the garden and permitted her to use a small cauldron and the cook fire to heat some water. When Oddny mentioned being Yrsa's daughter, a look of recognition passed over the older woman's face.

"Can you make anything to cure my joints of their aching?" she asked eagerly. "I've lived with this for a long time, so I never thought it was worth bothering your mother over—there was always something bigger going on to bring her here. But since you're here now . . ."

Oddny shook her head as she tilted the hot water into her cup and let the ingredients steep. "I'm sorry. Illnesses and injuries can be healed, but I can't cure ongoing conditions of the body."

Otherwise, she added silently, *I would cure whatever curses my womb.* Gods, sometimes she wished she could just rip the damned thing out.

"But I can make you something for the pain," Oddny went on. "Make it a little more bearable. That's what I do for myself. I know all my mother's recipes." She'd always been skilled at memorization. At times she'd recited the recipes back to Yrsa in the exact tone of voice her mother had used while explaining them the first time, even if it had been many winters prior.

"If you could, I'd like that very much." Vigdis suddenly seemed a little less bitter about having her around, but Oddny studiously avoided the eyes of the thrall women who also worked in the cookhouse. Ozur treated them well enough—their hair was kept long, their clothing worn but patched—but enslavement was enslavement. *Is this to be Signy's fate? Or worse?*

Oddny had not grown up with thralls. But in the north, and in much of the known world beyond it, the labor of the unfree was the backbone of society. It made her feel guilty that their predicament was something she'd seldom thought about before Signy's kidnapping.

"It puts a bad taste in my mouth," she'd overheard her mother telling her father one day when he'd suggested bringing home a thrall to help her with the laundry, Yrsa's most onerous chore. "Any person can become enslaved at any time—if they're captured, if they can't pay a debt. One bad day, and that could be us instead. No. It feels like tempting fate."

Oddny wondered, not for the first time, if Yrsa had possessed some foresight she'd never spoken of.

Finally Oddny's tea was done, and she drank it down. It would be some time before she felt its effects, but at least she knew they would come.

Suddenly there were shouts outside as a horn blew once. Vigdis and Oddny gave each other a weighty look that said: *Raiders? Again?*

"I'll go see what's going on," said Oddny. Before she turned to leave she saw Vigdis reach for a large kitchen knife.

When Oddny went outside, she saw a group of people coming up the slope from the docks. With relief, she realized they were familiar faces: Ozur's men. But between the two in front was a smaller man with an arm slung over each of their shoulders, head hanging, hair covering his face. He half walked with them, either hurt or semiconscious, dripping wet as if he'd just been pulled from the sea.

This newcomer might be in need of healing, so Oddny started toward the group, prepared to offer her services. As she rounded the corner of the longhouse, she saw Ozur come out to meet them, leaning heavily on his cane and asking, "What's going on?"

"He washed ashore near the cliffs," said one of the watchmen to the hersir. "We sent a boat out to get him."

"What's your name, son?" Ozur asked.

"Halldor Hallgrimsson," said the man, raising his head, and Oddny saw his face: square jaw, high cheekbones, russet hair that tumbled down to his shoulders in damp waves. Like her late brother, Vestein, he wore no beard; and, like most free men, he had a seax—a single-edged short sword—hanging horizontally from his belt by two loops attached to the sheath. From what she could see, she guessed he was about her age.

Then she noticed his pale green eyes and the three small, scabbing vertical slits crossing his eyebrow on one side, as if something had recently tried to take his eye out.

Something with small, sharp talons.

Something like a bird. A swallow, even.

"*You,*" she snarled, and his eyes widened in recognition at the exact moment she lunged forward and slapped him across the face.

"Oddny Ketilsdottir, what *has* gotten into you?" Ozur asked, aghast. The rest of the men, who'd had only the barest of interactions with their old friend Ketil's reticent younger daughter, looked equally shocked.

Oddny drew back, head buzzing. Her hands shook violently as she drew her small utility knife from her belt.

"This man is one of the raiders who destroyed my farm," she said. "I claim his life as compensation."

"Oddny, that's not how these things work," Ozur said.

She ignored him and started forward again, but the men holding Halldor dragged him back, giving her warning looks. One of them put his hand to his seax.

"You would defend one of my family's killers?" she said. When the men didn't respond, she gestured wildly with the knife and turned to Ozur in frustration. "If I were a man, you would let me slay him where he stood."

"Not unless it was a duel," said the man on Halldor's right, and a few of the others behind him nodded. "And I don't think you want that." Scattered laughter followed these words, and Oddny felt her face heat. Halldor remained silent, his expression betraying nothing, his eyes not leaving her.

Ozur chose a different tactic. "They defend him because they could very well have been in his place during our own exploits. We've all been on the raids. We've all done as he's done and haven't been put to death because of it."

"That's because you were never caught," Oddny spat.

Ozur stepped closer to her, his long white beard quivering as he tried to decide what to say. Finally he told her, so quietly that the other men couldn't hear, "We don't know who he is, where he comes from, and what kind of wealth he has to his name . . ."

Oddny realized at once what Ozur had in mind: He meant to extract her dowry from this man as compensation. The same sort of arrangement that Solveig had mentioned, one that would end with Oddny married off and Signy left to her fate. But perhaps, if this was indeed Ozur's intention, she could work it to her advantage. After all, her dowry would remain her property . . .

And thus a plan started coming together in her mind.

"We may be able to come to terms that will benefit you more than a mere moment's satisfaction at his death," Ozur said when she didn't speak.

"His death would satisfy me for more than just a moment," Oddny said through her teeth, but she sheathed her knife nonetheless.

If she had any hope of seeing her sister again, she needed Halldor alive.

ONCE A CLOAK HAD been placed over Halldor's shoulders and a steaming bowl of leftover stew shoved into his hands, Ozur bade the young man speak. Halldor sat on the platform, and Ozur, instead of taking his high seat, dragged over a stool and settled down directly in front of his visitor. Oddny sat on the platform across from them, hands white-knuckled on its edge.

The other men kept a respectful distance, but Oddny knew they were listening.

"Where are you from, Halldor Hallgrimsson?" Ozur asked.

"The south. Saeheim, in Vestfold," said Halldor after he'd wolfed down several spoonfuls of stew. "My father was a blacksmith for King Bjorn."

"Oh, yes? King Bjorn the Merchant?" Ozur said with interest. "Were you there when he was killed? You look old enough, but you may have been quite young when it happened."

From where Oddny hovered, she saw Halldor's eyes narrow. "You mean when his own brother stuck an axe in his chest?"

The hair on Oddny's arms stood on end; everyone knew that King Eirik had killed two of his brothers, but she'd never heard it spoken of with so much ire.

Ozur squinted at him. "That's precisely what I mean. That was—oh, how many winters ago?"

"Nine," Halldor said. "My parents were long dead by then. I only heard about it. Eirik was—"

"*King* Eirik is the next ruler of our young country," said Ozur with firm conviction, stamping his cane once on the ground.

"*King* Eirik. I forget myself. You must forgive me." Halldor sounded less than apologetic. "We're not overly fond of him where I come from."

Ozur said sharply, "King Eirik and his hird will be passing through here any day now on their way back from Bjarmaland. I hope you'll show them proper respect when they arrive."

Oddny thought she saw a sudden flash of hunger in Halldor's eyes, or something very close to it—but when she blinked, his face was carefully blank once more.

"You needn't worry about me," Halldor said. "I won't embarrass my host. May I ask whose hall has so graciously accepted me as a guest?"

Oddny grudgingly had to give the man credit—he knew the right words to say. Flattery could get you everywhere with the right people, and Gunnhild's father was one such person.

"Ozur Eyvindsson," said Ozur. "I am a hersir."

"It's an honor to have been rescued by such an esteemed man."

Oddny made a face, realized too late that Halldor had seen her do it, and continued to glare at him as he gave her a flat look.

Ozur said, "And how did you come to be parted from your raiding party?"

Halldor turned his attention back to his host. "I was thrown overboard after a disagreement with my captain."

"And do you have a trade, or are you a career fighter?"

"I was trained in smithing by Hallgrim—by my father. Back home in Vestfold. Before he died." Halldor eyed the old man warily, as if knowing exactly what Ozur was getting at. "I can forge rivets, repair cauldrons and the like, but nothing worthy of note. I'm better at fighting by far. Why do you ask?"

"Well, I have nothing against you personally, but I regret that you ended up at the wrong raid at the wrong farm," said Ozur. He jabbed his thumb over his shoulder to where Oddny sat. "You see, when my own youngest daughter was alive . . ." There was pain in the words, and he stopped and collected himself.

Oddny knew it was easier to pretend Gunnhild was dead than acknowledge whatever had truly happened to her. She hoped the old man felt guilty about it.

"Oddny here was her dear friend," Ozur went on. "Her sister, Signy, whom your party captured, was as well. Their father, Ketil, was an old friend of mine, and her mother, Yrsa, was in the process of healing my wife from a grievous illness when your people slew her."

Halldor's expression grew darker with each word as the gravity of his situation sank in. *Good,* Oddny thought.

"Which is all to say that I cannot let Oddny go uncared for," Ozur finished. "I feel it's only fair that you pay the price for your fellows' deeds, as you were the only one of them captured."

"Am I a prisoner here, Ozur Eyvindsson?" Halldor asked slowly.

"Until you compensate Oddny for her losses, yes."

Those pale green eyes flitted to the woman in question, then back to the hersir. "And how much do I owe her?"

Ozur sucked his teeth as he thought. Then he said, "Twelve marks of silver," and Oddny's jaw dropped. *One* mark of silver was a respectable dowry, but *twelve*?

Meanwhile, Halldor had gone pale. He spooned the last of the stew into his mouth, chewed, and swallowed. But, to his credit, he did not argue.

"Then I suppose I need to improve my smithing," he said.

"A fine idea," said Ozur as he rose, gripping his cane. "Or else you'll be here for a very long time. My men will show you to the forge. You may bunk there with the other smiths. Excuse me."

He made for the anteroom as Halldor stood as well and was led away. Oddny followed Ozur into the family's chamber and closed the door behind her. Solveig was asleep, looking paler than she had earlier. Her husband sat down heavily on the bed beside her and gave a tired sigh.

"Ozur, thank you—you didn't have to—*twelve marks* is—" Oddny began, but when the elderly hersir looked up at her, he had tears in his eyes.

"It was nothing. I wished to do for you what I couldn't for my little Gunna, Oddny Ketilsdottir," he whispered. "To give you a good life. Your father would have done the same for any of my girls. It doesn't absolve me of my role in driving Gunnhild to do what she did . . ." He looked to Solveig, then back to Oddny. "But it's something."

Oddny couldn't bring herself to confess to him what she intended to spend the silver on the moment Halldor put it in her hands. Better to let Ozur think he was securing her future.

She only nodded and ducked out of the room before he could see her cry.

TWELVE MARKS OF SILVER, Oddny thought to herself for the rest of the day as she sat spinning outside under the awning with Ulfrun and a few of the other women. Keeping her hands busy normally soothed her, but her mind was a storm.

Twelve marks. It was outrageous.

Outrageous enough to get her exactly what she wanted.

The horrors of the past few days had faded; the moment she'd realized that Halldor was her only link to Signy, it was as though a veil had lifted and she could see clearly once more. It allowed her to push aside the mountain of grief that threatened to crush her every time she thought too long about the raid and to replace it with a fierce determination to find her sister, the only family she had, one of the only people left in this world whom she cared about.

I'm of no use to her in this state, she told herself. *I must carry on.*

There would be time to mourn their family—together—once Signy was safe. But there was one more piece that had to fall into place, and it involved more than Halldor's silver: She'd need his cooperation, too.

So when she noticed him leaving the hall alone after supper the next evening, she followed.

"Halldor Hallgrimsson," she called just before he reached the smithy. "I would have a word with you."

He stopped and turned, eyes moving down to the blade at her belt. Now that his hair was fully dry, it was more curly than wavy, framing his sunburned face in a way that accentuated his sharp cheekbones. His mouth drew into a thin line as he regarded her.

"So long as you keep that little knife of yours in its sheath," he said warily. "Although it'd be unwise to maim me, as it could prevent me from paying you the exorbitant amount of silver I owe you."

"Exorbitant?" Oddny seethed. "I think it's a fair price for my losses."

"Well, I wouldn't even be here if I hadn't let you go," he shot back. "It lost us half our pay, so Kolfinna decided to feed me to Ran once we were far enough out at sea."

It took a moment for his words to sink in.

But when Oddny finally spoke, she *exploded*.

"Half your *pay*? You were *paid* to raid our farm?" She shouted the words so loudly that a flock of birds pecking about nearby took wing. "Why? By whom?"

"I don't—wait." Halldor took a step back from her, palms up, as she drew her knife and stalked toward him, leveling the tip at his throat. "Put that down."

"Not until you explain."

"Let's be civil about this, shall we?"

Oddny said nothing and kept her knife raised.

"I see we're past civility, then," Halldor said dryly.

"Well past," said Oddny. "Speak. Now."

"Listen. I'm sorry, all right?" he blurted. "For the part I played in what happened. It was nothing personal. Now could you please put that knife away?"

"Nothing personal?" she echoed shrilly.

Halldor's nostrils flared and he kept his hands up. "All I know is that a witch hired us to raid your farm. Said her friends would obscure our ship and grant us a swift wind. In and out—that was the deal. You and your sister were the targets, but we were told we could plunder the farm and kill or capture anyone else we wished."

"Who was this witch? And if you're telling the truth, you could very well kill me and cart me off in a rowboat to rejoin your friends and get out of your debt to me. How do I know you won't?"

Halldor eyed the knife. "I'm through with them."

"And why is that?"

"You'll just have to trust me."

"Forgive me if I don't. Now tell me about the witch."

Halldor shook his head. "She dealt only with Kolfinna. She was a fox."

"The *witch* was a fox?"

"Yes, and her friend was an eagle. Everyone knows witches can shapeshift. The fox seemed to talk to Kolfinna, but only in her head. If I were making this up, wouldn't I come up with something more plausible?"

Oddny was still skeptical. "All right. Let's say I believe you. But . . . what reason could anyone possibly have to attack us?" She hated the tears that sprang to her eyes, hated the way the knife shook in her hand as she continued to hold it aloft, and especially hated the way her voice cracked as she asked, "What did we do to deserve this?"

"Look, you're asking the wrong person. Now will you put the knife down? I can't pay you back if you cut my throat."

Oddny reluctantly lowered her weapon and sheathed it. "How do I know you won't try to escape in the night before your debt is paid?"

Halldor stiffened, offended. "You truly do think me *that* dishonorable, don't you?"

Oddny was silent.

"On my life, I'll pay you what I owe," he said after a beat. "I intend to join King Eirik's retinue when they pass through. I'll get richer raiding with them than I ever could've with Kolfinna. I'd be a fool to pass up such an opportunity. This way, I'm sure I can pay your debt off in a season or less."

"You wish to join the king's hird?" Oddny asked, raising her eyebrows. "But you spoke of him with such disdain. Why would you choose to swear yourself to him? And why would *he* trust *you*, especially after learning you're from Vestfold?"

Halldor raked a hand through his hair. "His reputation precedes him, but perhaps I wish to judge him for myself, in hopes that he'll do the same for me, no matter where I'm from. And the sooner I've paid off my debt to you, the sooner we never have to see each other again."

"Your smithing must be worse than you let on," Oddny observed, smirking.

Halldor only folded his arms and glowered at her.

Despite herself, Oddny had to admit that his plan made sense—judging by the finery that Eirik and his hirdsmen had worn at the feast she'd served, they were wealthy, without even factoring in the expensive weaponry they must've kept on their ship.

"Are we through here?" Halldor asked.

"No. There's still the reason I wished to speak with you." Oddny straightened. "If they didn't kill Signy, where would they have taken her?"

Halldor stared at her. "Why?"

"I mean to rescue her once you've paid me."

He seemed surprised, but shook his head. "I won't say. It'll only hurt you. There's no chance of saving her, Oddny. She's gone. I would rather stay silent and spare you the pain of this hopeless—"

"I'll take eleven and a half marks of silver instead of twelve if you tell me."

He eyed her. "Eleven."

"No. Eleven and a half or no deal."

"Done." He held his hand out, and Oddny hesitated a moment before shaking it once. His was cold, and calloused in different ways than her own, but that was all she noticed before he quickly let go of her and said, "Birka."

Oddny had heard of the town. It was on an island in Svealand, clear on the other side of the peninsula from Norway.

"But . . . why take her there?" she asked. "There are market towns much closer than that. Some even on the way."

"Birka is where we usually winter, so that's where she's most likely to be sold. But . . ."

"But . . . ?" Oddny prompted.

"At least one of the witches was still with them to hasten their escape. Even if I handed you your silver right this moment, and you hired a ship and a crew this very night and left tomorrow morning, you'd be too late to save her before she's sold."

"But I can buy her freedom once you pay me," Oddny said. "And if I find the raiders, I'll find who she's been sold to. You'll join Eirik's hird and pay me what you owe by the end of next summer, as you've said, and then I'll go to Birka and begin my search."

It wasn't soon enough, but for now it was all she could do.

"Wait," Halldor said. "Say I *am* able to pay off my debt to you by the end of next summer. By then, your sister could've been sold and sold again—"

"Yes, I know. Thank you." She turned to go, eager to get out of his presence, to have some time alone to go through her options.

Perhaps I could send out word of my healing services. If witches wander around the country peddling their magic, couldn't I do the same with my own skills? Maybe I could earn enough silver that I wouldn't even need Halldor's at all.

"Oddny," Halldor said to her retreating back. "I'm telling you, it's hopeless."

She stopped. Took a deep breath through her nose and out her mouth.

"Be that as it may," she said over her shoulder, "she's my sister. And she would do the same for me. Good night, Halldor Hallgrimsson."

She didn't wait to hear his response.

8

GUNNHILD DUG FOR A long time before she was satisfied with the depth of the grave, and she was sweating by the time she carefully laid her mentor's body down inside it. She'd dressed Heid in her finest garments, her shiniest rings and brooches, and had even painstakingly slipped the woman's gloves on over her stiff fingers. Once she'd positioned Heid, Gunnhild placed a bowl of henbane seeds by the old woman's head and set her hnefatafl board at her shins, arranging the smooth carved ivory and worn wooden pieces atop it as if preparing to play a round of the game. Heid deserved to go to the afterlife with all the best things she owned. In fact, a woman of her esteem deserved much more than Gunnhild had the ability to give her. She deserved a ceremony, wailing mourners, the proper sacrifices.

Instead, she was getting a sniffling young woman and a hole in the ground.

After setting the tafl board, Gunnhild nestled the wooden distaff in the crook of Heid's elbow. She would keep Heid's iron staff and what little remained of her silver, for Heid had no more need to be tethered to her body and no more need for wealth.

One last item gave Gunnhild pause: Heid's little wooden statue of the goddess Freyja. Gunnhild had fetched it from the small copse of trees where Heid had placed it when she'd returned from her last journey—twelve winters ago, with Gunnhild in tow. And now Gunnhild stared down at it.

The statue's blank eyes stared back, betraying nothing. Freyja's most recognizable attributes—her golden necklace and her cloak of falcon feathers—had been crudely carved by Heid as a girl. But something in the statue's face, in its stark and simple beauty, had called to Gunnhild from the moment she'd seen it.

It had been an exhilarating, terrifying thing to run away from home. Once the king's tax collector and his men had left the seeress and her stowaway on the mainland shore, it took Gunnhild and Heid days of walking to reach the cottage, Gunnhild pulling Heid's cart all the while. And when they'd arrived, Heid had instructed her to leave the cart at the cottage and had led her deeper into the woods. Gunnhild had been too exhausted to argue, but part of her had wondered if the witch had gone mad and perhaps her invitation to teach Gunnhild magic had been a farce; maybe Gunnhild truly was the foolish child her mother said she was, and she'd be better off going home and begging her parents' mercy than subjecting herself to the whims of a senile old woman in the middle of nowhere.

And then they'd reached the grove, where Heid had taken the statue from her bag and set it reverently in the hollow of a tree. One look at the goddess's face and Gunnhild had known she'd made the right choice.

"Freyja was the first witch," Heid had explained, and turned to Gunnhild with a glint of mischief in her eye. "Perhaps you'll get to meet her one day."

"Have *you* met her?"

Heid had only given her a small smile, turned back to the statue, and pricked her finger to offer the goddess a drop of her blood. Gunnhild herself would do the same many times over the dozen winters that followed.

For all the good it's done me, she thought sullenly at present. She'd never had a single sign that her offerings had been accepted.

In the end she tucked the statue under Heid's arm and picked up her spade. No goddess was going to appear out of the woods to help her; she was on her own.

It took her the rest of the night to fill the grave. Afterward, she lay on her straw mat—she couldn't bring herself to use Heid's bed pallet—and tried to memorize each gap in the thatched roof and every stone of the hearth, and tried to come to terms with the fact that this was her last night in the cottage where she'd spent half her life.

In the morning, she bathed and used the now broken-toothed comb she'd had since childhood to tame her hair before plaiting it. Then she packed her things: the henbane that she and Heid had cultivated, both dried flowers and seeds; a small box of potions, salves, and poisons; her earthenware cup; her sewing supplies; and finally, the iron staff. She'd long since outgrown the clothing she'd arrived in, and she'd repurposed some of it into a tight-fitting patchwork kaftan, which she pulled on over her dress and pinned closed at her breast with a rusty brooch before securing her belt overtop it.

Once she was ready, she uncovered Heid's rickety old pull cart from the lean-to where they'd kept it safe from the elements. Besides the knife and pouch at her belt, all her possessions fit into her haversack, which she loaded onto the cart along with Heid's last small chest of silver. The furs from the bed pallet she'd also shaken out and packed, intending to give them to the Sámi to add to their tribute for King Harald.

She looked at the empty cottage, the barren garden, and the stone-covered plot beside it where Heid's body lay.

"Goodbye," she whispered to the grave.

It was around midday when she reached her destination. The woods slowly began to thin, giving way to rolling plains beyond. There were no reindeer in sight; they might be grazing over the next hill. In the direction she was headed, she could see smoke drifting lazily into the sky from a cluster of tents near the edge of another wooded area, the trees acting as a windbreak.

A few heads turned as she entered the Sámi encampment, and she nodded and stopped to greet the people who approached her. After distributing the furs, she made a beeline through the cluster of hide-covered open-topped tents and came to the largest one, where her two friends lived: a testament to their importance within their community as well as a shared space for rituals. Juoksa and his apprentice, Mielat, were noaidi, Sámi practitioners of magic, and old friends of Heid who often came to visit her—and by extension Gunnhild—at the cottage. Over time Gunnhild had learned their language, customs, and a bit about their magic, which had many similarities to her own but also key differences.

Before she could make herself known, the door flap opened and Mielat appeared. He was dressed in a loose tunic of reindeer hide, tanned and finely stitched with colorful thread. His woven belt was bright blue, his hair dark, his eyes soft and kind.

But when he saw her, his face fell.

"So it's true," he whispered, letting the door fall closed behind him as he stepped out.

Gunnhild had intended to keep her composure, but as soon as he hugged her, she crumpled, dropping the cart's handle and returning the embrace.

"We sensed the moment when Heid's spirit moved on from the living world," he said when they broke apart. "How did it happen?"

"She was killed," Gunnhild said quietly.

"*Killed?* By whom?"

"I have more questions than answers. But—"

"I'll fetch Juoksa and our drums. We'll ask the spirits at once."

"There will be no need for that." Juoksa stepped out from the tent, dressed similarly to his apprentice but with a red belt. He was taller, paler, with lighter hair and sharp, dark eyes. When his gaze fell on Gunnhild, she nodded once. He nodded back in understanding: She did not want them involved.

"Why not?" Mielat asked, looking from Juoksa to Gunnhild.

"Because it isn't safe," she said. She explained to them everything that had happened, and finished with, "I fear that these witches are tracking me, and that if you're caught doing a ritual with me, or on my behalf, they'll attack you, too. I must return to my father's as soon as possible. I was hoping to come west with you to meet the king's tax collectors."

Juoksa made a face, and Gunnhild wanted to say that King Harald was as much her king as theirs—which was to say, not much of a king at all—but instead she said, "When are you leaving?"

"A moon from now," he replied.

Gunnhild cursed internally. That was too long. If she wished to find Signy before winter—

"But why would your own kind attack you? And what do your friends from childhood have to do with anything?" Mielat asked.

"That's what I need to find out." Gunnhild sighed. "If I must wait, I'll wait. But I'm eager to see that my friend is safe."

The noaidi exchanged a meaningful look.

Gunnhild narrowed her eyes. "What is it?"

"There may be a quicker way for you to get back to your father's," said Mielat, looking at Juoksa as if waiting for permission to continue.

"A group of Norsemen have made camp on the beach." Juoksa gestured north, in the direction of the water, which was far enough away from their own camp that it could not be seen.

"What?" Gunnhild hardly dared to believe her luck. "Norsemen? You're certain?"

Juoksa nodded. "Some of our trappers met them at dawn. They say they're on their way home from the summer raids."

"There are thirty or so men. They got caught in a storm," Mielat added. "They'll be here at midday to trade some of their plunder for supplies."

Gunnhild peered up at the sky. "But it's midday now."

As if on cue, she heard a commotion from the other end of the camp— men speaking another language, *her* language, and the sound brought with it a swell of memories.

She was really going back, after half a lifetime away.

Five Norsemen had come. The largest of them seemed to be the leader, for he said something to the other four, who hauled sacks of goods to trade. She heard him give instructions for them to meet up later at the camp. After a last look at Mielat and Juoksa for reassurance, Gunnhild swallowed heavily and walked up to him.

"Hello," she said in Norse, and he turned.

When she met his eyes, they were warm and brown and curious, a stark contrast to his menacingly large frame. She realized then that he was younger than she'd first thought—maybe ten or so winters older than her own twenty-four. He wore a tunic and pants, and leg wraps over powerful calves; a seax hung at his belt, and a gold arm ring glimmered just above his elbow. His dark beard was thick, and his tunic was rolled up to expose muscled forearms and strong, broad hands.

"Hello," he said slowly, as though concerned that she was a figment of his imagination.

She set her shoulders. "My name is Gunnhild Ozurardottir. I need passage south. I can pay."

He seemed uncertain as his eyes roved over her patchwork garments and pointed reindeer-hide shoes. "Your accent—where do you come from?"

"Halogaland."

"Then what are you doing all the way out here?" He looked from her to Juoksa and Mielat, then back again. The Sámi regarded him impassively and Gunnhild raised her chin yet higher to look the big Norseman in the face.

"Learning magic." Gunnhild was losing patience, but she supposed if she were seeing things from his point of view, she might have questions, too.

He looked even more unsure at this, but said, "Well . . . we *are* going south. If you wish to come with us, you'll have to take it up with King Eirik. I can bring you to him."

Out of the corner of her eye, she saw Juoksa stiffen at the name.

"Thank you. I would appreciate that very much," Gunnhild said, and turned back to her friends. Juoksa's eyes blazed, while Mielat was doing his best to look reassuring, though he clearly had reservations. She threw an arm around each of their necks and hugged them close. Juoksa nearly jerked away, unused to such a show of affection from her, but Mielat laughed and clapped her on the back.

"You know how to find us if you have need," Mielat said as they parted.

Gunnhild made to break from Juoksa, but he suddenly brought his arm up and clamped it around her waist. Despite the fact that the Norseman likely couldn't understand their conversation, he lowered his voice to a whisper: "Eirik Haraldsson is a witch-killer. If this is the king he means, you must come straight back to us. Do you understand?"

Witch-killer? The very idea chilled her, but what was this Eirik Haraldsson compared with the rest of her problems? He was only a man.

"Heid taught me well. I can take care of myself," she said as she pulled away from Juoksa, who seemed concerned and a bit offended that she hadn't taken his warning seriously. "Farewell, my friends."

"Farewell, Gunnhild," said Mielat as she took up the handle of her cart and turned to go, following the Norseman into the trees. Once they were far enough away from the camp, the man fell into step beside her, and she realized she had not asked his name.

"Thorolf Skallagrimsson," he said when she did. He ran a hand through his shaggy dark hair. "I should have said that earlier. My apologies."

Gunnhild turned to him as they walked, raising her eyebrows at the inclusion of his father's nickname in his patronym. "Is your father truly called 'Bald Grim'?"

"There are a lot of men named Grim," Thorolf said with a smile and a shrug. "He doesn't take offense. It's not as though he's *not* bald."

Before she could stop herself, Gunnhild let out a bark of laughter and covered her mouth. When she looked sideways, Thorolf was now smiling at her so widely that the corners of his eyes crinkled, and she felt her traitorous face begin to heat.

But then he sobered, seeming uneasy. "So. You're a witch?"

"I am. Do you have a problem with witches, Thorolf Skallagrimsson?"

"Not on principle. It's just that the events of this summer have left us all a bit wary."

"What happened this summer?"

They walked in silence for several paces while he gathered his thoughts. She waited patiently, for his face had taken on a haunted cast. Even though they'd just met, she somehow felt that such an expression was uncharacteristic of him.

"We raided a port in Bjarmaland. It was well defended. During the battle, four of the king's hirdsmen turned on him. His foster brother and I were fighting closest to him and we had to—"

He couldn't bring himself to say the words "kill our friends," but she gathered as much.

Gunnhild winced. "I'm sorry. But why do you think their actions were the result of witchcraft? These men could've been traitors."

Thorolf shook his head. "No. I knew them well. And when it happened, their eyes were—strange. Different. As though someone else were looking out from behind them. They were amber, like a cat's. And once they were dead, their eyes returned to normal."

In her mind's eye Gunnhild saw the yellowish eyes of the fox, and a shiver ran down her spine. *Could this be a coincidence?*

"Curious," was all she could bring herself to say.

A long silence ensued as they continued to walk.

"I mean you no harm. I only wish to get home." She paused. "But after what you've just told me, do you think your king would allow me on your ship?"

"I think he'd at least be willing to talk. This was just the latest in a long string of mischiefs that have happened around him. He's been trying to hire a witch for some time now to defend against them, but all have refused. Even those among the Sámi."

"Well, then I'll be sorry to inform him that I'm not for hire, but I do have silver and can pay for my passage." Then the rest of his words sank in. *Not even the Sámi would help?* It was not uncommon for the Norse to seek out noaidi for magical assistance when necessary. But the fact that *everyone* had refused did not bode well.

"Why has no one agreed to help?" Gunnhild asked, feigning calm, Juoksa's words echoing in her head. "Surely if he's so desperate, he'd be willing to compensate them handsomely. So it must be something else." *Something worse.*

"Ah . . ." Thorolf rubbed the back of his neck.

Gunnhild stopped walking, stilled the cart behind her. "You'll tell me now, or I'm going back this instant."

He halted as well and ran a hand through his hair again. "It's just that

Eirik has had dealings with witches in the past"—*Damn it,* Gunnhild thought, *Juoksa was right*—"that have made him a bit unpopular among your kind."

He started to walk once more, but Gunnhild stayed rooted to the spot, hand tightly clasping the handle of her cart. When Thorolf noticed she wasn't following, he stopped again and turned around to face her.

"What dealings with witches has this king had?" Gunnhild asked through gritted teeth.

Thorolf looked away. "He killed his brother for practicing magic. But his father was the one who—"

"How?" Every hair on Gunnhild's body stood on end. *Witch-killer* was bad enough, but to kill one's own kin was an unimaginable crime. One for which not even gods could be forgiven. "How did he kill him?"

Thorolf hesitated. But he had an open, honest face, one that made her think he would tell her anything if she asked. And she needed to know what he was getting her into. Needed to know the price of getting to Oddny and finding Signy sooner rather than later.

"Eirik burned him in his hall," Thorolf said. When he saw her eye twitch, he started, "But—"

"A *burning-in*?" she exploded. "That's one of the worst and most cowardly ways to kill."

"He acted at his father's behest," Thorolf said, surprised. He clearly hadn't expected such a strong reaction from her. "King Harald was bewitched once and has no love of magic. But listen. Now—"

"I heard of King Harald's 'bewitchment' by one of his wives when I was a child," Gunnhild snapped. "They called her Snaefrid and she was Sámi—of a different kin group than my friends back there, but Sámi all the same. And they tell another story. They say King Harald loved her so much that he neglected his kingdom, became too obsessed with her to govern. But now that she's dead, she can be blamed for just about anything, can't she?" She began to turn her cart around. "I'm going back. I want nothing to do with this man."

I'll go west with Juoksa and Mielat instead. But every day that passed made it less likely that Gunnhild would be able to rescue Signy before winter. And if she wanted to find Signy, she needed a woman she trusted to sing the warding songs for her. She needed Oddny.

"Listen," Thorolf said hastily. "Just come and speak with him. He's in a dire position. He may be willing to strike a deal."

"I want nothing from a witch-killer and a kinslayer. And that you would serve such a king makes me doubt my initial impression of you as a good man. Goodbye, Thorolf Skallagrimsson."

She jerked the cart forward, but he stepped in front of her.

"Get out of my way or you'll be sorry," Gunnhild said.

Thorolf held his hands up in surrender. "Listen—"

"Let me be clear: I would rather curse your king's cock to shrivel up and fall off than assist him with anything. If I have to tell you once more to let me pass, you'll regret it."

"Please," he said, but stepped aside. "At least hear him out. More men could die without your help."

Maybe it was because of the pleading look in his eyes, the knowledge of what he'd witnessed that summer and what he'd had to do, but she felt her resolve begin to crumble despite herself. And these men were still her quickest way of getting home . . .

"I promise that no harm will befall you," Thorolf added softly. "On my honor."

Gunnhild considered this. She supposed she had nothing to lose by hearing him out and having the satisfaction of snubbing King Eirik to his brother-killing, witch-murdering face. There was no reason for him to refuse her passage if she could pay.

And despite herself, she found that she trusted Thorolf.

"Fine," she said. "Take me to your king."

9

AS THOROLF LED HER through the camp, Gunnhild was taken aback by the sight of so many boxes and tents and *men*, in all shapes and sizes and colors. Some were cooking, others attending to the ship or to their weapons, and still others were combing and plaiting their hair and beards. A few had darker complexions that hinted at origins much farther south; Gunnhild saw one such man who had wiry black hair braided close to his head. She knew it wasn't impossible that warriors from one land would throw in their lot with the king of another, for her own countrymen had been known to do the same when they traveled.

King Eirik's hirdsmen were all well-groomed and well-fed, and like Thorolf, each wore a gold arm ring outside their tunic just above the elbow, a wolf head snarling at each end of the twisted torque. Many had knotwork tattoos peeking out from the collars of their shirts and the cuffs of their sleeves.

They stared at her as she passed. She stopped looking around and kept her eyes trained forward on Thorolf's back, dragging the creaking cart behind her as they continued down the path between the sun-bleached woolen canvases of the tents. Most used the ship's oars for beams, but the one Thorolf was leading her to had proper beams, carved with swirling patterns and topped with dragon heads.

Behind the camp loomed the beached warship, its mast down and its red sail furled. Even from a distance, Gunnhild knew that it was the finest craft she had ever seen in her life. Although the dragon head had been removed so as not to offend the land spirits, the ship was beautiful, its gunnel painted red and carved with complex loops and whorls from prow to stern.

A campfire lay in front of the tent with the carved beams. Beside it, two men sat upon ship boxes, playing hnefatafl atop a third box in the middle. The man facing away from her had his dark brown hair cropped short and a bald spot on the crown of his head. Across from him sat a dark-skinned man with tight curls, strumming a lyre as he squinted furiously at the game board.

"Wait." Thorolf held a hand out to stop Gunnhild; they'd paused along the side of a tent, and from this angle they could look at the two men without being seen. "Let's see what kind of mood he's in first."

Gunnhild huffed and muttered, "Oh good. That's a wonderful sign."

"The king is cornered," the skald sang under his breath. He plucked the strings of his instrument in time with the next words: *"Perhaps it's time to give up."*

"You're not a quitter, Svein," the other man replied as he moved one of the ivory game pieces with a flourish. "But I just beat you anyway. Again."

Svein blinked a few times and sighed before playing three sad notes, the last one warbling in the air. "Best three out of five. And you're playing the king's side this time."

"Is that him?" Gunnhild whispered to Thorolf. "The one facing away from us?"

"No." Thorolf nodded at a new figure approaching the men from the other side of the tent they were hiding behind. "There."

"Hmm," Gunnhild said. She couldn't see his face, but he was tall—as tall as Thorolf, though a bit slimmer—with dark blond hair that just brushed his shoulders. His clothing wasn't much finer than his men's, but then again, a sea voyage was not the time to pull out one's best garments.

Eirik, his back still to Gunnhild and Thorolf, stopped behind the man with the bald spot and cleared his throat.

The man turned. In profile, he seemed to be around the same age as the others—which is to say, not much older than herself, maybe thirty winters—with a short dark beard, a receding hairline, and a smirk she would not have expected to see on the face of someone looking at his king.

"Yes?" he asked pleasantly.

"You're in my seat," said Eirik.

"I don't see your name on it," the man replied, which caused Svein to strum two quick, ominous notes over and over on the lyre. "And there's an empty stool right there."

"Is this really how it's going to be, Arinbjorn?"

Arinbjorn turned back to the game and said mildly, "It's how it already is."

"All right, then." Eirik squatted behind him, grabbed him around the shoulders, lifted him off the box, and set him on his feet next to it—or rather, dropped him, since Arinbjorn was almost a head shorter. Svein snickered. Arinbjorn gave a little bow at no one in particular, as though being simply picked up and placed somewhere else by the future ruler of one's country were a common occurrence for him.

"See?" The king slid away the thick sheepskin set atop the box like a cushion and gestured to the flat lid, upon which was carved in runes so big that Gunnhild could make them out even from her vantage point:

EIRIK'S

"Those look fresh," Arinbjorn said, eyeing them. "Did you *just* do that?"

"Yes, because you kept taking my seat," said Eirik as he slid the sheepskin back in place and sat down on the box. "I should outlaw you."

"The perks of being your foster brother," Arinbjorn replied, which to Gunnhild explained why he was addressing Eirik so irreverently. He leaned an elbow on one of Eirik's broad shoulders and waved a hand. "Have I not given you plenty of other reasons to outlaw me over the years?"

"The prank with the fish heads was definitely worthy of at *least* lesser outlawry," Svein pointed out. "I've been meaning to compose a poem about that one."

"I wouldn't pay you for it," said Eirik grouchily as he grabbed a jug of ale from where it sat beside the chest, then snatched Arinbjorn's cup out of his hand. "Also, this is my cup."

"I don't see your n—"

Eirik turned the cup over and showed him something on the bottom, which Gunnhild could only assume by the look on Arinbjorn's face was the king's name scratched in runes again.

"Oh, fine." Arinbjorn turned to Svein. "*I* would pay you. How much?"

"You're not paying him to compose a poem about the fish heads," said Eirik.

"We should speak with him before they start talking more about the pranks. That's a sure way to sink his mood," Thorolf whispered to Gunnhild as he started forward.

She followed—and as she did, the cart squeaked loudly and all three men turned to look in their direction, and Gunnhild got her first look at the king's face. His beard was trimmed short and neat, and he had a snarling wolf tattooed at each collarbone, noses nearly touching at the hollow of his throat. His eyes were a glacial pale blue, limned by the remnants of the charcoal-and-beeswax mix that many sailors smeared across their eyelids to protect against the sun.

He looked her up and down, taking in her piecemeal kaftan, her raggedy dress. She'd never had to worry much about her appearance, and Thorolf's geniality had put her at ease. Lulled her into a false sense of security. Now, before the king, she felt suddenly exposed.

She sucked in a breath. Yes, he was handsome. But that was of little consequence to her; even if she hadn't known of his past deeds, she would have detested him for the way he was looking at her right now, as though she were dung beneath his shoe.

Gunnhild had not realized that it was possible to loathe someone on sight. Yet here was Eirik Haraldsson.

He hadn't even spoken to her, and already she despised him.

"Thorolf," Eirik said, "who is this . . . person?"

"You sound unsure that I am in fact a person, King," said Gunnhild before Thorolf could answer. "If you want to know who I am, ask *me*, not him."

Thorolf let out a small sigh, as if this was going exactly as badly as he'd expected. Eirik's mouth hung open and he glared at her, offended, as though he somehow hadn't expected her to hear him—let alone admonish him.

She held his gaze. *The audacity of this man!*

Arinbjorn, however, looked at Gunnhild as though she were a gift from the gods as he walked up to her and took both her hands, smiling. "Hello. I'm Arinbjorn Thorisson. It's great to meet you, my new favorite person, whose name is . . . ?"

"Gunnhild," she said, and she couldn't help but smile back. He was of a height with her, his face open and kind but his eyes shrewd and full of mischief, and she decided that anyone who could rankle a king the way he did was likely a good ally to have. "My father is Ozur Eyvindsson, a hersir in Halogaland."

"Ah! We stayed with him on the way here. My father, Thorir, is a hersir in Fjordane," said Arinbjorn approvingly, dropping her hands. He gestured to an empty stool. "Have a seat."

Gunnhild sat. Thorolf hovered at her shoulder, equal parts awkward and protective, which she had to admit was endearing.

Arinbjorn reassumed his place at Eirik's shoulder. "I have so many questions. How did you come to be here? And for how long?"

"I've been studying witchcraft these past twelve winters. My teacher was—" *Killed yesterday.* She sat up straighter. She couldn't show weakness in front of these men, and especially not in front of the king, to whom she now turned. "She's gone now, and I must travel home as quickly as possible. Thorolf mentioned that you were going south and brought me here to ask you for passage. I can pay in silver."

Still looking at her with utmost disdain, Eirik leaned over with one elbow resting on his knee, the other hand holding the cup he'd swiped from Arinbjorn. "How do we know you're truly Ozur's daughter? You're a stranger to us. So my answer is no, and there's nothing you can offer me to change my mind. Keep your silver and take your mischief elsewhere."

Gunnhild was stunned at his refusal. Thorolf had made him out to be as desperate as she was. *Is he bluffing or just a fool?*

"Then Thorolf seems to have misled me." She affected as smooth a voice as she could muster under the circumstances. "He mentioned that you were in need of a witch's assistance, and I'm well versed in the magic arts."

The sneer dropped from Eirik's face and he cut a glare to Thorolf, who shrugged.

"She isn't wrong," said Arinbjorn, looking at her with interest. "We need a witch, brother."

"I know," Eirik said quietly. "But this is too convenient. It could be a trap."

"Or it could be fate." Arinbjorn lowered his voice, too, but Gunnhild could still make out his words: "You don't have to like her. You just have to strike a deal."

"She came out of nowhere," Eirik hissed back. "It could be another trick."

"She could be our last hope."

"Or she could be our doom."

"I surely could be, should you continue carrying on as though I'm not sitting right here," Gunnhild said loudly, and both men turned to her.

Arinbjorn said, "Please excuse my brother, Gunnhild. He can be a bit difficult"—Eirik grunted and folded his arms—"but we can grant you passage south. In exchange for—"

"No." Eirik stood, causing her to stand as well. "How do we know she's truly a witch? We've never heard of her, so it's clear she hasn't made a name for herself. How can we trust someone with no reputation? And if she *is* a witch, how do we know she's even any good?"

Like Thorolf, he towered over her. Gunnhild was a woman of average height, but in the shadow of these two giants, she suddenly felt very small.

And that made her angry.

I won't be intimidated by the likes of you. She stepped around the ship box holding the tafl board, bringing herself uncomfortably close to him. "Would you like me to curse you? Would that be proof enough for you to strike a deal with me? I do quite enjoy curses."

"Well, now, *that's* reassuring." Eirik rolled his eyes and moved away, gesturing at her. "You see, Arinbjorn? She's only proving my point. Go back where you came from, woman. You're trying my patience."

Gunnhild's temper flared. "Why, you horrible—"

"Eirik, think this through," Arinbjorn said, in a way that made Gunnhild feel like he'd said those exact words a thousand times before. "Gunnhild, peace. Ignore him. We can come to terms—"

"No, we can't," said Eirik. "How could we possibly trust that anything she's saying is the truth?"

Gunnhild tossed her thick auburn braid over her shoulder and folded her arms, trying to hide how badly her hands shook. "If I prove to you beyond a doubt that I'm a witch, would you be willing to treat with me?"

"Yes," said Arinbjorn at once. "Yes, that sounds like a fine idea. Eirik?"

The king stared at her for a moment before saying, "Fine. But no curses."

She began, "Well, I could conjure a storm—"

The men cringed in unison.

"No. We've had enough of that this summer," said Eirik darkly. "It was a storm that beached us here in the first place. Try something else."

If not curses or weather magic, and with no women there to sing for her and no other witches to travel with for safety—especially if Katla was still skulking around—her options were limited to healing. She could ask if any of the hirdsmen were wounded so that she could demonstrate her power on them, but she was hardly the healer she'd watched Oddny grow up to be under Yrsa's tutelage. Heid had taught her to brew teas and make potions and poultices for aches and pains, but when it came to injuries, the person Gunnhild had had the most practice healing was herself. It was how she'd learned in the first place.

With every moment that she didn't move, Eirik looked smugger. She wanted to slap the smirk off his face. But then she noticed that the other hirdsmen had wandered over to watch what was going on.

Thirty battle-hardened men were staring at her. Gunnhild needed to make an impression.

She reached into her belt pouch to make sure she had a spare linen bandage handy, and then pulled out one of the small, flat wooden staves she carried around for runic magic and stuck it between her teeth.

Then she drew the knife at her belt.

Several of the men stepped back or made noises of surprise, and some of them touched the seaxes at their own belts as if ready to draw. Even Eirik looked wary, but he held up a hand to still them, not looking away from her.

"Well?" he asked.

She looked down at her hand, fingers splayed and palm facing out, and positioned the knife, willing her grip and focus to remain steady. It had to be a quick, clean wound. A shallow cut wouldn't make enough of an impact, but if she severed something important, it would take too much of her magic to heal, and she might pass out. That was the last thing she needed.

This had to be done just right.

For Signy.

Arinbjorn was the first to realize what she meant to do. His gray eyes went wide. "Wait. Hold on. You don't have to—"

Gunnhild stabbed the knife through her hand and then ripped it out— much to the shock of the king's hird, who reacted with a mix of gasps and expletives.

The pain was instant and horrible and turned her vision red. She clenched her jaw so hard that she nearly cracked a molar on the stave between her teeth. She ignored the muffled noises of astonishment around her, doubled over, and swore loudly around the stave until the words would no longer come.

She heard Eirik say, "I knew it. She's an absolute madwoman."

"Give her a moment," Arinbjorn said.

Blood dripped down to her wrist and soiled the sleeve of her dress and kaftan. When her vision cleared, she took the stave out of her mouth and held it gently in her injured hand. With the knife, she carved runes into the wood, singing each one under her breath. Then she grabbed the bandage from her pouch and wrapped her hand with the rune stick still pressed against her bleeding wound.

The men were dead silent. Gunnhild finally straightened and looked up. Thorolf had gone pale, Arinbjorn looked curious, and Eirik stood with his arms folded dispassionately.

She held up her shaking hand. She was already bleeding through the bandage. Between the pain and blood loss, and the energy she'd expended on carving the runes to heal the wound more rapidly than she ordinarily would, she was spent.

"It'll be healed by suppertime," she said, fighting to keep her voice even. It was all she could do to remain standing.

Eirik was still glaring at her, but he realized a moment later when Arinbjorn nudged him in the ribs that all eyes were on him.

Gunnhild raised her chin.

"Fine," the king said at last. "Once I see the proof, we'll talk."

THOROLF ALLOWED HER TO rest in his tent. She barely made it to the bedroll before collapsing.

"Are you all right?" he asked worriedly as he crouched beside her. "That was . . . rather excessive. Was there really no other way to prove your skills?"

Well, it worked, didn't it? Gunnhild curled into a ball with her bound hand tucked against her chest and squeezed her eyes shut. *He'll be willing to make a deal now.*

"I pushed myself too far, and now I'm paying the price," she whispered. "It's common to feel fatigued when you do too much magic at once."

"Would eating something help? I could fetch—"

"I need rest. Wake me before supper, would you?"

"I—yes. Of course." He stood and moved to the doors.

Gunnhild gathered the last of her strength and said, "Thorolf."

He stopped and looked over his shoulder.

"Thank you," she said.

He lingered a moment too long before nodding and ducking out of the tent. She scooted forward to rest her head on the lumpy haversack he used as a pillow, and she soon sank into the warm embrace of sleep.

Gunnhild didn't know how long she dozed—only that when she woke up, she was no longer alone, and she jerked in surprise when her eyes fell upon her visitor. It took her a moment to realize what she was seeing.

The white fox sat an arm's length from her head and watched her with its uncanny amber eyes. Gunnhild sat up slowly, her uninjured hand moving to the knife at her belt.

It won't do you any good, said Thorbjorg. *You're only dreaming.*

Gunnhild believed her, if only because her hand no longer hurt; though she'd expedited the spell, she couldn't have been sleeping long enough for it to run its course.

"How are you doing this?" she asked in a small, horrified whisper. "Get out of my head."

I've only come to warn you, said Thorbjorg. *You must leave these men at once.*

"And why is that?"

You weren't supposed to be there. At the farm. Neither was your mentor. But you were, and we had to act. It was . . . unfortunate.

"Is that so? I thought you said it was fortuitous. Or was that only when you thought I'd be easy to kill?"

The fox said nothing, which was answer enough.

"Why did you attack Oddny and Signy? They haven't done anything wrong."

Things didn't go the way I intended. I didn't mean to make an enemy of you—just to preemptively ensure that you and your sworn sisters stayed out of my way. Heed my warning now, and no further harm will come to you—

"But why? We weren't *in* your way. We don't even know you—" Gunnhild stopped. *Preemptively?* "Unless—you've foreseen something. Something you *think* we're going to do."

The fox stared back at her, unblinking, and again said nothing.

A feeling bubbled in Gunnhild's chest as she recalled the carnage of the day before, heard Signy's screams ringing in her ears, felt the thin, cold skin of Heid's hands beneath hers as her mentor took her final breath:

Rage. Pure rage, deep and cold and vicious. Had the fox truly been sitting before her, she would've grabbed the creature and snapped its neck. Or worse.

"My teacher told me once that nothing would bring me greater grief than trying to fulfill or avoid a prophecy," she said. "I don't suppose yours ever told you the same thing, or we wouldn't be having this conversation. We might have never even crossed paths if not for your actions."

The fox's eyes narrowed, and Gunnhild knew that she was right: Thorbjorg was well aware that she'd made a mistake—several of them, and big ones at that—but was not willing to admit it. Instead, she'd chosen to double down.

Leave now, said Thorbjorg. *Go back the way you came. Or we'll shadow your every step, as we've shadowed the men whose company you now find yourself in. Stay with them, and we'll make your life miserable.*

Gunnhild was startled. When Thorolf had described the men he'd had to kill this summer and their yellow eyes, her first thought had been of Thorbjorg. But to hear the other witch admit outright that she was harrying the hird—did this change things? This couldn't be a coincidence. But that wasn't Gunnhild's immediate concern.

If Thorbjorg thought she could threaten her into submission, she was dead wrong.

She leaned in and whispered, "I hope you realize that you've done the exact opposite of what you set out to do. Once I've assured that my friends are safe, I'm going to find you, and I'm going to end you. And that's a promise."

The fox growled and lunged for her throat.

Gunnhild jolted awake, panting, drenched in cold sweat. Her hand throbbed beneath its bandage, crusted with dried blood, and she held it to her chest and tried to slow her breathing.

Invading a person's dreams—that was a skill Heid hadn't taught her. How had Thorbjorg done it? More important, how could Gunnhild prevent it from happening again?

Her first thought was a protection charm. *I could come up with something—maybe a bindrune?—that will form a barrier around my mind so she can't get in. It'll be complicated, but if I do it right . . . if I keep it on my person at all times, or*—she looked down at her hand—*carve it or tattoo it on myself so it can't be taken away . . . yes. That will work.*

But that would take her some time to do, and her more immediate task was securing a way home, so she put it to the back of her mind. Once she'd salvaged some semblance of calm, she stood on wobbling legs, smoothed her hair, and looked down at her hand. It didn't hurt as much as earlier. That was a good sign.

She squared her shoulders and strode out of the tent with her head held high. Dusk was near; this far north, the sun was still up despite the lateness of the day, although the nights had been steadily growing longer for the past three moons.

Eirik, Thorolf, Arinbjorn, and Svein sat talking around the fire before Eirik's tent. All of them turned to her as she approached.

She stopped directly in front of Eirik, held up her hand, and unwound the crusty linen wrappings to reveal a pink scar where, a short time earlier, there had been a bleeding wound. The stave that had been tucked into the bandage clattered to the ground, a crack bisecting the bloodied runes Gunnhild had carved into it. She picked it up and tossed it into the fire, then held her hand up again so that all could see.

Thorolf's shoulders sagged fractionally in relief. Arinbjorn and Svein looked impressed. But Eirik's face was completely inscrutable as he stood and regarded her.

She met his eyes and didn't look away. "Well?"

The king pressed his lips into a thin line, jerked his head sideways as if to indicate she should follow him, and started walking. She looked at Arinbjorn, hopeful that he would be coming along, too—it seemed to her that he was Eirik's voice of reason—but he didn't move. But Thorolf gave her an encouraging nod and she turned to follow Eirik.

10

---◆---

EIRIK LED HER TO a small copse of pines over the next hill, keeping the camp within sight but out of earshot. Gunnhild sat down on a stump and crossed one knee over the other. The king remained standing, leaning against a tree.

"So," he said.

"So," she echoed. "Let's outline the situation, shall we? I've proven I'm a witch. I need to go home. You don't want my silver. You *do* want to hire a witch to work for you, but I regret to inform you that I have more important matters requiring my immediate attention—"

"Then why are you wasting my time? Why bother proving your skills if you didn't intend to offer them up in exchange for your passage?"

"Let me finish."

He folded his arms and waited.

Gunnhild took a moment to consider her options. What could she offer that wouldn't help him *too* much but might at least help his men? They seemed decent enough despite having made the questionable choice to swear themselves to him. She remembered with a pang the look on Thorolf's face as he'd told her of the friends he'd had to kill.

Then she recalled her dream: Thorbjorg's admission that she'd been shadowing the hird, her undeniable skill with mind magic, the defense Gunnhild had thought up when she'd awoken.

It was a finite task. Something she could stomach. Something she'd already planned on doing anyway, which would assuage her guilt at stooping so low as to aid a witch-killer.

"Thorolf told me what he and Arinbjorn had to do this summer when several of your men turned on you during a battle," she said at last. "He said it was as though someone else were controlling them. That their eyes looked strange."

Eirik's expression darkened and he looked away, which was enough to confirm that Thorolf had told her the truth.

"I can create a bindrune that will prevent this from happening again. To protect their minds from witchcraft," she continued. "Will that suffice as payment?"

"A bindrune?" Eirik repeated.

"Yes. I'll combine several runes into one unique sigil, and unlike the rune stick I carved earlier to heal myself, its magic won't run out—it'll work as long as I'm alive."

He nodded at her hand. "Will it weaken you, like your healing spell did?"

"Yes and no," she said. "What I carved on that stave were individual runes, a spell that I poured power into at once. Bindrunes feed on a witch's power little by little. One must be careful not to create too many in one's lifetime." She fixed him with a stern look. "I'm only trying to impress upon you that I don't make this offer lightly. It's more than worth the price of you taking me to my father's."

Eirik didn't argue that point. "How will it work, exactly?"

"I'll have to find the right combination," Gunnhild said. "Once I'm done, I can either carve them onto bits of wood or antler that your men can wear as necklaces, or they can have it tattooed on their bodies so it can never be lost or stolen from them."

Eirik thought for a moment. "I have a tattooist in Hordaland, where we're wintering. She'll surely be up to the task. Will you need to be present for the bindrune to be effective?"

A woman tattooist? Gunnhild fought down her curiosity and answered, "Yes. Unless . . . I could pour all the magic into one carving and she can keep it with her as she works. But it's one or the other—I can't make thirty individual necklaces *and* one carving with the power of thirty bindrunes for the tattooist to use. It would be too much."

"I'd rather it be permanent, if the men consent to it," Eirik said. "I'll take the risk of waiting until we make it back to Hordaland."

"Understood. One bindrune for passage to my father's. Do we have a deal?"

She stood and stuck out her hand; he took it and shook once. His touch sent a jolt up her arm, but she didn't dare pull away before it was proper, and was grateful when he withdrew first. She didn't want him to have the satisfaction of knowing he'd unnerved her.

"I'll get to work first thing tomorrow," Gunnhild said. "I'm worried about overexerting myself tonight after my spell earlier."

"Fine. We're preparing the ship to leave at first light." Eirik turned to head back toward camp.

"Good." She grimaced and muttered to herself, "I just have to hope that damned Thorbjorg stays out of my head until I'm finished."

Eirik stopped short and whirled around, his pale eyes wide and full of the same suspicion with which he'd first looked upon her earlier that day. "How do you know that name?"

Though she feared she already knew, she said, "Why do you ask?"

"Because it's the name of a woman who works for my brother," he said through his teeth. "She's been after me for years. She's the cause of all my troubles."

Thorbjorg works for his brother?! "So it's not a coincidence after all," Gunnhild said under her breath. She sat back down on the stump, resting her chin in her hand as she considered this.

Eirik did not share her calm.

"I knew it. I was right," he blustered. "This was all a trick—you're working together. I should never have listened to Arinbjorn. I should have killed you the moment I saw you."

He drew his seax, and she looked up at him, then at his weapon, and back to his face, which was contorted with loathing.

"Sheathe that blade," she said, wrinkling her nose in disgust. "Honestly. Were you even listening? I'm using the bindrune on myself, too. To protect *against* her."

Eirik blinked a few times, put the seax away, and then sat down heavily on the fallen tree across from where Gunnhild sat on the stump.

"What has she done to you?" he asked warily.

"You first," she said. "I only just met her yesterday. You said she's been after you for years—why?"

"It's a long story."

"And I would hear you tell it."

"I wouldn't know where to start."

"The beginning should suffice."

Eirik looked down at his feet. Gunnhild waited.

"My father has many children with many different wives," he said at last. "When my eldest brothers were old enough, they started making noise about all of us having our own regions to govern. He divided up the country and placed us above the jarls but beneath him."

Gunnhild knew this from her childhood—though by her reckoning, Eirik must have been young indeed when his father placed upon him and his brothers the title of petty king.

"But he's always favored me, and he'd already chosen me as his successor," Eirik went on. "As you can imagine, my brothers have never been particularly happy about this. My strengths lie in fighting, not politics. It's all I know. I've been raiding since I was twelve winters old. I've killed more men than I can count."

Gunnhild had to admit she was surprised by his self-awareness, but she couldn't stop herself from adding, "Including your own brother."

"Two of them, actually," Eirik said. When Gunnhild's eyes widened, he told her about the deaths of King Bjorn of Vestfold nine winters ago, and the witch Rognvald two winters later. The explanation for Rognvald's death was not a surprise after what Thorolf had told her, but the other—

"So, let me get this straight," she said. "You killed King Bjorn and looted his town because he refused to let *you* be the one to bring *his* taxes to your father? What were you trying to prove?"

"Back then, I would've done anything to look superior to my brothers, if only to show my father that he was right in choosing me to succeed him. That's why when he told me he wanted Rognvald killed, I had no choice but to do it. If I hadn't, one of my other brothers would've, and then he'd be the favorite."

"Oh, and we couldn't have that, now, could we?"

He glared at her but let the comment slide. "My slaying of Rognvald is also the reason not even witches from among the Sámi will aid us. I've sent out messengers to entreat every group we know of, but all of them have refused."

"Yes, I don't suppose you endeared yourself to the Sámi by murdering one of Snaefrid's sons. Tell me—*did* your father make the right decision in choosing you? It seems you solve all your problems at the point of a sword, and care little for the bonds of kinship."

"Don't pass judgment on me. All my brothers are half brothers. We didn't grow up together. We only see each other a few times a year, if that. My hirdsmen are brothers to me more than anyone. Just because my father's other sons are kin to me doesn't mean I hold any love for them."

Gunnhild almost knew how he felt. Her siblings had always been no better than strangers to her. Still, she couldn't see herself ever *killing* them—or anyone else, for that matter.

Besides Thorbjorg, of course.

"The law doesn't care whether or not you loved them. They were still your kin," she said.

"And when my brothers kill me, they'll be kinslayers, too. Your point?"

"What does any of this have to do with Thorbjorg?"

"I'm getting there." Eirik heaved an aggravated sigh. "My half brother Olaf took over rule of Vestfold upon Bjorn's death. He's Bjorn's full brother and swore vengeance upon me. My brother Halfdan has taken up the cause as well. He's one of the kings of Trondheim, and he's also my father's oldest living son, so he believes the rule of Norway should belong to him."

Gunnhild was beginning to see how bad this situation truly was. Trondheim and Vestfold were two of the most powerful districts in the country. It was unwise to make enemies of their kings.

"Did you offer Olaf compensation?" It wasn't uncommon to settle killings through the legal system rather than revenge, though doing so wouldn't necessarily end a blood feud. And if a feud started *within* a family, things could get complicated very quickly; it was part of why kinslaying was such an ugly crime.

"I have," Eirik said sullenly. "Many times. And he's refused."

Gunnhild grimaced. "I see. Well, if it's been nine winters, why wait so long to attack?"

"Because my father would be furious enough to dethrone both of them. As I said, I'm his favorite. But he's getting older, and soon he'll be *too* old to intervene on my behalf. So in the meantime, my brothers send their witches to toy with me and sow chaos and mistrust wherever I go. Until this summer, it's only been small things: farms I own being blighted when the others in the region are unaffected. Holes appearing in the hulls of my ships in the middle of the sea when I know for certain they'd been checked and checked again before departure. But the attack on me and on my men in Bjarmaland—that was too far. It makes me think that things are about to escalate."

"Which brother does Thorbjorg work for?"

"Olaf. Another one, Katla, works for Halfdan," Eirik said. "But it gets worse."

Katla. Gunnhild felt like she'd been kicked in the chest. During the raid, Thorbjorg was clearly in charge, but Katla had been the one who'd fought Heid. The one who'd killed her.

I'll kill her, too, once I'm done with Thorbjorg.

"I fail to see how it could possibly get worse," Gunnhild said.

"Rognvald was Thorbjorg's mentor."

Gunnhild pinched the bridge of her nose between thumb and forefinger. "I stand corrected."

He looked past her, seeming lost. "After we— After Rognvald— As his hall was burning, I saw a girl standing at the tree line with a bag over her shoulder. Staring right at me. Then I blinked and she was gone. I thought I'd imagined her, but she's haunted my steps ever since."

"So it's not just that she's in your brother's employ. She's also seeking vengeance. It's personal," Gunnhild said. She stood and faced away from him, folding her arms, digging her fingernails into her biceps, biting her lip hard enough to draw blood.

What can all of this mean?

She had a feeling she knew. But she didn't want to admit to herself that the most likely answer was that her fate and the king's were somehow inextricably linked.

"It's your turn," Eirik said from behind her, sounding very tired, as though he were unused to speaking so much at once. "How do you know her? What did she do to you?"

Gunnhild took a deep breath and let it out. "Yesterday I was traveling in the way that witches do and checking in on some dear friends when their farm was raided and their family murdered by Thorbjorg's design. One of my friends was kidnapped and the other has likely taken refuge with her closest neighbor: my father. As we tried to help them, the witches attacked my mentor and me, and they—they killed her."

Eirik waited a long moment before saying, "So that's why you're in such a hurry to get home. But what was the reason for this attack? Were your friends powerful? Were they some sort of threat to her?"

She was glad to still be facing away from him, for it was all she could do to hold back her tears.

"One of you clouds the futures of the others." Heid's words echoed to her from a lifetime ago, and along with them, Thorbjorg's from her dream: *I didn't mean to make an enemy of you—just to preemptively ensure that you and your sworn sisters stayed out of my way.*

"No," she whispered. "But I'm starting to think that *I* am, or at least Thorbjorg thinks I am, and that my friends were targeted by association. I'm still trying to make sense of it all. But first I need to get to my father's."

Eirik stood. "Earlier you said you weren't for hire, but it's clear now that we have the same enemy. If you'll work for me—"

She swiped at her tears and turned at last to face him, stony-eyed, try-ing to shrug off the mantle of grief that had settled upon her shoulders.

"No," she said.

"Why not? It would make sense. And I'd make you rich, besides. You'd never want for anything. You'd have all my resources behind you, as Thorbjorg has Olaf's. You'd be foolish not to accept. You can't possi-bly hope to destroy her alone."

The last of her sadness turned to anger in an instant.

"I don't care about getting rich, and I care less about vengeance than about rescuing my friend," Gunnhild said hotly. "And furthermore, I have no wish to throw in my lot with the likes of you. I believe Thorbjorg is after me for something I *might* do, but you *did* the things she hates you for. You killed your own brothers, and if Rognvald was as dear to Thor-bjorg as Heid was to me, I can't deny that if I were her I'd be out for your blood, too."

By this point Eirik was shaking with rage, fists balled and muscles coiled as though he might strike her, but she stepped toward him anyway.

"If you raise your hand to me, Eirik Haraldsson," Gunnhild said in a low voice, "know that I can kill you nine times over in nine different ways before your blow even lands. As far as I'm concerned, you've dug your own grave. Our association will be brief, and past that, I've no wish to see your face ever again."

"Fine," he said tightly as he took a step back from her. "We've made our deal. Now get out of my sight."

11

WHEN SHE RETURNED TO camp, the men were eating supper. Gunnhild had thought herself too angry to have an appetite until Thorolf pressed a wooden bowl of steaming stew into her hands, at which point she found herself suddenly ravenous.

"How did it go?" Arinbjorn asked as they sat around the fire.

Gunnhild confirmed that Eirik was nowhere in sight before replying, "We came to terms."

When she didn't elaborate, Arinbjorn prompted, "And those terms were . . .?"

She explained about the bindrune and its effects.

"That's quite a trade," he said quietly when she was done. "And it's appreciated."

"It'll make a big difference to us," Thorolf added. "Not to have to worry that what happened will happen again. Thank you, Gunnhild."

She swallowed the lump in her throat and they finished eating, washed their bowls, and went back to the fire. The sun had set by now, but nobody seemed intent on going to sleep, even though they were to leave at dawn. Instead, Thorolf fetched more ale, Svein took out his lyre, and Arinbjorn reset the hnefatafl board.

Eirik still had not returned.

"He does this sometimes," Arinbjorn said blandly when she questioned him about the king's absence. He gave her a knowing look. "Did you make him angry?"

"I'd say we made each other angry," Gunnhild grumbled.

"And yet you still were able to work out a deal without coming to blows. I'd call that personal growth on his part."

"He did pull out his seax at one point."

"Yes, well, he tends to strike first and think later."

"If that's the case, why didn't you come with us? You seem to temper him."

Arinbjorn raised an eyebrow. "You didn't need me—you stood your ground with him yesterday, after all. I love Eirik, I truly do, but I can't deny that it's satisfying to see him humbled every once in a while." He gestured at the tafl board. "You know how to play?"

Gunnhild nodded. Heid had favored the game as a way to keep her wits about her in her advanced age, and they'd spent many nights playing together. Gunnhild had become a skilled player as a result.

"Excellent," Arinbjorn said as she sat down on the box across from him. "Do you want to be the king and his defenders, or the enemies?"

She thought for a moment. "The king."

Arinbjorn grinned. "All right, then," he said, and made the first move.

His cheerful mood did not last long. A very short time later, a dozen men had gathered around to watch him sweat. Gunnhild nearly had him beaten, but a few surprise moves by Arinbjorn won him the game.

She scowled. "I suppose it's a good thing for Eirik to have you on his side if you're so good at capturing kings."

"I was losing for a moment there," Arinbjorn said, but he seemed downright exhilarated. "Do you want to go again? It's been a long time since anyone has given me a challenge."

"Oh, come off it." Svein played three notes on the lyre, which, paired with his thin-lipped grimace, managed to sound annoyed. Thorolf, sitting on the box to Gunnhild's side, looked impressed at her near win. When she turned and met his eyes, he smiled, and her heart fluttered. Their knees were very close together. Just a nudge and they'd be touching.

She shook herself, shifted away, and said to Arinbjorn, "Yes. Let's go again."

Gunnhild came closer and closer to winning over a few more games. During their final game, she almost succeeded in moving her king to the safety of his corner—and then Eirik appeared. Thorolf, sitting on the king's ship box, got out of his seat before he could be asked to move, and Eirik sat down and immediately knocked his knee into hers like *she* was the one taking up too much space. He took one look at the board and gave Gunnhild a condescending smile. "Don't feel bad about it. No one wins against Arinbjorn."

Disgusted, she pivoted her legs the other way. She wanted to smack him upside the head with the tafl board. She wanted to curse him with pustules while he slept. "I *almost* won."

Arinbjorn reached down for the jug sitting next to him, refilled his cup with ale, and refilled the borrowed cup someone had handed Gunnhild during the second game. She gave him a nod of thanks and drank, and he said to Eirik, "It's true. She nearly beat me this time, until a horse's ass showed up and ruined her concentration."

"What do I have to do with anything?" Eirik asked. When Gunnhild stifled a laugh with the back of her hand, he gave her a murderous look. "What?"

"If you don't understand, I won't explain it to you," she shot back.

Arinbjorn looked back and forth between the two of them, then looked up at the sky as if asking the gods for help.

As the evening wore on, Eirik and Arinbjorn went off to speak alone somewhere—for Eirik to relay their earlier conversation, Gunnhild assumed—but apparently word that Gunnhild would be helping them had spread around camp, for the mood had lightened. As Svein led the group in singing bawdy drinking songs, she found herself sitting shoulder to shoulder on a ship box with Thorolf, who didn't seem particularly keen to leave her side.

She found that she didn't want him to go anywhere, either. In fact, the longer they sat together, the more she felt a strange sort of hope—the kind that made her heart race, made her feel like a foolish child again. But she was a grown woman, and she told herself that even if she did fancy him, she shouldn't act rashly. She knew that much even after a lifetime living in the woods with an old woman.

Not that Heid hadn't been good company, and not that Gunnhild hadn't enjoyed spending time with Juoksa and Mielat. But the yearning to enjoy the company of others in that most intimate sense had become almost unbearable as the years passed. On those nights when Heid couldn't sleep and went wandering in the woods, which happened increasingly often as she got older, Gunnhild would lie there in her nest of blankets on the floor and imagine what it would be like to have someone touch her the way she did herself.

And now a man she desired was within reach—and, she admitted to herself, she *did* desire him—and she had no idea what to do. They'd met only today, so she certainly didn't know him well enough to know how he would react to an advance. Besides that, she couldn't stomach the thought of being spurned.

They sat there in companionable silence, watching the men around them getting steadily more drunk, before he finally spoke.

"It's bold of you to treat with Eirik the way you do," Thorolf said. His tone was heavy, thoughtful, as if he'd been working out how to say the words to her for some time. "If any harm befalls you while you're with us, it will be my fault for bringing you into our company."

"If any harm befalls me while in this company, it will be your king's fault, not yours," said Gunnhild. "I'm not afraid of him."

He didn't reply. She wondered if he wanted to say, *Perhaps you should be.*

"Why do you care so much?" she asked. "We're strangers. Is it just for the sake of your own conscience that you care what happens to me? Or do you . . ." A pause. "Do you feel another way about how things stand between us?"

It was the only way she could think to ask the question. She feared his response.

"Both, I think, in equal measure," he said. Which was not a rejection, but neither was it an explicit invitation.

But it was enough to encourage her to try.

After draining her ale cup, she said, with forced nonchalance, eyes trained on the fire, "During my nap I noticed that your bedroll was quite comfortable. I wondered if I might sleep there tonight."

Out of the corner of her eye she saw him freeze with his cup halfway to his mouth, and for a moment Gunnhild felt a stab of fear that she'd completely misread the situation.

But then he lowered the cup and said softly, "I don't see why not, provided that you'd allow me to share it."

The singing and chatter around them seemed to fade away as she turned to him, and he to her, and when their eyes met Gunnhild was certain beyond a shadow of a doubt that the rest of this night was going to go exactly as she'd hoped. All attempts at subtlety forgotten, she allowed herself a small smile.

"That seems reasonable to me," she said.

Thorolf stood and cast a cursory glance around them to make sure no one was watching, then turned to her, his back to the fire and the rest of the men. "As it happens, I was just about to retire."

He offered his hand. She took it.

LATER THEY HUDDLED UNDER his cloak in exhausted silence. The fog of desire had cleared, and she felt sore and tender in places she hadn't anticipated. Her expectations had been met in some ways and thwarted in others. She'd known there would be pain, but she hadn't expected its extent. And she certainly hadn't expected to feel the same release as she did on her own—she was more realistic than that, for Heid had always been honest with her when she'd asked about such things in her adolescence.

But as it turned out, Thorolf had been nothing if not attentive throughout the entire encounter. At first she'd been embarrassed, flustered, unwilling to admit that she had no idea what she was doing. He'd made not a single comment on her obvious lack of experience, and that had given her the confidence to finally stop thinking and to enjoy herself.

Gunnhild hadn't realized that she had fallen asleep until she awoke with a full bladder thanks to the ale. Beyond the tent's walls, the camp was silent. She slipped reluctantly from Thorolf's embrace and dressed, then left the tent, slunk far enough away from the camp that she couldn't be seen, relieved herself, and headed back.

As she was untying the tent doors so she could reenter it, a voice from behind her said, "I see you found somewhere to sleep."

Gunnhild jumped and clutched her chest as she turned to glare at Eirik, who was sitting on the ground by the dying fire, leaning against his ship box with a cup dangling from his hand, two cats sleeping on him: a large black one on his lap, and a small tortoiseshell on his shoulder. Someone had told her earlier that these were the ship's cats, but for some reason she found it jarring to see two innocent creatures so at ease with a man like him.

Gunnhild stepped closer and said in a furious whisper, "It's none of your business where I choose to sleep."

Eirik didn't bother lowering his voice. "I didn't say it was. I was only making an observation—"

"Don't tell me you're jealous."

She expected him to deny it and call her mad, but instead he rose to his feet and stalked off toward his tent. The cats, after mewling in protest at being disturbed, followed.

"He's insufferable," Gunnhild said softly to no one in particular once she had tucked herself snugly under the cloak with Thorolf.

"He's something—that's certain," Thorolf murmured. He'd been facing away from her, but he rolled over onto his back as he spoke.

She lay on her side, an elbow on the bedroll, her cheek resting on one palm, the fingertips of the other hand running up and down his battle-scarred chest until he reached up and put his hand over hers.

"I'm sorry," she said. "I didn't mean to wake you."

"You didn't. Eirik did."

"What was he doing out there? Waiting for me to leave the tent so he could try to shame me?"

"It's not about you," Thorolf said gently, but she felt a flush of embarrassment all the same. "It's normal for him. He's never slept well."

"Why is that?"

Thorolf was quiet for so long that Gunnhild thought he'd fallen back asleep.

"You can't do what we do, for as long as we've done it, without the consequences of such heavy amounts of violence and death catching up with you. And Eirik has done it longer than any of the rest of us have. Save for Arinbjorn, but he's . . . well, he's also something else."

Gunnhild gave a short, quiet laugh despite the weight of his words. "That's putting it lightly."

She couldn't see his face in the darkness, but she could tell he was smiling. "Having a sense of humor isn't a terrible way of coping."

"What's it like? Battle, I mean."

Thorolf was quiet again for a time before speaking: "You notice nothing but what'll keep you alive. Everything else is secondary. The blood, the smell, the screaming—none of it matters. Only the edge of your opponent's blade, and the knowledge that it's either him or you who'll feed the ravens that day. The fact that Arinbjorn and I even noticed something was amiss during the battle in Bjarmaland with enough time to come to Eirik's aid was a miracle in itself."

This seemed a lot more honest and a lot less poetic than what the skalds spoke of, but Gunnhild hid her surprise. "And yet you continue to raid. To fight. Why?"

"Because it's what we do," Thorolf said simply.

"But *why*?" she pressed. She thought of the night of Heid's ritual in Halogaland: how later, around that fire on the beach, the neighbor boys had spoken so eagerly of becoming great warriors. The poems they recited had the same themes: "Honor? Glory? Valhalla?"

"Those are all well and good," said Thorolf. "But the bigger question is, when the battle is over, how do we carry on? How do we put the

horror behind us and go on living? It eats away at a person, little by little."
There was undeniable pain in his voice as he added, "Sometimes I fear
that by the time the valkyries come for Eirik, there'll be nothing left
of him."

Gunnhild had nothing to say to that. But as much as she found herself
warming to the hird, there was one thing she had trouble reconciling:
"Were any of you with him? For Bjorn or Rognvald? How could you
have stomached his actions?"

"None of us were there. It was too long ago. Eirik has outlived all the
men who've been part of his retinue over the years, save for the current
hird and Arinbjorn. And Arinbjorn splits his time between Fjordane and
wherever Eirik is. It was mere chance that Arinbjorn wasn't present when
Eirik killed Bjorn and sacked his hall."

"He would've talked Eirik out of it."

"Yes." Thorolf lowered his voice. "And I also believe that the timing
of his father's ordering Rognvald's death was purposeful, so that Arinbjorn wasn't there to stop it. It's bad business, killing one's own kin."

"But King Harald knew this, and ordered it anyway," Gunnhild said
at the same volume. What they were saying was no less than treason, and
the tent's walls were thin. "Could he not have predicted that such a deed
would reflect badly on himself and Eirik both?"

"I don't think he sees it that way. In his mind, it probably looks worse
for him to have a witch for a son. Everything is about appearances."
Thorolf added darkly, "The more time I spend in Norway, the more I
understand why my father and grandfather fled when King Harald took
power. Eirik is the only reason I've been here so long. If I didn't love him,
I would have gone home a long time ago."

Gunnhild hadn't realized that he wasn't from Norway. "And where is
home?"

"Iceland."

"I see." She didn't know much about this island to the west, in the
middle of the open sea. But now that he mentioned it, she did recall hearing from her parents that many Norwegian malcontents had relocated
there after King Harald unified the country. "And did your family leave

because they were unwilling to live under the king's rule or because they made an enemy of him?"

"My family has a long history with King Harald," Thorolf said. "He killed my uncle Thorolf, who was in his service, and for whom I'm named. My father made sure to make his displeasure known before he left the country. It's a good thing he was already planning on leaving *before* he was outlawed."

Gunnhild was aghast. "And you came to Norway to serve the son of a man who killed your uncle?"

"That wasn't my intention when I left home, but it's how things happened. And I don't regret it." Thorolf gave her hand a squeeze. "I'm going to Iceland for the winter, for the first time since I left. I wish for you to come with me."

She was glad of the darkness so he couldn't see the dubious look on her face.

"When we arrive at your father's," he continued, "I mean to ask him for your hand. But first I want to make sure it's what you want as well."

"After just this one time, you wish to marry me?" she asked, trying to sound teasing, but her voice was tight. "We just met *today*. Well, yesterday, but—"

"Some couples don't even get the chance to meet before they marry, let alone lie together to see how things go in that regard."

"Was it really so good for you?" This both surprised and pleased her.

Thorolf's voice sounded a bit panicked. "Was it not for you?"

"No, it was. That is not what I meant," she said hastily. "It's just— This is . . . unexpected."

"You're the most remarkable person I've ever met," he said with such sincerity that she flushed at the compliment. "And I've been thinking— once we return to your father's hall, he may force you to marry. At least this way you have a choice. You can ensure your fate before he even gets the chance to force another man upon you."

Gunnhild frowned at this. In her determination to get to Oddny and rescue Signy, she hadn't considered her own prospects. Next summer, Heid had meant to take Gunnhild around Norway and introduce her as her successor. After that, Gunnhild would have taken the name Heid and let her mentor retire to the woods for good.

But for all that Eirik had overreacted when she'd first walked into the camp, he'd had a point: She was nobody. She had no reputation. Her own family thought her dead. Without Heid's endorsement of her skills, who would consider her prophecies trustworthy? And because she had no social standing as a seeress, her father would be well within his legal rights to take control of her life the moment she walked back through his door.

Thorolf was still waiting for her to go on, and when she didn't speak, he squeezed her hand again.

"If you came with me, I wouldn't leave Iceland again," he said. "Not even on the raids. Iceland is not an easy place for many, but it's what you make of it. I've earned enough by now to give us a comfortable life. My family would be glad to see me stay—my father especially. And I haven't seen my brother since he was very small." A pause. "I mean, since he was very young. I can't say he was ever small."

For a moment Gunnhild allowed herself to imagine a life with him. She didn't think it would be a bad one by any means—but she hadn't given half her life to learning witchcraft only to become a housewife. She didn't know the first thing about running a household, and it had been more than a decade since she'd touched a spindle, let alone a loom.

And what's more, her friends needed her. She wouldn't give up on them.

"I can't accept," she said. Before he could argue, she took his hand and pressed his fingertips to the scar on her palm from her blood oath with Oddny and Signy. "I swore to my friends a long time ago that we would always be there for each other. They're in trouble and it may be my fault. It would be so easy for me to say yes to you and to forget them, but I'm no oath-breaker."

"I don't understand. You've been gone twelve winters. How could anything that happened to them be your fault?"

She told him everything. About the circumstances that drove her away from home, her mother's cruelty, and the solace she took in her friends and the oath they swore the night of Heid's ritual; about her stealing away, learning witchcraft, spying, and being present for the raid; of the witches, of Heid's death; and finally, of what she had learned from Eirik and of the details of their conversation.

When she was finished, Thorolf said, "But shouldn't you and Eirik work together against your common enemy?"

Gunnhild felt a spark of anger—he said it so plainly, as if it were the obvious choice—but extinguished it. Despite Thorolf's admitting the king's failings, she suspected he was too fond of Eirik to understand why she would find it impossible to work with him, and she was too tired to defend her choice.

"No. After the terms of our deal are fulfilled, I hope to never see him again." She tucked her head into the crook of his neck and shoulder and pressed her body against his. "I don't refuse your offer because I don't care for you. Ask me again when my sworn sisters are safe and Thorbjorg and her friends have answered for their crimes. Until then, can we not enjoy this while it lasts?"

He tightened his arm around her. "I've heard worse ideas."

12

ODDNY WAS WORKING IN the cookhouse when she heard a
long horn burst from outside, signaling an approaching ship, then a
shorter burst to indicate that it was friendly.

"That'll be the king's men," said Vigdis. "They'll be a ways out yet if
the watchmen have only just spotted them." Still, she wasted no time giving the girls their tasks to prepare for the feast. Oddny chopped turnips
and parsnips for the stew until Vigdis told her to go see if Ulfrun needed
any help in the hall, so she wiped her knife on the hem of her dress and
sheathed it, then slipped out into the brisk air and hurried into the longhouse to find it a hive of activity as Ulfrun delegated tasks.

"Would you be a dear and make me more of that tea?" she said when
Oddny asked how she could help. Ulfrun, like many of the older women
Oddny knew, had terrible pain in her hands, wrists, and elbows from years
of textile work.

Oddny went to the bunk room, where she now kept her supplies inside
Gunnhild's old chest. She grabbed a linen bag of dried herbs and walked
back into the larger room belonging to Ozur and his wife. Solveig was
asleep and did not stir at the noise from the hall, nor at Oddny's footsteps.

Oddny built up the fire in the chamber, boiled some water, and
brewed the tea. As she waited for it to steep, she looked at Solveig and
grimaced. The woman's condition had gotten worse again since the day
Oddny had arrived, but she'd checked her mother's runes and found no

fault with them, so she wasn't sure what else she could do. And even if there *was* something . . . she thought of Gunnhild, her proud and stubborn friend who was cowed only by her fearsome mother, and found she couldn't summon much pity for Solveig.

By the time the tea was done, the noise on the other side of the wall had picked up. Oddny's hand tightened on the steaming clay cup as she stood.

She emerged back into the hall to find it full of men, their faces vaguely familiar from when she'd served them at the beginning of summer. Each flitted in and out of her vision as she made her way through the crowd. When she finally found Ulfrun, she was standing near Ozur, in his best tunic and arm rings, and Eirik, who said something and nodded at the door.

Oddny, Ozur, and Ulfrun turned as the last few people from the ship filed in. A large, dark-haired, bearded man took off his sea-cloak and gave it to the servant collecting the hird's outerwear at the door, then moved aside as the person behind him tugged off their own cloak and handed it over.

Before Oddny even realized this person was a woman, she saw the hair: tossed over one shoulder, a thick red braid glowing orange in the lanternlight.

The servant holding the sea-cloaks gasped at the sight of the woman's face. Ulfrun gasped as well and held one shaking liver-spotted hand over her mouth. Ozur dropped his cane, which clattered to the floor.

The woman turned at the sound.

And when her eyes met Oddny's from across the hall, the cup slipped from Oddny's grip and shattered into a thousand pieces, hot liquid splashing her shoes.

The scar on her palm burned.

Oddny moved forward, weaving through the throng as the other woman did the same, and Oddny's face was already wet with tears when they crashed into each other and sank to the floor in a tight embrace. She sobbed freely and loudly into the shoulder of Gunnhild's kaftan and didn't care who saw or heard.

"Shh," said her friend, petting her hair. "It's all right. I'm here. I'm here now. Oh, Oddny, I'm so, so sorry. I did everything I could, but I couldn't stop them."

Oddny was beside herself. Gods, Gunnhild was real and solid and *here*—but *how* was she here? And she *couldn't stop them* . . . Could she mean—?

"How . . . ?" Oddny pulled away long enough to look her in the face— a face she remembered so well, a face she'd thought she'd never see again, pale and spotted here and there with freckles, keen eyes the deep blue of the ocean framed by hair the dark coppery red of dried blood. But there were differences, too: Gunnhild had lost the round cheeks of her childhood, for one. She had become something starker, hungrier, fiercer than the child Oddny remembered. It was in her face, her eyes, the very set of her shoulders: Whatever had happened to Gunnhild, wherever she'd been these past twelve winters, it had sharpened her like a blade.

Oddny had so many questions and not the faintest idea where to start. The men gave them a wide berth. Oddny could hear the clack of Ozur's cane on the floor nearby. When Gunnhild looked past Oddny and saw him, she squeezed Oddny's shoulder and whispered, "Later."

Then she stood, helped Oddny up, and turned to her father.

"Hello, Papa," she said. Oddny noticed that the corners of her mouth trembled the way they did when she was small, when she was trying not to cry while being scolded by her mother.

The hersir took a step toward her and whispered, "Is it . . . is it truly . . . ?"

"It is," said Gunnhild. "Your youngest daughter, back from the dead."

He sprang forward to hug her, managing to hold on to his cane. Oddny saw Gunnhild close her eyes briefly as she gave him a small pat on the back.

"How can this be? Where have you been all this time?" Ozur said, pulling away to stare at Gunnhild's face before looking over his shoulder to where Eirik now stood. "How did you find her?"

"*She* found *us*," Eirik said, and Oddny did not miss the icy look that passed between Gunnhild and the king. "In Finnmark, on our way back from Bjarmaland. She was most adamant to return home."

"I can speak for myself," Gunnhild said testily.

"You'll have to excuse them, Ozur." A short, balding young man had elbowed his way into the circle. Oddny recognized him as the king's foster brother, whose name escaped her. "We've been long away from polite company, and these two seem unable to rein in their contempt toward one another for any length of time." He gave the old man a winning smile. "I'll see to it that my brother behaves himself, if you'll ensure your daughter does the same."

Eirik shook his head slowly, every bit of him promising murder, though the other man remained serene in the face of the threat. Gunnhild rolled her eyes, and Oddny swiped at her tears and fought back a laugh, surprising herself. When was the last time she'd laughed?

"Yes. Yes, of course, Arinbjorn." Ozur shook himself and cleared his throat. "Come, make yourselves comfortable. Supper should be ready soon."

He led Gunnhild toward the high seat, with Oddny trailing behind, but Ulfrun intercepted them, her rheumy eyes wet, her thin arms outstretched. Gunnhild fell into her embrace without hesitation.

"Oh, lamb," Ulfrun murmured, putting her hands on either side of Gunnhild's face. "You are a sight for these old eyes."

"I'm so sorry," Gunnhild said. "You know why I had to go."

"I do. Oh, dear—your mother is very ill. She's been sleeping since yesterday afternoon. Do you wish to see her?"

A bit of the light in Gunnhild's eyes dimmed. "Perhaps when she wakes."

"Of course, of course." Ulfrun dropped her hands. "I must go tell Vigdis."

"Vigdis! Is she well?"

"Thanks to Oddny," Ulfrun said, "we're all doing just fine."

Before following Gunnhild to the high seat, Oddny looked over her shoulder to see Eirik berating Arinbjorn in a low voice, gesticulating furiously, while the latter stared back at him, completely unconcerned. The dark-haired man who'd preceded Gunnhild into the hall was standing awkwardly beside them; he did not take his eyes off Gunnhild as she was led away.

Arinbjorn caught Oddny's eye and winked just before she turned back around.

IT FELT STRANGE TO Oddny to feast as a guest in Ozur's hall when she was so used to serving, but Gunnhild insisted Oddny dine beside her on her bench. The two of them, along with Eirik, Arinbjorn, Ozur, and the dark-haired man—whose name Oddny learned was Thorolf—all sat in the section of the hall containing the high seat, talking among themselves.

Ozur told Gunnhild of the raid on Oddny's farm. Gunnhild did not take this news with any sort of surprise, which seemed to shock her father—and it chilled Oddny, too, but she knew she'd hear the truth when they were able to speak in private.

Then Ozur asked Gunnhild again where she'd been. And she told him.

"But I sent men after the tax collector's ship," he said in surprise when she was finished. "They checked every box on board."

"Heid carved runes on it to hide me from unwelcome eyes," Gunnhild said simply.

Eirik sat on the platform in front of them, lounging against a post, one leg on the floor and the other bent with his wrist resting atop it, the soft glow of the hearth fires and braziers sharpening the planes of his face. This was a man who was at ease wherever he went, because he knew the world would bow to him simply by virtue of his birth.

Even if she hadn't known him to be a kinslayer, Oddny would have found him repulsive, and one look at Gunnhild told her that her friend felt the same way. This made her feel infinitely better. *What had Signy seen in him?*

"Ozur," Eirik said, standing. "It would please my hird to stay three nights, if that suits you." That was custom; a longer visit would risk overstaying their welcome unless it had been planned in advance.

Gunnhild leaned over to Oddny and said under her breath, "I would have been here sooner had Eirik not chosen for us to stay three nights with the jarl at Borg. I think he did it just to spite me. Thorolf had to stop me from poisoning him at the feast, I was so angry."

"It's not polite to poison people at feasts," Thorolf returned in kind. "Also, as I've told you, we'd been planning on stopping there for three nights anyway. Eirik wished for us to rest a few days with a roof over our heads, and I can't fault him for that."

"Don't defend him," she hissed.

"I'm part of his hird. It's literally my job to defend him." He nudged her, so imperceptibly that Oddny might not have noticed if she hadn't been looking straight at them. "And don't tell me you regret spending three extra nights together."

Ah, Oddny thought, looking back and forth between them. So that was how it was.

"Besides, you're a witch—could you not have summoned a strong wind to carry us here faster if you were so worried?" he asked.

Gunnhild huffed but said nothing. Oddny didn't know what to make of any of this, and a look from her friend told her all would be explained later.

"You have my eternal thanks for returning Gunnhild to me," Ozur said to Eirik. If he'd heard his daughter and Thorolf whispering, he'd ignored them, but Oddny rather doubted he had; the old man's hearing wasn't what it used to be. "What do you desire as compensation?"

Eirik looked at Gunnhild, then back at the hersir, and surprised Oddny by saying, "Nothing."

"Are you certain?" Ozur asked.

"Of course. We came to our own terms. She was no trouble at all." He smirked at Gunnhild, and she tensed like she wanted to throw her entire bowl of stew at his head.

"Papa, if I may take my leave of you, I wish to go thank Vigdis in person for preparing such a fine feast," Gunnhild said. Ozur gestured that she was free to go, and after Gunnhild subtly jerked her head at the door, Oddny stood to follow. Gunnhild purposely bumped Eirik with her shoulder as she passed, and he gave her a look of deep disgust, which he quickly wiped away before he turned back to speak to Ozur and the other men.

Once they were outside, Gunnhild heaved a sigh of relief. "Thank Freyja. I don't know how much more of his posturing I can take. Gods, how I loathe that man."

"Gunna—," Oddny began.

"Cookhouse first," Gunnhild said. "I meant what I said about seeing Vigdis." She looped her arm through Oddny's. "And then I thought we could build a fire if the pit is still there, and sit out for a bit like we used to. Unless it's too cold for you."

"Not at all," Oddny said, for she wore her shawl, and she was relieved to be free of the commotion of the hall. As they walked, she clung to Gunnhild out of a childish worry that if she let her friend go for one moment, she would vanish just as she'd done the last time they'd parted.

Ulfrun was in the cookhouse as well when they arrived. After a tearful reunion with Vigdis, Gunnhild said, "I need your help tomorrow night with a ritual."

Vigdis and Ulfrun looked at each other. Oddny, who had reattached herself to Gunnhild's side the moment she'd broken from Vigdis, said, "A ritual?"

"Yes. After supper, will the three of you sing the warding songs for me? Right here in the cookhouse, with any of the other girls here who know the songs?"

"No seeress has been through here since the one who took you away," said Vigdis carefully. "It's only the three of us, I think. Solveig has forbidden us to teach the songs to the younger ones. She thinks them cursed."

Gunnhild scowled. "She *would* think that."

"We'll do it," said Ulfrun. "If only because we've let you down in every other way, lamb." Her eyes were misty again as she came forward and took Gunnhild's hand. "I'm so sorry we couldn't protect you from her."

Vigdis's lower lip trembled. "Have you seen her yet?"

"I must go. Oddny and I have much to discuss. Thank you for your help," Gunnhild said stiffly. She slid her hand from Ulfrun's. "I'll see you tomorrow."

Once they were clear of the cookhouse, Oddny said, very quietly, "Would that my mother had gotten you away from her. She tried—"

"I know," Gunnhild said, staring straight ahead as they made their way across the darkening yard, ignoring the clamor from within the hall. "Yrsa was a good woman. She didn't deserve her fate."

"Which raises the question," Oddny said, "of how you already seemed to know what had happened to her before your father told you."

"From the moment I was taught to leave my body and travel as witches do, I came back as often as I could. As a bird." Gunnhild looped their arms together again as they continued onto the beach, the grass giving way to pebbles. "I've been keeping watch on you for many years. That I happened to be there for the raid was a coincidence: a good one for you, because I could help you escape, but a poor one for my mentor. She died that day. I wish I could have done more for you both. And for Signy."

"A bird?" Oddny's steps faltered. "You were the swallow? The one who attacked—?"

Both of them stopped. Farther down the beach, someone had already started a fire in the pit. The two women exchanged a look and approached with cautious steps until the shape of Halldor materialized.

"And would that I'd succeeded in taking out his eye," Gunnhild said coldly. "What is *he* doing here?"

"And here I thought that one random bird simply had it out for me," Halldor said. "Interesting to know the truth."

"How did you—?" Gunnhild began.

"You talk very loudly for two people attempting to have a private conversation." Halldor added another log to the fire, then sat back against the rock behind him.

"Halldor, this is Gunnhild," Oddny said, "the long-lost daughter of our host."

"So I've heard," he said. "The whole place is talking about her."

Oddny gestured at him. "Gunnhild, this is Halldor. He was thrown overboard after the raid and washed up here. Your father is making him pay me compensation on behalf of all his fellows. Twelve marks of silver."

"Eleven and a half," Halldor said. "Remember?"

"Right." Oddny sat down near the fire, opposite him, and bade Gunnhild do the same. "Why aren't you at the feast, Halldor? If you mean to join the king's hird, it would seem prudent to introduce yourself."

"I don't like crowds." Halldor shifted. "And I'll introduce myself tomorrow on the practice field, with a weapon in my hand. It'll make a more memorable impression."

Gunnhild looked back and forth between them. "I'm sorry. I haven't been spying since the raid, so I believe I'm missing something: How is it that we're sitting here so comfortably with one of the men responsible for what befell your family?"

"Halldor and I have an understanding," Oddny said. "Your father thinks I'm going to use the silver he pays me to find a husband and rebuild my life, but I intend to use it to rescue Signy. Halldor says she'll most likely be sold at Birka, because that's where the raiders winter."

Gunnhild cut him a suspicious look. "But there are other market towns well before—"

"Well, Kolfinna is banned from Denmark," Halldor said. "She wouldn't stop there. She's . . . noticeable."

"How is that possible?" Gunnhild asked. "Women can't be outlawed."

"I didn't say she was outlawed. It was more that she was asked to leave and never come back. Politely. At sword point." Halldor shrugged a shoulder. "It happens when you kill enough people during alehouse brawls without paying their families compensation. Anyway, as I've already told Oddny, even if you went to Birka, the chances of finding Signy would be very slim. She would only be passing through. Even if you got there before the start of winter, you'd be stranded there before picking up the trail."

"He also told me that the crew were paid to raid my farm," Oddny said. "By some witch who takes the form of a white fox and communicated only with Kolfinna."

Gunnhild pursed her lips. "This all aligns with what I witnessed that day. Kolfinna was furious that this man let you escape, Oddny. I'm not surprised she gave him to Ran's daughters. Thorbjorg cut half their pay."

"Thorbjorg?"

"That's her name. The white fox," said Gunnhild. "I learned from Eirik that she works for King Olaf of Vestfold, and studied witchcraft under Eirik's brother Rognvald, whom he killed."

"If that's so, I understand her anger," Oddny said slowly. "But what does any of that have to do with you, and with Signy and me?"

Gunnhild looked away. "All I know is that she foresaw something. Something to do with . . . us. I haven't pieced it all together yet, but I will." There was fire in her eyes when she looked back to Oddny. "The reason I'm doing the ritual tomorrow is to ask the spirits where Signy has been taken. The dead don't just know the future—they know everything. And once they've told me where to find her, we *will* bring her home."

Oddny stared hard at her, willing herself not to cry. More than a week had passed since the raid, and every day she'd put on her bravest face as she helped around the farm and made teas and tinctures for those who needed them. But every night her grief, and the guilt at surviving the raid unharmed—a free woman still, while somewhere far away her sister was surely in shackles—threatened to crush the air from her lungs. For all that she itched to put her rescue plan into motion the moment Halldor paid her, there were times when none of it seemed real: that Signy was gone; that her mother and brother were dead; that if she looked across the strait she would be able to make out the mound where they lay instead of the outline of her father's hall.

But Signy was alive. Oddny knew it. And she had kept her plan close to her chest, as though cupping her hands around a tiny flame in the darkness, shielding it from her own despair. She'd assumed beyond a doubt that she would be finding her sister on her own. But now . . .

"You're going to help me save her?" she whispered.

Gunnhild's eyebrows shot up in surprise, as though anything less were out of the question. "We swore an oath, Oddny. I don't intend to break it. And since Eirik didn't want my silver, I can put it toward Signy's rescue."

Oddny took a quavering breath. "Thank you."

Gunnhild smiled. "Of course. And hopefully what I find out from the spirits will corroborate what Halldor has told you, if he knows what's good for him."

"I'm telling the truth," Halldor said, exasperated.

"We'll see," said Gunnhild, rising to her feet. "And so help me, if you're lying to us, I *will* know, and you *will* pay for it."

Halldor did not seem intimidated in the least. "Duly noted."

"Gunna," Oddny said, hope flaring bright in her chest, "if you have the silver, then—once we know where she is, do you think we can make it to her before winter?"

"That was my plan," Gunnhild said. "Why do you think I was in such a hurry to get back here?"

Oddny let out a sob and clamped a hand over her mouth, but Halldor said, "No sailor in their right mind would agree to a long voyage so late in the season unless you plan to winter at your destination—"

"We'll worry about that once we know precisely where she is." Gunnhild's gaze moved to a dark figure making its way across the lawn toward the boathouse. "Now, if you two will excuse me, I have something to attend to. Oddny, shall I walk you back to the hall first?"

Oddny stood. "Yes. Good night, Halldor."

"Good night, Oddny. Gunnhild," Halldor replied, and when Oddny looked over her shoulder at him, he was still watching her as they walked away.

Once they were out of earshot, Gunnhild said, "You trust this man?"

"I do," Oddny said after a moment's hesitation. "He could've been long gone by now. I truly think he means to pay me back, which makes me think he has no reason to lie."

"Then that's good enough for me." Gunnhild stopped just around the corner from the door near the hanging lantern that illuminated the threshold, and she gave her a firm hug, which Oddny returned with feeling. "I'll see you in the morning. Good night, Oddny."

"Good night." With that, Gunnhild rounded the corner, leaving Oddny with a renewed sense of determination.

We will find you, Signy, she thought as she went back inside. *Together. Just hold on.*

13

MORNING FOUND GUNNHILD CURLED up in Oddny's bunk, back to back with her, just as they'd sometimes slept as children when visiting each other's farms.

Oddny sat up slowly and assessed her body for aches and pains. Her cycle was almost over, so today was the first day since she'd arrived at Ozur's that she thought she might be able to skip her tea. But she'd certainly have to wash out the makeshift contraption she'd sewn hastily to catch her blood; the garment was made up of wool layers that ran from her navel to the small of her back, both ends sewn to a thin whipcord-braided belt. Wearing it made walking a bit awkward, but at least she wouldn't bleed through it and ruin the only dress she owned.

She crawled over Gunnhild and out of bed. The servants who slept in the bunk room were still asleep. As Oddny pulled on her socks and shoes, Gunnhild stirred.

"I'm fetching breakfast," Oddny said softly. "Would you like anything?"

"No, thank you. I'm going to fast until the ritual tonight."

"So you're going to be grumpy all day."

Gunnhild yanked the pillow over her head. "Yes. I'm used to going without food as part of my training, but a week among these men has spoiled me."

"That's not surprising—you can tell by looking at them that they don't skip meals." Oddny bent over and fastened the toggles on her shoes. "Why must you fast? Spiritual reasons?"

"Yes, yes," Gunnhild said with a wave of her hand, voice muffled by the pillow. "But more practically, because if I have an empty stomach, I'll need less henbane to dislodge my mind from my body."

"Henbane? Gunna, that's *poisonous*."

Gunnhild lifted the pillow enough to peek up at her. "Yes, if you take too much. So—fasting. And meditation. I'll have to find someplace quiet to sit out and think before the ritual as well. Clear my mind and all that, and work on my payment for Eirik for taking me here. I've nearly finished it, and I can't wait to be free of any obligation to that man."

Once Oddny had done her laundry, she ate a boiled egg in the cookhouse and helped Vigdis and the other girls prepare food for their guests. Soon enough her arm was sore from turning the quern to grind grain. It was difficult for her to believe that serving this many additional people would hardly put a dent in Ozur's winter stores, but no one seemed particularly concerned about feeding thirty extra mouths for three entire days.

She was so busy working that when Gunnhild arrived at midday and asked if she wanted to come watch the men spar, Oddny was surprised at how much time had passed. Vigdis gave her leave to go and thanked her for her help.

The practice yard next to the armory was a wide fenced-in circle of dirt in the grass, completely unremarkable except for the men who fought within it, weapons glinting in the sun. Eirik's hird and Ozur's men were there, along with several men Oddny had never seen before, as well as a cluster of serving women and the teenage boys who tended Ozur's armory.

"Match to Svein!" they heard Arinbjorn shout as they approached.

"What happened to meditating?" Oddny asked Gunnhild.

Her friend waved a hand. "I can do that later. I want to see Eirik get smacked with sharp objects, but I'll settle for blunt ones. One good hit and I'll be satisfied."

They wove between the gathered men and claimed a spot next to Arinbjorn against the fence.

"So, what's all this?" Gunnhild asked him, gesturing to where Svein the skald and a man Oddny didn't recognize were exiting the field.

"A rite of passage," Arinbjorn replied. "The man Svein just fought came from one of the islands nearby, trying to join the hird. And more will arrive before we leave. First comes a steel test, then a probationary period, and *then*, if Eirik likes them well enough, they get one of these." He flicked the gold arm ring on his bicep. "To make it official."

"I see," Oddny said, thinking of Halldor—and mere moments later, he strode up to the fence farther down on her right. His hair had been pulled back into a short braid, his sleeves rolled up to his elbows to reveal forearms smeared with soot from the forge. He stared straight ahead at Eirik, who lounged on a bench just outside the field.

"King Eirik," Halldor said. "I wish to join your hird."

"You're not the first today," Eirik said, without turning to face him, as he took a proffered cup of ale from a serving girl, who blushed and giggled. Beside Oddny, Gunnhild made a loud retching noise that made Eirik turn and glare at her.

Then he got a good look at Halldor—who hopped lithely over the fence to stand before him in the practice yard—and raised his eyebrows. "How old are you, boy? Come back when you've grown your beard."

Most of the men laughed, and even the armory boys looked amused. But despite her dislike of Halldor, Oddny found herself insulted on his behalf. Her brother, Vestein, had never grown a beard, either, and in her opinion it hadn't made him any less a man.

"I'm a man grown, not a boy," said Halldor, chin raised. "My name is Halldor Hallgrimsson."

Eirik considered him. "You're not very big."

"I'm no smaller than many of your valued hirdsmen," said Halldor, with a pointed look at Arinbjorn, who inclined his head to acknowledge that Halldor was the taller of them.

The king looked at his foster brother, then back at Halldor, and said,

"All right, Halldor Hallgrimsson. Let's see if your skill with a blade lives up to your bold words. Arinbjorn?"

Arinbjorn leapt the fence. He had two seaxes at his belt, one in front and one in back, and he drew them both at once with liquid grace. Halldor drew his own seax just as one of the armory boys handed him a shield over the fence.

"You don't use one of these?" Halldor asked Arinbjorn, gesturing with the shield.

The shorter man shrugged and spun his seaxes with a flourish before settling into fighting stance. "I'd rather block with something that could hurt you."

"Have you ever been hit with a shield? It definitely hurts."

"I suppose it could, if you know how to use it. Do you?"

"You're about to find out."

"Oh, this'll be fun."

Gunnhild cupped her hands around her mouth and yelled, "Arinbjorn, if you kill him you have to pay my friend the twelve marks of silver he owes her."

"Eleven and a half," Halldor and Oddny said in unison, and Halldor added dryly, "Thank you for your confidence, Gunnhild."

"If we're through with the interruptions," Eirik said, raising his voice, "you may begin at will. To first blood."

Arinbjorn made the first move, bringing the butt of one seax down to try to hook the side of Halldor's shield while slashing the other seax toward his flank, but Halldor was quicker: He brought his own seax down to deflect the other man's blade and brought his shield in close, keeping a firm hold on it. Arinbjorn stepped back to reassess, and the two men circled each other.

This time Halldor was first to move, but Arinbjorn dodged his slash with ease and attempted to deliver a blow of his own, which Halldor parried with his seax. Oddny stood riveted to the spot, entranced, as she watched them—every move seemed calculated as they twisted around each other, strangely light on their feet. A feint here, a swing there, and they'd fall back, each looking for an opening, and, finding it, lunge again.

Oddny had at first agreed with Halldor that Arinbjorn would be at a disadvantage without a shield, but the smaller man used his seaxes defensively, moving as fluidly as though the weapons were extensions of his arms, blocking every hit until finally Halldor rushed at him, attempting to land a blow with the boss of his shield. Arinbjorn dodged and knocked the shield sideways with both seaxes, but Halldor stopped and jerked the shield back up and—

Its rawhide edge hit Arinbjorn in the nose with a sickening crunch that elicited shouts of shock from among the onlookers. One of the serving girls near Eirik fainted; one of the armory lads clutched his own crooked nose as if feeling the same pain. Arinbjorn stumbled backward a few steps before dropping his seaxes and falling back on his ass in the dirt, blood running from his nostrils and down his chin to splatter the front of his tunic.

He reached up to assess the damage and seemed surprised by the sight of his own blood when he pulled his hand away.

"Well," Arinbjorn said thickly, "that's first blood. Match to Halldor." The assembly clapped, and Oddny had not realized that applause could sound so uncertain. More than one person was looking at Eirik—who sat stone-faced on the bench, his ale forgotten—as if waiting to see how he would react.

Oddny said, "I'll set his nose," at the exact same moment Arinbjorn did it himself and swore loudly. "Never mind."

"That isn't the first time this has happened," said Thorolf, who had appeared at Gunnhild's elbow at some point during the fight. "But this *is* the first time I've seen Arinbjorn lose to anyone but Eirik."

Halldor sheathed his seax and dropped his shield, picked up Arinbjorn's weapons, and stepped forward, offering a hand to help him to his feet. The other man took it and gave a nod of thanks when Halldor handed both seaxes back to him, hilts first. Once they were safely in their sheaths, Arinbjorn grinned, teeth bloody, and clapped Halldor on the shoulder.

"Well done," the smaller man said. "I underestimated you this time, but it won't happen again."

"I look forward to our rematch, then," said Halldor, but Oddny thought he seemed nervous. And, a moment later, she understood why.

Eirik had risen from his bench, and the crowd had hushed.

"You all right?" he asked Arinbjorn as his foster brother left the field. Arinbjorn waved him off.

The king turned to Halldor and said to the armory boys without looking at them: "Bring me my axes." Several of the men chuckled; a few of them said, "Ooh," as if Halldor were a sibling about to get reprimanded by their father.

"He certainly loves a bit of drama, doesn't he?" Gunnhild drawled.

Arinbjorn, who had positioned himself against the fence on Thorolf's other side, leaned forward and looked around him at Gunnhild. "I watched you literally stab yourself the other day just to prove a point."

"He watched you *what*?" Oddny said, and when her friend offered no explanation, she turned back to the ring. "Thorolf, what is Eirik doing?"

The big man gave her a somber look over Gunnhild's head. "I don't know. He doesn't usually test them himself. Halldor made an impression."

"Exactly as he intended," said Gunnhild, folding both arms on the fence and leaning forward. "I hope he breaks Eirik's nose, too."

"This isn't fair," Oddny said as the king entered the ring, weapons in hand. "Halldor hasn't even caught his breath from the last fight, and Eirik is fresh."

"It won't matter either way," Thorolf said grimly. "Just watch."

Halldor swiftly picked up his shield and drew his seax, taking a defensive stance as Eirik came toward him. There was a look of firm resolve on Halldor's face, and something else, which Oddny couldn't place.

"When you're ready," Arinbjorn called, for the sake of formality. "To first blood."

Eirik let Halldor take the first few swings, which he deflected almost lazily. No sooner had Halldor paused to look for an opening than Eirik hooked the beard of one axe over the rim of Halldor's shield, sending it flying from his hand. Before Halldor could react, Eirik swung low and fast with the other axe, snagged Halldor's ankle with its beard, and yanked the other man's foot out from under him. Halldor dropped his seax as he fell hard onto his side.

Before Oddny could so much as blink, Eirik had an axe to Halldor's throat.

"Two moves," Gunnhild said, hands clenched on the edge of the fence. "He took him down in *two moves*, that son of a bitch."

"Not so much," Oddny said, stunned. "Look."

Halldor was staring up at his opponent, one corner of his mouth tilted up in a half smile. In the heartbeat between his falling and Eirik's leveling the axe at his neck, he'd managed to draw the utility knife from his belt, and the tip of the blade hovered a hairsbreadth from Eirik's groin.

"First blood, wasn't it?" Halldor said.

"It's a draw," Arinbjorn said hurriedly. "Match to no one. It's over. Eirik, did you hear me? Halldor?"

Eirik withdrew his axe and Halldor put his knife away. When the king dropped his weapons and offered a hand, Halldor regarded him for a moment too long before taking it, and once he was on his feet, the two men sized each other up.

"Keep it up and you're in," Eirik said after a beat. Turning to go, he barked to the armory boys, "Clean up my axes," before slipping through the gap in the fence and disappearing into the crowd.

"Shame," Gunnhild grumped. "I wanted to see him bleed."

"So that's it?" Oddny asked Thorolf. "Halldor is in the hird?"

"He's on his way. First one of the day that Eirik has accepted, too," Arinbjorn confirmed, but his usual look of cheer had shifted into something calculating. "A man that good—we have to keep him close or risk seeing him on the other side of the battlefield."

"A *draw*. Unbelievable," Oddny heard Svein moan from farther down the fence, echoing the sentiment that seemed to be bleeding through the crowd. She wasn't sure why this was cause for concern until Thorolf said, "Eirik is going to be in a very bad mood after this."

"Who *is* that man?" Arinbjorn muttered as he watched Halldor leave the ring. "I like him. It's the"—he paused and counted on his fingers—"fourth time I've had someone break my nose, but I like him."

"Were the first three times Eirik's doing?" Gunnhild asked wryly.

Arinbjorn affected a look of mock surprise. "How did you guess?"

"I have brothers."

"Fair enough."

As he exited the field, Halldor turned for just a moment, caught Oddny's eye, and nodded. Oddny nodded in return as several of the men clapped him on the back and congratulated him, same as Arinbjorn had. Oddny couldn't help but smile at that. *Made an impression, indeed.*

Arinbjorn turned to Thorolf. "Is my nose straight? It doesn't feel straight."

"It's not." Oddny sighed. "Come here. I'll fix you up."

ODDNY SPENT THE REST of the day scouring the kitchen's garden for healing supplies and scavenging more from the hillside. She made a poultice to hasten the healing of Arinbjorn's nose and delivered it to him just as he was heading into the armory, and he accepted it with gratitude. When he went inside, he left the door slightly ajar behind him—so as she turned to walk away, Oddny caught a snatch of conversation and paused to listen out of curiosity.

"—anyway, I still think it's a terrible idea," Arinbjorn said. "You don't even know if this bindrune will work—"

Eirik's voice cut in. "She seemed confident enough when she told me of it, and you saw the way she healed her hand. Thorbjorg will only devise worse ways to attack once the bindrunes are in place and she realizes her madness has no effect on us. And when that happens, we'll need Gunnhild."

"Still—she'll never agree, and when she turns you down, she'll brag about it."

"I could arrange it with her father. Then she'll have no choice."

"That's the worst idea you've ever had. She might *actually* kill you if you did that. She's already made you look like a fool more than once, and I don't dislike her for that, especially considering I do the same on a regular basis. But—"

"But she's not my brother. You undermine me for fun. She does it out of malice."

"Exactly. And do you really want to give her more fodder?"

"Well, what if I had fodder, too?"

Arinbjorn's tone turned thoughtful. "That's a fair point—we don't really know anything about this woman. I don't think it would be a terrible idea to talk to the others around here first. Get their opinions on things. Subtly. You do know the meaning of the word, don't you?"

"Thorolf won't be happy about it." Eirik actually sounded sad. "If she says yes."

"And while we both care about Thorolf, what's more important? His feelings or the safety and well-being of the lot of us?"

Oddny fled when she heard Eirik's heavy footsteps heading toward the door.

She had her suspicions about the conversation, but she put them from her mind and went to help Vigdis with the evening's meal. Gunnhild had gone off to the other side of the island to meditate in solitude and, Oddny supposed, to work on that task for Eirik, which she guessed had something to do with the bindrune the men had mentioned. Unwilling to brave the noisy feast hall without her friend, Oddny decided to eat supper in the cookhouse, where she heard from one of the serving girls that Halldor was eating with the king's inner circle. *Good. The sooner they accept him, the sooner he'll pay me back.*

Once they'd cleaned up from supper, Gunnhild arrived at the cookhouse for the ritual, and it was nothing like the last one Oddny had witnessed: She, Vigdis, and Ulfrun formed a triangle around Gunnhild in the cramped room and sang, as Gunnhild—after drinking her poison tea—sat atop a stool, the old seeress's iron staff tucked under her arm, and mimed spinning.

Like when she was a child, Oddny saw the thread that formed and dropped into the ground. But this time it sprang back up immediately and disappeared as Gunnhild jerked out of her trance and fell sideways off the stool, swearing up a storm.

She wouldn't let anybody help her up. The hand that clutched her staff was white. "Thank you for your assistance," she said to the three of them once she was on her feet. "That will be all." Then she swept from the cookhouse, shoulders hunched and shaking.

Ulfrun and Vigdis exchanged a helpless look, and Oddny said, "I'll talk to her," and grabbed a lantern.

"What happened?" she asked, trailing at Gunnhild's heels as they crossed the yard. It was dark, but the feast inside the hall was still going strong. "Gunna, say something. What did you do?"

They were on the other side of the longhouse before Gunnhild stopped in her tracks and turned around, her eyes wild in the lantern-light. "Nothing. I did nothing. I couldn't reach the sprits. I couldn't reach *anyone*. I should have known. When I tried before, right after the raid, Katla was there in the dark place, which is why I didn't try again—not alone—but she was there again and . . . I'm not . . . I'm not strong enough—"

Though Oddny did not understand half of this and had no idea who Katla was, she thought she understood the problem. "That's why you got that look on your face at the feast when Thorolf suggested you could've summoned a wind—you can't, because you need to leave your body to cast the spell?"

"Right. So it seems that even with the songs, I can't risk traveling. I have the runes and I have my curses, but without sending out my mind or being able to contact the dead . . . I'm not even a witch, am I, if I can't do those things? How will we ever find Signy now?"

"Start at Birka and go from there, as Halldor said? We're no worse off than when you arrived." Though Oddny had to admit she was disappointed—a precise lead would mean finding Signy that much more quickly. "Do you still think we can get to her before winter?"

"I asked my father earlier today if he would give me a ship and crew. He refused. Said we'd never make it there and back in time." Gunnhild rubbed her forehead, seeming to calm down a bit. "But we'll find another way. I swear it to you."

Before Oddny could reply, a figure came toward them out of the darkness and resolved itself into the shape of—

"His timing is abhorrent," Oddny muttered.

"What do you want?" Gunnhild asked Eirik as the flickering light from Oddny's lantern illuminated his face.

"A word," said the king. He looked to Oddny. "A *private* word. Leave the lantern, please, if you would."

Oddny shoved it at him, barely allowing him to get a grip on the rope before she let go of it. There was no time to relay the conversation she'd heard between him and Arinbjorn in the armory earlier, so all she could say to Gunnhild was, "Be careful."

Then she stomped back toward the cookhouse with her fists clenched at her sides, her mind a storm, irritated at Eirik's interruption and Ozur's reluctance to spare them a ship.

I'm sorry, she thought, wishing Signy could hear her. *We won't give up. I promise.*

14

"YOU HAVE A LOT of nerve," Gunnhild said, rounding on Eirik once Oddny was far enough away. "What is it?"

"You still owe me payment for taking you here," he said, seeming oddly unruffled by her tone. That was her first clue that this conversation was going to take a turn.

"You'll have it by first light the morning after next, and then our dealings will be done," she said tersely. "Is that all?"

"No. You see, I learned some things today."

"Oh yes? Congratulations. How many things? One, two? That makes, what, four things total that you know?"

Eirik ignored the jab. "I talked to some of your father's old watchmen. And then I stopped by the cookhouse and had a little chat with Ulfrun and Vigdis, and they had a lot to say."

Gunnhild fought the urge to bludgeon him in the head with her staff. Give him the beating she'd wanted to see him take earlier on the practice field. "About what?"

"About you. About your childhood. About your relationship with your mother."

Every hair on her body stood on end.

"You are steering this conversation onto thin ice, King Eirik," Gunnhild said through her teeth. "Tread carefully. Say what you're going to say and be done with it."

"I asked you for help once, and we came to terms. I was hoping to do so again. For a . . . longer engagement."

"No," Gunnhild said without hesitation. "I told you, I have more important things to do. The moment I hand you that bindrune is the last moment I wish to spend in your presence."

"As I've said, I can pay you."

"I don't want your silver."

"I thought as much. And if I can't appeal to your coin purse"—he stepped closer, holding the lantern aloft between them—"perhaps I can appeal to your ambition."

"You know nothing of my ambition."

"Oh, don't I? Let's see . . ." He began to circle her with long, lazy strides, and she turned with him, never letting him see her back. "A child whose mother tired of daughters and never wanted her. No one to stand up for her, even though everyone knows what's happening—her father and brothers don't care, and the servants are just as scared of her mother as she is. The one person who should have always been looking out for her was, instead, her biggest villain. Only her neighbors' mother ever attempted to save her, so she had to save herself in the end. To what lengths would such a person go in order to make something of themselves, to prove their mother wrong?"

Halfway through she'd stopped turning and stood frozen in place, both hands tight on her staff, his words slipping under her skin like needle pricks.

"This is low, even for you," she said. "You've snooped around in my life only to take my pain and shove it in my face in a sorry attempt to bend me to your will—it's reprehensible. Give me one good reason not to send you on your way with a curse for my troubles."

Eirik stopped in front of her, shaking his head. "You think I'm trying to insult you. I'm not. They didn't deserve you, Gunnhild."

She opened her mouth and shut it again. This, coming from him, was so unexpected that it rendered her utterly at a loss.

"I've lost some respect for your father—that's certain," he continued.

"He did nothing to stop her. Your friend Oddny's mother was the only one who ever tried to help you, and Thorbjorg is the reason she's dead—yet you *still* don't wish to ally with me against her?"

"That's correct," Gunnhild said frostily.

"Don't you see? Whatever Thorbjorg has against you, she's Olaf's right hand. She's my enemy, too. So if you don't want to work *for* me, perhaps if we work together—"

"How many times must I refuse you before you take the hint?" She jabbed her staff at his chest and he took a step back. "I want nothing to do with you. You may paint such an alliance as beneficial to us both, but there's nothing you could possibly offer me that would make me want to help you. How does *any* of this appeal to my *ambition*?"

Eirik hesitated, as if he were trying to force the next words out of his mouth.

"Get to your point," she snapped. "My patience wears thin, and—"

"Marry me."

She searched his face for a long moment and saw no hint of a jest. His jaw was set, his lips in a thin line. It was the unhappiest marriage proposal she'd ever heard of, so much so that she couldn't help but laugh: big, doubled-over belly laughs that echoed across the empty yard and sent a flock of seagulls scattering from the other end of the beach.

"Are you done?" he demanded after she'd gone on for quite some time. His expression had only grown harder in the face of her mirth.

"Why," she said, wiping tears from her eyes as she tried to catch her breath, "in all the Nine Worlds would you think I would *ever* want to marry *you*?" She turned to go. "Never mind. It doesn't matter. The answer is no."

"I don't think you're thinking this through."

"Have you missed the part where I don't want anything to do with you?" she said over her shoulder as she walked away.

Eirik called after her, "If you marry me, you'll be a queen."

Gunnhild stopped dead.

"Queen of the districts I govern, to start, which include your own Halogaland. But when I become *the* king instead of *a* king, it would make you one of the most powerful women in the country," Eirik went on. "I wonder what your mother would say about that."

One arm held her staff limply at her side while the other formed a fist.

"She's an ungrateful little whelp . . . stubborn and insubordinate . . . should be ashamed of herself."

Those were not even the worst things Solveig had said of her.

"It's your choice," Eirik continued. "I'll only ask you once. If you refuse, you have my word that I won't bring this matter to you again."

Gunnhild began to truly consider his offer. If she accepted it, Thorolf would hate her. And Oddny would think she'd lost her mind. But Eirik had succeeded in appealing to her ambition after all—just not in the way he'd expected.

Eirik's title aside, he and her father were both rich, and once they each handed over her bride-price and dowry—both of which she'd keep, as was custom—it would likely amount to more silver than she could amass in *years* trying to establish herself as a reputable seeress.

And in the short term, Eirik was more desperate than she'd thought if he was coming to her with such an extreme proposition. Which meant that he might be willing to agree to equally extreme terms.

He had ships and men. They were already traveling.

Maybe she could get them to travel just a little bit farther before winter was upon them.

Whatever Thorbjorg had against Gunnhild was trivial in the face of what Eirik was promising her. The resources she'd have at her disposal would be beyond her wildest dreams. Regardless of whether she could travel as a witch, she would have the means not only to save Signy but to hunt down Thorbjorg and Katla and make them pay for what they'd done to Heid and to Oddny's family.

She would kill them both in the worst way possible.

And then, just out of spite, she would make that damned fox into a fine fur hat.

All that aside—marrying a king would be a very satisfying thing to throw in her mother's face if Solveig ever woke up again.

"Fine." Gunnhild turned. "I accept."

Eirik recoiled in surprise. "You . . . accept?"

"Yes. And you will negotiate the bride-price and dowry with my father as the law dictates. However, I have my own terms as well."

"Oh good. Great." Eirik scrubbed a hand down his face. "Go on, then."

She couldn't lead with the most important thing, her most desperate want. She had to seem reasonable. She thought about what he'd told her in the woods in Finnmark, and that shaped her answer.

It occurred to her to ask first, though: "How many wives do you have so far? And children?"

"None and none. That I know of. Why?"

The answer didn't surprise her, for reasons she couldn't quite put her finger on. Nonetheless she raised her eyebrows, unable to resist a dig at him: "Really? But you're a *king*, and you're, what, thirty winters old already?"

Eirik fixed her with a long look before saying, "Get on with it already."

"Fine," Gunnhild said when it was clear he wouldn't take the bait. "In that case: If we're to marry, you shall take no other wives but me and sire no other children but mine. And when you succeed your father, I'll be queen not just of your districts but queen of Norway—not consort, nor queen consort, but *queen*. The *only* queen."

Some of King Harald's highborn wives were called *queen*, but none were considered queen over the entire country alongside him. She was asking to become the very first woman to assume this position.

Asking more of Eirik than was proper.

Asking to be publicly recognized as his equal.

Eirik folded his arms. "You must be jesting. It's every free man's right to take as many wives and sire as many children as he can support."

"Exactly," said Gunnhild, undeterred. "In Finnmark, you told me how you grew up. Do you wish for your sons to love each other as you and Arinbjorn do, or do you want them to be like you and your half brothers, so you can watch them fight over Norway like scavengers over a corpse before you're even in the ground? Are you going to repeat your father's mistakes?"

"My father does not make mistakes," Eirik said through his teeth.

"Your brothers would disagree," she said, and savored the look of fury on his face. "Anyway. That's my first term. My second—"

"Dear gods, what *else*?"

"As you said before, my friend Oddny's mother was the only one who tried to help me as a child—I don't know if you've met Oddny herself, but she was just here. You're holding her lantern."

"She was familiar, but no, I don't know that we've officially met. Why?"

"The raid I mentioned to you back in Finnmark, the one my father spoke of the night we arrived—it was her farm that was destroyed. Her sister was the one kidnapped, and we mean to rescue her before the start of winter. So my final term is that you'll take me and Oddny straight to Birka from here."

Eirik stared at her. "Have you lost your mind? We've been traveling all summer. We want to go home."

"Those are my terms," Gunnhild said. "Take them or leave them."

"You're mad." Eirik rubbed both hands down his face now. "You're delusional if you think—"

She stepped closer to him so they were nose to nose. "How badly do you need my help?"

He dropped his hands.

"No," he said firmly enough that she reared back. "Absolutely not. You don't know what you're asking for, Gunnhild. It's too late in the season to travel so far. Do you know what it's like to sail in the winter? By day, it'll be so cold that you may lose fingers or toes. And the nights are even colder, and longer. We'd have to dock at a settlement or stop to make camp every single night or risk us all freezing to death on the water, and at that rate it would take us at least two moons to get there. Two long, miserable moons. I won't risk my life, or my ship, or my men. I would rather take my chances dealing with Thorbjorg on my own than agree to something so utterly foolish."

Gunnhild bit her lip and sighed through her nose, but this was one area where she couldn't exactly argue with him. He was the more experienced sailor by far, and more traveled than possibly anyone else she knew. If even he wouldn't agree to making this journey, then she might be forced to admit that no one would. And if that were so, she couldn't fault her father for refusing her request as well.

"I suppose if no one goes anywhere during the winter, Oddny's sister won't, either," she said. "You said before that you're wintering in Horda-land?"

"At my father's estate at Alreksstadir, yes."

"Could we leave straight from there in the spring?"

He considered this. "What happened this summer means my broth-ers' plotting has escalated. I'd thought to forgo raiding in favor of making the royal progress, to reaffirm the loyalty of the jarls and hersar who've sworn to me . . ."

"Well, you could do that as well," Gunnhild said. "After Birka. How long would it take to get there from Alreksstadir?"

Another pause, this one more contemplative than troubled. "Just over a week, but that's with perfect weather and a fair wind, and provided we don't stop."

"That sounds much better than two moons," Gunnhild admitted. "Fine. Then that's my second term: Take me and Oddny to Birka in the spring, as soon as it's possible to sail."

"Fine."

"Fine." She plucked the knife from its sheath at her belt and grinned when he took a full step back. "Let's swear on it."

His revulsion was palpable. "I'm not taking an oath with you. My word should be good enough. And besides, have you ever been cut across the palm? It's terribly inconvenient."

Gunnhild winced as she made a shallow slice across her left palm, bisecting the scar where she'd stabbed herself in Finnmark. "What's wrong? Scared of a little blood?"

Eirik didn't dignify that with a response. Instead he said, "Don't you usually shake with your right?"

"I already did a blood oath on that hand with Oddny and Signy."

A brief look of recognition crossed his face. "Signy being her kidnapped sister, I assume?"

"Yes. We swore ourselves to each other as children."

"I see." Eirik put the lantern down on the grass between them, took out his own knife, and cut his hand as well. He held it out, but stopped just short of hers, looking uncertain. "I have one more term."

"I'm listening."

"Will this bindrune of yours work against your own powers should you choose to inflict them upon me or any of my men?"

Of course he'd fear such a thing after what happened with his father and Snaefrid, though Gunnhild still didn't believe that story the way the Norse told it. She began, "No, but I wouldn't do that—"

"Then swear it," he said flatly.

"Fine. I swear to never influence you with my witchcraft." *Even if I did have Thorbjorg's skill, there are other ways.* "Listen—there's nothing more important to me than rescuing Signy. Don't you think that if I *could* simply cast a spell and control your mind to make you take me to her, I would've already done it?"

Eirik's lips thinned but he didn't argue.

"Now, can we get this over with?" She reached for his hand, but he pulled it away.

"To reiterate," he said, "you're not just agreeing to marry me. You're agreeing to make my enemies *your* enemies and my fate *your* fate. You're agreeing to use your power to protect me and my men, and to never sway me with your magic. In exchange, you will be *the* queen. I'll take no other wives but you and sire no other children but yours—"

He made a face, clearly feeling just as sick as she was at the thought of what creating said children would entail. This was a small comfort; at least they were still on familiar ground. He hadn't suddenly decided he was in *love* with her. That would be even more disturbing than his proposing marriage in the first place.

"—and I'll also take you and your friend Oddny to Birka come spring."

"I agree to those terms."

"As do I. Wonderful," Eirik said with deep sarcasm. "Have I missed anything?"

"I don't think so," Gunnhild said cheerfully.

"Good."

"Fine."

They shook on the oath only as long as was proper before ripping their hands apart, and Gunnhild looked down at her palm, disquieted. She felt slightly singed, like the time she'd caught the end of her braid in the hearth fire when she was in trance and had awoken to Heid throwing a bucket of water on her. But when she glanced up, the coldness in Eirik's eyes likewise doused whatever feeling his touch had stirred in her.

"There," she said evenly. "Our fates are bound now. Exactly as you wished."

Eirik flexed the fingers of his bleeding hand while he bent to pick up the lantern with the other. "It's too late in the evening for me to speak with your father. I'll do so tomorrow before supper. I'd prefer you keep this between us until then."

"Do as you will," she said, looking past him toward the boathouse, her heart sinking into the pit of her stomach. "But there's someone who deserves to hear this from me first."

15

AFTER LEAVING GUNNHILD, ODDNY was so wrapped up in her thoughts that she didn't see Halldor exiting the cookhouse as she entered, and when she threw the door open she barreled straight into him.

He let out a yelp of surprise at their collision and a small object flew from his hand, but he managed to step back and right himself. Oddny, however, caught the toe of her shoe on the door's raised threshold and fell forward, hands out to break her fall—but Halldor grabbed her arm and tugged her back to standing. She hadn't had a chance to brace for impact; it took her a moment to realize that both her feet were firmly planted on the ground.

"Oh dear," Ulfrun said mildly from where she sat by the hearth with Vigdis, who glanced up from the wool sock she was mending and raised her eyebrows. Oddny flushed and took a deep breath to calm her racing heart.

"You can let go of me now," she said through her teeth, and Halldor—seeming surprised to find his hand still around her elbow—obeyed. Then, feeling a bit abashed, Oddny added, "Thank you. I'm sorry. My mind was elsewhere."

"I was just coming to look for you." Halldor's eyes searched the packed-dirt floor. "Where did—? Oh. Thanks."

Ulfrun had gotten up and laboriously bent to pick up what he'd dropped—an apple—from where it had rolled under a table, and she handed it back to him. Halldor dusted it off on his sleeve, raised it to his open mouth, then paused and offered it to Oddny. She shook her head, and he shrugged and took a bite.

"Why were you going to look for me?" she asked.

"I wanted to know if I should expect to wake up in the middle of the night to find Gunnhild standing over me with a knife," Halldor replied through a mouthful of apple. When Oddny gave him a blank look, he swallowed and clarified, "The ritual? The one that was supposedly going to tell her whether or not I was a lying sack of dog shit?"

"Yes, what did she say, lamb?" Ulfrun asked Oddny. "Did she tell you what happened?"

"Not so much." Oddny didn't have the energy to convey to them what Gunnhild had only half explained to her, for she wouldn't be able to answer any questions they had. And what's more, she didn't want to mention Gunnhild's powers' being hindered with Halldor standing right there, for fear this information would get back to Eirik and damage Gunnhild's credibility with the hird. "But we appreciate your help. Thank you."

This seemed to satisfy Ulfrun and Vigdis. Oddny turned to leave and Halldor followed, thanking Vigdis for the apple and grabbing his lantern from a table before closing the door behind Oddny and himself.

"Gunnhild would be more subtle than that if she were going to kill you," Oddny said once they'd emerged into the chilly night air and were walking toward the longhouse. Eirik and Gunnhild were probably still arguing around the other side of it, but Oddny could neither see nor hear them.

"Right," Halldor said dryly. "She wouldn't be *standing* over me. She'd be a swallow, flying at me with a knife clutched in those little talons of hers."

"That's rather specific. I was thinking she'd just poison you."

"I'll take care not to accept any drinks from her."

"Halldor." Oddny stopped and looked at him as he finished the apple and tossed the core aside. "Listen. I believe you. And—what did you do to your hair?"

The wind had picked up and blown his loose curls over the top of his head, revealing that he'd unevenly shaved the area just around his left ear, where he sported a very faded tattoo: A hook-jawed knotwork salmon leapt from his nape to his temple.

"Oh," Oddny said, squinting at it in the lanternlight. "What does it mean?"

"Must a tattoo always mean something?"

"You missed a few spots when you shaved it."

"I couldn't exactly see what I was doing. I'd borrowed Ulfrun's bronze mirror, but it's the size of my thumb, so it didn't help much."

Oddny didn't know what made her say it, but she offered, "I could touch it up for you if you'd like once we're inside."

"Thank you, but I think I'll pass. After all, the last two times you were holding a knife in my presence, you were threatening me with it."

"Well, if I kill you now, I won't get my silver, will I?"

"True enough," he allowed after a beat. "Lead the way."

With Svein performing and the men drunker and rowdier than when Oddny left, it was easy enough for her and Halldor to slip inside, cross the hall, and enter the antechamber without much notice. Solveig was asleep; Oddny spared her a passing glance as she led Halldor to the bunk room, where someone had left a lit soapstone lamp atop one of the chests.

Before Oddny could draw her knife, Halldor reached into his pouch and pulled out a smaller one in a scuffed leather sheath with tarnished, stamped brass fittings, attached to a broken chain. It was the kind of tool a lady of the house could hang from her brooches if she were lucky enough to own a pair. She wondered if it had belonged to a family member—or maybe even a lover.

"I just sharpened it," he said. "Be careful."

"All right." Oddny gestured to Gunnhild's old chest. "Sit."

He did, and she got to work. The knife *was* very sharp—the sheath had seen better days, but the blade itself was pristine—and they both winced at the scratching sound it made as she drew it across his scalp. She had to pause every time he fidgeted.

"Whose knife was this?" she said after a time.

He hesitated for a moment before replying, "My grandmother's. She gave it to me when I was small."

"She must've been very dear to you if you still carry it."

"She was," Halldor said shortly.

Oddny worked a few moments longer. "What was her name?"

His shoulders tensed. "Are you almost done?"

Oddny pursed her lips and decided not to press the subject despite her curiosity. She knew what it was like to lose family, and that he didn't wish to speak of his own made her think that he carried as deep a pain as her own. With a last scrape of the knife, she finished evening out the shave along his hairline, then wiped the blade on her sleeve, sheathed it, and handed it back to him. He took it wordlessly and stuffed it back into his pouch as he stood.

"I didn't mean to offend you," she said as he made to go.

Halldor stopped just before the curtain that divided the bunk room from the rest of the antechamber, but he didn't turn around. "I'm not offended. Just confused as to why you wanted to know."

"I was only curious. I'm sorry. I—"

"Svanhild," he said quietly. "Her name was Svanhild. My grandmother."

Swan-battle. "That's a strong name."

He turned so that she saw him in profile, the side with the tattoo facing her. "What was your mother's?"

Oddny clasped her hands together to still their shaking.

"Yrsa," she whispered.

"*She-bear.* A strong name as well." Halldor turned once more to leave. "Good night, Oddny."

"Good night, Halldor," she replied, sinking down to sit on Gunnhild's chest, and it was long after he'd gone that she realized her hands were still trembling. A strange feeling had risen in her tonight, a feeling both wildly unexpected and wholly undesired, and she vowed then and there to stamp it back down. Until she rescued Signy, she could not afford to become distracted—least of all by one of the men who'd been responsible for her sister's plight.

16

GUNNHILD'S LAST DAY IN Halogaland passed in a blur. She spent most of it sitting on the edge of the cliff on the north side of the island, working on her bindrune and trying to put the previous night from her mind.

Thorolf hadn't been able to look her in the eye after she told him of her conversation with Eirik and the decision she'd made, and he'd fled back to the hall without a word. She hoped he'd gotten drunk with the rest of the men to dull his pain; part of her wished she'd done the same to assuage her guilt, but instead she'd gone straight to bed and hadn't even told Oddny what happened.

By the time the sun was low in the sky, she was exhausted, but the spell was complete: She'd found the perfect combination of runes. First, she took a needle and some charcoal dust and water, and hand poked it into her own arm just above the elbow, her deep concentration numbing her to the pain as she sang the runes. It was hardly the work of a professional tattooist, but the moment she'd made her last poke and stopped singing, a thrum ran through her and she smiled—hopefully that meant it would work. Her mind and her dreams were safe.

Afterward, she carved her creation deliberately and with care onto a circular cutting from the antler of a deer, pouring as much intent as she could with each stroke, then chanting the runes at least thirty times, once for each man in the hird. When she was satisfied, she put the bone in her pouch and stood, swaying on her feet, and made her way back across the island to her father's hall. She sat on the bench next to Oddny and studiously avoided looking at Thorolf, who sat with Svein. The skald glared openly at her; she ignored him.

"Are you all right?" Oddny asked her during supper when she slumped in her seat and nearly dropped her stew bowl.

"I think I need to lie down," Gunnhild muttered, but before she could, Eirik stood and turned to her father, and her stomach dropped.

"Ozur," he said. Even amid the clamor of the feast, she could hear the stiffness in his voice. "I've a matter to take up with you."

Thorolf stood wordlessly and left. Svein followed after one last glance at Gunnhild. Anyone who hadn't known of her involvement with Thorolf would have thought little of this, but Gunnhild knew better—and by the look on Eirik's face, and the fact that he did not so much as turn to acknowledge their departure, he did, too. Next to where they'd been sitting, Arinbjorn smiled tightly. Eirik looked at him as if for reassurance, and his foster brother gave him the tiniest nod of encouragement.

Eirik turned back to the hersir. "I wish to marry your daughter."

It was almost embarrassing, Gunnhild thought, how Ozur fell all over himself to accept without even asking her. She clenched her bandaged hand, a twin to Eirik's own, into a fist in her lap as the two men negotiated the dowry and bride-price.

It was no less than a small fortune. And it was hers.

"Gunnhild," Oddny hissed from the bench beside her, "did you *know* about this?"

"You think Eirik would've done it without asking me first?" Gunnhild said out of the corner of her mouth. "Even he's smarter than that."

"So this is what last night was about. Why didn't you tell me?"

"Because you would have talked me out of it," Gunnhild admitted. "And because you were sleeping this morning when I left to work on my bindrune."

Before Oddny could reply, Ozur stood and announced, quieting the chatter in the hall, "A toast! To the betrothal of my daughter and King Eirik!"

He had the servants take down the ceremonial drinking horn—a massive thing as long as Gunnhild's arm, carved and painted with elaborate scenes and whorls, its rim and tip gilded—from where it was displayed on the lintel with the statutes of Odin, Thor, and Frey, and told them to fill it with mead from his stores. This got everyone's attention: Mead was sacred to the gods, and due to the sheer amount of honey that went into its brewing, it was passed around only on special occasions. Eirik's hird and Ozur's men roared their approval as the hersir's orders were carried out.

"To our marriage." Eirik took the first swig of mead from the horn before passing it to Gunnhild, and for a moment both their bandaged hands remained on it, not touching, before he let it go. She hoped that any onlookers took the grim looks on their faces for nervousness instead of what it really was.

"To our marriage." She forced a smile, took a sip, and passed it on to Oddny. The sweet mead slid down her throat like sludge and left a lingering dryness in her mouth, which she washed down with ale.

"I don't like this" was Oddny's quiet toast before drinking and passing the horn on to Arinbjorn.

"Then I suppose you can stay here instead of coming with us to Hordaland and then, in the spring, Birka," said Gunnhild, more brusquely than she intended.

Oddny's mouth opened and closed a few times before she choked out, "I—you—*what*?"

"It was part of our marriage agreement. We leave tomorrow morning to overwinter at King Harald's estate at Alreksstadir. We took a blood oath, and Eirik has sworn to take us to Birka as soon as—"

She stopped talking when Oddny threw her arms around her and squeezed tightly.

"Oh, Gunna, thank you," she whispered.

"All I do, I do for Signy," Gunnhild whispered back. "And for vengeance."

"Take care that the latter doesn't become more important than the former," said Arinbjorn from Oddny's other side.

A short time later, when the horn had been passed several times and the drink flowed freely, Ulfrun took Gunnhild aside. "Your mother is awake. She wishes to see you." The old woman wrung her hands. "But don't feel that you must. I can make an excuse for you. I could tell her that—"

"I'll see her." Gunnhild rose and put her cup down on the bench with a clumsy hand. She swayed and Oddny grabbed her arm.

"You don't have to," Oddny said.

"Yes, I do," Gunnhild replied without looking at her.

"Don't do this to yourself. You've come so far."

"I need to confront her."

"It won't satisfy you. She's weak."

"This may be my last chance."

Oddny sighed, gave her a squeeze, and let go. "As you wish."

Gunnhild's legs felt heavy as she followed Ulfrun to the antechamber. Despite sleeping in the adjacent bunk room for the past two nights, Gunnhild had been diligently avoiding looking in the direction of the master bed during her comings and goings. As such, she had not looked upon her mother's face in over a decade.

But now there was no avoiding it. She stepped into the room and there was Solveig, propped up with a pillow behind her head, staring at Gunnhild as though she were an apparition.

Then Ulfrun closed the door behind her with a snap, and mother and daughter were alone.

Gunnhild strode forward woodenly—back straight, hands clasped to still their shaking—and lowered herself onto the stool next to the bed. As she took in her mother's skeletal face and withered limbs, she realized Oddny was right: It gave her no satisfaction to see Solveig this way. She wished she were dealing with the monster she remembered instead of this sick and dying woman.

But the monster was still in there somewhere, and she knew it.

"Little Gunna," Solveig wheezed, eyes watering, reaching for her. "My darling."

"You've never called me either of those things before," Gunnhild said. "Not a nickname. Not a term of endearment. Not even once."

Solveig's lower lip trembled. "Of course I did. You're my daughter."

Ah. There she is. "Name one time."

In her annoyance, Solveig's voice gained strength. "You've been gone how many years, and you expect me to remember everything I ever said to you? Ridiculous."

"Curious, isn't it, the things that stay with us, and the things we choose to forget?" Gunnhild fought to keep her tone level. She would not lose her temper. Not now. She had to stay in control.

Solveig's hand dropped. "I don't know what you're talking about."

"Oh, don't you? Do you remember the last words you spoke to me, Mother?" Gunnhild's voice was deadly quiet. "Did you ever wonder *why* I ran away?"

Solveig sniffed. "You were a difficult child."

Gunnhild remembered Heid's hand on her shoulder. *"You are not a bad child. You are not a burden. I'm sorry that you've been made to feel that way."*

"Was I?" she asked. "Or were you a difficult parent?"

"I should have expected this from you. Such ingratitude." Solveig waved a hand, her thin voice quavering with anger. "You run away. Worry us sick. Make us believe you're dead. And then you say it was *our* fault that you ran off with that old witch and became—what, a witch, too? Is that what I'm to believe?"

It was clear to Gunnhild now that no good would come of this conversation; it was time to end it before she lost her composure. She could relay each memory to her mother one by one in extensive detail, and the woman would tell her she was wrong—that she was only a child; she was misremembering.

If not for Heid, Gunnhild might have even started to agree.

You may have birthed me, Solveig, but you are not my mother.

"Yes. And King Harald's successor has asked me to marry him," she said. "King Eirik. He and Father have already shaken on it."

Solveig's gaze sharpened. "Is that so?"

"It is. Eirik has many powerful enemies, some of whom wield magic. He requires the assistance of an equally powerful witch to fight them off.

And that, you see, is me." Gunnhild's voice rose with pride. "I'm to be queen, Mother. I'm to become the most powerful woman in Norway. And it's all in spite of you."

After a long moment, Solveig gave a deep, rasping chuckle, and Gunnhild's hackles rose.

"Oh, my dear girl," her mother drawled, "you're confused. If that's the case, it's *because* of me that you're in the position you're in. If you hadn't been so desperate to escape me, if I hadn't driven you into the arms of that seeress, where would you be now?"

Gunnhild's chest felt so tight she could barely breathe.

"So which is it, Mother?" she said. "Did you mistreat me or not?"

"But now you'll be queen," said Solveig, ignoring the questions. She was smug, but tiring; her head sank deeper into the pillow behind it. "You should be thanking me. It's due to my so-called mistreatment that you've become what you are today. It made you stronger."

Gunnhild could not believe her ears. She leaned over her mother and looked her dead in the eyes. She could feel the tears forming, but she did not blink, did not let them fall.

This woman would never see her cry. Not ever again.

"I would rather have been loved," Gunnhild said, her voice breaking on the last word.

Solveig stared at her, wide-eyed, as if struck. Before she could react, Gunnhild reached under her pillow and slid out the rune stick she'd seen Yrsa create when she'd been spying as a swallow in the rafters.

The runes were correct. Yrsa had done her job well. But Solveig was too sick, and Yrsa was no witch. Whatever power she'd imbued into the carvings had run its course: A shallow crack had appeared down the length of the stick as proof. There was nothing more a healer on her own could do for Solveig. But Gunnhild could easily add her own power to the spell. Flip the stick over, carve some runes of her own. It would take only a moment. It could even save the woman's life.

Or.

"These are well carved." Gunnhild slid the rune stick back under her mother's pillow and stood. "It's a pity that their magic is spent."

"Forgive me," Solveig said, reaching for her again, her eyes half-lidded as fatigue claimed her once more. "Gunnhild. My daughter. Forgive me."

Gunnhild was already halfway across the room by then.

"Goodbye, Mother."

She did not look back.

SOLVEIG WAS DEAD BY morning. Gunnhild awoke to her father's wailing, soon joined by that of Solveig's loyal serving women as they stumbled from the bunk room and into their lady's chamber, crowding the bed. Oddny and Gunnhild took this opportunity to dress, pack their things, and slip away without being noticed. Oddny said nothing, offering the same silent support as she had when they were children, and Gunnhild loved her for it.

What she loved less was that Oddny had to support her as she walked. She was paying the price of overexerting herself the day before, and would be for some days to come. But as they left the hall and approached Eirik and his men, Gunnhild bade Oddny move away; she couldn't appear weak in front of them.

"The ship is ready to sail. We leave after breakfast," Eirik said. He and the hird were eating outside, likely to escape the melancholy that Solveig's death had cast over the household.

"Good," said Gunnhild. "Excellent." She reached into her pouch and pulled out the antler coin along with a small clay jar. "The bindrune, as promised. And a bit of salve for your palm. When I took the oath with Oddny and Signy, my cut began to fester before Heid healed it. I'm certain my friends' mother did the same for them."

"I told you palm wounds were inconvenient." He took the salve but not the bit of antler. "Hold on to that for now. You can give it to Runfrid yourself when we arrive, now that you're coming with us."

She nodded and tucked it away, and when she looked back up, he was regarding her with a look she found impossible to decipher.

"Do you wish to stay to see her buried?" he asked.

No preamble, no softness, no condolences. She couldn't tell him how much she appreciated that.

"No," she said. "I don't. I wish to go south today as planned."

"As you say," said the king, turning to his men. "Meet at the ship when you're finished eating." He started toward the dock, and Gunnhild found herself stumbling after him.

"Eirik," she said.

He turned back to her.

"Thank you," she said, straightening. "For not saying you're sorry for my loss. For not saying 'but she's your mother.' For not—for not making me feel like a monster. If you would continue to treat with me as though nothing has changed, I'd be glad of it."

He looked unsure for a moment. "I—you're welcome. Of course." And as she turned to go, he added, "Do you know what they intend to bury her in?"

Gunnhild stopped. "Her best clothes, I would imagine. Why?"

"I'd advise you to go through what's left." He regarded her shabby, patched dress. "Unless, of course, you intend to meet my father in *that*."

Her mouth hung open.

"What?" he asked. "It's not like she's using them—"

"You insensitive— *My mother just died.*"

He blinked. "Yes, and you told me to act like nothing has changed, so which is it? Do you want me to be sensitive or not?"

Gunnhild pressed the heels of her palms into her eyes and took a breath. How could she even begin to untangle the complicated feelings she was having about her mother's death, let alone explain them to someone else? Luckily, she didn't have to: When she slid her hands down her face and let them drop to her sides, she saw that Eirik had quietly moved on and Oddny had come forward to stand beside her.

"Gunna," Oddny said. "Are you ready?"

"Yes," Gunnhild replied, taking her hand and squeezing it. "Come. Let's go."

17

GUNNHILD KNEW THAT ODDNY had never traveled on such a large ship before, but she could tell that the novelty of it had worn off for her friend as quickly as it had for her when she'd first come on board. They were cold and miserable as they sat huddled under their sea-cloaks against the biting wind and sea spray.

But the weather was good and the sailing was easy, the coast always within sight. When the sun was low on the horizon, a few of the men expressed surprise that they weren't going to seek hospitality with a farmer or nearby jarl, but all Eirik said was, "I'm tired of being around people."

"But what if there's another storm?" one of the men asked uneasily, looking up at the clear sky as if certain the weather would change at any moment.

"We have a witch with us now," Eirik said. "She'll handle it. I wish to enjoy some peace while I can."

This was met with grumbling, but no one argued.

"You're not going to tell him?" Oddny mumbled to Gunnhild. "That you can't—"

"If it comes to it, you can sing for me," she replied in kind.

"But the witches! It could be dangerous for you—"

"That's the price for saving Signy. I'll gladly risk it."

Oddny had nothing to say to that.

The men took out a large tent canvas from below the deck and ran the ropes necessary to set it up, after which a sack of stockfish was passed around for supper. One of the ship's cats, the tortoiseshell, came up to Gunnhild and complained until Gunnhild gave her a scrap of food. The two creatures had taken a liking to her, and she could tell it irritated Eirik, so she made sure to give the cats extra attention.

"The black one is Hnoss and this one is Gersemi," Arinbjorn said as he came up and gave the tortoiseshell a scratch behind the ears.

After Freyja's daughters, Gunnhild thought with a smile, though she was a bit perplexed; no one in the hird seemed particularly devoted to the goddess. "Who named them?"

"Eirik. They're his, after all," Arinbjorn replied. "This is the original Hnoss, but we're on—what—the third or fourth Gersemi? Their mother keeps having kittens in the stables at Alreksstadir, and it seems there's a new one that looks exactly like the last Gersemi every time we lose her. Hnoss is smart, which is how she stays alive. Gersemi, not so much."

"She's the fifth Gersemi," Eirik said from a bit farther down the ship. Hnoss perched on his shoulder, making valiant attempts to steal a piece of his stockfish.

"Why not come up with new names?" Gunnhild asked.

Eirik looked at her as if this were the most preposterous suggestion he'd ever heard. "What else am I supposed to call a companion to Hnoss? They go together. Like Ask and Embla, Sol and Mani, Hugin and Munin..."

"How unoriginal." Gunnhild rolled her eyes. "Next you'll tell me your axes are named Geri and Freki after Odin's wolves."

The tips of Eirik's ears went pink and he stared at her for so long and with such furious irritation that she thought the vein at his temple was going to burst.

"I can name my things whatever I want," he barked, several beats too late.

Gunnhild made a face. "That's just as well, but it took you *that* long to come up with such a dismal retort?"

Eirik turned on his heel and stalked to the other side of the ship without another word. Arinbjorn's shoulders shook with silent laughter as he followed.

"I didn't know his axes had names," Oddny said from beside her, and when Gunnhild nudged her shoulder they both burst into giggles.

At night, Oddny and Gunnhild slept in the tent on bedrolls placed atop the oars to keep them dry. The men took turns sleeping around them, those on watch using the stars to keep their bearings when it was too dark to make out the shape of the coast in the distance.

Halldor proved to be a better sailor than the other five prospective hirdsmen who had accompanied the hird from Ozur's farm. He worked without complaint, always volunteered for first watch, and seemed to sleep just about as little as Eirik did. Often when Gunnhild got up to relieve herself in the night, she'd spot Halldor and Eirik keeping watch in what seemed like companionable silence.

"He's good," Gunnhild heard Arinbjorn say to Eirik over their breakfast of stockfish on the second morning. "Experienced—he told me he's been raiding for nine summers. The rest of them can sail, but he's a *sailor*. *And* he can fight. You'd better give him an arm ring before he decides to swear himself to someone else, brother."

Eirik cast a look to where Halldor sat talking quietly with Svein and the steersman, but he said nothing except, "Then all he has left to prove is his loyalty." A pause. "And his footwork can use some improvement."

"Looks like things are going well for Halldor," Gunnhild said to Oddny after she'd relayed what she'd heard. "He'll have paid off his debt to you in no time. And now that I'm here, you can keep it—we'll have Signy back before he's managed to earn that twelve marks anyway."

Oddny took her hand and squeezed, and the look of hope on her face was almost too much for Gunnhild to bear. She leaned her shoulder against Oddny's and let out a long sigh, confident that the worst was behind them.

The last day of their trip dawned bright and clear, and the mood was cheerful: They were to reach Alreksstadir well before nightfall, maybe even by suppertime. The men lounged on their ship boxes, playing dice games and talking among themselves while the cats moved from person to person to pilfer scraps of food, eventually settling down near where Eirik and Arinbjorn sat near the bow, Eirik staring out over the water and Arinbjorn patching a hole in the side of his shoe with an awl and sinew. Nearby, Svein and Thorolf played tafl, neither of them speaking with the king or his foster brother. Halldor sat with them, observing the game as he sharpened his seax with a whetstone.

But Svein was facing the women, and Gunnhild saw him exchange troubled looks with Arinbjorn every now and then, which the other man returned. She appreciated that the skald was trying to keep Thorolf distracted, but she couldn't help but wonder how things stood between Thorolf and Eirik. Eirik had known they'd shared a bed, but had he known that Thorolf had proposed to Gunnhild first?

In hushed tones she told Oddny of the situation, and all Oddny had to say was, "I think Eirik did know. I overheard him and Arinbjorn talking about it. Eirik seemed remorseful because he knew Thorolf would be upset, but they decided it was for the greater good."

That threw Gunnhild for a moment, but she supposed it made sense— for all his faults, Eirik was protective of his hird. But it frustrated her that she couldn't quite parse him, this man she'd at first taken for nothing more than a violent brute. When the hird had stopped with the jarl, Gunnhild had witnessed their host bending over backward to please Eirik, and watched the same thing happen again at her father's. Eirik had seemed to expect and even appreciate the attention. But when they departed each time, he seemed to cave in on himself, no longer the self-important, posturing king, but once more the brooding, taciturn creature she'd first met on the beach in Finnmark.

Perhaps he was just tired from the long summer, or the expectations of his status affected him more than he was letting on. Gunnhild felt no pity for him either way.

It was midday when something in the air shifted, and suddenly the ship tilted violently to one side, causing the men to fall off their boxes. Gunnhild, who'd been looking out over the horizon, careened into

Oddny, knocking her over and sending them both sprawling. As the sailors picked themselves up, wind came at them from all directions as the sky darkened at a supernatural speed. The waves began to churn, spraying water over the side of the deck, threatening to flood the ship.

"Not again," Svein moaned. Several of the other men echoed this response.

Ice flooded Gunnhild's veins. A few moments ago there hadn't been a single cloud in the sky, the sun high and bright, but now—

"Clear the deck!" Eirik shouted over the roaring wind. "Secure the sail!" As Gunnhild watched, he scooped up Hnoss and Gersemi, dumped both yowling felines into a ship box, and slid it to the closest man to stow beneath the deck.

The hird knew exactly who was doing what without Eirik delegating further. The tent came down, boards came up, and boxes and oars went below. Some men checked the rigging while others tied up the sail.

"And you two," Eirik bellowed at the women as he grabbed a stack of buckets and tossed one to Arinbjorn and the other to Thorolf, "stay down, and stay to the center—we have to stabilize the ship!"

Gunnhild and Oddny scurried to obey, splaying themselves flat on their bellies on the wet boards, crushing their bags beneath them. Gunnhild never risked stowing her haversack belowdecks, as it contained her staff and henbane and all the tools of her trade, and at sea it seemed wise to keep it on her person in case a crisis arose; Oddny, likewise, always had her bag of healing supplies slung around her shoulders.

One by one the men completed their tasks and hit the deck as well.

"We just have to ride it out!" Svein said as he threw himself down beside Oddny and Gunnhild.

"It came out of nowhere," Gunnhild said, raising her head, searching the dark clouds. "The storm—"

"It's been happening all summer," Svein said grimly.

The ship rocked and a wave of freezing water hit them, stealing the breath from Gunnhild's lungs as she and Oddny clung to each other for dear life. She lifted her head again to see Eirik, Arinbjorn, and Thorolf bailing water, and watched as Thorolf lost his footing and almost went overboard when the ship rocked the other way, but Eirik grabbed him by the collar and flung him back onto the deck.

"Get down!" Gunnhild shrieked at them. "What are you doing?!"

"Trying not to drown!" Arinbjorn yelled as he flung a bucketful of water over the side of the ship, at the same time Eirik said, "You don't give the orders!"

But the three men couldn't bail fast enough, and more water flooded the deck as the ship cut through the choppy waves. Several shields came loose from where they'd been secured on the gunnel. She didn't know how much more the ship could take.

"*. . . been happening all summer . . .*"

Gunnhild lifted her head and searched the darkened sky until she found it: the eagle. Soaring in a circle overhead, each wing tip seeming to summon black clouds from nowhere.

Katla.

Gunnhild clamped a hand down on Oddny's arm and pointed up.

"That's the witch who killed Heid!" Gunnhild yelled. "Katla—she works for King Halfdan! She made the fog in your fjord!"

Oddny's eyes widened. "She's causing the storm? What do we do?"

Gunnhild raised herself to all fours and dug frantically in her witching bag. Oddny grabbed her elbow and hooked a leg around her knee to keep her from sliding off the deck, Svein bracing her from the other side. Gunnhild pulled out her staff and a small leather canteen waterproofed with beeswax—she'd filled the canteen with water and stuffed it with henbane before the ship had set sail. Once she had the objects in her hands, she flipped over onto her side.

"What are you doing?" Halldor shouted. He'd appeared on Oddny's other side and looked just as confused as Svein did.

"Saving our lives!" Gunnhild popped the waxed linen stopper from the leather canteen and turned to Oddny. "I need you to sing for me!"

Oddny's eyes went, if possible, even wider. "If Vigdis, Ulfrun, and I weren't strong enough to defend against them with the warding songs, how could you possibly think I could protect you on my own?"

Gunnhild grimaced. She hadn't tried to send out her mind as a bird since Heid's death, fearful that the witches were stalking her steps in the waking world just as they seemed to be doing in the void. For all she knew, the moment she left her body, Thorbjorg's fox would appear out of nowhere and have itself a swallow for supper.

But she had to try.

"If things go badly, pull me back," Gunnhild said.

"Pull you back?" Oddny echoed, incredulous.

"You can see the threads." Gunnhild turned and grabbed her shoulder as they lay there on their sides in the cold water of the deck. "Oddny—you can still see the threads, can't you?"

Oddny was panicking, tears mixing with the salt water soaking her face and hair as another wave crashed over the side of the ship. "Yes—but—"

"If you see any other animals—like a fox—pull me back. Do you understand?" Gunnhild said. "There are worse things than drowning. If they manage to sever my thread, I die, and I die slowly. Oddny, do you understand me?"

Oddny nodded feverishly.

Gunnhild tried to keep a clear head, though she thought she might vomit. Several of the men, seasoned sailors though they were, had become sick as they clung to the deck for dear life. The wind had not abated. Another wave knocked Arinbjorn's feet from under him, but he clung to a rope, his bailing bucket washed out to sea; the same wave almost wrested Gunnhild from Oddny's grasp, but Svein's arm clamped down hard around Gunnhild's waist and held her tightly as the ship continued to rock.

"Whatever you're going to do," Svein shouted, "do it fast!"

Halldor grabbed on to Oddny in the same way, bracing her. Over her friend's shoulder, Gunnhild could see that the man's face was set in determination.

"We'll keep you both safe as long as we can," said Halldor. "Go!"

Gunnhild downed the cold tea, shoved the canteen into her bag, and rolled onto her back with her staff in hand. The tea tasted worse than usual but was no less effective. The last thing she felt was Svein and Oddny hanging on to her before Oddny began to sing, her mouth next to Gunnhild's ear, her high, soft voice rising above the whipping of the wind, grounding Gunnhild, making her feel as though she were safe and warm and surrounded by light and not trapped on a ship during a bizarre storm.

And the moment Gunnhild started to mime spinning and chant the spell to stop the storm, the swallow soared from her chest and up into the maelstrom, and she heard sounds of disbelief from Svein and Halldor and the others who'd been watching. Oddny's breath hitched for just a moment, but her song didn't falter, nor did Gunnhild's body cease its whispered incantations.

Gunnhild beat her wings against the wind—so strong that it would have sent an ordinary bird flailing into the water—and anger burned in her as she rose. But there was relief there, too, relief that she was still able to travel this way. That even if no spirits came to her in the dark place, she still had this skill. And she was going to make the most of it.

She caught one of the winds and spread her wings, let it carry her up above and behind the eagle. Katla was so focused on her work that she didn't notice the much smaller bird until Gunnhild dove down and slammed into her, knocking her off balance.

The eagle squawked and listed to the side. The unexpected blow had been enough to disrupt Katla's spell, for wherever Katla's body was, it was chanting, the same as Gunnhild's. The darkness in the sky faded slightly, the waves beneath them calming just enough that the ship stopped taking on water.

The swallow and the eagle faced each other, beating their wings in the air, hovering high above the ship on either side.

Gunnhild noticed something interesting then: The eagle seemed to be flagging. Katla must be exhausted from a summer of harrying the hird. Leaving one's body for extended periods of time took its toll, and when Katla came to bother them, her bird would have to fly from wherever her body was. And if the other witch had stretched herself too thin, her fatigue would be to Gunnhild's advantage.

I hope someone is singing for you, wherever you are, Gunnhild snarled. *Because you're going to need all the protection you can get.*

I could say the same for you, came Katla's gravelly voice in response. *You don't have the old woman here to watch your back anymore.*

Thanks to you, Gunnhild said, and dove for her again.

They were a tangle of feathers and wings, snapping beaks, flashing claws—and then Gunnhild, the smaller and more agile of the two, shoved her tiny foot at the eagle's eye and felt something squish beneath her talons as she curled them.

The wind instantly died down, the waves sank back into the sea and the water went still, and the dark clouds began to clear. Shouts of surprise greeted her ears from the ship.

But Katla's agonized cry echoed in Gunnhild's head as the eagle veered backward, flailing in anguish as though wanting to touch the ruin of her eye but finding herself without hands to do it.

That was for Heid, Gunnhild said viciously. The eagle ignored her, still screeching in pain. She imagined Katla, wherever she was, bleeding from a similar wound. If she did have women singing for her wherever her body was, Gunnhild could not imagine what it must look like to them.

Before Gunnhild could land another blow, the eagle tucked its wings to it sides and dropped like a stone. Blood and fluid streamed from its eye as its plummeted toward the surface of the water.

You'll pay for this, Katla said, and the pain in her voice made the threat all the more chilling as the eagle disappeared into the sea.

Gunnhild felt a yank, then another, then another; she was being tugged down. She turned and saw that her body lay on the deck of the ship where she'd left it, and the men were on their feet, looking up at her.

And Oddny—Oddny was no longer singing. She was standing, pulling on Gunnhild's thread as frantically as a starving person hauling up a fishing line, Halldor holding her around the waist to keep her steady as her feet slid on the slippery deck.

"There's something in the water!" Oddny cried.

Gunnhild felt a trill of fear as she remembered. The raid—the third witch, in the water, the one she hadn't known, hadn't seen—

Katla hadn't been alone after all.

She dove back for her body.

And at the exact moment her swallow form buried itself in her chest and she released her staff, a wave slammed into the side of the ship and sent her hurtling over the gunnel and into the dark water.

Her eyes snapped open as the cold hit her, and she struggled for a moment before regaining her bearings: She was underwater and sinking fast, her heavy wool kaftan and sea-cloak weighing her down. Her fingers and toes had already been going numb on deck, but now, in the frigid water, she had no feeling in them at all.

But as her stiff, clumsy fingers struggled to unfasten the penannular brooch holding her sea-cloak in place, something bit down hard on her ankle with razor-sharp teeth and *pulled*.

Gunnhild screamed, the sound coming out of her mouth as a torrent of bubbles. Whatever had bitten her was hauling her downward and the pain was excruciating, and when she tried to twist her leg and free herself, the creature only dug its teeth in deeper. She screamed again and tried to jerk her foot away. She felt something tear.

A splash far above her, but she didn't look up. Instead she looked down and saw, through the deepening gloom, a pair of human eyes staring up at her from the face of the seal that was attempting to drag her down to her watery grave. Nine more pairs of huge, reflective eyes lurked in the darkness far below: Ran's daughters waited to escort her to their mother's hall.

Her vision darkened at the edges. Even the pain of the seal's bite had started to dim.

Just as everything went black, she felt movement in the water beside her—swift, like a kick or a punch—and heard a wet, bubbling, animal cry of pain from below, and those vicious little teeth released her ankle, and someone was hauling her up.

She hit a hard surface and threw up a stream of salty water onto the deck of the ship.

Oddny's arms were around her in an instant. "Gunna, oh, Gunna, oh gods—can we get them something dry?"

Vaguely Gunnhild heard Arinbjorn give orders. But why him? Where was Eirik? Everything was blurry. She guzzled down a few gasps of air before sitting up. The bite mark on her ankle was bleeding and Oddny was already fussing over it, digging around in her own sodden haversack for some poultice and a bandage.

Teeth chattering, Gunnhild wiped the water from her eyes and blinked a few times before her vision came into focus.

Beside her was Eirik, soaked and shivering as he clambered to his feet. And when he looked down at her, his usual piercing gaze was clouded with weariness and concern.

"Are you all right?" he asked.

Gunnhild's jaw dropped. *He was the one who—who—?*

No. This can't be. I can't owe him.

She dragged herself to a standing position despite Oddny's outrage, and she stumbled on her mangled ankle as pain shot up her leg. She ignored it and demanded, "Why did you do that?"

Eirik stared at her as though she were speaking a different language. "Because you were drowning?"

"I didn't ask for your help. I had things well in hand."

His eyes hardened to ice. "I think what you meant to say was 'Thank you, Eirik, for saving my life.'"

"I could have handled it myself."

"I doubt that. You were practically dead when I kicked that seal in the face."

"I was not! I was saving my strength for one last attempt to free myself—"

He drew back in mock offense. "Well, then, forgive me for not waiting until your last gasp to intervene—"

"You are *not* forgiven! I don't need your help—"

"I still haven't heard a 'thank you'—"

"Stop. For the love of all the gods, *stop*," Arinbjorn said as he forced himself between them, hands up. "Gunnhild. Thank you. You saved all our lives. Eirik. Thank you for saving Gunnhild's life. You're even, and we can all go on to fight another day."

"Is that what you're so worried about?" Eirik peered at her around Arinbjorn. "Keeping score?"

Gunnhild sniffed and looked away as he stepped close to her.

"I'm going to ask you, in earnest, to get rid of that mind-set by the time we're married," he said, with an intensity in his voice that made her less keen to meet his eyes. "Or we'll both be miserable for the rest of our lives."

"Or as long as our marriage lasts," Gunnhild said under her breath. Her anger had fizzled out and now all she felt was cold and wet and miserable. Her ankle burned. Oddny had given up trying to tend it and stood beside her, waiting, exasperated.

Eirik hesitated for a long moment before storming away toward the prow of the ship. "Where are my cats?"

Someone lifted a board and Eirik dragged out the box where he'd thrown them, and as soon as the lid was opened both felines leapt out, making their anger known loudly. The wind started to pick up again and Eirik ordered the sail let down, and before long the ship was headed once again toward Hordaland.

Thorolf appeared at Oddny's elbow with a stack of dry pelts, blankets, and cloaks that had been sealed up in a tent canvas. He didn't look at Gunnhild as he handed them over. Oddny thanked him and he went to give the rest of the pile to Eirik.

Gunnhild's heart hurt. *He'll never speak to me again, will he?*

Oddny held up a blanket for her to change behind, and Gunnhild peeled off her wet clothes and wrapped herself in a cloak and several furs. Out of the corner of her eye, she saw that Eirik was doing the same at the other end of the ship, with far less concern for who saw him.

She pointedly averted her eyes and sank down heavily onto the box that had been hauled up for her to sit on. Something shiny came into her line of sight; Oddny was laying her staff across her lap. Gunnhild blinked back tears. She hadn't even realized that it was missing.

"Svein grabbed this and your bag before they went overboard. It got caught on a shield," Oddny said. "I tried to catch you, too, but Halldor held me back."

"That was probably for the best," Gunnhild said.

Oddny crouched at her feet and began tending to her ankle.

"Did Eirik say that he . . . kicked a seal in the face?" Oddny asked once she'd applied the poultice and had started to wrap the wound in a damp linen bandage. "I just saw this—shape—in the water, looking up at you, and that's when I started pulling your thread—"

The seal.

Gunnhild's head snapped up and she gripped her staff as she scanned the waves. She half expected to see the creature's head bobbing there in the water, fixing her with those horrible eyes, but nothing broke the surface. She sagged, having expended her very last bit of energy anticipating yet another attack. She was so tired, so cold.

"The third witch," she murmured.

"Gunnhild?" Oddny's thin, dark eyebrows drew together in worry. "What are you talking about?"

"There were three of them. The day of the raid. Thorbjorg, the fox. Katla, the eagle. And a third in the water—one that I never saw."

Oddny tied off the bandage and sat back on her haunches. "Well, I suppose now you know what form this third witch takes. But who are they?"

Who, indeed? Gunnhild looked out over the water once more, tightening her hands around her staff, the events of the day hitting her all at once—making it difficult to breathe, making her hands shake.

Eirik *had* saved her, though she'd never admit it to him. She'd never come so close to death before. It took everything in her to tamp down the fear creeping up her spine like ice. Thorbjorg and Katla invoked only anger in her, not fear—but their companion had nearly succeeded in taking her life. Until now, she'd been unwilling to admit that she was outmatched.

That she could lose.

And she hated it.

PART III

18

ALREKSSTADIR LAY AT THE innermost point of a fjord and extended back into the valley, beyond Oddny's sight. Lush trees clung to the cliffs that rose on either side of the estate, leaves painted in the vibrant oranges and yellows and reds of autumn. From a distance, the landscape seemed to cradle the massive hall and clusters of outbuildings like cupped hands.

The sight stole Oddny's breath away; this place was so big yet so familiar. Smoke wafted from the holes in the roofs of the buildings. The chatter of people going about their day soon reached her ears, along with the sounds of dogs and livestock and children running and playing. It made her chest constrict as she longed for a home that no longer existed.

As the ship docked, a group of servants—at least Oddny suspected they were servants, since they were too well-dressed to be thralls—arrived to unload it once the hird disembarked. A few smaller ships were moored to the left of Eirik's, and along the shore, Oddny could see that several other vessels had been hauled up on land, likely to be moved to boat sheds for maintenance and repairs over the winter.

The mood had lightened among the men as they'd gotten closer to the estate. Even Eirik had seemed to be in better spirits, though that wasn't saying much. Gunnhild, on the other hand, had not said a word since Oddny had bound her ankle, and her eyes had taken on a vacant cast.

"It's all right to be afraid, you know," Oddny said softly as they followed the trail of men up the gentle slope from the docks to the main hall. "What happened today—"

"I'm not afraid," Gunnhild said without looking at her.

Before Oddny could reply, they were inside the longhouse, and her jaw dropped. It was impressive enough from the outside, but inside, it proved to be at least four times bigger than Ozur's hall. It had three hearths running down the middle and a row of posts along either side to support the high ceiling; the posts, each fixed with a hanging brazier, were decorated with stamped golden squares that seemed to glow in the firelight, making the space much brighter than any hall Oddny was accustomed to. At the far end, massive wooden statues of Odin, Thor, and Frey were lofted to loom over the cavernous room, and beneath them were two doors that Oddny guessed led to private chambers: a luxury she knew she'd never experience.

With servants sweeping the clean floors and not even the faintest hint of foul smells on the air, Oddny could tell at once, with a twinge of jealousy, that no livestock had ever set foot inside this place. Even at Ozur's farm, the sheep, cows, goats, and horses were brought inside to winter at the opposite end of the longhouse from the family's chambers, keeping the animals warm while also adding heat to the hall; at Oddny's own farm there had been no room for such division, and the family and their workers lived amid the smell of manure all winter in a cramped, dimly lit space.

What must it be like, she wondered, to have the resources to live so comfortably? To have warmth and light all winter long with no worry that the oil or wood would run out?

She almost asked Gunnhild as much before remembering that her friend had grown up with similar comforts—until she'd run away, at least. Moreover, Gunnhild was still staring straight ahead as though not really seeing, so the two of them stood awkwardly near one of the hearths as the crowd milled about. Serving women circled the hall, offering pitchers of ale and sly smiles to the tired sailors.

At last Arinbjorn and Svein appeared next to Oddny and Gunnhild, each man holding two cups of ale.

"Welcome to Alreksstadir," Arinbjorn said as he handed one cup to Gunnhild and then knocked the other against it in a toast. "Drink up. It's thanks to you we made it here in one piece."

Gunnhild's eyes seemed to focus at last and she gave him a wan smile. Oddny took a cup from Svein and asked, "Where are we to sleep?"

"I heard Eirik ordering your things taken to the textile workshop," said Svein. "That's where a lot of the women go when they're between places."

Oddny brightened. "Textile workshop?"

"Between what places?" Gunnhild asked with suspicion.

Arinbjorn waved a hand vaguely. "You'll see. Saeunn takes all kinds: older women who never married, widows conned out of their farms by their children's in-laws, daughters who have to earn their own dowry because they had too many older sisters . . ." At the look on Oddny's face, he grinned. "There are plenty of eligible men coming and going in a place like this. A small dowry doesn't matter much to some of these drunken fools, so long as the summer's plunder was good."

"And so long as she's pretty!" one of the nearby men chimed in, and several of the others laughed. Oddny and Gunnhild traded a droll look.

"We're going to get cleaned up before supper." Arinbjorn took a swig of ale and scanned the crowd over the rim of his cup. "Have you seen— Oh no."

Oddny turned. A woman was watching the grimy men file in with a look of mild distaste, as though she were the one who'd have to sweep up the dirt they were tracking into her hall. But no, Oddny thought—this was not someone who'd ever held a broom. The woman had at least seventy winters, if Oddny had to guess, and she wore a deep red gown with a bright blue apron-dress, the latter secured with a pair of enormous, intricate oval brooches strung with several strands of beads. She wore a thin golden circlet on her brow, and her hair was bound back in a silk scarf, with a few gray wisps escaping at her nape.

Eirik approached her and said something, and her mouth turned down in a scowl as she replied. With the noise in the hall and with the considerable distance separating them, Oddny couldn't hear what was said, but she could tell that the conversation was not going well. Whoever this woman was, she was not happy to see Eirik. And whatever he was saying was causing her expression to grow angrier with each moment.

Gunnhild observed this interaction with interest. "Don't tell me that's his mother."

"Ah, no," Arinbjorn said. "His mother died when we were young. That's Queen Gyda."

Oddny stifled a gasp. Queen Gyda's father had ruled Hordaland when Norway was made up of petty kingdoms, and she was almost as much of a legend as her husband. In his youth, King Harald had asked for her hand, and she'd refused him, instead daring him to bring all of Norway under one rule before she would marry him. He'd sworn an oath to neither cut nor comb his hair until he'd carried out this task. Oddny, though a bit terrified, found herself awestruck as well.

Gunnhild, on the other hand, blinked once before draining her entire cup of ale in one go. Arinbjorn, Oddny, and Svein watched in impressed silence until she lowered the empty cup and said, "Right. My future mother-in-law."

"One of many," Arinbjorn reminded her.

Gunnhild glared down at her cup as though willing it to refill itself.

Svein asked, "Arinbjorn, aren't you going to go rescue him?"

But before he could reply, both Eirik and Queen Gyda turned to look at them.

"Not this time," Arinbjorn said. He nudged Gunnhild, who in turn gave Oddny a pleading look, and the two of them linked arms and went forward.

"This is she. My betrothed. Gunnhild Ozurardottir of Halogaland," Eirik said, gesturing at her and completely ignoring Oddny, which didn't at all surprise Oddny. "Gunnhild, this is Queen Gyda, my father's foremost wife if not presently his favorite."

Queen Gyda ignored the jab. Her lips curled into a mirthless smile as she looked Gunnhild up and down. "And does your father know that you mean to marry a witch, Eirik?"

"How would he possibly know that?" Eirik shot back. "He isn't here yet."

"He won't be happy. It would behoove you to remain in his favor if you still wish to become king of Norway, boy. And this?" Queen Gyda looked again to Gunnhild—her shabby clothes stiff and crusted with salt, her hair wild and windswept, her cheeks and nose sunburned—and scoffed. "This is not the way to do it."

Gunnhild tensed and Eirik squared his shoulders, but to Oddny's surprise it seemed that for once neither of them knew what to say.

Queen Gyda huffed and waved them off. "I must return to preparations for Winternights. Things have gotten considerably more—complicated—now that I have a *wedding* on my hands." She said the word as though it were the name of a disease. After a last scathing look at Gunnhild, she swept out of the hall without so much as a goodbye.

"Well," Oddny said into the awkward silence that followed. "That went well."

Eirik scrubbed a hand down his face. "Unfortunately, I don't think it could have gone any better."

Gunnhild whirled on him. "We're getting married at Winternights, now, are we? I didn't agree to this. It's too soon."

Though Oddny followed the moon's phases rigorously to know when to expect her blood, her sense of time had been thwarted since the raid, and she'd all but forgotten that the full moons that marked the Winternights festival were so near. The three feast days heralded the start of winter and the beginning of a new year, and served to usher in the season of darkness and magic and rest: a direct contrast to the sunlight and traveling and raiding—not to mention the farmwork—that dominated the summer for most people in the north.

"There was nothing in our terms about *when* we're getting married. Besides, it'll soften the blow not to ask for a separate wedding feast," Eirik returned. "Weddings often happen at Winternights. The timing is auspicious."

"'Soften the blow'—'the blow' being me?" Gunnhild said. The hurt in her voice took Oddny by surprise. That Gunnhild was showing any measure of vulnerability in front of him meant that her near-death experience on the ship had brought her lower than Oddny had realized.

And the way Queen Gyda had looked at Gunnhild—similar to the way Oddny had witnessed Solveig looking at her daughter many times before—had clearly not helped.

"I wish you would've mentioned that your family would hate me when we were making our terms," Gunnhild continued bitterly. "Although I suppose I should've expected it, given your father's history with witches. It was my folly to expect any better of you. Any of you."

Eirik seemed about to argue, but instead he turned on his heel and stormed toward Arinbjorn, spoke to him briefly with some angry gesturing, then stalked into the chamber on the left and slammed the door behind him. Hnoss and Gersemi ran up to the door and pawed at it, and it opened a crack to let the cats enter before slamming shut again.

At least Eirik knew when to walk away, Oddny thought, because Gunnhild clearly did not: She tried to follow him before Oddny grabbed her by the arm. "You should probably let him be until he's calmed down."

Gunnhild tore out of her grasp and glared at her. "Whose side are you on?"

"Oddny has the right of things," Arinbjorn said as he came up beside them; Svein had disappeared along with many of the other hirdsmen, leaving only the servants who endlessly swept the hall. "Come. I'm to take you to Runfrid to give her the bindrune first thing—some of the men have long journeys home and plan to leave before the festival, so the sooner she can start tattooing them, the better. I'll point out the workshop on the way. They'll take care of you from there."

Oddny was about to ask if she'd heard correctly—that this tattooist they were going to see was, in fact, a woman—when Gunnhild said, "Not so fast, Arinbjorn. What did he say to you before he went off to sulk?"

Arinbjorn smoothed back his short dark hair and gave her a smile that didn't reach his eyes. "King Harald is on his way here from Vestfold, where he was visiting Olaf, who was also being visited by Halfdan at the time. And they're all accompanying King Harald here for the festival."

"Are they wintering here?" Oddny was confused; back in Haloga-land, Winternights was more intimate, with only close neighbors assem-bling. "It doesn't seem sensible to cross the country for a feast at this time of year."

Though, she supposed, Halfdan *did* employ a witch who seemed to have a knack for weather magic, and the west coast of Norway never froze, so perhaps he wasn't overly concerned about getting back to Trond-heim before the season turned.

"Only King Harald is wintering here, as far as I know," Arinbjorn said. "But apparently Queen Gyda accused Eirik of spreading rumors about his brothers using witchcraft against him. She suspects Olaf and Halfdan were trying to convince King Harald that he's lying. She's not completely convinced herself that it's true, but she dislikes Olaf and Halfdan more than she does Eirik, so it remains to be seen whose side she falls on."

"But we've seen the witches' tricks with our own eyes," Oddny pro-tested.

Arinbjorn grimaced. "And speaking of which, Thorbjorg and Katla are with them, and Queen Gyda was considering having one of them per-form the disablot during the festival."

Gunnhild and Oddny looked at each other, dismayed—and not just at the prospect of meeting the witches face-to-face. The sacrifice to the disir, minor goddesses whose whims could grant both good fortunes and bad deaths, was a huge responsibility that would affect the fortunes of all present at the feast, at least for the coming year. If Thorbjorg or Katla was put in charge of such an important task, the fates of their enemies would be sure to take a foul turn—and Oddny didn't know how many more of those she, Gunnhild, and especially Signy could handle.

"Who usually does it?" Oddny cut in. Back home, the sacrifice was performed by either the lady of the house or whichever devotee of the gods felt most up to the task. "Can't they just do it again?"

"It depends. Queen Gyda, or someone from the temple, usually," Arinbjorn said. "But she suggested one of the seeresses because there hasn't been one here in decades, and she thinks King Harald wouldn't object to a good prophecy to keep people happy. But obviously Eirik doesn't trust Thorbjorg or Katla, so he volunteered Gunnhild to perform the disablot instead."

Gunnhild could not have looked more shocked if someone had come up behind her and dumped a bucket of freezing seawater over her head. Oddny tightened her hold on Gunnhild's arm in reassurance, even knowing it was futile.

If this sacrifice went as poorly as the ritual Gunnhild had tried in her father's cookhouse, it would not only compromise Gunnhild's career as a seeress but complicate her terms with Eirik if he were to realize that she wasn't at her full power. And should he divorce her before spring, she and Oddny would lose their ride to Birka. To Signy. Gunnhild would still have her dowry and bride-price to get them there and to buy Signy's freedom, but finding a new ship and crew to hire would cost them valuable time.

"I take it that this is not, in fact, good news," Arinbjorn observed, not without sympathy.

Gunnhild pulled herself together enough to grumble, "Would that he'd consulted me first."

Arinbjorn raised an eyebrow. "You don't strike me as one to balk at the chance to prove yourself. Is everything all right?"

"Everything is fine," said Oddny before Gunnhild could speak. "We're all tired from the journey. The sooner you take us to this Runfrid so Gunnhild can deliver her bindrune, the sooner we can get to the textile workshop and someone can tell us the best place for a woman to bathe."

Arinbjorn's keen gray eyes regarded her a moment too long, as if he were trying to detect a lie, but then his smile returned. "Right, then. Follow me."

ARINBJORN LED THEM ACROSS the grounds, pointing out the textile workshop and a few other buildings as they went. Each was larger than Oddny's father's hall. The people they passed on the way looked healthy enough, their clothing worn but of good quality—not humble

farmers, Oddny thought, but not wealthy, either—and they greeted Arinbjorn and spared a curious look at the women before continuing on
their way.

Once they reached the armory, Oddny was not surprised to find that
it, too, was larger than the home she'd grown up in. The space was lined
with racks of spears and axes, with retired splintered shields fixed to the
walls above them. Small wooden icons of Odin, Tyr, and Thor sat on a
shelf over the spear rack. The statues were splattered with dried blood,
probably from previous rituals—or so Oddny hoped. There was a loft at
the far end of the room, but Oddny could not see anyone or anything up
there.

The hird bustled about, dropping off their weapons and ship boxes in
haphazard piles. Oddny saw no sign of Halldor, Svein, or Thorolf, but
assumed they'd gone to bathe. Several of the hirdsmen were already
wearing clean, dry clothes and brushing out their wet hair and beards.

Oddny felt a stab of jealousy. At this moment she wanted nothing
more than a bath.

"It's usually not as much of a mess," Arinbjorn said, gesturing at the
chaos around them, "but then I suppose everyone is eager to get cleaned
up before supper."

"We can relate to that," Oddny said pointedly.

"All in due time, Oddny Ketilsdottir." Arinbjorn went to the ladder
leading up to the loft. "Oi, Runa!"

"Just a moment!" came a woman's voice from above.

"You know, most people would be more eager to see their beloved
return from a summer of dangerous adventure, but my ship just got in and
you weren't even at the docks," Arinbjorn said conversationally, leaning
against the ladder with his arms folded.

Beloved? Gunnhild mouthed to Oddny, who shrugged. This was the
first either of them had heard of Arinbjorn being romantically attached.

"I did hear that the ship was coming," came the mystery woman's voice,
along with her light footsteps, "but you know where to find me, Arri."

Arinbjorn pouted. "That's not the point."

A woman poked her head over the edge of the loft, her features in shadow. "Forgive me for wanting to enjoy my last moments of peace and quiet before you lot returned—and just when I thought I'd cleared this place of the smell."

Smoke wafted down from the loft. The woman was burning something—juniper, to Oddny's nose—to battle the damp, musky odors that had followed the sailors to the armory.

"Fair enough," Arinbjorn said. "Also, I brought friends, and a task from Eirik."

"How much is he paying?" the woman asked.

"Would you just come down here, please?"

The person who descended the ladder was unlike anyone Oddny had seen before. She was small, roughly Oddny's size, and dressed in a pale green woolen tunic and gray pants, with light blue leg wraps secured over thick nalbound socks. Her hair was black as pitch and thicker even than Gunnhild's, and it was pulled into a braid roughly the same size as her forearm; her skin was a deep copper brown and covered in tattoos, some faded and others bright and richly pigmented.

She threw herself at Arinbjorn before she'd made it all the way down the ladder, and he swung her in a circle. Oddny and Gunnhild looked at the ceiling politely and let them have their moment, though Oddny decided that if they didn't hurry things along so she and Gunnhild could go get cleaned up and settled in, she was going to make a bad impression. The thin smile on Gunnhild's face indicated that she was of a similar mind.

"I *am* glad you're alive," said the woman when Arinbjorn set her down. "Thorolf and Svein told me what happened . . ." She pulled away and looked him over as if searching for visible wounds. "How are you?"

"Later," he said, and gestured at Gunnhild and Oddny. "Runfrid, this is Gunnhild Ozurardottir and Oddny Ketilsdottir of Halogaland."

"Runfrid Asgeirsdottir." She shook Oddny's hand, then Gunnhild's.

"Oddny is a healer, and Gunnhild is a witch. And she's also marrying Eirik at Winternights."

"Ah! They told me that, too. This is her, then?" Runfrid froze with

Gunnhild's hand still in hers. She put her other hand over Gunnhild's as well, looked her in the eyes, and said with mock seriousness, "I am so sorry." When Gunnhild's smile only became more strained, she added, "I'm only kidding. I say that because Eirik's like a brother to me. The big, moody, prickly brother I never had. He'll grow on you. Like a fungus."

She dropped Gunnhild's hand and looked to Arinbjorn as though waiting for him to back her up. He shrugged a shoulder. "You said it, not me. Gunnhild, the bindrune?"

Without preamble, Gunnhild reached into her belt pouch and pulled out the antler coin she'd carved with the symbol she'd created. She explained what it was for and how to use it—all of which was new to Oddny, who listened with interest—and Runfrid nodded along until Gunnhild dropped it into her palm, causing her to gasp in surprise.

"I felt something," Runfrid said in awe as she ran a finger over the carving. "Incredible."

"Eirik will talk to you about payment later," Arinbjorn said. "For now—"

"If this is the task you were talking about, I'll do it for free. For all our sakes." Runfrid closed her hand into a fist around the bindrune and turned her head over her shoulder to the freshly bathed hirdsmen trickling back into the armory. "All right, who's first?"

Oddny and Gunnhild took their leave after that and headed to the building Arinbjorn had pointed out as the textile workshop.

"Gunna," Oddny said as they stopped just outside the door. "Are you all right?"

Gunnhild chewed her lip. "I was just thinking. About the sacrifice—"

"I'm sure if you just talk to Eirik about it—"

"Oh, gods, that's the last thing I want to do. Talk to *him*?" Gunnhild made a face. "No. But I think we could use this situation to our advantage."

"How? You told me that the spirits wouldn't come—"

"Hush!" Gunnhild looked around wildly to ensure they weren't overheard, and lowered her voice. "No. Listen: If Thorbjorg and Katla are *here* during the disablot, and King Harald allows me to do a ritual as well, then that means neither of them will be able to get to the dark place."

"The dark place?"

"The place a seeress goes to when she sinks down and meets with the dead. Anyway—whatever those two are doing to prevent me from communing with the spirits, they won't be able to, because they can't go into trance right there in the hall."

"Not without suspicion," Oddny said, eyes widening in understanding. "And their absence would be noticed on such an important day. *And* if Olaf and Halfdan are trying to convince King Harald of their innocence—"

"They wouldn't dare try anything right under his nose," Gunnhild finished. She reached forward and squeezed Oddny's shoulders. "Every woman here will be singing for me. I'll be safe, and the spirits *will* come, and I *will* find out exactly where Signy is. We won't have to go to Birka at all come spring—we can just go straight to wherever she's been sold off to, as I told you we would back at my father's. I won't fail again, Oddny. I swear it."

"And if King Harald won't allow you to perform the ritual along with the sacrifice?"

Gunnhild grimaced and dropped her hands. "Then we'll figure something else out."

"Yes. We will." Oddny took a deep, shaky breath, unwilling to get her hopes up again but desperate to stay optimistic for her sister's sake. And for Gunnhild's.

She turned back to the door. "Shall we?"

THE MOMENT THEY ENTERED the workshop, a sense of peace settled onto Oddny's shoulders. The merry crackling of the hearth fire and the soft chatter of the working women were a soothing balm to her ears; the brush and tap of the heddle rods moving and the clink of the loom weights knocking together were songs she knew by heart. Oil braziers hung from the posts here, too, making the smaller space as bright as the main hall. Beneath each brazier hung bunches of dried wildflowers and herbs, their heady fragrances mixing with the smell of woodsmoke to envelop her like a warm embrace.

Statues of Frigg and her handmaidens were perched on the lintel, offering bowls set out in front of them, and soapstone lamps burning high between each figure. Oddny smiled to recognize Eir by the bouquet of angelica clutched in her hands—her kind face so similar to Yrsa's statue of Eir, stowed safely in Oddny's bag—and she realized, at the sight of her goddess, that this was the first time she'd felt truly safe since the raid.

But Gunnhild looked uncomfortable. Oddny understood why at once—when was the last time Gunnhild had touched a loom? Probably not since she'd run away from home. And at a glance, Oddny could not identify any of the figures on the lintel as representing Freyja, who was almost certainly Gunnhild's patron.

Once they entered, a woman came up to them, leaning on a cane. She had maybe forty winters and was tall, with curly dark brown hair and a kind face. Oddny, feeling fully in her element, introduced herself and Gunnhild and explained why they were there.

The woman in turn introduced herself as Saeunn Hrolfsdottir, the workshop's head. She seemed happy to have them and began explaining the weavers' daily routine. As she did, many of the women stopped working to peer at the newcomers; some whispered behind their hands and gave Oddny and Gunnhild—especially Gunnhild—strange looks. But a dark-haired, bright-eyed woman at the loom closest to the door was smiling with unconcealed interest, and Oddny found herself smiling back.

"We make sailcloths, mainly," Saeunn said, and Oddny's attention snapped back to her. "Alreksstadir is the king's shipbuilding center, at least until they've felled all the trees they can use and they move on. But as long as the sheep are here, so are we." She smiled. "We sleep here in the workshop. I can have the girls dig out some extra bedrolls for you both."

"Thank you," Oddny said sincerely. "We'd love to have a bath before we get settled in, though."

Saeunn bobbed her head in understanding. "Ulla here can take you to the bathhouse. She could also show you around, if you'd—"

"I'd love to," said the smiling woman at the closest loom, leaping down from the platform. Before Oddny and Gunnhild knew it, Ulla was ushering them both out the door to begin their tour.

"That's the cookhouse. Hrafnhild is in charge there. Hello, Hrafnhild!" Ulla said, waving cheerfully at a hefty red-faced woman having an animated argument with a reedy man brandishing a piece of birch bark with runes and tallies on it. The woman ignored her, but Ulla wasn't deterred. Some of the cookhouse girls, however, returned Ulla's wave with smiles and hellos.

"That building over there with the little stream running through it is the brewhouse. Hrafnhild usually poaches a few of us from the workshop to help get the ale ready for Yule. There's the armory. Over there—*way* over there—is the latrine. That's the new one they built after the sickness last winter. Very nasty. And there's the temple, but it's dedicated mainly to Odin, so we don't go there often. And over here—oh."

Downstream from the brewhouse was the bathhouse, which they could see was packed with Eirik's hirdsmen coming and going.

"We'll come back later, if that's all right?" Ulla said. Despite their want of a bath, Oddny and Gunnhild agreed it would be better to take one when there was less of a crowd.

Ulla pointed out more buildings as they walked: the storehouses, the stables. Everywhere they went, she greeted people by name, and everyone looked happy to see her. As they continued on, Oddny stopped short at the sight of a cluster of ramshackle huts. Through the open doorways, she could see women with shorn hair and raggedy dresses spinning wool, eyes downcast, their movements stiff and hollow.

Thralls. Her stomach twisted as she pictured Signy among them.

Gunnhild and Ulla had stopped walking as well, and Ulla's cheery expression shifted into something darker. "Those women supplement our production at the workshop and work the dye vats. More than once we've had to chase off the men who try to pester them. Poor dears. I wish there was more I could do for them."

Oddny wished the same.

"Come along, friends," Ulla said gently. "We'll head back toward the bathhouse down this other path." She waved them along and started walking again. After a last lingering look at the huts, Oddny and Gunnhild followed.

Ulla pointed out the well-tended cottages where artisans and farm-workers lived year-round, the plots where the winter barley had been planted, and the pasture where the livestock grazed; beyond that lay the woods, and beyond *that* the mountains. The three women walked along the pasture's fence to their next destination instead of going any closer to the trees, though Oddny could see a path cutting through the field, where a team of men was hauling a massive log out of the forest.

Wondering about the woods, and knowing she would need to make her tea again sooner rather than later—she could hardly believe it had nearly been an entire moon since the raid—Oddny asked Ulla where she could go about getting the ingredients.

"Oddny here is a very skilled healer," Gunnhild added. "I've got a few tricks myself, but her talent is well beyond mine."

"You're being modest," Oddny said, but she was secretly pleased.

Gunnhild waved a hand. "Magic can't fix everything. You have the practical skills." She stopped and rolled her bandaged ankle. "I'm not even limping thanks to you."

"You could ask Hrafnhild about using the estate's garden," Ulla suggested. "I'm sure she'd agree. There are plenty of people in need of help around here. And I'd be happy to take you foraging, too—I know the woods well."

Next they came to the charcoal pit and the forges, where they saw Halldor observing the smiths and chatting with one of the younger boys working the bellows. Halldor looked like he hadn't washed yet, and Oddny wondered why he wasn't bathing with the other men before she remembered that he didn't care for crowded spaces. He'd probably chosen to explore the estate on his own first and wait for the bathhouse to empty, same as her and Gunnhild.

Halldor caught her eye and nodded, and she nodded back, tried to ignore the flush creeping up her neck at the thought of his arm around her on the deck of the ship. She'd been able to put it from her mind ever since it had happened—gods, had it really been only that morning that they'd come so close to death?—but now that she was safely on land, the sight of him caused the memory of his body pressed against hers to worm its way back into her mind. As soon as he'd followed orders and cleared the deck, he'd gone straight to Oddny, had kept such a firm hold on her that the wave that had knocked Gunnhild overboard hadn't budged her from his arms, and had held her back when she'd foolishly tried to jump into the water and save her friend.

Why did he do that?

Perhaps she was dwelling too much on the whole episode. After all, this had been the closest she'd been to a man save for a few encounters she'd had at feasts and assemblies, which had not been particularly enjoyable. But Halldor's closeness to her on the deck, born out of desperation and not sexual in the least, seemed to have affected her in ways she hadn't anticipated.

Oddny did not like this one bit. She liked even less that a part of her hoped he'd show up at the bathhouse at the same time as her and Gunnhild—

No. It's not like that. We're bound until he pays me, she told herself firmly. *After that, I never have to think about him again.*

Oddny half listened as Ulla pointed out the woodworking shop, where carpenters shaped the keel of a warship and several coopers carved staves for barrels and buckets. Before long, Ulla had led them back to the bathhouse, which had mercifully emptied.

There was no sign of Halldor when they got there. Oddny hated that she felt even the slightest twinge of disappointment about it.

Ulla took her leave and told them she'd see them in the main hall for supper. The fire was already built up inside the bathhouse, and Oddny almost cried when she entered; it was the warmest she'd been in days. After she and Gunnhild had washed themselves and combed their hair, they sat inside in comfortable silence, hoping to enjoy this peace until someone else arrived.

Gunnhild leaned her head against the wall and closed her eyes. "This is the best I've felt in ages."

Oddny, sitting across from her, folded her knees up to her chest and wrapped her arms around her legs. "This place—I never imagined I'd live in such comfort."

"You can say that again," said Gunnhild with feeling. "I've spent the last twelve winters sleeping on a straw mat on the cold, hard ground—"

"I wonder where Signy will be sleeping this winter," Oddny said.

Gunnhild looked away. Between nearly dying earlier trying to stop the storm, the mystery of the third witch and her seal form, and her disaster of an introduction to Queen Gyda—as well as dwelling on her impending and probably worse introduction to King Harald, Eirik's brothers, and the enemy witches when they arrived—she was having a bad enough day.

But Oddny had to get this off her chest.

"I can't stop thinking about them, Gunna. Those women in the huts. If Signy's circumstances are anywhere near that bad—or worse—I wish we could've gotten to her before winter."

Gunnhild slumped against the wall. "I know. But we have a plan. There's no sense in feeling so guilty that we can't enjoy ourselves at least a little. Things are only going to get more difficult from here."

"Especially with Thorbjorg and Katla heading our way as we speak," Oddny said darkly.

Fear flitted across Gunnhild's face for a brief moment before it hardened into resolve.

"Exactly," she said.

By the time they'd dressed and left the bathhouse, both cursing at the cold air that struck them the moment they opened the door, it was clear they'd missed supper. They went straight to the cookhouse and scavenged some leftovers, then retired to the textile workshop, took to their borrowed bedrolls, and fell into a heavy, well-deserved sleep.

19

GUNNHILD DREAMED THAT SHE was drowning.

The water around her was dark as the void, and she was being dragged down, arms flailing, sharp teeth clamped around her ankle as the other foot kicked out.

She was so cold.

She couldn't breathe.

Gunnhild!

Movement above her, and her heart leapt as she looked up, but it wasn't the shape of Eirik that materialized—it was a white fox, and it bit down hard on her arm, and another shape was diving toward her and it was the eagle, blood and fluid streaming from its hollow eye socket, its remaining eye glaring hatefully, as Ran's daughters laughed far below in the deep—

And then two hands grabbed her shoulders.

"Gunnhild!"

She was shaking, sweating, and Oddny was standing over her, looking down in concern. "Are you all right?"

"Yes," Gunnhild managed. "Yes. It was only a dream."

Oddny looked skeptical, but released her.

They breakfasted with the workshop women, after which Oddny jumped at the chance to share a loom with Ulla, and Gunnhild went off to work on a spell she had in mind, born of her terrible dream.

The woods were her first choice for some privacy. The problem was that she was hesitant to veer from the path for fear of getting lost, so she kept running into carpenters or thralls at work, marking trees or hauling out logs.

Her second choice was a copse of oaks behind the armory, where she hid herself behind the thickest tree and got started on her task. Crafting a spell from scratch was tedious work; at this beginning stage, it involved little more than scratching runes on a piece of birch bark with a lump of charcoal until she figured out the right combination to use. Men sparred on the practice field nearby, and their chatter and laughter and shouting, paired with the clash of steel, became distant as she worked.

But when several voices floated into her immediate vicinity, she froze.

Eirik's was first. It was tight, worried: "Are you sure you don't wish to winter here? It's late in the season to be crossing the open sea. And it's bad luck to travel during Winternights. It's dangerous—"

Then Thorolf, sounding stiffer, more formal than Gunnhild had ever heard him: "There's a cargo ship of Icelanders here waiting for me, as I arranged at the beginning of summer. If I decide to stay now, they'll have tarried these past few weeks for nothing. They've made the crossing many times before. We'll be fine."

Arinbjorn, pacifying as always: "He needs to get away for a time, Eirik. From her."

And finally, Svein: "And from you."

Gunnhild's guilt threatened to suffocate her. In the silence that followed the skald's words, she took a chance and leaned over to peer out from behind the tree, and saw that the three other men had turned to look at Svein.

"What?" the skald asked, folding his arms. "Everyone knows by now that Thorolf asked her first." When no one spoke, he sighed, said, "I'll go get it," and walked into the armory.

"I don't wish to get into this again," Eirik said wearily to Thorolf once Svein was gone. "I've already explained myself and apologized. What more would you have of me?"

"Time," said Thorolf. "Distance."

His voice was heavy with words left unsaid, and Gunnhild didn't miss the look that passed between the two men, how Eirik very nearly managed to cover a wince, how he was the one to break eye contact first.

The significance of this moment was either lost on Arinbjorn or else he was dutifully ignoring it. Gunnhild guessed the latter. "Don't mind him, Thorolf. It's just that so many of us are leaving for the winter, and it makes him nervous—"

This didn't improve Eirik's mood. "Yes, thank you for reminding me."

"Come, now," Arinbjorn said. "You'll have Svein. And Halldor. He was up before dawn practicing, remember? The other hopefuls drank themselves silly with the rest of us and were still drunk this morning."

"But isn't it better to get to know the men you'll be fighting with?" Thorolf asked. "I don't dislike Halldor, but he seems a bit . . . standoffish, doesn't he?"

"And Eirik *isn't* standoffish? He didn't drink with us, either, and he was also up before dawn." Arinbjorn gave his foster brother a bracing pat on the shoulder.

"That's because I never went to sleep," Eirik said without inflection.

Arinbjorn pointed a thumb sideways at him and continued, as if he hadn't spoken, "This one would be living in a troll cave with no one else but his cats if we let him. Halldor will fit right in. Go, enjoy yourself this winter, Thorolf. And tell your father that my father says hello." Gunnhild vaguely remembered someone mentioning that his father and Thorolf's father had been foster brothers.

At this point Svein emerged from the armory carrying an axe and handed it to Eirik. The king took it and held it out to Thorolf, who gawped but didn't move to take it. It was a glorious piece with a crescent-shaped blade, gold inlays, and silver plating on the shaft: a weapon clearly more for show than for practical use.

"You've been a good friend to me for many years," Eirik said, still proffering the axe. "You gave me my first ship when we were young. And you did so in full awareness of the strife between our families, in hopes of healing the rift. Yet over the past moon, I've torn it open once again. I can't regret what I did, or why I did it. What I do regret, however, is negating all your hard work. Let me at least make up for that."

"But that axe," Thorolf said. "Isn't it the one your father gave you when he named you his successor? You can't possibly mean to—"

"It is, and I do. I don't know about our fathers, but in my mind, between you and me, there can be no question of our friendship. You haven't returned home to Iceland since we met, and I wish for you to take this with you."

"I can't," Thorolf said, his dark eyes huge. "It's too much."

"Give this to Skallagrim," Eirik replied firmly. "From my father to me, from me to you, and from you to *your* father. With my thanks."

Thorolf shook his head until Eirik added, "Please," the single word loaded with emotion, and Gunnhild saw Thorolf's resolve crumble as he took the weapon.

Gunnhild turned away. She couldn't watch anymore, couldn't bear to hear them say their goodbyes. Guilt burrowed itself deep in her chest, squirming, telling her to run.

But she held her ground and covered her ears until she was sure they must be gone—and then she raised her head to see Thorolf standing over her, alone. She scrambled to her feet and looked into his sad brown eyes. Every breath she drew made her chest feel tighter.

He was a good man. Kind, and sweet, and brave. He'd done nothing wrong except to care for her too much. In time, she thought she might have even come to love him. What kind of person was she to forsake him for another? For someone who was his complete opposite, at that?

"Things are bad between you and Eirik, and everyone knows it." These were the first words Thorolf had said to her since the boathouse. "You can still abandon your oath to him and come with me to Iceland. You could leave this all behind if you wanted to."

Gunnhild shook her head. "Signy needs me. Nothing has changed. There was never a choice at all, Thorolf. I need to stay and see this through."

He set his jaw. "Is that truly what it is?"

"What do you mean?" she asked, miffed by his tone. "You were the one who told me I should work with Eirik in the first place—"

"But not like this. You didn't have to marry him to work together. He didn't appeal to your ambition—he appealed to your selfishness. Your desire to be someone. To prove your mother wrong. But to me, you've been someone all along. You never had anything to prove. Do you not see that?"

His words rendered her speechless, for they stung as though he'd rubbed salt in an open wound. Yes, things *were* bad with Eirik—and if she proceeded down this path, surely she would rescue Signy and avenge Heid if it was the last thing she did, but at what personal cost? If she were to go through with marrying Eirik, would she ever know the tender embrace of another person again?

No words came, and that was just as well. They'd already said all they could say to each other.

She waited until he was gone before she slumped back down against the tree and sobbed quietly until she could no longer breathe. A short time later she watched his ship depart.

That night she dreamed for the second time that she was drowning, and she awoke with a renewed determination to succeed. It didn't matter where she worked on the spell; she just had to *work*. So after breakfast she headed back into the woods, went a little ways off the path, and though the sounds of human activity nearby told her she wasn't completely alone, she blocked them out as best she could and tried to focus.

She was certain that her bindrune tattoo had worked and her mind was protected from Thorbjorg. Which meant that these dreams were not being sent by someone else to scare her: Her terror was entirely her own. She needed to come up with something to protect her body as well, a spell that would keep her from all harm. Thanks to that damned seal—that godsforsaken third witch and those teeth around Gunnhild's ankle—the fear of death had taken root in her and buried itself in her bones, and she wanted it gone.

I am not weak. I am not afraid.

Maybe, once she felt she was safe again, the dreams would stop.

But the spell proved more complicated than she'd anticipated. There was too much potential damage to ward against, too many things that could injure or kill a person, all of which Gunnhild needed to account for. As a result, she soon became frustrated, and switched to the other task she'd set for herself that day: a curse.

Curses had always come as naturally to her as breathing. She gathered a pile of deer rib bones from the forest, and upon each she carved her intent in runes. Then she waited until the dead of night to bury them at the threshold of each of the thrall women's huts.

As she placed her last curse and made to fill in the hole, the tattered cloth that served as the hut's door parted, and one of the pale, wan thrall women appeared. Understandably disturbed at the sight of her, the woman gasped and made a strange gesture, moving the tips of her fingers from her forehead to the center of her chest and to each shoulder, saying something in a foreign tongue. Gunnhild tried to explain and saw no recognition in the woman's eyes, but then a second woman—perhaps one who understood Norse—dragged the first back inside and let Gunnhild finish her work.

The next morning she heard talk of a man who'd broken into horrible pustules the moment he attempted to enter one of the huts, and she smiled to herself. Ulla, seeing the dark bags under her eyes and the dirt under her nails, smiled as well.

Gunnhild told Oddny about the curses that afternoon when Oddny took a break from the weaving workshop to mend one of her socks. The two of them sat on a bench near the armory. It was an unseasonably warm day, but there were rain clouds on the horizon.

"I didn't know you could do things like that—*oh!*" Oddny jerked at the sound of a yell and stabbed herself with her needle. She cut a glare to the two men sparring on the practice field. "Could you keep it down?"

"Could you go sit somewhere else?" Eirik countered, and leapt back into action.

"Terrible retort," Gunnhild said under her breath.

"Absolutely horrendous," Oddny agreed.

Eirik and Halldor were practicing with, of all things, sticks, and they'd been at it since Gunnhild had trudged back to the textile workshop just as the sun came up. Both were so fast that her eyes could barely follow them. After the conversation she'd witnessed two days before, she was surprised to see that Eirik seemed to be having—fun?

Fun? That simply wouldn't do.

"What happened, Eirik? Did you lose your axes?" Gunnhild taunted from the bench.

"If you must know, I'm teaching Halldor how to improve his footwork," Eirik said from the other side of the fence. "You don't need blades for that." He stopped to catch his breath and gestured at Halldor with his stick, which Gunnhild realized was actually a short spear shaft without its metal tip. Halldor's was a spear shaft as well. Potentially injurious, but better than a blade, Gunnhild thought.

"My footwork has gotten me through nine summers of raiding, thank you *very* much," Halldor returned, leaning on his own stick, panting. "I need little improvement."

"Oh?" Eirik smirked. "Why are you up and training every day before the rooster crows if you're already the perfect fighter?"

"I could ask you the same question, considering we've been the only two out here before breakfast."

"I'll give you that—you *are* making the rest of my men look bad. Except, as I said, for your footwork."

"Well, now I know to look down when you're swinging an axe at me." Halldor smirked as well. "I never said I was the perfect fighter. But you're the only one I have yet to beat."

Eirik looked to the women, smugly. "He's a big talker yet, but still a liability on the field."

Halldor scoffed and took a swing at him with his stick, which Eirik blocked. Before long the two men turned into a blur, moving toward the other side of the yard amid the *clack-clack-clack* of their weapons' clashing.

"That's the closest Halldor's gotten to a smile since we met," Oddny observed in a strange tone.

Gunnhild would often think of that moment afterward—the way

Oddny seemed to soften when she said his name—for she couldn't puzzle out why her friend was so fond of the man who'd helped ruin her life. But for now she let the matter drop.

THE DREAMS CAME AGAIN and again, until a few mornings later Gunnhild awoke to see Ulla crouching over her, eyes wide with concern. As always, it took her a moment to realize that she was safe in the textile workshop—which was empty save for herself and Ulla. She sagged in relief. Her linen underdress was soaked in sweat, and as soon as she sat up and shrugged the blanket off, she was cold. She'd been the only one still asleep; the other women had already cleared their bedding from the platform lining the hall, where they slept tucked around the looms.

"The dream again?" Ulla asked, troubled. "When I visit my family, I can ask our noaidi to—"

"I have things under control," Gunnhild said. And then her words sank in. "You're Sámi?"

"I am," said Ulla proudly. "My family will be just over the mountain at this time of year. I'm going to see them after Yule, but I can go sooner if it would help you."

Gunnhild almost said something to her in the language she knew, but Ulla and her kin likely spoke an entirely different one so far south—she remembered her friends in Finnmark once telling her that there were considerable differences between the Sámi tongues. The thought of Juoksa and Mielat made her heart heavy with guilt. What would they think if they could see her now, marrying the very man they'd warned her against?

But just as she'd been determined to leave her noaidi friends out of her troubles for their own safety, she would not allow Ulla's family to become involved, either.

"Thank you, but it's nothing. I promise." Gunnhild raked her hand through her damp hair until it snagged on her sleep-tousled braid. "Where has Oddny gone?"

"To fetch breakfast with the others," Ulla said. "We should clear your bedroll so we can be ready to work when they get back. And you still have your dresses to make, don't you?"

Gunnhild looked down at the fraying cuffs of the linen dress she'd worn to sleep. "Right. You're right." She reached into her haversack and took out a plain, soft, undyed linen gown nearly identical to the one she was wearing, then turned to change into it. She'd never in her life had a spare linen underdress, and it was a luxury she appreciated today.

Her garments from Finnmark had officially been retired, due both to their state and to the fact that they barely fit anymore. Luckily Gunnhild had indeed sneaked back into her parents' chamber after Solveig's body had been removed—realizing the logic of Eirik's ill-timed yet reasonable suggestion, not that she would ever admit as much to him—and grabbed a few of her mother's dresses. All would've fit her well when she lived in Finnmark, but a few weeks of eating full meals had rendered them tight, especially as Solveig had been smaller than her to begin with. The old linen dresses had stretched with age, but the wool ones remained snug.

So when she took out a wool overdress in faded red and pulled it over her head, Ulla stepped forward without asking and helped her drag it down the rest of her body.

"Can you breathe in that?" Ulla asked, stepping back to regard her.

"I don't have a choice." Gunnhild hopped off the platform, the movement causing the loom weights nearest her to sway and clack gently.

Just then, Oddny entered the workshop with a bowl of porridge in her hand. She also wore one of Solveig's old woolen gowns, this one in a garish yellow-green, which she'd hemmed to a more appropriate length for her diminutive height. "How's your ankle, Gunna? Still all right?"

"Thanks to you," Gunnhild said. The wound she'd sustained on the last day of the voyage a week ago had already healed to a scar of teeth marks ringing her ankle.

Darkness all around—the seal's eyes—
Don't. Don't think of it.

"Good." Oddny handed her the bowl and looked her up and down before echoing Ulla's earlier question: "Can you even breathe in that dress?"

"Barely. I'll have to sew myself some new ones once I've finished my wedding gown," Gunnhild grumbled as she took a bite of porridge. She hated sewing, possibly more than weaving.

"You're not finished with it? You only have a few more days!"

Gunnhild thought for a moment as she chewed and swallowed. "If I give you some silver, will you finish it? You've a better hand for these things than I do."

"True. From what I've seen, you're rather terrible at sewing."

"Thank you," Gunnhild said sarcastically. "I'll need that confidence as I cobble together a queenly new wardrobe for myself. All that fine fabric I bought from Saeunn is about to be wasted on my pitiful skills with a needle and thread."

Oddny thought for a moment before snapping her fingers. "I'll sew the rest of your dresses if you give me the ones we got from your mother once I'm done."

"Deal," said Gunnhild, and they shook on it.

"Saeunn will probably give you a break to do it, Oddny," Ulla said. "Gunnhild will need them sooner rather than later, what with King Harald arriving anytime now."

"Gods, don't remind me." Gunnhild finished off her porridge. "With that said, Oddny, could you maybe start with the duck dress?"

"The duck dress?" Ulla repeated with interest.

Gunnhild put her bowl down, reached into her chest, and pulled out a madder-dyed diamond twill apron-dress: one of her mother's, which Solveig must've worn while pregnant, for it was not only larger than the rest, but it had also sat in storage for so long that it had holes where mice and moths had gotten to it. Thankfully the damage was confined to the top and front of the garment and its linen straps. Gunnhild had already sewn new straps, but as for the rest—

"Oh dear," said Ulla worriedly. "That dress has seen better days, hasn't it?"

"Saeunn suggested a solution," Gunnhild said, and from the chest she took out a panel of silk patterned with—of all things—ducks, and slapped it over the top of the dress.

At the time, Saeunn had admitted, "It was from one of my grand-mother's gowns. I always thought it looked a little ridiculous, but I held on to it. It's probably a hundred winters old." Though she'd gladly taken Gunnhild's silver, she'd seemed perturbed by the future queen's evil lit-tle giggle at the sight of the brightly colored ducks.

"See? I just have to sew it on," Gunnhild went on when Oddny and Ulla only stared. "It covers all the damage and adds a bit of—I don't know—"

"Absurdity?" Oddny suggested.

"Exactly. Eirik is going to hate it," Gunnhild said gleefully.

"*I* will sew this on." Oddny snatched both dress and panel from her in one fell swoop. "I don't trust you working with silk."

Gunnhild pretended to be ashamed, but privately she was relieved that she wouldn't have to do any sewing in the near future. She grabbed her witching bag and thanked Oddny for breakfast, then went to wash her dirty bowl in the stream and return it to the cookhouse, after which she headed to the woods once again to work on the protection spell. At this point she thought she'd figured out the correct runes, so she carved them on a stick and held it while she made a shallow cut across the back of her hand, hoping that the blade wouldn't bite, wincing when it did, then swearing and tossing the stick aside.

By midafternoon she had a nice little pile of failed attempts and de-cided to stop for the day. She gathered the sticks up to use for kindling, rubbed some healing salve on her cuts, and went back to the workshop.

She was nearly there when Oddny ran up to her.

"There you are!" she panted. "Everyone's been looking for you. King Harald is here—his ship is docking right now!"

Before Gunnhild could react, Oddny grabbed her by the arm and dragged her inside.

"I finished your apron-dress," Oddny said, thrusting the red dress with its cheerful ducks into her arms. "Wear the pleated linen one under-neath since none of the wool ones fit right. Saeunn, can she borrow your good cloak? And Ulla, can you help me with her hair?"

Saeunn nodded and went to fetch it. Ulla pulled a comb seemingly from out of nowhere and grinned.

Gunnhild raised her chin. "I can take care of my own—"

"Sit," said Oddny as she practically shoved her friend to sit atop the platform. "We have a lot to do and not long to do it. And it'll go more quickly if you hold still."

20

A SHORT TIME LATER Gunnhild was wearing Saeunn's cloak, the pleated underdress, and the duck apron-dress, along with her childhood brooches. She'd hastily polished them while Oddny strung together some of the beads from Gunnhild's little pouch of baubles used in the horn game so long ago; Oddny had kept it in Gunnhild's old chest from Halogaland when she'd repurposed it for her healing supplies.

"I remember some of these," Oddny said as she handed the finished string over. Gunnhild slipped the looped ends over the pin backs of her brooches and secured the straps of the apron-dress. Ulla finished fussing over her hair, which she'd plaited into a crown, with smaller braids twisting around it like a wreath. When Gunnhild saw her own reflection in Saeunn's polished bronze mirror, she had no idea how Ulla had accomplished it.

"Oh! The cobbler dropped these off for you earlier." Ulla handed over a pair of leather shoes Gunnhild had commissioned, which had toggles in the same style as Oddny's and many of the other women's. Gunnhild took off her pointed-toe reindeer-hide boots from Finnmark and tried on the new pair; they were a perfect fit.

"Thank you for your help," she said to both women. Then, to Ulla, "Do you want these boots? They're only a season old."

"As a matter of fact, yes." Ulla took off her shoes and pulled on the reindeer-hide boots, considering them with a broad smile. "They fit well. My old ones are worn out and I'll need them for skiing this winter—I'd meant to ask my family for a new pair, but now I won't have to." She looked back to Gunnhild, touched. "Thank you."

Gunnhild nodded, and Oddny said gravely, "Good luck, Gunna."

Eirik found Gunnhild standing outside the longhouse moments later. He looked her up and down and said, "Good enough. Come."

"Good *enough*?" Gunnhild seethed.

His eyes strayed momentarily to her chest—more specifically to the silk facing on the front of her apron-dress. "Are those . . . ducks? You're meeting my father wearing *ducks*?"

She folded her arms, purposely pushing up her ample breasts to make said ducks bulge. "Do you have a problem with my ducks?"

Eirik stared a moment too long, seemed to shake himself, and took off down the hill. Gunnhild huffed and followed.

They headed for the two splendid warships at the jetties, the first with a blue sail and the second with a yellow-and-white-striped one. The former was a statement in itself: As with Eirik's deep red sails, dye in such quantities was an obnoxious display of wealth. The ingredients needed to achieve such a rich blue were especially expensive, so she figured the first ship must belong to King Harald.

Eirik said, "Your hair looks good, at least. I'm assuming you didn't do it yourself?"

"You are *asking* to be cursed right now."

"And you perhaps need to sew yourself some larger dresses—"

"I'm working on it."

"—though I'm not complaining." This with a sideways glance in her direction.

Gunnhild raised her eyebrows. "I do hope you're not making a comment about my body. You see, when one goes from subsistence eating to big meals that other people cook *for* you—"

The tips of his ears turned pink. "I'm not trying to insult you. I'm saying I *like* it, Gunnhild. But if one of the seams on that duck dress busts during this meeting with my father, it's your own fault for not sewing others sooner."

"So you're complimenting me? Are you feeling all right?"

Eirik looked as though he were trying to compose himself. "I should've chosen my words more carefully. I didn't mean for you to take offense. I'm sorry."

An *apology*? Before she could question it, he said, "Do you see the warship with yellow-and-white sails? That belongs to Olaf. Halfdan isn't here yet. Hopefully he decided to do the wise thing and go straight back to Trondheim."

Gunnhild said through her teeth, "Right. Thorbjorg and Olaf are bad enough—"

"*King* Olaf to you. Until we're married, at which point you can call him whatever you want."

"I feel the word 'king' is used entirely too loosely in this country," she quipped.

Eirik nearly cracked a smile at that, but when he caught her eye, his mouth flattened, as though he was unwilling to give her the satisfaction of knowing that she'd amused him. "I wouldn't say that in front of my father."

"That reminds me—Arinbjorn mentioned that your father is wintering with us after the festival?" King Harald had no permanent residence, but had estates such as this one where he would spend varying lengths of time.

"Yes," Eirik said. "And his latest wife is with him."

Gunnhild's eyes widened. "Wait—there are only the two private chambers in the hall. Yours"—*soon to be* ours, *which I have yet to set foot in*—"and Gyda's. Are he and the wife *both* staying in Gyda's chamber?"

"My father and *Queen* Gyda have been married for fifty winters. I assure you she's not offended. His wives all usually stay at their own estates and he visits them on his progress, but there's little ill will between them. Except for the ones he cast aside when he married *my* mother, and then took back up when she died. They're still a little bitter, I think. Understandably."

When Gunnhild didn't say anything, Eirik gave her a sidelong look. "Part of the reason my father was able to unite the country was that he went around marrying the daughters of important men."

"Hmm."

"It's called strategy, Gunnhild. And need I remind you that *this* strategy in particular is one that I myself am forsaking in accordance with *your* marriage terms?"

"You didn't have to agree to them."

"You took advantage of my desperation."

Gunnhild stopped and glared at him. "I wasn't trying to deny you anything. I wish to prevent the same strife happening in your family now from happening again. Clearly, you yourself wouldn't know strategy if it jumped out of the latrine and bit you in the—"

He stopped as well and put his hands on her shoulders. "We can quarrel about this to your heart's content later."

"There's nothing to quarrel about." His touch seemed to burn her through her clothes, and the fresh scar on her left palm started to prickle. She ignored both and stuck her chin in the air. "We already swore upon it."

"I meant—never mind. Listen. We have to present a united front to my father. Once he finds out about you and about our marriage terms, and of your profession, he's going to be furious. You only have one chance to make a good impression. It might lessen his anger."

"Take your hands off me," she said. When he did, they started walking again, and she decided to change the subject. "So, what's so special about this new wife that he takes her with him when he travels?"

"Who knows? Maybe it's his old age, but he seems especially attached to her. And their son. He's maybe four winters old. He'll be fostered somewhere else soon, I'm sure."

Gunnhild hadn't realized that Eirik had brothers who were so young. "*Another* son? Will your father never quit?"

"He's over seventy winters old. If he hasn't quit by now, I doubt he ever will."

"Has he claimed the child? Did he name it?"

"He did. His name is Hakon. The mother is Thora. She hasn't the title of queen, but she's of good enough birth. And they're no threat, if that's what you're thinking."

"Good. At least you have one brother who doesn't want to kill you."
Yet, she added mentally, but he glared at her as if she'd said the word
aloud.

Queen Gyda waited at the jetty, a light blue fur-lined cape on her
shoulders. She seemed tense, and Gunnhild could imagine why: The old
queen experienced a certain degree of autonomy by running the estate on
her own. King Harald's visits were doubtless more of a bother to her than
anything else; she was likely already counting the days until he left at
winter's end.

She looked Gunnhild up and down, much the same as Eirik had, but
only sniffed and turned back to search the crowd milling about the ships.
Gunnhild's cheeks burned. She could only assume Queen Gyda disap-
proved of the ducks.

And then a man, followed by a servant wielding three massive hounds
on thick leather leashes, came toward them amid the throng. Gunnhild
had never met him before but recognized him by his posture, his clothing, and his uncanny resemblance to Eirik.

Fifty years ago, as a man of some twenty winters, King Harald had
united the petty kingdoms of Norway under one rule. Tall and broad
shouldered with a full head of silver hair, he was now old and a bit
hunched, but he had the air of someone who had, in his prime, been im-
mensely strong. Gunnhild got the distinct impression that she was looking
at the spitting image of Eirik forty winters from now.

The king's rich blue cloak was lined with fur and hid most of his
body, but when he waved an arm to direct the servant with the dogs to
the hall and then embraced Queen Gyda, Gunnhild saw the fine garments beneath: a blue tunic and pants, trimmed with gold-threaded
tablet-woven bands and faced with silk at the neck and cuffs. The belt
over his tunic was studded with stylized gold fittings, the blue leg wraps
around his calves secured with gold hooks just below the knees. A simple
but thick gold circlet rested atop his head. The dye for his clothing had
probably been more costly than the clothing itself, Gunnhild thought.

King Harald broke from his wife and turned to his son, clapping him
on the shoulder. "Ah, Eirik. I heard you won a great victory this summer

on the Dvina River. I trust your skald will regale us all with a more detailed account of your exploits soon enough."

"That's what I pay him for," Eirik said, his smile becoming strained. Gunnhild knew from Runfrid that the hirdsmen still refused to speak of that battle. Svein would have his work cut out for him trying to make it into a poem that would entertain the hall without causing himself and his friends an undue amount of pain; for all that the skald now seemed to hate her on Thorolf's behalf, Gunnhild felt for him.

Then King Harald's eyes were upon her. "And who is this?"

"Gunnhild Ozurardottir." She held his gaze and kept her spine straight. "My father is one of your hersar in Halogaland. It's truly an honor to meet you."

"Gunnhild and I are to be married on the second feast day," said Eirik.

King Harald seemed surprised. "The daughter of a hersir isn't a bad match by any means, but it's hardly the most advantageous for the future king of Norway." He looked at Gunnhild askance, then back to Eirik. "Still, she's beautiful, and for a first wife—don't tell me this is for love?"

"We have much to discuss, Father," Eirik said tightly.

King Harald turned back to Gunnhild. "The silk you're wearing—is it an heirloom?"

"I—" Gunnhild looked down at the ducks, surprised, then back up at him. "Yes, but not my own. I bought it from Saeunn Hrolfsdottir. It was once part of a dress belonging to her grandmother, or so she said."

To her surprise, King Harald smiled. "Her grandmother was a friend of my mother's and often cared for me when I was very small. I remember her having a dress with that pattern of silk. It's a fond memory." He looked at her approvingly, as if this were a good omen.

Gunnhild resisted the urge to gloat—*He likes the ducks!*—but King Harald had already returned his attention to his chosen heir.

"I expect you to behave yourself once your brothers arrive," the old king said sagely, but with the undercurrent of a threat.

The smile dropped from Eirik's face. "I will if they will."

"You can discuss this later, along with the circumstances surrounding

Eirik's marriage," said Queen Gyda, who caught Gunnhild's eye and gave her a withering look. "Come. It's cold down here in the wind. We— ah, dear me, he's gotten big, hasn't he?"

The chatter on the dock was broken by a young child's high-pitched whining. A short, homely woman came up behind King Harald, dragging the source of the noise behind her. Harald introduced her as Thora and the red-faced child as Hakon. Queen Gyda approached Thora with genuine warmth and bent to embrace her, then to hug Hakon, who allowed himself to be kissed on the cheek before squirming out of her arms.

"It's a pleasure to meet you both," Thora said to Gunnhild and Eirik, who replied in kind. Gunnhild immediately liked the woman despite herself; she had a gentle disposition.

Hakon brandished a small wooden sword and began smacking Queen Gyda in the leg, and Thora chuckled as she waved him away.

"He's a rambunctious little fellow. Obsessed with that sword!" Thora smiled at Eirik, her cheeks dimpling. "Perhaps his older brother will show him how to swing it properly on the field this winter?"

"I—yes, of course." Eirik seemed a bit taken aback, as though he were unused to being spoken to with any sort of fondness. This stirred up a feeling within Gunnhild that troubled her, so she shoved it back down into the crevice in her mind from whence it came.

Reunion complete, Queen Gyda ushered King Harald, Thora, and Hakon toward the warm hall, following the train of servants and thralls with their possessions.

Eirik and Gunnhild looked at each other once they were out of earshot.

"You're right," she said. "Thora and the boy seem quite . . . wholesome."

"I *told* you they're nothing to worry about," he replied.

Gunnhild looked past him and said darkly, "Speaking of worries, this must be Olaf."

"*King* Olaf." Eirik turned around to face his brother. "You have a lot of nerve showing up here."

"I can't say I have any idea what you mean," said Olaf. He was dressed in finery similar to his father's, as if he'd anticipated presiding over a great feast the moment he stepped off the boat. But as far as faces went, his was nondescript. There were hints of Eirik and Harald there, but only just. He was of a shorter build than his father and brother as well, round faced with a receding hairline, but with those same cold blue eyes.

"Father invited us," Olaf continued. "This *is*, after all, *his* estate. Not yours." He turned to Gunnhild and looked her up and down. "And you are—"

"My betrothed," Eirik said flatly.

Olaf arched an eyebrow. "I always assumed you'd marry someone prettier."

Gunnhild gave him a bland smile. "And I assumed a brother of Eirik's would be taller, considering your stock. But I think we both know that looks aren't everything, don't we, King Olaf?"

Olaf studied her for a long moment before he threw his head back and let out a short, humorless laugh. "Well, at least this one's got some wit. Let's hope she has enough for both of you, eh, Eirik?"

With that he shoved past the two of them, and Eirik said to his retreating back, "I don't see my nephews here. Did Father not invite them as well?"

Olaf turned back to face them, his mouth twisted with scorn. "You think Gudrod wanted to come to a wedding to celebrate the man who killed his father? No—he and Tryggvi are enjoying the Winternights festivities back in Vestfold, where I'll have no worries for their safety. I don't want those boys anywhere near the likes of you."

Eirik took a menacing step toward him, and Gunnhild reached for his bicep in a vain attempt to hold him back. "Stop. This is exactly what he wants."

To her surprise, Eirik relaxed.

But then, from behind them came an airy, whimsical, *familiar* voice: "Yes, King Eirik. To trade blows the moment your guest steps off a ship will only reflect badly upon you. And we don't want that, do we?"

Gunnhild's blood ran cold.

A tiny woman approached them from the ship, her white woolen dress seeming to glow in the midday sun. She had no cloak despite the chill but wore fine gloves, a fur cap, and a belt laden with pouches and feathers and bones. She carried a sack over her shoulder with one hand and held an iron staff in the other. Underneath the cap she had long, straight white-blond hair that flowed past her waist. Her wide eyes were a honeyed brown beneath pale lashes.

And though she had addressed Eirik, she was staring directly at Gunnhild, who drew in a sharp breath when their eyes met.

Thorbjorg.

The woman grinned, revealing small, pearly white teeth as she came toward Gunnhild, who had released Eirik's arm and stepped forward to meet her. "Why, whatever is the matter? You look as if you've just seen a revenant."

What Gunnhild *saw* in her mind's eye was Heid's corpse and Oddny's burning farm. Vestein Ketilsson falling into the water with an arrow through his windpipe. Yrsa cut down with her own axe. Thorolf's haunted look as he remembered the friends he'd slain on the battlefield, blighted by Thorbjorg's madness, in order to save his king's life. And Signy's bound feet slamming down onto the head of a small white fox.

Would that I could strangle you with my bare hands, Gunnhild wanted to say. But no; they were witches. And they had quicker, cleaner ways to kill.

She gave Thorbjorg a placid look and said, "I'm sorry. Have we met?"

The corners of Thorbjorg's amber eyes crinkled with distaste as she struggled to keep smiling. "We haven't met face-to-face, no—but your reputation precedes you, Gunnhild."

"Strange, isn't that, considering I've yet to make a name for myself? You seem to know something I don't." Gunnhild tilted her head sideways, catlike, feigning confusion. "And yet I've never even *heard* of you . . ."

"Thorbjorg," said the other witch through clenched teeth, lips barely moving.

"A pleasure, Thorbjorg. That's a very fine cap. Is it fox fur? Red fox?"

"It is."

"I should like to have one of my own someday." Gunnhild took a step closer and pitched her voice low enough that not even Eirik, still standing nearby, could hear. "But I think I'd prefer mine to be white."

"Thorbjorg," Olaf called. He'd continued toward the longhouse but had stopped to witness the witches' conversation, though he was out of earshot. "Come."

Thorbjorg didn't turn. She kept her eyes on Gunnhild for another beat before the smile dropped from her face, her composure suddenly lost.

"You can't prove *anything*," she spat, looking as though she'd like nothing more than to strike Gunnhild down on the spot. "Whatever you think you know, you don't."

"Thorbjorg," Olaf said again, warningly.

"Your papa is calling you," Gunnhild sneered.

"The closest person I've ever had to a father is *dead*. Killed by the very man you've so unwisely chosen to throw in your lot with," Thorbjorg said, her eyes blazing with hatred. "Eirik Haraldsson is a bully and a brute. He is no great sea king—he owns only what King Harald has handed to him and steals the rest. And on my life, he *will* get what he deserves. He's unworthy of being his father's successor, just as you yourself are unworthy of the staff you carry. You should have buried it with the old woman."

With that, Thorbjorg pushed past her and followed Olaf, leaving Gunnhild furious and, frankly, a bit put out by how quickly she'd lost control of the conversation.

"Olaf wasn't wrong about your wit," Eirik said from behind her as they watched his brother and Thorbjorg go, "but I don't need you to fight my battles for me."

"I *beg your pardon*?" Gunnhild rounded on him. "Is that not the entire reason we're getting married?"

She saw him tense, as if he were holding himself back from hitting her with one of his clenched fists.

"Stay your hand. It's not I whom you wish to strike." She raised her chin and stared him down. "And if you do, I'll make you sorry you were ever born."

The tension released. "I'm sorry. My brothers bring out the worst in me. Olaf in particular . . ." He shook his head and ran a hand through his windswept hair, and they started walking back toward the longhouse.

"I know. And Thorbjorg all but admitted to enacting her petty vengeances just now," Gunnhild said.

Eirik perked up. "Can we prove it? Bring the matter to my father and the Lawspeaker?"

"No. It's only my word against hers, and I have a feeling it won't be enough for your father."

"At least we won't have to worry about her causing any mischief with him in residence," Eirik said bitterly.

"Any *overt* mischief, that is." Gunnhild sighed. "While we're on the topic of people who wish to kill you, what of the boys he mentioned, your nephews? Gudrod and Tryggvi?"

Eirik shook his head. "Gudrod is Bjorn's son. Olaf fosters him."

"Was Gudrod Bjorn's only son?"

"Yes. There was a daughter, too, a few winters older than Gudrod, but long dead as far as I know. We never met. Bjorn's wife died giving birth to Gudrod and he never married again."

"I see. Well, is there anyone else coming to our wedding who wants to kill you? And will you scold me for defending you against *them*, too?"

"Enough," he said, his voice loud enough to scatter the seabirds that had been congregating nearby. He stopped walking and gestured wildly with his hands, more annoyed than angry. "You're to fight only *specific* battles for me, and only at my *express* command."

"Your command? Ha!" Gunnhild poked a finger at his chest. "What happened to 'perhaps we can work *together*'? I'm going to be your wife, not your servant. You didn't hire me. You don't command me. Am I understood?"

Eirik waved her hand away. "Be that as it may—"

"Am I *understood*?"

"Gunnhild," barked Queen Gyda from the door of the longhouse. "Is that how you would speak to your husband, let alone your king?" She turned to someone in the shadows behind her. "You see? It's just as I told you."

King Harald appeared beside her, his expression like thunder, pale eyes fixed on Eirik, and with one jerk of his head he ordered his son inside and disappeared without waiting to see if Eirik would follow.

Eirik and Gunnhild stood completely still, but out of the corner of her eye, she saw him swallow and step forward to heed his father's summons.

"*I* was going to tell him everything," Eirik said to Queen Gyda.

"Now you don't have to," said his stepmother sweetly, stepping aside to let him pass. "You need only explain yourself."

When the queen's eyes turned to her, Gunnhild's heart dropped into the pit of her stomach and she followed Eirik inside.

21

KING HARALD AT LEAST had the decency to berate his son in private, which was more than Gunnhild's mother had ever done for her. She stood outside the door to his chamber and strained to listen above the noise that two more kings' retinues had added to the hall.

She caught the words "bewitched" and "ensorcelled," along with "Have you learned nothing?" and "How could you be so foolish?" and pressed her ear more firmly against the door. It seemed King Harald was pacing, for his voice faded in and out.

"A king should take as many wives and sire as many children as he pleases," he said. "And she seeks to deny you this, *and* wishes to be seen as your peer? As *the* queen? That's absurd. How could you have ever thought to agree to such madness? Marrying a witch. And for what? To protect against threats that don't exist? She's cast some sort of spell on you—"

Eirik cut in. "She hasn't. I was the one who approached *her* about this, Father. My hird are sworn to protect me, and I must do the same for them. My brothers—"

"Have vowed to me that they are guilty of no wrongdoing."

"They're lying. You don't believe what my men and I have witnessed with our own eyes? Ask Arinbjorn. He and Thorolf—"

"Do not speak to me of Skallagrim's son," said King Harald in disgust. "I've told you before that one day you'd regret your friendship with him. I should have never allowed it in the first place."

"That you did is the reason I'm alive. He and Arinbjorn killed four of my other hirdsmen to save me. They were—it wasn't natural. I watched them die, Father."

"Men die," King Harald said flippantly.

"Not like this." Eirik's voice was thick with emotion. "You won't stop this. And I can't prove anything to you without Gunnhild's help. What else am I to do?"

"Put that woman aside and cease this nonsense immediately, or you'll force me to find a new successor. You can't be trusted to rule if your mind is under the sway of some paltry sorceress."

"And you would know, wouldn't you?" Eirik shot back.

The silence that followed was so fraught that it made the hairs on Gunnhild's arms stand on end; she could feel the tension even on the other side of the door. Something told her that Eirik had never spoken to his father that way before.

"Get out of my sight, boy," King Harald said at last, venom in every word. "We'll speak on this again when you've come to your senses and apologized for your disrespect."

The door swung open so abruptly that it very nearly smacked Gunnhild in the face, but she managed to step aside in time to avoid it. When Eirik halted in the doorway, pain and rage and frustration warred on his face.

She almost said something, almost reached for him, and then—

"See what happens, King," said Queen Gyda to her husband, "when you let his leash slacken?"

Eirik's countenance became a storm, and he fled as quickly as his dignity would allow.

Gunnhild did not know what came over her in the moments that followed. As she'd listened to the old king carrying on, suddenly she'd been a child again, shouted down by her own mother for some perceived slight.

She realized then how lucky she'd been to escape Solveig so young. She knew that Eirik had been raised with Arinbjorn, and Arinbjorn himself seemed to have turned out well enough—but it was clear that the expectation to obey the king, to please the king, to follow his orders, to respect him no matter what, had been beaten into Eirik, most likely from birth. His loyalty to, his respect for, and his fear of King Harald were things that had not been earned. They had been expected.

And what had his father given him in return, save for the promise of a power that Eirik had never asked for, and that so far had caused only misfortune for those around him?

She remembered her words to Solveig—*I would rather have been loved*—and realized it was entirely possible that Eirik felt the same.

Gunnhild stepped into the doorway and peered into the chamber, and its lavish trappings faded into nothing as she regarded the king and queen. They'd been talking to each other, saying things she couldn't hear for the blood roaring in her ears, and when they noticed her, they startled. The dogs sleeping at King Harald's feet looked up impassively, and the king opened his mouth to reprimand her for her interruption, but Gunnhild spoke first.

"Perhaps it is you, King, who has been disrespectful," she said. "Eirik is your chosen successor, not one of your hounds. And if this is how you would treat your favorite son, I shudder to think how you treat the rest of them."

She left without waiting for either of them to respond and went to find Eirik.

GUNNHILD FOLLOWED HIM TO the stables, where she saw him leap onto a horse and ride bareback in the direction of the woods.

"Damn," she said. And then, to one of the stable hands: "Saddle one for me, please." While Eirik was obviously a skilled rider, she was the opposite. But she'd never catch him on foot.

The horse that was brought out for her looked as excited about being ridden as she felt about riding it. She waved the stable hands away when they tried to help her up onto the saddle; instead she used a fence as a foothold as she clambered onto the creature's back.

It launched straight into a gallop the moment she flicked the reins, and she found herself barely able to steer it toward the path leading into the trees. People leapt out of the way, dropping baskets of food and laundry and whatever else they'd been carrying, squawking in outrage as she passed by.

"Sorry!" Gunnhild called, but her voice was lost to the wind as she flew down the path and through the pasture. Soon she was among the trees, enveloped by the warm, comforting hues of the autumn foliage around her.

She saw movement ahead and pulled hard on the reins, causing her mount to halt with an irritated whinny. Eirik had steered his horse down a deer path that Gunnhild would most definitely have missed if she weren't tracking him, and she guided her own horse down it. When she got to where his horse was tied to a tree, she slid gracelessly off her own and tied it up as well. Eirik was nowhere in sight, but the path was there, though narrower now.

She followed it until it opened up into a clearing, in the center of which lay a grove of silver birch trees; their leaves were green yet, and Gunnhild could not help but notice how *still* the woods felt here, how peaceful. No animal noises, not even the rustling of underbrush save for that caused by her own steps. She stopped to stare, then took a hesitant step forward, leaves crunching underfoot.

Eirik sat on a stump just inside the clearing, facing the birch grove.

"Go away," he said without turning around.

"What is this place?" she asked breathlessly. "I don't—*oh*."

In the centermost tree of the grove there was a hollow, and inside the hollow was a weathered effigy of Freyja. It looked much different than Heid's old statue, but it felt the same.

"Ah," Gunnhild whispered. "I wondered why she wasn't in the workshop."

The small wooden figure wore a cloak of feathers and her famous necklace, both attributes intricately, lovingly carved. Stashed around the idol was an assortment of feathers, beads, brass trinkets, and coins that looked to be from distant lands.

"I come here to be alone," Eirik said grumpily without getting up, and she could feel his eyes on her as she stepped past him to examine the shrine. "But it looks like others visit, too—those amber beads weren't here last time."

"Hush for a moment," she said without rancor. "I wish to make an offering."

She could sense the retort on his tongue—You're *the one disturbing* me—but he said nothing, which worried her. He must be feeling lower than she'd thought. But she didn't question it. There would be time for that later.

Gunnhild took the small knife from her belt, pricked her pinkie finger without so much as a wince, and allowed her blood to drip onto the top of the figure. Watched it run down through the grooves of Freyja's hair and necklace and cloak until it reached the statue's flat base. She closed her eyes.

Lend me the strength to deal with my new in-laws and my husband, and to defeat Thorbjorg and avenge Heid, one of your most dedicated devotees, she prayed. *You may consider Thorbjorg just as much your daughter as I am, but if blood and terror and greatness are in my future, then I will at least dedicate the blood to you.*

Let it sate you. Let it result in more bodies in your hall, a bigger army for when you battle your foes at Ragnarok.

If I am to be the cause of much death, then let that death serve you.

And let it begin with Thorbjorg's.

When she opened her eyes, she turned around to see that Eirik had stood, and he was looking at her with minor concern. She smirked. "Have you forgotten how Freyja receives half the battle-slain in her own hall? My goddess enjoys her flowers and baubles as much as the next, but sometimes she prefers blood."

Eirik folded his arms and raised his eyebrows. "The duality of woman?"

"You're catching on." Gunnhild gestured around them. "Whose place is this? Whose statue?"

For a moment she thought he wouldn't answer, would stalk away to go brood somewhere else, but he surprised her.

"I wish I knew," Eirik said, looking up at the unseasonably green canopy of birch leaves. "My mother used to bring me here when the seeresses passed through. I was so small when she died, and those are the only memories I have of her."

"You mentioned your father put some of his other wives aside for her," Gunnhild said, not quite knowing what else to say. "She must've been quite a woman for him to do something like that."

"She was the daughter of a Danish king, so if I had to guess, I'd say her father worked it into their marriage terms." He gave her the ghost of a smile. "She moved to Alreksstadir after the wedding. She was here for only a short time before she died, but she was popular. So if you ever hear people speak of Queen Ragnhild—that was her."

"So she lived on this estate, too?" Gunnhild asked. "With Queen Gyda? And there were no bitter feelings?"

"Queen Gyda wasn't one of the wives my father divorced in order to marry her, so no."

"But that's why there are two separate bedchambers?"

"Yes. The one we're staying in once belonged to my mother. As did this grove. She had a special interest in the workings of witches. Not that it saved her in the end." He looked away. "But every time I'm here, I come to this place at least once. My father ordered that it remain untouched in my mother's memory."

"I see," Gunnhild said. That was rather more sentimental than she would've expected from King Harald, but then again, this was a man who'd accused his wife of witchcraft when he'd fallen too deeply in love with her. It was little wonder that Eirik seemed just as scared of his own feelings. Gunnhild figured it must run in the family.

"It still feels like my mother here," Eirik said, gesturing at the still, empty air around them. "Maybe she's one of the fylgjur now, one of the fate spirits looking out for our family line. I suppose it's comforting, in a way, to think of my foremothers keeping watch while my forefathers feast in Valhalla."

Gunnhild suppressed a shudder. "They say you see your fylgja when something terrible is about to happen. If that's true, I have even more reason to hope I never see my mother again." She shifted. "Ever since I was a child, it's troubled me that only people who die in battle can hope for a glorious afterlife with the gods. Ending up with Hel or Ran always sounded terribly dull—that can't be what most women expect, can it? I quite like the idea of becoming a fylgja instead when I die."

"Well, you're a witch. I'm sure Freyja would welcome you into her hall. Would she not give her own kind the afterlife you deserve?"

Gunnhild was both touched and alarmed that he spoke of Freyja with such reverence, especially after every witch in the north had turned against him. While she supposed his interest in her goddess explained why he'd dubbed his cats Hnoss and Gersemi, it didn't explain something that had been bothering her since she'd learned the creatures' names.

"It seems to me that you hold more respect for the magic arts than I thought. But," she ventured, "if that's true, how could you have gone through with killing your brother Rognvald?"

Eirik's face darkened. "Because it's not right for men to practice magic. Men are meant to pick up swords and fight out their problems. Magic is for cowards and women."

"And yet," Gunnhild said, "you honor the likeness of Odin in the main hall *and* the armory *and* the temple. Is he not also a witch? Did Freyja not also teach him magic?"

"Odin is different," Eirik said stiffly, with an infuriating matter-of-factness that made her suspect that he was regurgitating the words of another. She had a strong suspicion as to who. "He's also the patron of kings."

"But did Rognvald not also honor him?" she pressed. "Tell me—before you burned him alive in his hall, did you see whose statue your brother had lofted upon *his* lintel?"

Eirik's eyes went wide and he drew away from her. She didn't know what he was seeing in that moment in his mind's eye, but she could hazard a guess.

"I don't know what you wish me to say," he said, voice hushed. "There's no way to undo what I've done, and now I'm paying the price. I regret—"

"Do you? Would you still regret it if Thorbjorg weren't so intent on avenging him?"

"Yes, I would. Would *you* care about the enslaved women on this estate if you didn't picture your friend as one of them? I've heard about that charm of yours—men seem to have been blighted with pustules upon trying to enter the weaving huts. It was noble enough of you, but whatever you do for them won't help Signy Ketilsdottir."

"You're a beast," she said, because he wasn't wrong, and she hated it.

Eirik was silent. Then he said, "That's not the worst I've been called."

Any pity she'd felt for him when he was being castigated by his father and stepmother had evaporated. "I find you endlessly vexing. It's clear to me now that you've never had an original thought in your entire life. You're King Harald's creature through and through. You're lucky to have Arinbjorn at your side—he sees the need to humble you, lest your head get as big as your father's."

"Don't speak of my father that way," Eirik snapped.

"And why shouldn't I, after hearing the way he speaks to you? He says, *Go kill your brother,* and you say, *Yes, my king,* and then you say ridiculous things like *Magic is for cowards and women.* Do you hear yourself? He's tried to make you in his exact image."

Eirik was visibly uncomfortable now, his reddened face twisted up like that of a child about to throw a tantrum. "Is that such a bad thing?"

"Yes. Because if you can't admit that your father isn't perfect, how are you ever supposed to become better than him?"

He flinched as if she'd struck him, and she braced herself for him to rage at her or order her to go away. But instead he only looked at her, and didn't move, and didn't speak.

She wanted to smack some sense into him. She wanted to grab his hair with both fists and—

No. The next thought was horrifying, exciting, and completely unwelcome. *No, no, no.* It was better, easier, to think of him as a heartless monster.

But he was scared. He was *vulnerable.* She saw it now. This, from a man who had never known anything soft in all his days, who probably had only the faintest memories of a gentle presence in his life, unnerved her more than anything else.

And then the moment passed, and he was himself again.

"You are steering this conversation onto thin ice," he said. "Tread carefully." The words, her own words thrown back at her, were low, harsh, clipped. He regarded her now with his usual contempt, which she returned in kind, with an anger stronger than anything else she'd ever felt—because it was born of disappointment, of the dashing of her own optimism.

She saw her foolishness now. It was folly to think for even one moment that this man could be anything other than what he was. What he had been born to be, and molded into.

It was only when his horse's hoofbeats faded into the distance that her heart slowed its rapid pounding and she sat down on the stump, put her head in her hands.

What have I gotten myself into?

BY THE TIME SHE'D returned the horse to its stall and walked back to the workshop, it was past suppertime and her stomach growled ferociously. It seemed the workshop women had gotten their hands on some hot cider, for Gunnhild recognized the smell of apples wafting from the cauldron over the center hearth. She went to sit by Oddny, who sat sewing, while Ulla was nalbinding a sock—and surprisingly, Runfrid the tattooist was there, too, sewing a rip in the sleeve of a kaftan.

"The whole hird's in the armory to make room in the hall for the other kings and their guests," Runfrid explained when Gunnhild expressed surprise at her presence. "Oddny invited me here for some quiet. I figured since you were all done working for the day, no one would try to shove a spindle or shuttle into my hands."

"What happened, Gunna?" Oddny asked. "Where have you been all day? How did it go with King Harald?"

The moment Gunnhild entered, Ulla had gotten up and returned with a steaming cup of cider, which Gunnhild accepted with gratitude. Ulla settled back in beside Oddny and went back to her nalbinding.

"Judging by the mood Eirik was in when he returned to the armory," said Runfrid, "I'm thinking it didn't go well."

Gunnhild looked at Runfrid and Ulla, then at Oddny, and grimaced. "I'll say this much: I doubt King Harald will let me do the sacrifice now, let alone a ritual on top of it."

"You were going to do a ritual?" Ulla asked, eyes huge. "I've never seen a Norse seeress tell the future before."

"But you're still getting married, aren't you?" Oddny asked, her eyes searching Gunnhild's. "He hasn't made Eirik put you aside?"

Not if Eirik doesn't decide to do it himself first, after the conversation we just had, Gunnhild thought. But she said, "Not yet. For now, I'm still to be married in a few days' time, which means we're still going to Birka in the spring." She leaned against the post behind her and took a sip of cider. "Winternights would still be the perfect time to do this. Yule would work as well, but the fact that Katla and Thorbjorg are here gives us an advantage now that we won't have then."

Oddny worried at the skin of her bottom lip with her teeth as she thought. "What if we did the ritual right here in the workshop and kept it private instead? Everyone will be at the feast. We can ask one of the men to keep an eye on Thorbjorg and Katla to make sure they don't leave the longhouse to interfere."

"Who are Thorbjorg and Katla?" Ulla asked, cocking her head.

Runfrid lowered her sewing. "Wait, isn't the point of a ritual to tell everyone's futures? Why make it private?"

Oddny and Gunnhild exchanged a long look. Neither of them were sure whom they could trust here, especially with the identity of the third witch still a mystery. As for Runfrid and Ulla, Gunnhild had come to like them over the course of their very short acquaintance, and both were now looking at her with sincere concern and confusion. Oddny, who seemed to have spent more time with the two than Gunnhild had, nodded and elbowed her softly in the arm as if to say, *Tell them.*

Gunnhild relayed everything from the beginning, from her leaving home and learning magic, with Oddny helping to fill in the gaps until she got to the day of the raid and everything that had happened since she'd met Eirik, ending with the conversation she'd overheard between Eirik and his father, and what she'd said to King Harald before following her betrothed into the woods.

"But I lost sight of him in the trees, and haven't seen him since," she finished. It was the only untruth she'd told. What had happened in the grove had stirred something in her, something she wished to keep private until she could either rid herself of it or put it into words.

By then Gunnhild's cider had gone completely cool, and Runfrid was so furious that she threw down her sewing and dug her fingers into her knees.

The tattooist said, "To say nothing of how King Harald has treated Eirik—which I can speak to *at length*, and by the gods, Gunnhild, you were right to say to him what you did, even if you pay for it later—I can't believe *that's* what happened in Bjarmaland. The men still won't speak of that battle. Not even Arinbjorn will tell me anything. By Skadi's bow, it kills me to see him like this, that look he gets when he thinks I'm not watching him—and it's all because of *her*? This *witch*?"

Ulla was more contemplative than angry. "This Thorbjorg. Can we not simply"—she splayed her hands innocently—"poison her breakfast?"

"No," said Oddny, turning to Gunnhild. "You confronted her publicly at the docks. If she were to be found dead, you'd be the first person they suspected. And if that happens, there'll be more proof of your wrongdoing against her than of hers against you."

Ulla sighed. "I suppose that's true. And Thorbjorg is replaceable, isn't she? King Olaf could always hire another witch."

"Right," said Runfrid. "So you need to keep her and her friend distracted while you ask the spirits to help you find Oddny's sister, and you need us to sing for you while you do it. Is that correct?"

Gunnhild's lack of ability to commune with the spirits was something she'd left out of the story—something *no one* could know besides herself and Oddny, lest it somehow get back to Eirik that her powers were hampered. She could only hope that this time, with so many voices and at such a powerful time of year, things would be different. They had to be.

"Yes," Gunnhild said. "Exactly."

Ulla clapped her hands together. "Well, then, I'm sure we'll make it a great success."

"I can ask Arinbjorn to keep an eye on Thorbjorg and Katla," said Runfrid. She turned to Oddny. "Why don't you ask Halldor to watch them, too? That way if one or the other of the men gets drunk or falls asleep—"

"Why—why would I be the one to ask Halldor?" Oddny stammered.

Runfrid blinked at her. "Ah, well, when I was doing his bindrune tattoo, he spoke very highly of you. I'd thought you were friends—"

"Friends?" Gunnhild scoffed. "He was one of the raiders who destroyed her farm. He owes her twelve marks of silver."

"Eleven and a half," Oddny said.

"Maybe I misinterpreted what he was saying." Runfrid did not sound convinced.

"I've barely spoken to him since we arrived," Oddny said. "But—yes, I suppose I could ask him. It's a good idea to have a few of the men know what we're up to, in case things go badly. But we shouldn't tell anyone else, just in case."

"We could ask more of the women here to sing, couldn't we?" Ulla asked. "Isn't that how the warding songs work? More voices, more protection?"

Gunnhild cast a furtive glance around them before replying. "We have reason not to trust everyone here. Because of the third witch, like we told you."

Ulla looked troubled. "Who do you suspect?"

"No one, so far," Gunnhild assured her. "But what happens to you once you send your mind out is reflected in your physical body, so if we see anyone with a bruise on their face—"

"But Arinbjorn told me how fast you were able to heal your hand with magic back in Finnmark, Gunnhild—if Eirik's kick had left a visible mark on this witch when she was a seal, couldn't she have just healed it herself before anyone noticed?" said Runfrid.

Gunnhild was quiet, seeing the reason in this.

Ulla added, "In terms of who to trust, there are a few of the new girls that I'm not too sure about. But the rest I'd vouch for without question."

Runfrid shrugged. "Well, that's good enough for me. I'm friendly with some of the artisans around the estate. Hrafnhild and the cookhouse girls, too. I could invite them as well. The ones I don't suspect of being murderous sorceresses."

"We can't let this get too big," Gunnhild said, raising her hands. "The way King Harald talked about me—about witchcraft—I suspect worse things than a broken engagement will happen to me if he catches even a whisper of this."

"He won't," said Ulla with conviction. "Saeunn told me once that there hasn't been a seeress at Alreksstadir since the days of Queen Ragnhild. People will be too excited to want to spoil it, even though they won't be hearing their own fortunes. Just to sing and to bear witness—I think that would be enough."

"Let us help you," Runfrid said softly, and Ulla added, "Please."

Gunnhild took a deep breath and set her hands in her lap, curled one around her cold cup of cider. "Right, then. Tell them it will be here, on the third night of the festival."

The other women nodded. The first day of Winternights was the disablot, during which Gunnhild, were she still to perform it, would likely be too visible to sneak away; on the second, the most extravagant of the feast days, with the heaviest drinking, she would be married; and the third was only a feast day. Guests would be so tired by the third night that it wouldn't be notable if some of the women retired early or otherwise slipped away.

Yes, Gunnhild thought. *This plan will succeed. It must.*

The alternative, the loss of the power that made her not just a sorceress but a seeress as well, would be too much to bear. She thought of Heid's staff—her staff, now—hidden safely in her chest below the platform, thought of the blood she'd offered to Freyja that afternoon.

Thorbjorg was wrong. She *was* worthy of the staff. She'd given up half her life to earn it, and earn it she had.

But if she couldn't conduct a successful ritual, then everything she and her friends had been through would be for nothing.

She could not fail.

BY THE EVENING PRIOR to the Winternights festivities, the dock was full of ships lashed to one another. Gunnhild suspected that Olaf and Halfdan weren't the only guests whom King Harald had unexpectedly invited to Alreksstadir for the festival.

For the next few nights after meeting Eirik's father, Gunnhild had sequestered herself in the textile workshop with Oddny and the other women, and worked on her protection spell in the corner. In doing so she managed to avoid both King Harald and Eirik. It had seemed wise to give them both a chance to calm down.

But at this point she could only assume that Eirik had worked things out with his father. The fact that she hadn't been summoned to King Harald and admonished for the way she'd spoken to him made her wonder if perhaps her words had swayed him in his decision to let Eirik go through with marrying her. No one had come to tell her that she was being removed, that the wedding was off, that she wouldn't be performing the disablot. In fact, Queen Gyda herself came by the day before the festival to speak to her about how everything would go, seeming peeved all the while.

"I trust you have a gown you use for sacrifices and such. One that could stand to get bloody," Queen Gyda finished. "But until the disablot, you must look like and behave as women of your status should, even for people who don't yet know your face. They'll recognize you after tomorrow night and remember if you looked slovenly. So you must dress well. Anything less will be frowned upon."

By whom? Gunnhild wanted to ask, but she decided not to press her luck. She made a show of compliance, thanking the queen for her advice and her generosity, and spat on the ground as soon as the woman closed the door behind her.

On the morning of the first feast day Gunnhild awoke to Saeunn cooking porridge in a small cauldron over the hearth fire, the smell making her regret that she wouldn't be eating until after the sacrifice that night. After breakfast, the women went off in groups to socialize until only Gunnhild and Oddny remained, Gunnhild sitting cross-legged on the platform to nervously braid and rebraid her hair, Oddny sitting steadfastly beside her, her own mousy hair already in its thin, orderly braid.

When she was satisfied, Gunnhild stood. "Is it time?"

"It's time," Oddny said.

Gunnhild nodded and shrugged off her dress—the last of Solveig's too-small ones she'd brought from Halogaland—and passed it to Oddny, as promised, who folded it and stuck it in her own chest with the rest of Gunnhild's mother's old clothing. Oddny passed over the last dress she'd sewn: a muted blue woolen underdress dyed from woad, as well as the duck-silk apron-dress. Gunnhild secured the straps with her brooches and the beads Oddny had put together. She'd decided to go without a belt, for she felt it would distract from the rest of her outfit.

"How do I look?" she asked, turning to face Oddny, who had changed into one of the old dresses she'd already hemmed: dyed from nettles, it was a brownish green that matched her eyes.

"Like a queen." Oddny buckled her thin leather belt over her dress, her pouch and knife dangling from it as always. "Shall we?"

Benches and stools had been taken from the longhouse, and guests congregated in packs outside, drinking and catching up and trading gossip, for there were few opportunities to do so outside of sacred festivals and regional assemblies. It was a pleasantly cool day, and Gunnhild and Oddny walked arm in arm through the crowd.

The festival's games were well underway. People had formed a circle around two men locked in a wrestling match, and they were hooting and cheering the combatants on. Runfrid appeared to be winning the archery competition, and raised a hand in greeting as Oddny and Gunnhild passed, then went back to arguing with a woman who seemed to be demanding a rematch. Finally, Oddny and Gunnhild passed two groups of people playing a ball-and-stick game in the practice yard.

Once Gunnhild had scanned the players and determined that Eirik was not among them, she and Oddny drifted toward the field. The first group was made up of adults—mostly young men, but a few young women Gunnhild hadn't seen before—and the second group were all children, with just as many girls as boys. They seemed to be playing rougher than the adults were.

"I don't quite remember the rules," Gunnhild said as they stopped to watch for a while, "but the girls are winning, I think. Do you remember how Vestein and his friends used to beat us when we were kids?"

"Yes. Mostly because I wasn't interested, and you capitulate when you're not immediately the best at something."

"That's not—" Gunnhild paused at the brief memory of Heid whacking her over the hands with a stick every time she complained about wanting, for the exact reason Oddny mentioned, to give up on whatever exercise she was learning. "All right. Fine. That's true."

"That's why Signy would always be the last one standing," Oddny said.

They both sobered at that, but then a roar went up from the other side of the armory. They went around the building and found the source of the noise: Eirik's hirdsmen, cleaner and more well-dressed than she'd ever seen them, gathered near the copse of oak trees where Gunnhild had last seen Thorolf. Against the thickest trunk leaned a wooden board, on which circles of charcoal had been drawn to serve as targets.

"Hah! I win again!" Arinbjorn shouted at Svein as he retrieved his throwing axe from the center of one board. "I think it's time for you to give up, my friend."

"Best four out of seven," Svein said. He, too, held a throwing axe in his hand.

"If you want to lose again, that's fine by me. It'll give you something to remember me by this winter, eh?" Arinbjorn made a kissing face as he

walked to the other side of the line someone had drawn in the dirt, and
Svein laughed and shoved him.

Eirik lounged on a bench, leaning against the outer wall of the armory
and drinking directly out of a pitcher of ale, with two finely dressed
young women—daughters of some rich visitor, Gunnhild guessed—
practically trying to climb into his lap. He wore a tunic in the same pale
blue as her underdress, and a madder red cloak was pinned at his shoulder with an obnoxiously large and intricate brooch. She hated to admit it,
but he cleaned up as well as the rest of his hird.

"Should we let the women take a turn?" Svein asked, turning to the
two sitting with Eirik. Then, as soon as he'd spoken, he noticed that
Gunnhild and Oddny had approached, and he extended his axe to them,
handle out. "How about you two?"

Oddny began, "I don't think we—"

"We'd love to give it a try." Gunnhild saw Eirik's attention turn to
her, but he did not push the women away from him. She ignored him and
took the axe from Svein. After a few moments of trying to reckon the distance, she threw it toward the tree.

It didn't even make it halfway to the target before embedding itself in
the ground with a sad *whump*.

The people around her laughed, the women sitting with Eirik snicker-
ing behind their hands, until Gunnhild whirled around to face them all
with a death glare and they went suddenly quiet. She heard someone
whisper, *"Pustules."*

Oddny stepped up beside her, looking furious on her behalf.

"Give me that," Oddny said, and Arinbjorn handed his axe over.

Gunnhild noted the amused looks on the faces around her. Of course
the hird didn't think that tiny Oddny could do any better than Gunnhild
had done, but Gunnhild knew better.

Oddny barely looked at the target before she threw.

The axe thudded into the centermost circle.

She turned to the small crowd of shocked faces, shrugged, and said,
"Farm girl."

Utter silence followed this pronouncement.

"Well," Arinbjorn said at last, "it seems Oddny Coal-brow has quite an arm."

Svein pumped a fist and said, "Coal-brow!" And the rest of the men joined the chant: *"Coal-brow! Coal-brow! Coal-brow!"*

Oddny laughed, seeming both nervous and delighted, until Eirik got up—much to the offense of the women doting on him, who shot Oddny dirty looks as they left—and handed her the pitcher he'd been drinking out of, and at the men's encouragement she took a long draught. They cheered and Eirik clapped her hard on the back, causing her to spill some of the ale.

Gunnhild, not at all offended by Oddny's showing her up, took this opportunity to steal away to Freyja's grove, where she could enjoy what remained of her time out of the public eye, and collect the bundle of twigs she'd need for the sacrifice. Queen Gyda had been right about one thing: After the disablot, people would know her face.

Tonight, everything would change.

22

ODDNY LOST GUNNHILD IN the chaos that erupted after her
first axe throw. In spite of drinking far too much ale, she managed to best
Arinbjorn six out of ten. After, Svein asked if he could put Oddny up on
his shoulders for a victory lap, and she allowed herself to be paraded
around the estate amid shouts of *"Coal-brow!"* She didn't know how the
hird had come to learn her nickname, but she didn't care. The guests,
many already drunk by midday, took up the chant as they passed, despite
not having the slightest idea what had happened.

When Oddny returned to the workshop near suppertime, she found
that Gunnhild had already changed into her ritual gown and was combing her hair, which fell in gentle waves to her waist. The plain linen dress
that Oddny had sewn for her was stiff in its newness, sun bleached to a
bone white, and soon to be dappled with sacrificial blood.

"How do I look?" Gunnhild asked her for the second time that day.

After a moment's contemplation, Oddny said, "Like a woman in her
underclothes. Who, in a very short time, is going to become someone to
fear."

"That's the idea," Gunnhild said with a grin.

As they left the workshop, Oddny could see Hrafnhild and the other
kitchen staff filing toward the longhouse, carrying pitchers of ale, while
Hrafnhild herself led a healthy-looking bull by a rope. Oddny felt for the

poor creature, but knew that it would feel no pain, and its sacrifice would please the disir and nourish all the guests in attendance.

"Well," said Oddny, "shall we?"

ODDNY HAD NEVER SEEN anywhere else lit so brightly at night-time. As there were too many guests to fit into the temple, the disablot would occur in the longhouse, and the air was thick with the scents of woodsmoke and sweat and alcohol. Trestle tables and benches had been set up all around the hall, except for the spaces marked out for the sacrifice and for the skalds' performances later. The gold stamps adorning the posts seemed to glow in the light from the hearth fires, the hanging braziers, and the lamps on each table.

Oddny hovered near the door with Runfrid and Ulla, who were holding lanterns, waiting to aid in the short procession that would follow the ceremony. Oddny had left her belt and knife outside the door, as no weapons were allowed save for the one that would be used to carry out the sacrifice. Like many of the other guests, the two women had stripped down to their linen underlayers so as not to mar their everyday clothing with blood, and Oddny followed suit. She held her wool dress wadded in a ball under one arm, her mother's statue of Eir tucked under the other, and waited between Runfrid and Ulla, the three of them silent and anxious on Gunnhild's behalf.

They didn't have to wait long. A shallow dais had been built at the front of the hall, and atop it stood Gunnhild next to a massive flat stone that had been hauled in to serve as an altar, and to which the stunned bull had been tied. The statues of the gods lurked above and behind her on the lintel.

Once the hall had filled up and gone quiet, Gunnhild began.

She was a sight to behold, the firelight casting her hair in red-gold and turning her eyes to glowing embers. But what Oddny found most arresting was Gunnhild's confidence, as well as her utter lack of expression, as though she was a woman possessed. The way Gunnhild carried herself reminded Oddny distinctly of the old seeress on that night so long ago, the booming of her voice harking back to Heid's own as Gunnhild said all the right words: thanking the disir for granting good fortunes this past year, dedicating the bull to them, and asking them to bestow health and prosperity upon everyone present. Then Eirik—dressed similarly to her in a simple linen undertunic and pants—came forward with a plain but wickedly sharp axe and took off the creature's head with one swing, sending a spray of blood across himself and the people seated nearby.

Oddny always winced at that part, for it could go horribly wrong if the axe wasn't sharp enough or its wielder wasn't strong enough, but by and large decapitation was better than other ways of killing, which would prolong the animal's suffering. Its blood ran down the altar stone and into a large clay bowl etched with runes, but soon the dais was also soaked, a red puddle spreading to where Gunnhild stood, soaking her bare feet and the hem of her underdress bright red.

Eirik set the axe—now dented from where it had hit the stone—against the altar, and returned to his seat. Next to him, King Harald and Thora sat together on a bench, its back and arms carved and painted with knotwork dragons. A few children in the hall started bawling, Hakon included, and Thora held him in her lap, murmuring soothing words. On the king's other side, Queen Gyda sat in her own carved chair and looked on with cool detachment.

Across the hall, Oddny spotted a woman who could only be Thorbjorg: small, pale haired, clad in all the trappings of her profession, face carefully blank as she observed the spectacle. Beside Thorbjorg sat a tall woman, older, with dark brown hair and an eye patch. She was dressed similarly to Thorbjorg and glared at Gunnhild with such open hatred that Oddny was surprised that her friend hadn't yet burst into flames from the intensity of her stare.

This was Katla, Oddny realized. She'd watched Gunnhild's swallow take the eagle's eye herself.

Gunnhild gave no indication that she noticed the other witches—or anyone else in the hall, focused as she was on her work. And it was not lost on Oddny that the moments Eirik fulfilled his part of the ceremony were the only time he'd taken his eyes off Gunnhild.

When the bowl was full, Gunnhild lifted it over her head. The three hearth fires, along with the flames of every lamp and brazier, suddenly rose in unison—causing the crowd to gasp—and then returned to normal as Gunnhild brought the bowl back down. She extracted a bundle of twigs from her sleeve, dipped them in the blood, dabbed them across her own forehead, then dipped them once more and flung the red droplets out onto the assembly; she did this again and again as she moved around the hall, making sure each person was touched. Many guests held up effigies of the gods from their own homes and altars to be blessed. Oddny raised her mother's statue of Eir, and next to her, Runfrid did the same with a small figure carved in the likeness of the bow-hunting goddess Skadi.

At last, Gunnhild went back to the front of the hall to fling blood up onto the statues of Thor, Odin, and Frey—and suddenly all three hearth fires rose again. The assembly cried out in wonder and, duly blessed, they started to cheer as Hrafnhild's servants began making their rounds with pitchers of ale. Several large horns of mead were filled and passed around after Gunnhild smeared blood across the runes carved upon them. The bull was hauled out to be butchered for the feast.

Heads turned when Gunnhild made her way to the doors, still holding the bowl and bundle of twigs. At her sideways look and nod, Oddny, Runfrid, and Ulla followed her out into the night and donned their wools, and the few of them who carried weapons grabbed them from the pile. Oddny, thinking of the enemy witches with a shudder, felt instantly better after she'd put her belt and knife back on.

She cradled her mother's statue in the crook of her arm as they waited for stragglers. To her surprise, more than a few of the other women joined them, including Thora and Saeunn—and then, shockingly, Katla and Thorbjorg materialized out of the crowd and went to stand at the head of the procession with Gunnhild. No one questioned this—they were seeresses, after all, and their presence would seem appropriate enough to anyone who didn't know their true motivations.

Gunnhild made a very good show of ignoring them, but Oddny saw the way her shoulders stiffened at their approach. Oddny shifted closer to the front, scarcely daring to breathe, as though the witches would startle if they took notice of her.

Thorbjorg seemed to sense she was being watched: She looked over her shoulder at Oddny for the briefest moment before turning back around, the confidence in the motion indicating that she did not consider Oddny a threat.

Oddny thought of her mother and her brother and Signy, and had the sudden urge to drive her knife into the woman's back. The only thing that staunched this impulse was the memory of her own words: Without proof of wrongdoing on the witches' part, murdering them would be a futile gesture that would do nothing to add to Eirik and Gunnhild's credibility.

Gunnhild led them all in a silent procession to each of the outbuildings, where she flung blood onto the statues of Frigg and the goddesses in the workshop, and then onto the statues of Tyr and Thor and Odin in the empty armory, and then onto the massive icon of Odin in the temple. And then, inexplicably, she headed toward the woods. The rest of the women traded uncertain looks before trailing her—all except for Thorbjorg and Katla, who'd followed without hesitation, and Saeunn, whose knee was giving her trouble, as Oddny's tea from earlier had worn off. Thora opted to stay behind to help her back to the workshop.

Oddny's trepidation built as the procession continued, Gunnhild leading them farther from the main hall than many would dare to go during a sacred feast night.

"Gunnhild," Oddny said warily as they passed the artisans' cottages, "where are we going? It's cold. We should go back inside."

"There's one more statue I have to bless," Gunnhild said without turning around.

As she watched the back of Gunnhild's head and the witches who flanked her a step behind, Oddny's anxiety continued to escalate. Who would strike first? Would Thorbjorg or Katla choose now to make their move? Would Gunnhild be dead before the sun came up, and with her, Oddny's hope of finding Signy?

This isn't a ceremonial procession anymore, Oddny thought as she swiped at the cold sweat on her forehead. *It feels like we're being escorted to our deaths.*

None of the other women seemed concerned except for Ulla and Runfrid, who walked on either side of Oddny, holding their lanterns aloft. Runfrid's hand rested on the hilt of the small seax she wore at her belt.

Once they were deep enough in the woods, Gunnhild led them off the main path and to a birch grove in the center of a clearing. The largest tree had a hollow in it, in which sat a small wooden statue of Freyja. Gunnhild flicked it with blood from the offering bowl before wedging the bowl itself into the hollow.

"I'm sorry to bring you all so far out here, but my goddess has been too long neglected in this place," Gunnhild said to the rest of them, again without turning around. "You may return to the hall and enjoy the feast. Thank you for joining me tonight."

The women whispered among themselves and began to disperse. To Oddny's surprise, even Thorbjorg and Katla—after pricking their fingers and leaving their own personal blood offerings to Freyja—followed. Only Oddny, Runfrid, and Ulla lingered with Gunnhild and watched them go, and it wasn't until the witches were out of sight that Gunnhild let out an audible sigh of relief.

"That was them, wasn't it?" Runfrid asked.

"Yes," said Oddny, "but why didn't they do anything? What was that all about? Why even—?"

"They wouldn't," said Gunnhild flatly. The last traces of the night's formality were gone, and there was anger in her eyes. "It would be too suspicious, same as if we were to strike against them first. If something were to happen to me, with so many witnesses, it would only prove Eirik right. They're more subtle than that, Oddny. They have to be, and so do we. They were only trying to intimidate me."

"Did it work?" Ulla asked in a small voice, but Gunnhild offered no response. She turned on her heel and stalked out of the clearing, her blood-spattered dress and her wild hair fading out of their lanternlight and into the darkness before the other three women could utter another word.

Runfrid shifted, hand still on the hilt of her seax. "Is she going to be all right?"

Oddny didn't know. She motioned for them to follow, and they kept Gunnhild's shape in their sight all the way back to the workshop to ensure nothing happened to her.

"Saeunn will be in there, and probably some of the other women by now, so she'll be safe," Ulla said when they saw Gunnhild disappear inside the workshop. After a short discussion they realized none of them were in the mood to attend the feast, so Oddny and Ulla walked Runfrid back to the armory with the intention to retire to the workshop afterward.

But when Runfrid opened the door to the armory to reveal Halldor sitting inside, she turned to Oddny and whispered, "Have you asked him yet if he'll help Arinbjorn keep an eye on the witches during the ritual?" At the look on Oddny's face, she smirked. "Well, now's your chance."

HALLDOR WAS THE ONLY one in the armory. He sat on a stool near the fire, fletching arrows, their wooden shafts sticking out of a bucket at his feet. On his left sat a bowl of arrowheads, a roll of twine, and a pile of split and trimmed feathers.

"Tired of the feast already?" Runfrid asked him, tousling his hair as she crossed the room to the loft's ladder. "It sounds as though everyone is already good and drunk."

Halldor waved her off, but one corner of his mouth twitched up in amusement, though he didn't look up from his work. "I hate crowds, and I only get drunk at Yule. The rest of the year I prefer to keep my wits about me and let others make fools of themselves."

"No wonder Arinbjorn likes you so much," Runfrid said. "Tea?" When they all said yes, she fetched a small clean pot from the loft, filled it with water, and stuck it in the fire, all the while shooting Oddny pointed looks as if to say, *Ask him!*

Oddny gave a silent, horrified shake of her head, so Runfrid said loudly, "Ulla, will you come help me choose a tea? I've got them up in the loft."

Once they'd ascended, both of them looked over the edge and made encouraging motions at Oddny. *Traitors*, she thought indignantly.

With a silent sigh, Oddny approached the hearth and sat down on the stool opposite Halldor. He'd been at the disablot, for a few specks of blood dotted the side of his face, but now he was dressed in clothing she hadn't seen him wear before: a tunic of heavy green wool, and brown pants. Both items were of good quality, but patched in places and slightly oversized for his slim frame. His worn shoes, his faded red leg wraps, and the seax in its scuffed sheath at his belt remained just as shabby as on the fateful day she'd met him. His sleeves were rolled up to reveal sinewy forearms, and as he worked, she caught a glimpse of Gunnhild's tiny bindrune where it had been tattooed just below his elbow.

When Halldor spoke to her at last, his tone was dry.

"These clothes are borrowed, if that's what you're going to say." He still hadn't looked up from his work. "I haven't earned any silver yet, so you needn't worry that I'm trying to get out of what I owe, or spending what should be in your coin pouch."

"That's not what I was going to say," Oddny said defensively.

His pale green eyes flitted up, and she hated the feeling that stirred in her belly when his piercing gaze met hers. Someone had reshaved the side of his head to reveal the salmon in all its faded glory, though the hair hadn't grown in much since Oddny had shaved it in the bunk room at Ozur's hall.

She asked, "Did you do that yourself? It looks better."

Halldor reached up and touched the shaved patch. "Runfrid did it. She's going to freshen up my tattoo before she leaves for the winter." He held up one of the half-finished arrows and added, "And before you say anything about how I can afford it, we came to terms."

A shuffling sound from the loft, and Runfrid's voice: "It's more than a fair trade to me. I love shooting arrows but hate making them."

Oddny picked up one of the arrowheads and examined it. "Did you smith these yourself?"

"I did." Halldor lowered his voice. "They're not very good. Don't tell her."

"I heard that," said Runfrid from above.

Halldor set his unfinished arrow in the bucket and looked to Oddny. "But none of that is why you sat down to talk to me."

Oddny cleared her throat. "No, it's not. I need a favor."

"Oh?" He raised an eyebrow—the one shot through with the scars from Gunnhild's tiny talons. "What kind of favor? And would you be willing to lower my debt if I agree?"

"A relatively easy one, and yes," Oddny said. "By a mark."

Now he raised both eyebrows. "A whole mark?"

"Gunnhild can use her own silver to rescue Signy now, so I can spare mine for a task this important," Oddny said. "I trust you saw Olaf's and Halfdan's witches at the sacrifice tonight."

"They're difficult to miss," Halldor said. "The hird's been on edge since they arrived, and from what Eirik has said, his father doesn't believe they're at fault for anything that's happened." He rubbed his chin. "Which is curious, because King Harald hates witchcraft. You'd think he'd be more prone to believing such accusations if it meant he could swing a sword at a witch first and investigate the truth of her crimes later."

"I hadn't thought about that." Runfrid descended the ladder with a small linen sack clutched between her teeth, Ulla following close behind her with a small clay pot of honey, and dumped the contents of the sack into the now-boiling water. "It does seem odd, doesn't it?"

"Maybe something is staying his hand. Do you think someone is trying to discredit Eirik?" Ulla suggested. "Whispering in his father's ear?"

"It wouldn't be the first time King Harald's mind has been swayed by nothing but rumors," Runfrid said, a dark look crossing her face. "Remind me to tell you sometime what happened to Thorolf's uncle."

From her tone of voice alone, Oddny decided she didn't want to know.

Runfrid ladled the tea into cups and handed them out, and as Ulla passed around the honeypot, Halldor said, "So, you were saying, Oddny . . .? This favor you need . . .?"

"Right." Oddny inhaled the scent of the tea—dandelion root—and lowered her steaming cup. "I need you to watch the witches on the third feast night. Make sure they don't leave the hall, and if they do, follow them. And if they're up to anything suspicious, come to the workshop immediately and tell us."

"Why?" Halldor asked.

"Because Gunnhild is going to be performing a ritual to see if the spirits will tell her where Signy has been sold to. With luck, we won't need to go to Birka at all. But King Harald will be furious if he finds out, so no one can know. And Gunnhild says Thorbjorg and Katla might wish to cause some mischief for her, so we need to make sure they stay put until the ritual is complete."

Halldor bit the inside of his cheek and considered this. "Lower it by a mark and a half—make it an even ten marks that I owe you—and it's a deal."

"Fine. I'll cut your debt to ten marks. Will you do it?"

After a moment, Halldor nodded once and stuck out his hand, and Oddny shook it. Unlike the first time they'd shaken on a deal—when she'd agreed to decrease his debt in exchange for what was still currently the only lead they had on Signy—she found that the feel of his hand in hers wasn't entirely unpleasant.

Once she and Ulla had finished their tea, they bade Runfrid and Halldor good night and went back out into the cold. Halldor gave her a lingering look as the door shut behind them, and Oddny shook herself, thinking she'd seen something there that she must have imagined.

But she couldn't get Halldor's eyes out of her mind, or that simple, innocent touch of his hand. Why was she thinking of him this way? This man had participated in the heinous act that had resulted in the destruction of her family and farm and the kidnapping of her sister—and yet, hadn't Ozur been right that any raider could have easily ended up in the same position? Hadn't nearly every free man on this very estate gone on the raids at least once?

Besides, Halldor had apologized. He was honorable—he'd made that much clear. But he couldn't undo the raid. He couldn't bring her mother and brother back.

I'm not fond of him, she told herself, and not for the first time. *He owes me money and he's agreed to do me a favor. That's all.*

Ulla stopped halfway to the workshop and tilted her head back to admire the full moon. "What a strange night."

Oddny stopped beside her and grimaced. "I have a feeling it's only the first of many."

23

THE SECOND FESTIVAL DAY was much the same as the first, with plenty of drinking, gossiping, and games—except that now, instead of drifting unnoticed through the crowds, Gunnhild seemed to draw some-one's attention everywhere she turned.

It started the moment she stepped out of the textile workshop that morning. She seemed to have impressed the guests at the disablot, for many wanted to introduce themselves and their families to the future queen, to compliment her on the power of the sacrifice the night before and comment on how they just *knew* that good fortune would come their way thanks to her. Now they knew her face, knew her name.

They saw her. They wanted to know her.

She wished she could be happier about it. Her smile was forced, her replies empty, and every name slipped out of her head the moment she turned to greet the next person.

At first the day dragged on, but before long she had to go back to the workshop and get ready for her wedding, which was to take place at dusk. Oddny had sewn another linen dress for her, identical to the one she'd worn to the ritual but with the cuffs, hem, and neckline adorned with stitches of pale blue wool thread.

Instead, Gunnhild opted to wear her ritual gown. The blood from the sacrifice the previous day had dried to the same dark copper red as her hair. When Oddny asked about the sudden change of mind regarding her wardrobe, Gunnhild lied and said she'd coordinated it with Eirik. But in truth she wanted to remind everyone who she was. Remind her enemies, remind those who doubted her—King Harald, Queen Gyda, Thorbjorg, Katla, even Olaf, and Halfdan, whom she'd yet to meet—exactly whom they were dealing with.

And that was not some waif in a pristine white gown, but a witch who was not afraid to spill blood if fate demanded it of her. Looking down at the stains as she combed out her hair, she was now more certain than ever that she was walking the path that was meant for her, both because of and despite Thorbjorg's interference.

A path that, she was no longer able to deny, led straight to Eirik.

This was a truth she couldn't have told Oddny even if she'd asked. Though Eirik hadn't spoken to her since that day in the grove, and Gunnhild still wasn't certain that he didn't despise her, during the disablot she'd felt a shift—everyone else had been riveted by the sacrifice, but his eyes had been on *her*.

And she found that she wanted him to look. To recognize her for what she was. He, more than anyone else, needed to see her. Maybe then he would listen to her, too.

She finished combing her hair and stood, took the juniper crown that Ulla offered her, and placed it atop her head. Oddny stepped forward to ensure that it was straight.

And then it was time.

Gunnhild was struck by the deep red of the sunset as a dozen of the weavers, including Oddny and Ulla, escorted her to the temple. As they approached the people who'd gathered to witness the marriage ceremony—which would be taking place outside—the crowd hushed and parted for them.

When they reached the front of the assembly, she saw that a fire had been built outside the temple doors. The women broke off from her and only Gunnhild continued forward, though she almost stopped in her tracks when she realized she hadn't lied to Oddny after all: Eirik stood before her in the very same plain tunic and pants he'd worn for the ritual, his hair pulled back at his nape and his beard trimmed, this neatness at odds with the dried blood on his clothes. He stared at her as though he was equally shaken that they'd separately made the same decision to forgo their finery for something even more powerful.

They were married by a priest of Frey, the ceremony cast in shades of blood by the setting sun. She didn't dare look out onto the crowd. She couldn't bring herself to care what any of them thought. Not anymore.

Her vision had narrowed until it encompassed only Eirik. It was as though they were the only people in the Nine Worlds. They didn't speak, didn't even touch until the priest bound their clasped forearms together in a lovely gold-threaded tablet-woven band Saeunn had made. He bestowed the gods' blessings upon them as he tied it, all the while calling on Thor to consecrate the marriage, on Odin for the wisdom to guide their rule, on Frey and Freyja for fertility.

Gunnhild heard the priest as though from a distance. He passed Gunnhild a large, shallow cup full of golden mead, and with her free hand she took it and sipped.

You don't have to like me. She held Eirik's gaze over the rim as she lowered it, recalling Arinbjorn's words from the day they'd met. *But I'm your last hope, as you're mine.*

She passed him the cup and he took a drink as well. Then the priest took it and poured the rest of the mead into the fire before them as an offering to the gods. Everyone in the crowd cheered, save for a select few.

Gunnhild barely heard any of them.

Beneath the binding of the band, she squeezed Eirik's arm and whispered, "Your enemies are my enemies."

At once he recognized his own words from the day they'd bound themselves with blood nearly a moon ago, and a ghost of a grim, determined smile played at his lips. This wedding was for his family, the people, the gods. But these words were a reminder of the oath they'd already taken, a reminder for just the two of them.

"And your fate is my fate," he said.

THE FEAST THAT FOLLOWED felt like a fever dream Gunnhild couldn't wake from.

A table had replaced the altar stone atop the bloodstained dais, and Eirik and Gunnhild sat there under the statues of the gods. To their left sat King Harald in the high seat, with Thora and Hakon, and next to them, Queen Gyda ate in watchful silence.

Gunnhild took a long swig of grape wine from the large wooden cup she and Eirik shared: the same one from the ceremony, an elaborately carved dragon head sprouting from each side. The wine was a precious commodity imported from far to the south, brought out for this very special occasion. She was enjoying the drink perhaps too much.

Despite what she'd perceived as a positive development in their relationship during the wedding, Eirik had not spoken to her or shown her any affection since. She was beginning to think that it was merely a fluke, that he really did loathe her, and the wine wasn't helping her mood. On top of that, the guests simply would not stop coming up to greet them, congratulate them, and occasionally present them with lavish gifts.

The more she drank, the less she felt. And she wished to feel nothing at all, so she kept drinking, which was very convenient, as the wine seemed to be in endless supply.

As yet another guest ended their long string of praise and blessedly returned to their seat, a servant approached the table and refilled the dragon-headed cup with wine. Gunnhild nabbed it just as Eirik went to pick it up.

He gave her a sharp look. "I'm not sure if you're aware of this, but I would also like to drink on my wedding day."

Gunnhild waved the cup at him and wine sloshed over the rim. "Aha! He speaks! And here I'd thought you'd forgotten I was here—wait." She squinted. "Are you biting your nails?"

He hid his hand in his lap and glowered at her. "A nervous habit from childhood. It comes back every now and then when I'm under duress."

"Oh, you're under duress, are you?"

"Yes," Eirik said, reaching for the cup. "Give that here. You can have more later, when you've sobered up."

She held it away from him. "You can't tell me what to do."

"I can tell you that you're going to make a fool of yourself in front of my family if you keep drinking. Hand over the cup."

"Now, Eirik," said a voice as two men approached the table, "who are you to tell your wife that she can't drink at her wedding feast?"

"I didn't tell her she can't drink, just that she should stop," Eirik said with forced nonchalance as he stood and clasped forearms with the tall black-haired man who stepped forward first. Neither looked happy about having to touch the other in anything resembling a friendly way. It was very clear to Gunnhild that they were putting on a show for the rest of the guests. Keeping the peace, as it were. From his pale blue eyes she knew on sight that this was one of Eirik's brothers. The man with him was Olaf, whose acquaintance she had already made.

Gunnhild wanted to snap that she was *right here*, but she forced herself to hold her tongue when she realized that this man was Halfdan Haraldsson, Eirik's oldest brother. He must have been here yesterday, since Katla was present for the sacrifice, but he hadn't announced himself; Gunnhild assumed he was waiting to make a scene. It would've been an insult to the disir to do it the night before, but the wedding was a different story.

"You nearly missed the disablot yesterday," Eirik said, dropping his hands to his sides and forcing a smile.

"The seeress in my employ sustained an injury and was too weak to sail," said Halfdan. "That's why we were a few days behind."

Gunnhild looked past him to where Katla was staring daggers at her, and then back to the men in front of them. She didn't regret what she'd done—only that she hadn't finished the job.

"How unfortunate," Eirik said rigidly.

Out of the corner of her eye, Gunnhild saw King Harald sit forward on his bench, watching the exchange through narrowed eyes.

"Father's told us of your marriage terms," said Halfdan, smirking. "Just one wife, eh, brother? Don't tell me she has you under some spell."

It had been a joke—or so she'd thought—but when Halfdan's eyes cut to her, Gunnhild saw the malice in them. Her hand tightened on her cup.

Eirik scoffed. "You think me so empty-headed as to fall for such trickery?"

Both men's expressions said yes, but it was Olaf who spoke. He put a hand to his chest, feigning offense. "Is that a jab at Father's previous bewitchment? Such disrespect coming from his *chosen successor*."

Eirik's throat worked but he seemed unable to speak, and he looked angrier for it.

Before he could dig himself a deeper hole, something shifted in Gunnhild, as if a cold snap had blown through her mind and scattered the mist that had settled upon her from the wine. She said, loudly enough for the people around her to quiet, loudly enough for King Harald to hear: "If you're referring to Snaefrid—if she *was* in fact a witch, she must have been powerful indeed to have ensorcelled such a man as King Harald, and I'm flattered that you think me powerful enough to have done the same to such a man as my husband. You seek to insult King Eirik, yet by accusing me, you've paid us both a compliment. Perhaps I should thank you."

Her heart pounded as she felt many of the eyes in the hall turn to her, including Eirik's. But she kept her head high.

"Ah, but you *are* a sorceress, aren't you?" Halfdan jeered. "I don't suppose you've heard what happened to our brother Rognvald. I'd heard you were wise, but it seems foolish to me to throw in your lot with Eirik after what he's done."

"Especially since you're the only one of your kind who would," Olaf said. "Though I daresay, after seeing you last night, it seems to me your talents are wasted on serving him."

"I do not *serve* him," Gunnhild said.

"Nor should you," Halfdan said placatingly, making Gunnhild think he was perhaps the wiser of the two brothers. "It's not too late to call for a divorce, you know." He gave a sideways nod at Eirik. "Surely you know by now that no lantern is burning in the loft. He's no more than our father's attack dog. If you wish to be a queen, there are worthier kings in this country to marry."

Gunnhild rose to her feet.

Your enemies are my enemies.

She wouldn't need magic to unsheathe her claws, not this time. These enemies were not witches—they were only men.

"I suppose you're just taunting us because I've given you another reason to be jealous of Eirik. A marriage to a woman such as I is so beyond you two that I don't know if you deserve my ire or my pity for trying to spoil my wedding feast. I feel bad for your wives, if you have any at all."

By the end of her outburst, the hall had fallen dead silent. Even the skald had paused midpoem.

"Bitch," Olaf said after a beat.

Gunnhild threw her hands in the air and said to the ceiling, "Is there a single Haraldsson in this room capable of conjuring a decent retort? By the gods, you lot have all the imagination of a dead codfish. Am I to suffer this tediousness all the years of our marriage?"

This last part was directed to Eirik, who glared at her. Off to the side, Queen Gyda let out an extremely unqueenlike snort and covered her mouth. On King Harald's other side, Thora was smiling broadly, making no show of hiding her amusement.

"You'll pay for these insults," Halfdan growled.

Gunnhild made a face. "Oh, how boring. Thank you for proving my point. And funny that you should speak of disrespect toward your father when you're the ones who continue to disregard his express wishes. He's named Eirik his successor time and time again, has he not? And here you stand, right in front of the king, mocking his choice."

She looked over to King Harald and was relieved to see that, beneath his braided silver beard, he was giving her the smallest of smiles.

"Queen Gunnhild speaks truly," he said, standing, and the words "Queen Gunnhild" coming from him meant everything.

"Father—," Olaf began.

"She—," said Halfdan.

"You've lost this round, boys," said King Harald affably, holding up a hand to silence them. "You came to antagonize your brother, and I can't say it's not deserved, considering the baseless claims he's made against you—"

Eirik opened his mouth to argue against the baselessness of said claims, but Gunnhild kicked his foot under the table and his mouth snapped shut.

"—but it seems," King Harald continued, "you've only given his new wife a chance to prove her wit."

"It would've been a good plan had she been a lesser woman," added Queen Gyda, not without a hint of bitterness, as though the words tasted foul on her tongue. "But now it's time to take your seats."

Gunnhild couldn't believe it. *They're taking my side? Impossible.* But by the whispers around her, it was clear that it was the crowd she'd won over, and King Harald and Queen Gyda knew it. To side with Halfdan and Olaf against Eirik now would have made them look foolish.

Halfdan was shaking with rage. "But, Father—"

"Enjoy your drink. Find a woman," said the king. He waved a hand as he made to sit down again. "Set aside your grudges, if only for tonight, and let Eirik and his bride celebrate."

Olaf was not giving up. "But, Father, we—"

That was the last straw—King Harald's patience ran out. He straightened again and roared, forcefully enough to shake the bowls on the tables around him, *"Should I show you what will happen should you continue to disrespect me?"*

That finally shut the brothers up. King Harald sat back down heavily on the bench. When the hall remained silent, he barked, *"Well?"*

Straightaway, the baffled skald resumed his recitation of the poem about Thor and Loki dressing as the bride Freyja and her handmaiden, respectively, to get Thor's hammer back: a favorite for wedding feasts.

For their part, Halfdan and Olaf turned and stormed out of the hall, shoving people out of the way left and right as they went. Gunnhild took a deep, shaking breath and sat back down. Eirik did the same.

Slowly, the mood inside the longhouse regained its earlier merriment. The skald sang more loudly, the revelers laughed at his exaggerated impersonations of the gods, and the chatter rose.

Eirik still hadn't said a word; he was now drinking deeply from the cup. When Gunnhild reached for it, he clamped a hand down on her knee and squeezed, leaned in, and whispered, "Those are not the enemies I meant for you to fight."

Gunnhild took this opportunity to snatch the wine cup back from him, turned her head so that their noses were nearly touching, and replied in kind, "And what's the difference?"

"The difference is that they're men, and I can handle them myself."

"Well, you were doing a poor job of it. When we have an enemy you can strike down with those axes of yours, it'll be your turn to fight. I'm the mind. You're the muscle. Remember that, *husband*."

The word might have had a different effect on her if she'd spoken it during the ceremony, during that moment when she'd thought things were going to change between them, but now it made her feel ill. *I was a fool to hope for better from him.*

Eirik's lip curled and he pulled away from her, and did not speak to her the rest of the feast. Did not speak to her as, much later in the evening, they stood and went to the bedchamber amid the cheering and hollering of the crowd.

Gunnhild's chests had been moved into the room, and she quickly checked them to make sure all her things were present—especially her staff. Satisfied, she turned and took in the rest of the chamber: a few chests of Eirik's things; a few tapestries on the wall; and, of course, Hnoss and Gersemi, curled up together on the bed.

The *bed*. Its frame was even more beautifully carved than the one her parents had slept in. Gunnhild wanted to cry at the sight of it. After sleeping half her life on a dirt floor and the past few weeks on a bedroll the thickness of her finger, now she had an actual *mattress*, stuffed with feathers, which *she* would get to sleep in—

With her husband.

Who had swiftly changed into a clean tunic while she'd been checking her chests and now slid under the bedcovers. The cats moved to sit on top of him as he lay there on his side, facing the wall. While Eirik's back was turned, Gunnhild took off her juniper crown and her bloodstained ritual gown, trading them for a clean linen shift, then climbed under the furs and the thick blanket stuffed with eiderdown. A length of surprisingly soft wool had been placed over the mattress itself for added warmth.

It was the most comfortable she had ever been in her entire life. She actually wiped away a tear as she settled in, before she remembered that she should not get *too* comfortable in the face of what was still ahead of her tonight. She lay on her back and stared at the ceiling.

"Do you sleep like this all the time?" she asked, remembering too late that he rarely slept at all. She was still a bit drunk, but that had been purposeful. She didn't think she could manage the act sober. "No wonder kings think they're better than everyone else."

Eirik didn't turn around. "The servants will be in and out to tend the hearth. Please blow out the lantern. Good night."

Gunnhild sat up but ignored his request. One of the servants had blessedly left a full jug of the southern wine on the chest on Gunnhild's side of the bed, and she drank directly from it, leaning against the headboard. Through the wall behind her, she could hear the skald singing, the loud talk and laughter. Everyone was still celebrating the wedding—except for the newlyweds.

Annoyed by the intermittent *glug-glug-glug* sounds coming from the jug as she drained it, Eirik finally turned his head. "Stop drinking and go to sleep."

Gunnhild squinted, her vision swimming as she swiveled her head toward him, and slurred, "Are we consummating our marriage tonight, or are we not?"

Eirik sat up in bed faster than she would've thought possible, the cats yowling at being disturbed, and he snatched the nearly empty jug from her. "We are not. Especially now that you're so thoroughly intoxicated."

She made a face. Regardless of the fact that she'd been trying to convince herself that she didn't want him ever since their confrontation in the grove, her inebriated logic dictated that she should be offended that *he* didn't want *her*. She felt wounded. She felt *mean*.

"I prefer a willing partner of sound mind," he said, "and right now you're neither."

"Well, well," Gunnhild drawled. "The kinslayer has some honor after all—"

The jug flew past her head and smashed against a tapestry on the far wall.

The noise from the main hall quieted for just a moment, and then the people cheered.

Eirik curled his hand into a fist. He'd purposely thrown the jug wide, had never intended to harm her with it, but Gunnhild did not move a muscle. The bottom half of the tapestry, which she'd recently learned his own mother had woven, was now stained a deep purple.

Eirik lay back down and faced away from her again. After a few deep, quiet breaths to calm herself, she lay down as well and blew out the lantern.

Despite the wine, it took her a very long time to fall asleep.

24

ODDNY HAD SPENT MOST of the night with Runfrid and Ulla. Both women had proven extremely adept at thwarting unwanted advances, which had allowed Oddny to drink in peace. But Ulla had retired some time ago, and Gunnhild and Eirik had gone to bed looking rather too miserable to be a pair of newlyweds; and now Runfrid was engaged in a dice game with Halldor and Svein across the hall, while Oddny had opted to remain in her seat. She didn't think she could face Halldor, not with all these confusing feelings bumbling around in her head, knocking against the inside of her skull like trapped moths.

The woman sitting next to Oddny had been flirting with one of Eirik's hirdsmen throughout the night, and when she got up to follow him out of the hall, Arinbjorn immediately slid into her place.

"Finally," Arinbjorn said, motioning to a servant for a refill. He nodded his thanks and turned to Oddny. "I thought they'd never leave."

"You were waiting to sit with *me*?"

"Of course I was! You're one of the most interesting people here, Oddny Ketilsdottir." He cast a look to Eirik and Gunnhild's closed chamber door. "I saw you watching them. I was, too. What are your thoughts?"

"I'm worried," Oddny said, following his gaze. "The ceremony was so intense, but all night they've seemed unhappy."

"I know," Arinbjorn said. "I agree."

"You tried to talk him out of proposing to her, in the armory at Ozur's."

At his surprised look, she said sheepishly, "I heard. When I dropped off the poultice for your nose."

Arinbjorn reached up to touch it and grinned. "It's the first time breaking my nose has scarred. Halldor did well." He nodded at the chamber door. "If it's any consolation—Eirik has been different since they met, and I think it may be for the better. She's done something to him. Most of our lives, he's been indifferent toward women."

"Let me guess—he thinks us silly, frivolous creatures, unworthy of his important, manly attention?" Oddny asked dryly. She remembered how Eirik had conducted himself with Signy during that first feast at Ozur's, barely paying her advances any mind until he was very drunk.

"Something like that. But I wouldn't worry for Gunnhild. She's more than a match for him," Arinbjorn said. "You're a good friend, Oddny. That's part of why I was waiting to speak with you. Runfrid is awfully fond of you, and any friend of my beloved's is someone worth knowing better, in my opinion. She chooses her friends more carefully than anyone I know."

Oddny felt a surge of warmth in her chest. She didn't feel that she knew Runfrid all that well yet and she was touched that the tattooist thought so highly of her. But she noted Arinbjorn's avoidance of the word "wife" and said, "You two . . . aren't married, are you?"

"Oh, no. She doesn't want to."

"Won't her father force her, though? If he knows you're so—close?"

"Ha! He knows better than that. He made her the way she is, after all," Arinbjorn said. At Oddny's questioning look, he explained. "He found Runfrid wandering the streets after he and his raider friends sacked a town in Cordoba. She was maybe four winters old. He was a career warrior with no wife or children of his own, but he had a softness for her that to this day he can't explain. The problem was that he had no idea what to do with a daughter. He didn't want to adopt her only to drop her off with his relatives, so he took her along when he went on the summer raids, and she learned her trade on the way."

"That's incredible," Oddny breathed. It was the most unconventional upbringing she could imagine for a woman.

"I know," Arinbjorn said proudly. "So, while she won't legally marry me, in my heart she's my wife. We had a ceremony a few winters ago and swore an oath to each other, but she doesn't want the law involved. She said it would make her feel like she's my property. She doesn't want to be beholden to anyone. I respect that."

"But a woman gets to keep her dowry and bride-price," Oddny said. "A woman herself is not property."

"But both are provided by her kinsmen, so you see how she might feel that way?"

Oddny sat back and took a swig of ale. The truth was that she'd never considered a marriage agreement from that angle. The women she'd grown up around—her mother and Solveig—had always seemed so independent to her young eyes. But how much of their own authority had come from their husbands?

She cast a look at the closed door to the chamber that Gunnhild now shared with Eirik.

She might be a queen now, but only because of him, Oddny thought. *Her ritual tomorrow isn't just about finding Signy. It's about proving to herself that she still possesses a power no one can take away from her.*

Signy had been right all along, Oddny realized with a pang: While her sister had dreamed of adventure and freedom ever since they were young, Oddny had always doubted her, and with no real-life example to follow— only the legendary women in their father's tall tales—Signy hadn't known how to pursue what she wanted in any practical way, which is why she'd settled on trying to attract a rich man and moving far from Halogaland instead. Oddny, too, had never met another woman who'd done what her sister had wanted to do, until now. Until Runfrid. Once Signy was safe, Oddny would have to introduce them.

"And when *you're* made to marry?" she pressed, turning back to Arinbjorn. "What will happen to Runfrid then?"

"That's not a problem until it's a problem," he said. "There's no use worrying about it before then. Now, can I ask *you* a personal question?" When she nodded, he said, "You and Gunnhild are around the same age. Were you betrothed before the raid?"

Oddny shook her head. "No. My sister and I were thought to be cursed. But perhaps it all worked out in the end. If I were married, it's not likely I'd get a chance to rescue her. I'd be too busy running a farm."

"And is that what you wanted to do?"

"It's what I always *thought* I wanted to do." She took another sip of ale. "But I could never tell my mother of my doubts. I was too scared she wouldn't approve of me doing anything other than what was expected of me. What's more, people have been coming to me for remedies since I first made Saeunn her tea, and I find it . . . gratifying. To help people. I wonder if, once Signy is safe, I can follow my own path, like Runfrid is doing. Be a traveling healer, as Gunnhild had wanted to be a traveling seeress. And maybe Signy would even want to come with me. She's always longed for adventure."

"I think that's a grand idea," said Arinbjorn. "I didn't get to talk to your sister much when we stayed with Ozur on the way to Bjarmaland, considering she was too busy trying to get Eirik somewhere nice and quiet where she could get his pants off—"

Oddny guffawed into her cup. She wondered if Eirik even remembered that night, or if he'd mentioned it to Gunnhild, who thus far had given no indication that she knew her sworn sister had once attempted to bed her now-husband.

"—but it seems like you two are very different, no?"

"Yes," Oddny said emphatically, the ale loosening her tongue. "We are *very* different. For one, Signy's had a lot of dealings with men, where I've had few. I've tried being intimate with others, but it went poorly because I felt no . . . *connection* with them. I can't simply look at someone I've just met and decide to seduce them. I feel as though I have to *know* them to even want them in that way. Does that make any sense at all?"

When Arinbjorn didn't speak, Oddny became worried that she'd said too much, that he thought her foolish. But instead, he gave her a knowing smile. "I've met many people who feel the same. In fact, I'm one of them."

Oddny was stunned. "You have? You are?"

"Yes. There's nothing wrong with wanting to get to know a person first before deciding to be intimate with them. Few get the opportunity to do so." Arinbjorn leaned in close. "And if I may give you some advice? If you wish to get to know Halldor, you'd best go strike up a conversation with him before someone else catches his eye."

Oddny's jaw dropped and she smacked him on the shoulder. "Why would you say that? What has Runfrid told you?"

"Oh, this and that. Why don't you go over there and start forging a connection?"

"Was that a blacksmithing joke?" When he only grinned, she said, "No. He owes me ten marks of silver and that's all the connection I wish to have with him."

"Ah yes, how silly of me. It's only about the silver," Arinbjorn said sagely. "He's no catch. He's only devastatingly handsome, an accomplished fighter, a decent smith—and, oh, the next king of Norway is about to make him an official member of the hird."

"Already? It's been less than a moon!"

"The shortest probationary period Eirik has ever had for anyone, save for Svein. And myself, of course, but that was only by virtue of my fighting beside him practically since we could walk."

Oddny hesitated—but when she saw Halldor stand and start moving toward the exit, Arinbjorn said, "If you don't go now, you may miss your chance," and suddenly she had risen and her feet were moving of their own accord.

But when she followed him around the corner of the longhouse, she lost sight of him in the darkness and staggered to a halt, shoulders slumping. *Perhaps it's just as well. What would I have said to him anyway?*

A voice said from behind her, "Oddny Ketilsdottir. It's well past time we officially met."

Oddny whirled to find Thorbjorg standing there. The witch's expression was perfectly calm, innocent even. It made Oddny sick.

"Don't come any closer or you'll regret it," Oddny said, drawing her knife.

Thorbjorg stood her ground, but her eyes moved to the blade and her smile curved into something just as sharp. "Put that away. You're embarrassing yourself."

Oddny made no move to do so. "You had my family killed. My sister is gone because of you. Why? Tell me now and I may let you live."

"Oh, you'll let me live, will you?" The witch's laugh was entirely devoid of humor. "Listen, Oddny. I'll tell you the same thing I told *Queen* Gunnhild, and I'll only tell you once: You can walk away from all this."

"I can't. You've made that impossible."

"But what if I made it otherwise?" Thorbjorg produced a small coin purse from a pouch at her belt and dangled it between thumb and forefinger. "I didn't mean for things to turn out the way they did. I'll admit that much. My plan was rash."

Oddny scoffed and eyed the coin purse. "Don't tell me you want to compensate me for my family's deaths. There's not enough silver in the Nine Worlds that could—"

"Oh, no. But this *is* enough to buy your sister's freedom."

"Gunnhild can already do that. Try again."

"And if I put you on a ship right this moment and gave it a swift enough wind that it would take you to Signy's precise location, and get you both to safety before the worst of winter hits? Can Gunnhild do that, too?"

Oddny nearly dropped her knife—at the confirmation that Signy was indeed alive, and at the fact that Thorbjorg knew where she'd been taken.

"Where is she?" Oddny demanded.

"You'll be halfway to her by dawn if you agree to my terms."

"And what terms are those?"

Thorbjorg's smile flattened to a thin line. "Break your oath with Gunnhild."

"What?" Oddny whispered. "You want me to—?"

"To do nothing. To leave her. That's all. The only harm that will come to her, she'll have brought on herself. I'm not asking you to do anything terrible to her—"

"And breaking my oath isn't terrible?"

"She's the reason we even took notice of you and your family," Thorbjorg spat, growing frustrated. "We searched for her for years, but the old woman's magic protected her from our sight. So we had no choice but to strike against you instead. If you hadn't sworn that oath with her when you were children, your mother and brother might yet be alive."

The words were too horrible to believe. *Gunnhild was their real target after all?* Oddny's hand began to tremble on her knife, but she managed to bite out, "It's not Gunnhild's fault they're dead. It's yours. Why should I listen to a word you say?"

"You hadn't seen her for twelve winters, Oddny—how can you even be sure she's the same person as she was before? She'll show you her true self soon enough, and then you'll regret refusing my offer for the rest of your life."

Oddny could only shake her head in silent anguish.

"Forsake her," Thorbjorg snarled, "and swear a binding oath to me that neither you nor your sister will ever see her again, for as long as you live, and in return my oath will be that your safety and that of your sister will be ensured. That's the price." The witch thrust the coin purse out to her. "Will you pay it? For Signy?"

Slowly, Oddny sheathed her knife and looked down at her palms, at the scar from the blood oath.

I'm sorry, Signy. You'll have to hold on just a little longer.

I can't forsake one sister for the other.

And then something else occurred to her.

"That's not all there is to it, is there?" Oddny said. Despite how much she'd had to drink, she suddenly felt more sober than she ever had before. "Why are you so desperate to get Gunnhild alone? She said you'd foreseen something, but she didn't know what. And you didn't come after us to draw Gunnhild out—she told me you were surprised to see her on the day of the raid. Which means Signy and I are important somehow, aren't we? The three of us. Together." She looked up at Thorbjorg. "Listen—I understand wanting your revenge for Rognvald. I do. And so does Gunnhild. You had *her* mentor killed, after all. But—"

"You don't know what you're talking about," Thorbjorg said, but a hint of alarm had crept into her voice, and that was enough to convince Oddny that she was on the right path.

"Oh, but I think I do," Oddny said. "Your price for my sister's return is splitting us apart, but why? You said your plan with the raid was rash, which makes me think it was born of fear. And *that* makes me think that without us, you'll succeed and Gunnhild will die, but *with* us—she'll beat you. Maybe she'll even kill you."

Thorbjorg stared at her with something that wasn't fear, wasn't horror, wasn't rage, but was a mix of all three.

Then, in one fluid motion, the witch stuffed the purse back into her pouch and drew her knife: longer than Oddny's, antler handled, and wicked sharp. "Or maybe I could solve all my problems right here instead."

"Do it," Oddny snapped. "When they find my body, King Harald will know there's treachery afoot, and how long will Olaf vouch for you then? He'll never admit to anything. Not if he wants to remain king of Vestfold. And even if you escaped King Harald, Gunnhild would hunt you to the ends of the earth. Whatever you saw her do to you in your little prophecy, she'd do ten times worse if you kill me."

Thorbjorg drew back in disgust. "Do you truly have so much faith in her?"

"I do," said Oddny firmly.

"So be it," Thorbjorg said, and the knife flashed as she closed the distance between them. Oddny drew her own knife once more and held her ground—

"Oddny, there you are!" Halldor came up beside her, stumbling, and threw an arm around her shoulders. "I've been looking all over for you." He looked to Thorbjorg—who had stopped dead in her tracks—with the disinterest of the severely intoxicated. "What's going on here?"

His weight threatened to topple her as he leaned against her, but she didn't miss the fact that his free hand gripped the seax at his belt. Thorbjorg's eyes moved to it and narrowed; even if she believed Halldor to be drunk, she was outmatched, and she knew it.

Oddny discreetly sheathed her own weapon and played along. "We're only having a disagreement. Let's go."

They turned and shuffled away, Oddny bracing herself for the knife between her ribs with each step, but it never came. She made to stop, but Halldor moved her along until they reached the door to the textile workshop, where he suddenly removed his arm from her shoulders and stood up straight.

"You're very good at pretending to be drunk," she opined.

Halldor was not amused. "Are you all right?"

"I'm fine."

"If you say so," he said, and nodded at the door behind her. "Stay in there. If you have to leave, take someone else with you. All right?"

Looking up into his face, she could not think of a single thing to say to him. All thoughts of her conversation with Arinbjorn had fled, replaced by what Thorbjorg had unwittingly revealed to her: that Heid's prophecy from that night so long ago was true, that Gunnhild really had ruined Oddny's and Signy's futures by association. But Oddny's thoughts lingered most strongly on Thorbjorg's insinuation that Gunnhild wasn't to be trusted. That Oddny and Signy both were in danger and were better off accepting her offer and forsaking Gunnhild. That she *knew where to find Signy.*

But no. Thorbjorg was the one who wasn't trustworthy. And Gunnhild would find out Signy's location herself tomorrow night. Thorbjorg was trying to turn them against each other, and Oddny wouldn't let that happen.

"Oddny?" Halldor prompted. "Are you sure you're all right?"

"Yes." Oddny shook herself. "Thank you. For stepping in. It was good of you."

He shifted as though uncomfortable with the compliment. "Well, if anything happened to you, I don't . . ."

Oddny's breath caught, but when he didn't go on, she leaned in closer and prodded: "Yes?" *You don't know what you would do? Is that what you mean to say?* "You don't what?"

Halldor looked at her a moment too long before shifting away from her, rubbing the back of his neck. "Well, I don't know who I would owe that ten marks of silver to, eh?"

Oddny's heart dropped.

"Right." She cleared her throat. Earlier in the night she'd been uncertain of her desires, but now she only felt tired. She wanted him to stay. Wanted to work this out, whatever was happening between them. But she also wanted to be alone, and the latter was easier. "Well. Good night, then."

"Good night," he said. And when he turned to go, part of her wished he would look back. But then he rounded the corner and was gone.

25

ON THE MORNING OF the third feast day, Gunnhild woke up feeling like she'd been trampled by an ox. She was grateful but not surprised to find the other side of the bed empty. She didn't know how she was supposed to face Eirik after last night.

She sat up and pulled on the pair of thick nalbound socks that had been a wedding gift from Ulla. She didn't put on an overdress over her shift, nor did she do anything to tame her hair, which overnight had twisted itself into an angry red storm since she hadn't plaited it for bed. The servant who'd built up the fire had also left a pitcher of clean water atop one of the chests. Gunnhild drank all of it, used the chamber pot, and went over to examine the items that had appeared in the room overnight.

The wedding gifts, many of which had been presented to her and Eirik during the feast, had been brought inside while she slept, along with a chest of silver coins as the bride-price Eirik had paid, sitting next to the dowry from her father. She shoved both under the bed, where they would stay until she could have the silversmiths melt the coins down and render them into something more portable, like bracelets.

Queen Gyda and the workshop women had given Gunnhild more of a task than a present: a tapestry loom already fixed with a white cloth lashed to the beams, and some richly dyed thread to go with it.

"Saeunn mentioned that your weaving wasn't very strong," the old queen had said last night. "But embroidering a tapestry should be less difficult for you than weaving one. You could make it to celebrate one of Eirik's battles. Queens weave to immortalize our husbands' deeds for all to see, same as the skalds."

Gunnhild did not want to make a tapestry, much less one as a tribute to Eirik's glorious victories, but she'd put on a sunny smile and thanked her stepmother-in-law for such a gracious gift, and Queen Gyda had for once seemed pleased with her.

As she glared at the loom, there was a soft knock at the door. "Come in."

Oddny, looking just about as bad as Gunnhild felt, slipped inside, a bowl of porridge in each hand. She closed the door behind her with her foot, took one look at Gunnhild's face, and said, "Oh no."

Gunnhild's expression crumpled and she put her face in her hands.

"Oh, gods, Gunna." She put the bowls down, hurried over to where Gunnhild had sunk onto a stool, and knelt before her. "Did he hurt you? Do you need me to heal something? Or"—she pitched her voice lower—"do you need me to poison him?"

Gunnhild shook her head and dropped her hands. "I can't eat the porridge you brought. I'm fasting today. But it was very kind of you. Grab your bowl and I'll tell you about it."

And she did, while Oddny sat cross-legged on the floor and ate.

"Do you think you can repair things?" Oddny asked when Gunnhild was done.

"I don't know. But I'll attempt it just the same." Gunnhild studied her. "You don't look well, either. Are you all right?"

"Oh yes. It's just that I had too much to drink last night, same as you," Oddny said, too quickly. "Come. Let's go join the festivities. Runfrid is about to win the archery contest again."

The third day of Winternights passed as the first two had, but instead of mingling, Gunnhild feigned a headache and was able to sneak away by donning a nondescript cloak and pulling it up to form a hood to hide her face. She spent the day sitting out in Freyja's grove, and before she left she offered the goddess more blood. Afterward, she returned to her room, stuffed her braid under a kerchief, and dressed in her best for the feast before assuming her place beside her new husband. Eirik still didn't speak to her, nor did he comment on the fact that she refused food, claiming nausea from her heavy drinking the night before.

When she judged that everyone was too drunk to notice her absence, she grabbed her witching bag and slunk away to the textile workshop. She removed her fine outer clothing to reveal the blood-splattered gown from the disablot and her wedding, then she took off her kerchief, combed out her hair, and brewed her tea.

Soon afterward, the women trickled in: Saeunn first, then Oddny, Runfrid, and Ulla; Thora, smile twinkling as though she was grateful to be in on this secret; a few of the other workshop women, whose names Gunnhild didn't know; then Hrafnhild and a few of the other cookhouse girls.

The last person to arrive was none other than Queen Gyda, who took up a place beside Saeunn, her smooth expression revealing nothing of her thoughts. Gunnhild tried not to let the old queen's presence rattle her.

From her stool atop the platform that lined the hall, the looms at her back, she watched the women arrange themselves in a semicircle before her. Once they were all in place, Gunnhild stood, her staff in one hand and her steaming clay cup of henbane tea in the other, and realized that she didn't know what to say or how much to tell them. It wouldn't do to mention Thorbjorg's mischiefs, for fear Queen Gyda would step in and call her claims false. No—she would stick to her one and only goal. *And what would Heid say if she were me?*

"Welcome, my friends. Thank you for coming," Gunnhild said. "When I was a child, I took a blood oath with my dearest friends, Oddny and her sister, Signy. We swore to always be there for each other, no matter what happened. But now their farm has been destroyed and Signy sold away. The raiders who carried out this fell deed have not been found, and nor has she."

The women's reactions were varied: Thora gasped and put a hand over her mouth, looking as though she might cry; Hrafnhild and Saeunn seemed sympathetic; Queen Gyda's expression remained unchanged;

Runfrid and Ulla each put a hand on Oddny's shoulder; and Oddny met Gunnhild's eyes and nodded for her to continue.

"But Oddny and I mean to find and rescue her by seeking help from the spirits, and for that, we need your help. And so I must ask you all . . ." Gunnhild asked them the same questions Heid had asked the women in her father's hall so long ago: "Are you willing to help me summon the spirits tonight, to sing the warding songs? Will you call them here, and keep out any who mean us harm?"

"Yes," said the women in unison.

All except for one: Ulla. She stepped forward holding a leather bag, the outline of something round inside. When Ulla opened it and pulled out a drum, Gunnhild's throat constricted, for it was lovingly painted with figures of people and animals and other shapes, similar to the drums that Juoksa and Mielat used in their practice.

"Queen Gunnhild." Ulla raised her chin. "I don't know the songs. But if you would allow me to join this ritual by playing one of my family's sacred drums, it would mean very much to me to help you however I can."

"Yes," Gunnhild said as she blinked back tears. "Yes. Please. You would honor me."

Ulla nodded once, pleased. She dropped the carrying case, raised the smooth bone mallet to the stretched and painted skin of the drum, and waited.

Gunnhild addressed the circle: "Let us begin."

She sat back down on her stool. Ulla beat the drum, and the singing began.

Saeunn and Hrafnhild were the first to raise their voices in the haunting, ethereal melody. Then Runfrid's voice joined, then Oddny's, and at last the rest of them. The opening moments were difficult, their harmonies imperfect, the pacing off—Thora wanted to go faster, Runfrid more languidly, Oddny hitting different notes than the rest of them, for the songs varied in style by region—but Ulla's steady drumbeat forced them to settle into a rhythm before long.

Gunnhild closed her eyes and waited for the song to even out. Once she was satisfied, she took a deep breath and downed the tea in one gulp.

The effect was immediate and familiar, yet always a bit unsettling: She had a sudden sense of vertigo as her mind began to loosen itself from her body, and before it could get any worse, she stuck the iron staff under her arm and imitated the motions of spinning.

When she opened her eyes again, she was in the dark place.

SINGING VOICES HIGH ABOVE, joined by the drum.

But down here, Gunnhild was alone. Again. Just her and her internal glow, the gleaming thread extending from her chest and stretching upward into the darkness.

"Where are you?" she whispered. "Where *is* everyone? Why will you not come to me?"

"It's not too late to give up, you know," came a voice, and when Gunnhild turned she saw a woman standing before her, a cloak hiding her body and a hood hiding her face. Her voice was distorted, as though coming from underwater.

Gunnhild knew her presence, though. She'd recalled it every night in her dreams for weeks.

The seal. The third witch.

"Thorbjorg has made you this generous offer already," the hooded woman continued, "but this is your last chance. Flee and we may yet let you live. If you can't speak with the spirits, you're unworthy of taking on your mentor's name—but you can at least peddle your petty sorceries, no?"

"What are you doing to me?" Gunnhild snarled. "How are you keeping me from contacting the spirits?"

The woman giggled, the sound as warped as her voice. "You poor little fool. Nobody is keeping you from anything. You know as well as I do that the spirits choose for themselves whether or not they wish to appear, and for whom. And tell me—when was the last time you managed to speak with them? Were you working with your mentor? Or were you alone?"

Gunnhild startled. "I was—"

She'd been working with Heid. Every single time.

"Mmm," said the woman, clearly savoring the look of horror on Gunnhild's face. "You see, my dear, the dead know all. Which means that they know you for what you are: a selfish, foolish girl. A fraud. The reason you won't receive the knowledge you seek is because they don't wish to give it to you, not because of anything we've done."

"You're lying," Gunnhild said, but her voice was thick with panic and rage. She started toward the hooded woman, her hands curled into claws. "You're behind this. I know it. You're tracking me when I leave my body and you're—doing *something* now. You think I'm afraid of you? I am not afraid of *anything*—"

The woman took a step forward and vanished.

Gunnhild jerked to a sudden stop midstep as someone grabbed her from behind, an arm locked around her neck.

"And that," the woman hissed in her ear, squeezing, "is precisely your problem."

Her vision blurred at the edges as she struggled, kicking at the woman's shins as she was lifted into the air.

The song and drum echoing from above stopped abruptly.

Oh, gods—Oddny's voice sounded very far away.

We have to wake her up! Ulla, panicked.

Runfrid. *But how?!*

Oddny again. *Let me*—

Then with a jolt she felt herself being hauled upward through the darkness.

26

HER FRIEND BEING CHOKED by *nothing* was the most horrific thing Oddny had ever seen. Gunnhild clawed at her compressed throat, gasping, eyes bulging, lips turning blue.

Oddny pulled the glowing thread up from the floor.

The results were instant: Gunnhild took a huge breath and pitched forward on the stool; her clay cup hit the ground and shattered to pieces, her iron staff clattering beside it; and the thread dissipated. She would've fallen flat on her face if Runfrid hadn't caught her.

Once she'd helped Runfrid lay Gunnhild down on the platform, Oddny paused and stared. "Your neck. Good gods."

Gunnhild coughed a few times and croaked, "How does it look?"

"Like someone tried to strangle you," Oddny said, gingerly touching the bruised skin. "What *happened*, Gunna?"

Gunnhild looked away.

Oddny hopped off the platform, dragged her chest out, and rummaged through her healing supplies until she found a tonic in a little clay vial and a salve she'd stored in a small wooden cup, both stopped with waxed linen covers.

"Were you able to speak with the spirits?" Ulla asked, but the longer Gunnhild's silence lasted, the more the excitement drained from Ulla's face. Beyond her, Runfrid looked worried, Thora seemed on the verge of tears, and the other women hung back, their expressions a mixture of uncertainty and fear. Even Queen Gyda's brows had drawn together in concern.

Oddny massaged the salve into Gunnhild's throat with both hands, ignoring her friend's short, pained grunts of protest. "This will hasten your healing. And I'm giving you a draught, too, for the pain. You should feel better by the morning."

"Thank you," Gunnhild said hoarsely. "Will you . . . help me . . . back to my room?"

"But what *happened*?" Runfrid pressed.

"Not now," Oddny said, and hauled Gunnhild to her feet.

Thora came up beside her and put one of Gunnhild's arms over her surprisingly strong shoulders. "I'm headed to my chamber as well. I'll help."

Gunnhild did not say a word as they walked, and though the healing salve was visibly working, Oddny figured it probably hurt her to speak. The three women wove their way through the rowdy feast hall, most of the revelers too drunk to notice anything was wrong. Those who did probably thought the new queen had had too much to drink again.

Out of the corner of Oddny's eye, she saw Thorbjorg and Katla sitting and whispering with their heads close together—and though they snapped to attention as the women passed, they looked mildly confused at Gunnhild's state, and Oddny could tell at a glance that their reactions were genuine. She turned and saw Arinbjorn playing a dice game with Halldor. Each had a direct line of sight on the witches, and when Halldor's eyes met hers, he gave her the subtlest of nods.

Oddny tightened her hold on Gunnhild. *But if both of them were here—then what happened to her in there? Could it have been the third witch?*

Eirik was not in the bedchamber when they entered—nor, Oddny noted, had there been any of his hirdsmen present in the hall besides Arinbjorn and Halldor. Curious.

"Poor thing," Thora cooed as they helped Gunnhild lie down on the bed. She turned to Oddny and said softly, "I don't know what happened just now, but she wasn't in a fit state to begin with. This family can be very demanding . . ." Her hands were soft and warm when she gave Oddny's own a squeeze. "Is there anything else I can do?"

"No," Oddny said, touched. "I'll watch over her. Thank you for your help."

With a last concerned look at Gunnhild, Thora took her leave, and Oddny helped her friend into a clean dress and got her settled into her very nice, very soft bed.

"Reapply the salve before you go to sleep," Oddny said. "Do you wish me to stay with you?"

Gunnhild had already rolled over to face the wall. "No."

"Well, have a servant call for me if you change your mind."

"I'm sorry," Gunnhild whispered as Oddny turned to leave.

"Gunna—"

"I failed."

Oddny had suspected as much, but hadn't expected to hear it confirmed. She'd known Gunnhild long enough to know that she didn't easily admit defeat. Whatever had happened—wherever she had gone—the results had clearly been the opposite of what she'd wanted.

"Do you truly have so much faith in her?"

Oddny forced Thorbjorg's words from her mind. For all that the witch had offered to give Signy back to her, Thorbjorg was the reason she'd been taken in the first place. That Gunnhild's ritual had gone wrong tonight was probably likewise due to outside interference. *Somehow.* Oddny knew it in her bones: Her faith in Gunnhild was not misplaced. She'd reappeared at the exact moment Oddny had needed her most, and there was nothing they couldn't do together. That was exactly what Thorbjorg was afraid of.

She had to hold firm. She couldn't waver.

"It's all right," Oddny said without turning around. She couldn't let Gunnhild see the disappointment on her face.

"It's not," Gunnhild said miserably. "I've failed Signy. I've failed *you.*"

"We'll start the search at Birka as we planned," Oddny said. "It isn't a great loss."

It was, though. Gleaning Signy's exact location from the spirits could have shaved weeks or even moons off their search. But she didn't want to make Gunnhild feel worse, which was exactly why she had no plans to tell her of the conversation she'd had with Thorbjorg.

"Good night, Gunna," she said over her shoulder.

Gunnhild didn't reply. Oddny slunk out of the room and shut the door behind her. The heat and light and noise of the longhouse were stifling, so she made her way back through the crowd and into the cold night air outside, where she found Runfrid waiting.

"Is she all right?" she asked before Oddny had even closed the door behind her.

"No," Oddny said.

"Is there anything we can do?"

"Also no."

Runfrid sighed and shook herself. "Well, I'm going to the armory, then. It seems we haven't missed the ceremony—they were waiting for Arinbjorn and Halldor."

"Ceremony?" This was the first Oddny had heard of it.

Runfrid grinned. "Come."

THE ARMORY WAS FULL of Eirik's hirdsmen who hadn't yet gone home for the winter, plus a dozen hopefuls, including Halldor, all drinking and laughing. Runfrid dragged Oddny through the claustrophobic press of male bodies and toward the ladder to the loft. On the way, some of the men turned to give Oddny a curious look, until they realized Runfrid was with her, and moved to let the women pass.

When they ascended the ladder, Oddny saw that the loft was bare except for two bedrolls pushed together and a few chests, none of which could be seen from below. Tallow candles had melted into clusters on the floor near the smoke hole at the gable, and all were lit, illuminating Runfrid's charcoal sketches on the bare wood. The largest number of candles surrounded Runfrid's bloodstained wooden statue of the huntress Skadi, staring proudly and fiercely ahead, a bow clutched in her hand. It was exactly what Oddny had expected Runfrid's living space to look like.

There was a call for quiet, and silence fell upon the armory as Eirik beckoned the hopefuls forward. Oddny and Runfrid scooted to the edge of the loft, swung their legs over the side, and looked down on the proceedings.

Oddny hated to admit that Eirik looked good. For the first two feasts he'd been in plain bloody linens like Gunnhild, but now he was back in his finery, as were the rest of his men: combed hair and beards, clean tunics and pants and leg wraps, arm and finger rings and neck torques glinting in the glow of the hearth fire.

Eirik was holding two arm rings, and all eyes were on them.

"I'll make this short so you lot can go back to whatever company you're keeping tonight," he said. "I only have two of these to give out this time. One of them, some of you may say is premature. But the other is a long time coming."

Confused murmurs. These men were new recruits—who could he mean?

Eirik looked up toward the loft and said, "Runfrid, would you come down here, please?"

After a moment of shock, a roar of applause went up from below. "Oh, you must be kidding," one man said loudly, but he was smiling and clapping with the rest.

"Go!" Oddny said, for the tattooist's mouth was hanging open, but Oddny's encouragement roused her and she descended. Arinbjorn waited at the foot of the ladder, beaming, and gave her a big, wet kiss on the cheek even as she pushed him away, laughing, to strut up to Eirik. The crowd parted for her.

Runfrid stopped in front of the king and folded her arms. "Well, well. I may be the best archer in Hordaland, but what makes you think I *want* to join your silly little boys' gang?"

This was met with laughter, and Svein and several others yelled, "Boo!" Runfrid waved them off. Eirik raised his eyebrows and made to slowly retract the arm ring, but Runfrid huffed, snatched it out of his hand, and gave him a bear hug. The men cheered again as he patted her on the back, and she fixed the ring on her bicep just above the elbow like the rest of them and headed back to the ladder, avoiding another one of her beloved's sloppy kisses on her way up.

"You didn't know that was going to happen, did you?" Oddny asked her once she was in the loft.

"Well, Arinbjorn *did* tell me that Gunnhild has hassled Eirik once or twice about not having any women in his hird," Runfrid said with a brief roll of her eyes, "so *I* was the obvious choice to get her off his back. If there's one thing I know about Eirik, it's that he'll do anything for people to stop bothering him." She looked down at the arm ring and smiled. "It doesn't mean I don't appreciate the recognition, though."

Eirik waited until she was back in her seat before he held up the second arm ring and paced from one end of the line of hopefuls to the other. Some of them were staring eagerly at the king. Others, including Halldor, had their eyes on the floor, barely breathing for their nervousness.

"You've all trained well and are welcome to stay and keep improving, but the man I'm choosing to accept into my hird tonight has put even my most seasoned fighters to shame in terms of commitment and enthusiasm in just a few short weeks," Eirik said as he walked. "If he keeps it up, he should have a long career ahead of him. And I have every confidence that he will."

He stopped in front of Halldor.

Halldor looked up at him.

Eirik held out the arm ring. "Welcome to the hird."

The armory exploded once more with cheering. Halldor, stunned, took the ring from Eirik and looked down at it as though he'd never seen such a thing before in his life.

"Now go get drunk!" Eirik called, and his men enthusiastically began to trickle from the armory. But when he made to turn and follow the crowd, Halldor drew him aside, still holding the arm ring instead of putting it on, and they gravitated toward the back door.

Halldor was speaking quickly at first, but then he stopped and looked Eirik in the eye and said something else. Whatever it was, it caused Eirik to step back and look him up and down. Grimacing, Halldor held out the arm ring in one hand, the other hand twitching near the hilt of his seax.

What was going *on?* Oddny watched with bated breath.

After what seemed like an eternity but in reality was more of a moment, Eirik shook his head, took the arm ring out of Halldor's hand, fixed it onto Halldor's arm just above the elbow, and said something that made Halldor's expression go slack with shock.

Oddny caught only the last thing the king said, for he said it loudly: "And I mean it. Go have a drink, Halldor Hallgrimsson. Tonight is your night."

Then Eirik clapped him on the shoulder and left through the back door, leaving Halldor staring after him until Runfrid poked her head over the side of the loft and called, "Halldor! I've changed my mind. I know you haven't finished my arrows, but I'll do your tattoo tonight anyway. Just give me a moment to set up—and go fetch me a bucket of clean boiled water from the cookhouse, yes?"

Halldor regained himself. "I'll be right back," he said, and ducked out the door.

After a moment, Oddny scrambled down the ladder and followed him.

"Halldor," she called, and he stopped and turned just before entering the cookhouse, which was quiet inside, as if the place were breathing a sigh of relief that the feast days were at an end.

"Yes?" Halldor asked.

"Congratulations," Oddny managed, a beat too late for comfort.

"Thank you." He rubbed the back of his neck. "It was—unexpected."

"What happened just now?" she asked before she could stop herself. "With Eirik?"

"You saw that?" Halldor shifted. "It was—I told him something very personal to me. Something that some people might feel was a deception. And I needed to know if he was one of those people, because it's *not* a deception—it's who I am. But he—" He looked down at the arm ring as if surprised to see that it hadn't vanished into thin air. "He understood."

"Oh. Well, good," Oddny said half-heartedly, not understanding herself. Halldor went into the cookhouse and she stood outside until he emerged with the bucket of water. At the sight of her waiting there for him, he sighed.

"I'm not trying to be vague on purpose," he said. "But it's between us."

"I know." Oddny toed the dirt with the tip of her worn leather shoe. "I didn't mean to pry. It's just that I was worried."

"You were?"

"Yes. Despite everything, I—" The confession stuck in her throat, and she splayed her hands as she finally dislodged the words: "I care what happens to you."

He stared at her for what felt like a lifetime before giving her a wry half smile. "Right. Because I owe you a debt."

Oddny felt a prick of irritation, same as she had in the armory when he'd disclaimed how he'd gotten the clothes he was wearing, thinking she was coming to scold him for the crime of having new things when he owed her silver. "It's not about that. I don't care about the debt."

"Wait. What?" Halldor put the bucket down. "So I don't have to pay you back?"

"No. I mean, yes, you do!" Oddny huffed, folding her arms, flustered. "That's not what I meant and you know it."

"Do I?" Halldor asked mildly as he folded his arms as well. "You just said you don't care about it."

"I told you, that's not what I—" She squinted at him. "Oh. I see. You're jesting, aren't you?"

"I don't know, am I?"

Oddny sighed. Here she was, trying to get it off her chest that she was fond of him, only for him to deflect it by bringing up that godsforsaken debt yet again. But why had deflection been his reaction at all? Maybe he didn't feel the same way about her and didn't want to talk about it, and it was easier to change the subject than hurt her feelings.

Or maybe it was because of something else.

There was only one way to find out.

"Well, I do care about the debt," Oddny said. "But that's not why I care about *you*."

Halldor regarded her with suspicion. "Why, then?"

"Because you aren't who I thought you were."

"And who did you think I was?" he asked with what seemed like forced calm. "Besides dishonorable."

"Yes—no—but—" She waved her hands, searching for the words. "But, Halldor—can you blame me for thinking that? We met when your friends were burning down my home, murdering those closest to me—"

"I understand. And I've apologized for the pain it caused you. I feel guilty that I had any part in it. But it's—it's what we *do*, Oddny. Even Gunnhild's father knew that much. He couldn't condemn me without condemning himself and every other man he'd ever known."

Oddny's temper flared. How had this conversation taken such a turn?

"No wonder you get on so well with Eirik," she said. "But why is that? I've wondered about it. A moon ago you were only joining his hird to get rich and pay off your debt to me faster. And now you're up before the sun to spar with him on the field, and telling him your secrets? Explain that to me."

Halldor clenched his fists and squeezed his eyes shut, as if his next words were going to physically pain him to speak.

"He isn't who I thought he was, either," he said at last.

This brought Oddny up short, extinguished her anger as though pinching a candle flame, and all she could say was, "Oh."

Halldor said into the awkward silence that followed, "So, who do you think I am now?"

Oddny hugged her shawl more tightly around her shoulders and fiddled with the hem, looking at the ground. "I do think you're an honorable man. Because . . ."

"Yes?" he prompted.

"On the way here, when the storm hit, you did what you had to do and then you—you came to help me. I didn't even ask. You may have even saved my life that day," she said, and as she moved closer to him, she finally met his eyes. "When that big wave hit the ship and knocked Gunnhild overboard, you could have loosened your hold on me, let me drown, and everyone would've thought it was an accident. You could've let me go in after Gunnhild and drown myself, even. With me dead, you'd be released from your debt for good. But you didn't. You held on to me when you could have let go. Why?"

He seemed confused. "Because I didn't want you to die?"

"But why not?" Oddny insisted. "I'm no one to you. I'm—"

Halldor's next words erupted from him as forcefully as a dam breaking: "Because I care about you, too, all right?"

"You . . . do?"

"Yes. Because of who you've proven yourself to be," he said, still speaking quickly, as though afraid that if he didn't get the words out now, he never would. "Not just with those healing skills of yours, but with what you're doing for Signy. I hadn't expected it. You're a farm girl, and I—I thought for certain you'd stay at Ozur's and wait for my silver, find a husband, then settle down and spend the rest of your days raising children and wondering whatever became of your sister. But no. Even before Gunnhild came back to help you, you were determined to do the impossible. To rescue your sister no matter what. Oddny Ketilsdottir, you are extraordinary."

Oddny's mouth had gone dry.

"Extraordinary?" she echoed. "You think I'm—"

"Yes," said Halldor. "I do."

She gaped at him for another moment, then shook her head. "No. You don't mean that. I'm not—and if I am, it's only because of what happened. Before, I was . . . different. My entire life, all I thought I wanted was to follow in my mother's footsteps. I didn't know that I *could* want other things. But Signy always did. It didn't take desperation to change her, as it did me."

"But you did change," Halldor said. "The raid sent you down a path you never could have imagined for yourself otherwise. You have no idea how much I can relate to that."

Oddny swiped at her eyes with her shawl and let out a small wet laugh, looking down again. "Signy and I argued that day. The day of the raid. She told me I was boring. That the only thing that made me special was that I'd make a good little wife."

Eyes still downcast, she felt more than saw Halldor move closer to her, and then, to her surprise, his hand came up to brush away a tear from her eye, and he said softly, "Well, when you're the one to save her, she'll know just how wrong she was."

The silence between them felt as charged as the air before a thunderstorm. And when she raised her head, and her eyes found his, lightning struck.

Then their lips met and the rest of the world fell away.

She felt like she was floating, felt that it was *right*, as his hands moved down to her waist to pull her closer and her arm wrapped around his neck, the other hand pressing against his ribs, lingering momentarily in curiosity as her fingers found the outline of *something*—the bottom edge of what felt like a stiff, thick garment beneath his tunic, and then—

His breath hitched and he jerked away.

Oddny stepped back, confused. "Halldor?"

"Wait," he said, running a hand through his russet hair. His face was red, his breathing ragged. "Wait."

"Oh." Oddny's cheeks burned with shame. "Did I do something wrong? I—I don't have much experience in the way of—"

"It's not that. I'm—it's just—" Halldor rubbed his forehead. "Before this goes any further, I have to tell you what I told Eirik earlier."

Oddny blinked in surprise.

He straightened, seeming to steel himself. "But—but whatever you think of it, what I'm about to tell you must be kept to yourself, all right? I'm not ashamed, not even a little, but it wouldn't be safe for me if people knew. Even Eirik agreed on that. All right?"

"Of course," Oddny said with growing anxiousness. "Please just tell me."

And he said, "When I was born, my father gave me a daughter's name. And when he died, I took my own."

It took a moment for what he was saying to sink in, and then she realized several things at once: why he'd avoided the bathhouse when it was crowded, why Eirik had looked him up and down as though searching for a clue that would confirm the truth of his words. And once that truth had settled in her mind, she found that it changed nothing of her feelings for him, or her desire to be closer to him.

"Do you understand?" Halldor's eyes searched hers. "Say something."

"Yes. I understand." She hesitated. "What did Eirik say when you told him?"

Halldor clearly hadn't anticipated the question, but he looked down at his arm ring and said, "He said his decision stood. He said, 'You're not a man I want to see coming at me from the other side of the battlefield.'"

"That's wiser than I would have expected from him," Oddny said, impressed, though in those words she heard the echo of Arinbjorn's on the day Halldor had broken his nose. "No wonder you looked so surprised."

He gave her a strained smile and shifted. "I don't suppose you see me any differently now?"

Oddny tapped a finger against her chin. "Hmm. No. All I see when I look at you is a man who still owes me ten marks of silver." She looked up at him through her eyelashes. "And as a matter of fact, I happen to think you're pretty extraordinary yourself."

Halldor blinked at her a few times before breaking into a broad smile. It took her breath away. Made her heart feel too big for her chest.

And when he moved closer to her once more, it seemed the moon shone brighter.

"If that's so, perhaps that kiss was worth subtracting another mark?" Halldor said, cupping her face in his hands. His touch made her shiver and she put her arms around his waist, hardly daring to believe that this was really happening.

"Don't push your luck," Oddny said.

Before they could kiss again, Halldor broke from her and said, "Runfrid is waiting. If I want to get my tattoo touched up before she and Arinbjorn leave for Fjordane tomorrow, we'd better get back. It's already going to take most of the night."

"Right," Oddny said. It was difficult not to feel disappointed. Now that she'd actually enjoyed the touch of another person for once, it was hard not to want more, want everything, right this moment, as nervous as she was about what would come next. So when he went to pick up the bucket, she took his hand and smiled. "To Runfrid, then."

He smiled back at her and her heart soared. But as they walked back toward the armory, she thought of Signy again, suffering out there somewhere in the world while Oddny kissed a man who'd participated in the act that landed her there, and she felt the shame wash over her. It was too much to hold in her head at once.

She tried to tell herself that she and Gunnhild had done all they could for now, but then she remembered Thorbjorg's offer and the guilt reared up again like a wave, so high that it blocked out all the light that Halldor had brought into her life tonight.

She'd been foolish to turn Thorbjorg down, hadn't she? She could be halfway to Signy by now if Thorbjorg hadn't been lying, and if she truly wanted Signy back, shouldn't she have taken that risk? Had she made the right decision in rejecting the witch? How would she be able to live with herself if she'd been wrong?

Oddny could only hope that when she saw her sister again, Signy would understand.

27

GUNNHILD HAD SEPARATED HER wedding gifts from Eirik's. The ones meant for both of them—like the fine cloths—she'd left to him. She stacked them on the box chair that had been gifted to them, a magnificent thing with a high carved back and arms, the seat lifting up for storage beneath. Hnoss and Gersemi dozed on the pile of fabrics she'd set upon it, and over the back of the chair was draped another gift: a pristine polar bear pelt.

She'd included her bride-price with his things and crammed as much of her dowry as she could into her witching bag, though the silver weighed it down significantly and made the basket handle of her staff poke out. Then she took a pack basket and stuffed it with everything else she wished to take with her. She had, sadly, decided to leave her duck dress behind, as she would probably have to sell her tarnished old brooches as well as her much heavier, more extravagant, and more valuable new ones, which had been a wedding gift from King Harald himself.

Lastly, she considered the tapestry loom Queen Gyda had given her, and had the sudden urge to smash it to pieces and throw it into the hearth out of sheer spite—but then the door opened, momentarily admitting the racket of the rowdy feast, and then closed.

"What are you doing?" Eirik asked. "And what—what happened to your neck?"

She'd braided her hair over one shoulder, leaving the faint bruising visible, and now she cursed herself. Before she left she would need to put on a scarf to prevent more people from asking that question.

"I'm leaving," she said.

A clink as he set down his cup on one of the chests. "Leaving? Why?"

"I'm going back to Finnmark. Before the guests depart tomorrow, I'll find the ship headed farthest north and pay for passage on it. Discreetly. I'll stow away with Halfdan himself if I have to, to get me as far as Trondheim, and I'll make do from there." She gestured at the items piled on the box chair. "I've left you what's yours. Tell people what you will of my departure. I'll be too far away to care what they think of me."

"But *why*?"

She blinked back tears as she met his eyes. "Because I am a fraud."

Eirik folded his arms, leaned against the door, and regarded her suspiciously. "You stabbed yourself and healed the wound in an afternoon, and planted curses to protect the women in the weaving huts. Your power doesn't seem false to me. What's really going on?"

"I've been dishonest with you," she said. "I performed a failed ritual tonight, and it wasn't the first. Now I'm forced to face the fact that I'm unable to commune with the spirits on my own. My power is limited to charms and curses and a bit of healing. And that's all."

A peddler of petty sorceries. Without being able to commune with the dead and gain their knowledge, Gunnhild was only half a witch, maybe not even that. She couldn't even craft an effective protection charm; she'd tried and failed so many times already that it now seemed an impossible task. What else was beyond her?

Eirik shook his head. "I don't understand. What about the bird? During the storm? The one that came out of your chest? And what about Signy?"

Gunnhild curled her hands into fists. "Oddny will have better luck finding Signy in my absence. I'm a curse upon both of them."

Her throat was healing thanks to Oddny's salve, but her voice was still hoarse, and it cracked on the word "curse," which caused a few traitorous tears to escape her eyes. She wiped them hastily and motioned to one of the chests she was leaving behind, atop which sat a full haversack, stuffed with dowry silver that she couldn't fit in her own bag.

"This is for Oddny," Gunnhild said. "It'll be enough to get her to Birka, if you'll see her safely onto a ship heading that way. And, gods willing, after that it'll be enough to buy Signy's freedom once she's found."

"I'll see it done." Eirik rubbed his jaw. "You're not going to say good-bye to her?"

"No. It'll hurt too much." She picked up her pack basket.

He didn't reply, and when she turned to him, she saw that he was sullenly gnawing at the cuticles on his thumb. She put the basket back down, crossed the room, and ripped his hand away from his mouth. "Ask Oddny to make you something to help you stop that. A salve so nasty it'll keep you from biting them."

Eirik looked at her, then at their hands, which had not touched since they swore the blood oath in the woods of Finnmark. Not even during the wedding ceremony, when they'd clasped forearms as the priest bound them together with the woven band; not even when they'd been passing the dragon-headed cup back and forth during the feast afterward.

It was strange that this simple touch seemed such an intimate gesture. And yet.

She was suddenly reminded of the urge to grab him, the one she'd gotten in the grove. It was startling how much had changed between them since that conversation—and how little.

Then he pulled his hand away, and she suddenly remembered: He hated her. And rightly so.

"I'm sorry," she said. "About last night. I had thought during the wedding ceremony that something had changed between us. And when you were so cold to me for the rest of the day, and then got angry with me for sticking up for you, I was bitter."

Eirik, still slouched against the door with his arms folded, looked up at the ceiling. "I'm not used to showing affection, and people aren't used to seeing it from me. I was afraid that if I doted on you, my father and stepmother would think it so out of character as to prove I'm being bewitched. Better not to let them see that you mean anything to me."

Gunnhild stared at him. He'd wanted to show her affection? He'd wanted to *dote* on her? But he was worried that his parents would think it suspicious to see him *happy*?

He frowned at the puzzled look on her face. "Is that so surprising?"

"Yes, it is. It's just—I don't know." She flailed her hands. "Gods. You can be so *frustrating*."

Eirik stepped away from the door and stood up straighter. "Well, you're more frustrating by far. The first time I saw you, I thought to my-self, *That is the most beautiful woman I've ever seen.* And then you opened your mouth."

Beautiful? This was too much to untangle. She had to leave, and leave now. But something kept her feet rooted to the spot. "And yet you treated me as though I were some wild animal looking to murder you and your men in cold blood."

"It was a difficult summer. I was on edge. I was paranoid."

"Well, that hardly excuses your behavior."

"As you say. As to the rest—we're married. You're not leaving."

"And you would stop me?"

He held up his left hand to show her the scar across his palm. "We swore an oath, remember? So what if you can't prophesize? You created the bindrune—"

"Which you have yet to test. For all you know I've failed at that, too," she said bitterly. If Thorbjorg had realized that Eirik's men were no longer susceptible to her mind magic, she hadn't given any indication over the course of the festival. Not that Gunnhild would've expected her to.

"On the contrary, I have every confidence." He cast his eyes to the ceiling again. "And I—I don't wish for you to go."

Gunnhild felt as though the ground had rocked beneath her feet.

"You don't . . . *what*? But last night—" She gestured to the wine-stained tapestry. "I thought— Things between us have been *bad*, Eirik. Why would you possibly want me to stay?"

He met her eyes at last and moved toward her. "Ever since we met, my every waking thought has been of you, for better or worse," he said qui-etly. "I won't pretend I never despised you. I truly did, at first. But you have challenged me. You have complicated me. And I think, eventually, I'll be better for it—and better to *you*, if you'd only grant me the same courtesy."

This rendered her momentarily speechless. He was so near to her now that she could reach out and touch him, but he came no closer.

"I can't forget the reason I loathed you before we even met," she said, slowly. "The things you've done—"

"Can't be taken back. I can't change who I am, Gunnhild. I can't change what I do, what I was made to be. I'm good at one thing and one thing only. And that's violence. My brother called me our father's attack dog, and I fear it's not far from the truth. I don't know that I can ever be more. But maybe—together—*we* can."

Gunnhild was completely at a loss.

She could go back to the wilderness. Complete her training and take Heid's name. Live a long, happy, unremarkable life. Leave Oddny and Signy to their fates and hope their luck would be better in her absence. Forsake both oaths she'd sworn. Walk away.

Or she could choose this. Choose them. Choose *him*.

But what held her back was the understanding that if she chose him now, she might do so again and again until eventually there would be no question and no choice at all.

Until it would always be him.

That, she realized, was love. A different kind of love than she felt for her sworn sisters and for Heid. A love like fire, warm and bright and destructive all at once. And she wasn't certain she should kindle this feeling, for she didn't have to be a seeress to know that one day the resulting blaze might very well consume all else.

Eirik seemed unsettled by her long silence. "That is—if you choose to remain here. But if you truly wish to leave, then I won't make you stay."

Before she could stop herself, she reached forward and pushed his hair behind his ear. He inhaled sharply, and at first he twitched away as though the brush of her fingers repulsed him, frightened him even—but as she let her hand linger on the side of his face, she felt his resistance cave, felt him begin to lean into her hand. As though he'd been longing for a gentle touch, *her* touch, but was terrified of the feelings it might evoke in him.

Their oath had been the strike of flint against a fire steel, the spark. And she had decided that she would fan the flames.

"What are you doing?" he managed.

"Making my choice," she said, and kissed him.

When their lips met, the feeling that surged through her was unlike anything she'd ever felt—it was *certainty*, as though a piece of her had finally slid into place, two ends of a tether tied together, the last stitch in the tapestry of their interwoven fates.

He returned the kiss hesitantly, as if in disbelief, before reaching down to hold her closer, moving his hands from her waist down to her hips as she wrapped her arms around his neck, and suddenly his hands were on her thighs and he turned her, lifted her, crushed her against the wall. She gasped, both in surprise and at the feeling of the length of his body pressed against hers, and at the fierce hunger that flared in her as a result. She clung to him, fisting her hands in his hair as their mouths met again, as he braced her with a knee and started bunching up her dress and—

Fast, too fast. Gunnhild needed to get her bearings. She needed to stay in control, like she'd been during the sacrifice, when he'd been so enthralled by her that he couldn't bear to look away. And sex was just another ritual, wasn't it?

Gunnhild abruptly tore her mouth away from his and Eirik stilled, looking at her, his face flushed, a question in his eyes. She slid from his grip and planted both feet on the floor, grabbed him by the shirt collar, and guided him backward. When she pushed him to sit down on the box chair, the pile of fabric she'd stacked on the seat toppled and sent the cats bolting under the bed, though the bearskin remained in place on the chair's back. Eirik didn't resist, hands clasped on the arms of the chair, eyes wide and hungry.

He did not move as she hiked up her dress, climbed onto the chair, and straddled him, nor did he resist when she pulled his tunic over his head. Ran her fingertips over the battle scars that crisscrossed the slightly darker hair on his chest and belly, up to the snarling wolf tattoos near his collarbones, which were also slashed with long-healed injuries; at her touch, his breathing became heavier, quicker, and he grabbed her hips again and held her closer.

She moved one hand down to the drawstring on his pants while she twined the other hand in his hair. She pulled a little harder than she intended when she tilted his head back, and confusion and irritation and desire warred on his face—he was clearly used to being the one in control in these situations—but when she moved against him, she felt him react; desire had clearly won.

Gunnhild grinned. Arinbjorn had been right about one thing—it *was* satisfying to see Eirik humbled. *Enormously* satisfying.

She whispered, "Perhaps you should get used to looking up at me."

And he whispered back, "I can't say I mind the view."

28

THE ESTATE WENT SILENT after Winternights, but the armory was quietest; only half the hird had stayed for the winter, Svein and Halldor among them. Runfrid, having gone to Fjordane with Arinbjorn, had given Oddny permission to use the loft as a dedicated space for her healing work.

Gunnhild was more cheerful than Oddny expected her to be after the last failed ritual, and Oddny soon had a sneaking suspicion as to why. Now that there were so few people about—only the usual residents, Eirik's reduced hird, and his father's hird remained—everyone dined together in the longhouse, so she got a chance to witness Eirik and Gunnhild's interactions. The couple still argued incessantly about trivial things, but seeing the sudden lack of vitriol between them was downright startling to Oddny.

"Good to see them finally getting along, isn't it, dear?" she heard Thora say to King Harald one day after supper, during which the young king and queen had not had a single squabble.

"Yes, but would that we couldn't *hear* them getting along all night while we're trying to sleep," Queen Gyda muttered, earning a sideways look from her husband and a giggle from Thora.

That night, as always, little Hakon sat in his mother's lap, eating a boiled egg and talking excitedly about his sword fighting lessons from Eirik and the hird. Thora smiled indulgently as she listened, stroking the child's white hair. Thora might not have been of humble birth, but unlike many people born into similar wealth, she was of kind spirit, and like Ulla, she seemed to carry sunshine with her wherever she went.

Saeunn started excusing Oddny from weaving more and more often, for Oddny had become busy. As word got around that she'd brewed a tea to relieve Saeunn's knee pain, an increasing number of people began to enlist her services.

Oddny soon realized that she wouldn't have enough supplies to last the winter, even after Hrafnhild had given her unlimited access to the estate's stores in exchange for coming up with a potion to ease the cook's chronically irritable bowels. And there were some supplies that couldn't be found in the garden at all, so before Ulla left to visit her family, Oddny took her up on her offer to go foraging, and the two of them donned snowshoes and spent a short, cold afternoon gathering plants in the woods.

About two moons after Winternights came Yule, and after the Yule moons passed and the festivities were over with, Ulla went home for her visit. The workshop seemed colder in her absence, so Oddny took to spending more time in Runfrid's loft even when she wasn't grinding herbs or mixing teas. When Ulla returned a few weeks later, Oddny spent as much time at the workshop as she could between making and dispensing her remedies, and found that she'd missed the soothing, repetitive motions of weaving almost as much as she'd missed her friend.

It was hard not to feel the presence of the goddesses with her as she worked, their statues perched fierce and watchful on the lintel. When Oddny had first arrived, she'd left offerings for Eir in the workshop and continued to carry her mother's statue in her bag, but now that she had access to the loft, she took it out and placed it where Runfrid had kept the likeness of Skadi she'd taken with her to Fjordane. Oddny felt most connected with her patron when doing healing work, so the loft seemed a better place for it. Sometimes she thought she could feel Eir working beside her, guiding her hand, whispering in her ear.

The short days passed quickly, as did the long nights. Though Oddny spent most of her time in the loft, she was reluctant to sleep there; Eirik's hird had bedded down in the armory so that King Harald's retinue could have the main hall, and being alone with so many strange men made

Oddny ill at ease. Even knowing that Halldor and Svein would be among those asleep below her, she knew she'd be listening from the loft, hand on her knife, for any unexpected creak of the ladder.

But one night she was so exhausted that she fell asleep on Runfrid's bedroll, shivering under her thin shawl, and awoke to find Halldor shaking her shoulder, the pale morning light softening his face. For a moment she thought she was dreaming, until he leaned down to kiss her and said with a crooked smile, "You know, you could have at least invited me up if you were intending to spend the night. We could've kept each other warm."

Her heart skipped a beat. They'd had a few stolen kisses here and there, some heavier than others, but she still sometimes flinched at being touched for too long, no matter how much she wanted to be. Early on, she'd explained this to him just as she'd explained it to Arinbjorn at Winternights.

Halldor had pondered her words for a long time, and for a moment Oddny had felt a stab of terror that he'd lose interest in her. By the looks she'd seen some of the serving girls give him, she didn't think it'd be a difficult task to find another woman to take to bed.

Then at length he'd said, "Oddny, sex doesn't have to be the culmination of our affections."

"But I want it," she'd protested. "I do. I only need time."

One night after midwinter, Halldor broke his rule about drinking too much outside of Yule when he, Oddny, Ulla, and Svein found themselves embroiled in a particularly competitive dice game. After, Oddny and Halldor stumbled hand in hand to the loft, and once they made it up the ladder, he kissed her until she couldn't remember her name. Then his hand started wandering up her dress and he paused, remembering himself, and whispered, "Is this all right?"

Oddny, having had just enough ale to feel good while maintaining a clear head, smiled and whispered back, "Yes."

That was the way things continued between them: "Is this all right?" and "Can I touch you there?" both learning to navigate the other's body, what felt good and what didn't. As the winter wore on, Oddny took to spending most of her nights in the loft with him and spent the rest in the workshop with the women, unwilling to completely give herself over to this budding romance, afraid that if she did, there would be nothing left of her afterward.

If this was truly love, it was sweeter than she could have ever imagined—and more dangerous by far.

GUNNHILD NO LONGER FREQUENTED the workshop. Instead, she snowshoed to the grove in the afternoons, and in the mornings she sat down in the main hall and took lessons with the Lawspeaker— Saeunn's elderly father, a cheerful mustachioed man named Hrolf who always wore a bright yellow nalbound hat. When Oddny asked one day at breakfast if she planned on memorizing the entire law code, as the Lawspeakers did, Gunnhild laughed.

"Twelve winters away from society hasn't done me any favors," she said. "When we make the royal progress or go to assemblies, cases will be brought before Eirik. It'd help if I knew the laws as well as everyone else does."

"I suppose that's wise." Oddny wondered if Eirik knew that Gunnhild's reason for learning the law was to help him rule, but the fact that he wasn't stopping her meant he either didn't know or didn't care. Oddny suspected the latter.

But at least Gunnhild was keeping busy. Despite Oddny's best efforts to keep herself occupied as well, her sister was never far from her mind, and her anticipation for winter's end and the voyage to Birka grew with each passing day. Gunnhild felt the same, and did her best to distract both Oddny and herself by frequenting the loft with oatcakes and honey she'd cajoled from Hrafnhild in between her morning law lessons and afternoon witching work. Oddny wasn't used to having anything so sweet and rich, let alone having it between meals. But despite how much more she'd been eating since she left Halogaland, her body remained as thin and wiry as it had always been.

The opposite was true for Gunnhild, who told her one day at supper in the main hall, "It's a good thing you sewed these dresses a bit bigger, Oddny. Hrafnhild is quite a cook."

"I did it because I figured now that you're married, you'd be with child sooner or later," Oddny replied.

A strange look crossed Gunnhild's face. "I appreciate that, but I'm not trying to conceive until I know there's one less witch in the Nine Worlds who wants to kill me."

Oddny lowered her voice. "If you're brewing a contraceptive, you shouldn't be taking it every day. It could stop your blood from coming at all if you use it too frequently."

Gunnhild replied in kind. "I'm not. I've used a spell instead. I stuffed it in the mattress on my side of the bed." She cast a brief look at Eirik, and when she turned back to Oddny, her eyes were hard. "I'm not bringing a child into this world while Thorbjorg still walks it. I'm not giving myself one more thing to worry about."

Oddny couldn't fault her for that. She wondered if her friend was still having bad dreams, or if the horror of her near drowning had finally worn off. A week later, she got her answer.

On that day, Gunnhild deemed the weather too cold to make it to the grove, so she went to the loft to sit with Oddny, armed with her witching bag, which was filled with flat sticks she'd made from branches in the woods. She sat there carving on them and whispering to herself for some time, with Oddny grinding herbs with her mortar and pestle in silence on the other side. It was, despite her friend's muttering and the faint sounds of the men sparring outside, strangely peaceful.

Forgetting for a moment that she wasn't alone, Oddny began to sing under her breath, as she often did while she was at work.

A furrow appeared in Gunnhild's brow as her head snapped up. "Is that—?"

"Oh, it's—it's your chant from the storm," Oddny said, flushing. "The one you used to dispel it. I thought it was pretty."

Gunnhild sat back on her haunches and tilted her head. "You *were* a little mimic when we were children, weren't you? Always repeating things. Signy said once that you should be a Lawspeaker."

"I have a good memory," Oddny said with a shrug of her shoulder.

They went back to work on their respective tasks.

"Do you think you'd ever want to learn magic?" Gunnhild asked a short while later, with thinly veiled interest.

"Me?" Oddny didn't look up. "No."

"Why not? You can see the threads. That means you've got a touch of something in you. You don't want to cultivate it?"

Oddny shook her head. "I'd rather use it to do exactly what I'm doing now, if anything. Sorcery isn't for me." The pestle stilled in her hand. "But what is it like, to travel? To be a bird or—wherever you go when you go—*down*?"

"I can't fully explain it," Gunnhild said. "Part of it is instinctive. I've heard there are some witches whose minds can take more than one shape, but mine came out as a swallow, and I'm content with it." She gave Oddny a sideways look. "I wonder what form yours would take."

Oddny couldn't hope to speculate on that, so she went on. "And when you go down, how do the spirits speak through you? You didn't say anything when you were in trance at Winternights, but something must've been happening down there."

Gunnhild offered no clue as to what that something was, but answered her question: "There are two ways to do it. One is that you speak with them, and come back and tell people what was said. The other is that they come up and touch your thread, travel up it, and speak through your mouth as you wait below. You can hear what they're saying." Gunnhild looked down at her stick. "Heid preferred to do things that way in her old age. Said she couldn't remember what they told her, so it's best to let them say it themselves—like what she did at my father's, except she interrupted the spirit giving the prophecy about us."

Oddny shuddered. "But couldn't they—*possess* you? And couldn't witches possess each other that way?"

"That was my first question, too, but Heid told me it can't happen," Gunnhild said. "Your thread is your tether to *your* body, and it's not easily broken. If another witch wanted to possess you, they'd have to sever both your threads and then bind theirs to your body, which is impossible, because the moment they sever their own thread, they've doomed themselves. And as for spirits, who have no thread—this is why the warding songs are so important, Oddny. They don't just summon the spirits; they also keep out the ones that would hurt you. If a spirit did mean to possess you, the songs wouldn't let it anywhere near."

Oddny mulled this over. "You told me once that Thorbjorg had some kind of mind magic that Heid never taught you—hence the bindrune—but are there other things you might have never learned? Things she might have . . . kept from you?"

Gunnhild looked up sharply. "Are you *sure* you're not interested in becoming a witch?"

Oddny shook her head.

"Suit yourself," said Gunnhild with finality, and got back to work. Each time she completed a rune stick, she tucked it into her belt pocket, ran her knife across the back of her hand, swore at the sight of the resulting blood, extracted the stick, and threw it into a growing pile.

"Gunna," Oddny said after she'd watched this happen at least a dozen times out of the corner of her eye, "what exactly are you doing?"

"Trying to create a protection charm," Gunnhild responded. She heaved a ragged sigh and tossed her latest failed rune stick aside, slumping against the wall. "But it's slow going."

"A protection charm? But the bindrune—"

"Is to protect the mind. Now I need one to protect the body. But that's more—complicated," Gunnhild said. "If they were easy to make, whole armies would have them, wouldn't they?"

"I don't know about that. I think even if it were easy, no one would use them. We've spent our whole lives hearing warriors talk about Valhalla— you'd think some of them *wanted* to die. A glorious death is more appealing to them than growing old," Oddny said. "And I doubt that cheating to stay alive in battle would be seen as honorable, even if it granted your side victory."

"Then it's a good thing I'm not going to battle," Gunnhild said dismissively.

Oddny slid a small flat clay pot containing a healing salve over to her.

Gunnhild took it, thanked her, and smeared its contents over the cuts on the back of her hand. Oddny hedged: "I'm guessing you're making it for yourself, because you're afraid of—of what happened on the ship on the way here? Are you still having the dreams?"

"Less so these days." Gunnhild re-covered the pot with its waxed linen topper, and slid it back to her. "And no, I'm not afraid. It's just a precaution." As if eager for a change of subject, she cast a look at the two bedrolls sitting in the corner of the loft and gave Oddny a knowing smile. "Saeunn says you don't sleep in the workshop so often anymore."

Heat crept up Oddny's neck. "That's true."

Gunnhild scooted across the floor to her and took her hand. "I'm happy for you, Oddny. I really am. I know I wasn't sure if we could trust Halldor at first, but I trust your judgment." She waggled her eyebrows. "If you'd like to trade details, just say the word."

Oddny flushed but decided to say nothing. The privilege of getting to know the person she lay with before bedding them was one she knew many people weren't granted, and that made her cherish it all the more—enough to keep it close. It felt better that way, like something precious, a joy that was only hers and Halldor's to know. Telling another of their most private moments would feel too strange, even if that person were her best friend.

"If it's all the same, I'd rather not. But it's been—good." Oddny couldn't help but return her smile. "Very good."

"To each their own," Gunnhild said. "Do you think he'll marry you? He has no reason not to, if you two are getting along so well."

Oddny felt a twinge in her chest. "I hope so, maybe, one day. We haven't spoken of it."

Gunnhild sat back, thoughtful. "What do you think Signy will say when she sees you two together? She'll definitely remember him, even if it's just as the man Kolfinna tossed overboard."

Oddny grimaced. Gunnhild often spoke of Signy as though she were going to be waiting at the docks at Birka when they arrived. As though Birka were their final destination and not merely a starting point for the search. Oddny, on the other hand, remained more realistic. She knew it could take all summer to find Signy—longer, if Kolfinna and her crew had already set off on the raids by the time Oddny and Gunnhild arrived.

"I've thought about that. We'll have to be careful about how we tell her," Oddny said uneasily. "But I'm happy for you, too, Gunna. I know I had my doubts about Eirik, too, but it turns out he's not exactly as he seemed, is he? And here I'd thought that a man like him couldn't be changed by a tender hand."

Gunnhild was quiet for some time, gathering her thoughts.

"I don't think it's as easy as that," she said at last. "He's lived his life at the edge of a blade, and it's difficult to let others see him be soft. I don't know if that will ever change. Sometimes I feel we're getting somewhere, other times less so. But winter is a time for rest, and summer for action, so winter's end will be the real test."

Oddny glanced out the smoke hole in the gable to where the men were sparring on the snowy practice field. "I suppose you're right."

A moment after she looked away, a cry went up from the yard and little Hakon shrieked, "Halldor! Yay, Halldor!" as the dogs barked. Oddny looked again just in time to see Halldor helping Eirik up, and her breath caught.

"What?" Gunnhild asked, scrambling over to look as well. "What's happened?"

"I think Halldor just won a round against Eirik," Oddny said.

"I— Well, then. I suppose his footwork must've improved after all. Good for him." An odd look crossed Gunnhild's face before her mouth curved into a suggestive smile. "Congratulate him well tonight, will you?" to which Oddny responded by elbowing her lightly in the ribs.

Gunnhild took her leave soon after. Oddny worked through supper, preparing a batch of tea to help one of the carpenters' wives with the nausea brought on by pregnancy, and even after she'd lit Runfrid's candles, she hadn't realized how late in the day it had become until she heard the men below file in from supper, and Halldor ascended the ladder, balancing a stew bowl in one hand.

Once he'd crawled into the loft, he gave her a peck on the lips and sat down cross-legged beside her.

"Thank you," Oddny said, reaching for the bowl.

Halldor held it away from her and looked at her in exaggerated surprise. "Who said this was for you? Go get your own."

"Stop jesting and hand it over."

He did, smirking. "You've been busy up here, I take it? I wondered when I didn't see you in the hall."

"I've been *very* busy, yes. Did you truly beat Eirik today during practice?"

"I did. Barely. And just the once."

"That counts for something, doesn't it?" Oddny stuffed a spoonful of meat and turnip into her mouth and looked at him in profile. She'd freshly shaved the salmon tattoo again the night before, and now she nodded at it. "Are you ever going to tell me its significance, Halldor Salmonhead?"

"Maybe one day, Oddny Coal-brow," he said, which was the same answer he'd given her the last time she'd asked. He leaned against the chest behind him as she ate. When she finished, she put the bowl aside and rested her head on his shoulder, and he put an arm around her. Below, several of the hirdsmen were playing dice, and while their noise usually drowned out whatever she and Halldor got up to in the loft, tonight she wished for a bit of peace and quiet. No wonder Runfrid had complained when the hird had returned from the raids.

"What are you thinking about?" Oddny asked him at length. It was a common question they posed to each other, both being prone to long, comfortable silences.

"I was thinking . . ." Halldor looked down at the arm ring on his bicep. "Eirik has been talking about making the royal progress after Birka this summer instead of raiding. Which means that it might take me more than one season to make what I owe you."

Oddny smiled. "What a shame. We'll have to deal with each other for a little longer."

"And I was thinking," he went on, "that even though Eirik would never admit it, I have a feeling that his raiding days are over, or near to it. His father is getting on in years, and it's time for Eirik to actually act like a king. So I thought that I might get better at smithing, pay off your debt that way, and stay in the hird."

"You know, I really don't care about the debt—"

"Oddny, I'm being serious. I mean to pay you back."

"Well, if you're going to be stubborn about it, we can always just call it my bride-price."

The words had come out before she could fully think about their implications, and her eyes went wide when she realized what she'd just said. Halldor slipped his arm from around her shoulders and pulled away to stare at her.

Oddny's face heated. "I didn't mean—it's not as though I was assuming—I'm going to stop talking now."

Halldor leaned back against the chest again and ran a hand through his curls. His face was a mask, stony and unreadable and—worried? Was he truly so disquieted by the thought of marrying her? Oddny thought she might die of shame.

But then he said, "I just—I never thought—" Seeing the look on her face, he blanched. "Oh, gods, Oddny. It's not you. I promise. It's just that I never considered that my life would go this way. I spent nine summers learning to fight. I'm a raider. I'm a warrior. I always thought—"

"That you'd be dead by now," Oddny finished quietly.

"Something like that," Halldor said after a beat. "But now I know things don't have to be that way."

Oddny gave him a tentative smile. "You could live, and be happy."

"I *am* happy." Halldor smiled back, one of his soft smiles that made her heart melt, and put his arm around her again. "I was thinking—you should come with us when the hird goes on the progress. Gunnhild will be going, too, so I'm not the only one who will miss you if you stay behind. But I know it will depend on what Signy wants to do . . ."

It was Oddny's turn to go quiet. The truth was that she hadn't thought much past Signy's rescue. What would become of the two sisters then? Would they indeed stay with Gunnhild, or would Signy wish to go somewhere else? Would Oddny have to choose between them?

There was no use dwelling on it until Signy was safely by her side again.

"What are *you* thinking about?" Halldor asked.

"Signy."

He tightened his arm around her. "It won't be long now, Oddny. Winter is almost over."

"But part of me wishes it would never end," Oddny whispered, turning to him, raising a hand to cup his smooth cheek. "I know it's selfish of me, but—"

"I don't think it's selfish to cherish happiness when you find it, for as long as you can." Halldor put his hand over hers, seeming troubled—but why?

The question was on her lips, but he silenced it with a kiss, and the rest of the world faded away along with her worries.

29

GUNNHILD HAD ALWAYS CONSIDERED winter her least favorite season. Before now it had meant carving her runes with stiff fingers or sending out her mind with Heid, only to return to a body she could barely feel for the cold. And prior to that, she'd been trapped indoors, unable to escape her mother.

This winter was entirely different. Gunnhild had gone from spending the season sleeping on a frozen dirt floor to waking up and swinging her legs over the side of a bed, only for her toes to meet a plush bearskin rug. The only time she knew cold was when she went outside.

Was it selfish of her to savor these comforts? She knew Oddny thought so, but as much as Gunnhild had tried to distract her friend from her guilt, there was no running from her own. So she turned her mind to other things, like the frustrating protection charm she was trying to create. Even when she did get the runes right, in order to make the spell powerful she would need to pour weeks' worth of energy into it. Preventing shallow slashes on her arm was one thing, but what about stabbing blows or arrow wounds or the incoming swing of an axe? She wasn't going to run a blade through her own heart to test the charm's effectiveness.

She could only hope that it would hold up if Thorbjorg decided to do as much to her, or worse.

Late one night after her conversation with Oddny in the loft, she woke to find Eirik slouched on the box chair, deep in his cups, a lit soapstone lantern on the stool nearby, a half-mended tunic in his lap. He stared into the fire, looking lost.

This was a normal enough occurrence, but it was beginning to rankle her. *Am I not enough to make you happy?* she sometimes wanted to scream at him. *Am I not enough to keep the memories at bay, to keep you here with me?*

She slipped from bed and stripped off her pleated linen underdress. It was one of the only ones that still fit; winter had filled out her body in ways both she and Eirik appreciated, and also had created vivid red stretch marks on her breasts and hips and belly, of which she remained unselfconscious as she crossed the room. She took his mending from his limp hands and slid into his lap, leaning her head against his shoulder as he put one arm around her back and the other around her legs as she curled them up to her chest.

"Can I tempt you to bed?" Gunnhild asked, examining the half-mended tunic. "Or are you too busy not sewing? I don't think you've made a single stitch since I went to sleep."

Eirik gave her a flat look.

She secured the needle in the fabric and tossed the tunic onto the rug. "Peace, Eiki. I didn't mean to offend."

"There's a surprise." He said it with less venom than he might have a few moons earlier, and he nearly smiled at the diminutive. The first time she'd said it, he'd said, *"No one's ever shortened my name before,"* with the same wonder on his face as when Thora had been kind to him at the docks. *"Not even my mother. Not even Arinbjorn."*

"Why won't you take that sleeping draught Oddny made you?" she asked him.

"Stop trying to mother me, Gunnsa."

That nickname, the one only he called her, made her feel warm. But she wouldn't be deterred. "I could always sneak it into your ale at dinner."

"Without my consent?" Eirik rolled his eyes. "How honorable of you."

"As it happens, I'm not above such things if they're for your own good."

His lip curled slightly. "And you always know best, do you?"

"Yes. Haven't you realized by now?" She relaxed against him, and they stayed like that for some time, she looking at him worriedly as he stared into the middle distance. Then she sat up straighter, put her lips to his temple, reached to brush his hair behind his ear, fingertips lingering at the base of his jaw, and whispered, "Where are you?"

She had never asked before. If he was surprised by the question, he didn't show it.

"The same place I always am. The night I burned Rognvald and his men," he said, and it was the first time she'd heard him speak of it as something he had done rather than something that had simply happened. When he continued, his words were slow and deliberate, as though the scene were happening now, before his very eyes. "He had burned some herb to put the rest of them to sleep—the place stank of it. I only saw the shapes of them. But my brother, he—he sat there right in front of the hearth, facing the open door. He knew we were coming. He could have run. I left the door open as I ordered fire set to the hall. I watched him burn with my own two eyes. Why didn't he run? I've asked myself this question every day for the past seven winters."

Gunnhild felt chilled to the bone.

"Perhaps he knew there was no escape," she offered. "Perhaps he knew your father was determined to see him dead—"

"Maybe I should just let her kill me," Eirik said, so quietly that Gunnhild thought for a moment that she'd imagined it.

She gaped at him. How long had he been thinking this way? Was this truly what kept him up at night? "What? No. I won't hear of it."

"Why not? Thorbjorg is only doing what anyone else would do. If she were a man, or a warrior, she would've challenged me to a duel. But instead she has to do what she can, draw things out, target the people closest to me to ward off suspicion. And I'm tired of it. I'm tired of constantly looking over my shoulder. It would be better for everyone if I let her have what she wants. Does my brother not deserve to be avenged?"

"Of course he does," Gunnhild said fiercely. "No one deserves what you—what your father had you do to him. But if she kills you, it won't bring Rognvald back."

"Not any more than you killing Thorbjorg and Katla will bring Heid back."

"That's different," she said. "When I kill them, it won't just be for revenge, but to protect us. They won't stop until they've seen this through, so I have to stop them before they do."

"But at what cost?"

"At *any* cost. Eirik, stop this foolishness. If you were planning to offer yourself up as a sacrifice to ease your guilt, then you should have left me in the woods in Finnmark. The time for that has long passed. Our only option now is to do what we do best."

"And what's that?" Eirik asked dully.

Gunnhild grabbed him by the chin and turned him to face her.

"We fight," she said.

AS SOON AS THE worst of winter had passed and the air began to warm, King Harald spoke of returning to his favorite estate, at Avaldsnes, farther south. At the first thaw, his men began removing his ships from the sheds where they had been stored and maintained. They also uncovered and retarred the ones that had sat on the beach during the long season, Eirik's own ship among them, to ensure that all were seaworthy.

Eirik summoned the hird to the armory along with Oddny and Gunnhild. As the weather had improved, several ships had arrived from local farms and his hirdsmen had started to return, so a little over half of the hird was present when Gunnhild took her seat next to Oddny and Halldor.

No sooner had she sat down than a wave of nausea hit her, and she took deep, slow breaths through her nose as Oddny shot her a look of concern. Gunnhild shook her head and waited for it to pass. It had been happening for the past week but wasn't confined to just the morning, as she'd heard was the case when one was with child.

"Gunna," Oddny whispered, "do you think you're with—?"

"Impossible," Gunnhild replied in kind. "It must've been something I ate."

Oddny seemed unconvinced, but when Gunnhild offered no further information, she turned to face forward as the last few hirdsmen trickled into the armory.

"I know you've all been wondering whether or not we'll be raiding after our trip to Birka," Eirik said once the room quieted. "Between what happened last summer and the scene my brothers caused at my wedding, I'm wary of leaving Norway for any length of time. I have no doubt of my father's health and ability to rule, but should he happen to die while we're away, the consequences would be disastrous. I would hear your opinions on the matter."

"If we don't go raiding, do you intend to make the royal progress?" Svein asked. He shot a look in Gunnhild's direction. "To introduce your wife around the country?"

"Those were my thoughts exactly," Eirik said. "And we'd be away a few weeks at most before making the progress. All in favor?"

No one dissented. Oddny, however, looked concerned.

"And what if we don't find out where my sister has gone at Birka, or we find she's been sold somewhere so far away that it'll take us most of the summer to reach her?" she asked.

"We'll hire a crew at Birka and go from there," said Gunnhild.

"No," said Eirik at once. "Out of the question."

"What? Oddny and I would be safe. We can look after ourselves," Gunnhild said, and he cut her a glare, which she returned. If something terrible happened in the short time they were away from Norway and Eirik wasn't there to face it, she would never forgive herself. She'd go on without him if she had to—Signy was *her* sworn sister, after all.

"We'll talk about it if it comes to that," Eirik said with finality. "Anyone else? Other thoughts? Or are we in agreement?"

"Will we not wait for Arinbjorn to return?" Svein asked.

"We've word from Fjordane that his father has fallen ill, so he doesn't know when he'll be back," said Eirik. "Better to leave without him and return sooner."

Gunnhild didn't particularly like the idea of going without Arinbjorn—and by the looks on some of the men's faces, this was a popular opinion. She recalled Thorolf's words from the first night they'd lain together, about what Eirik was capable of when his foster brother wasn't there to hold him back, so Gunnhild knew she might have to step into that role should a fight break out or trouble arise.

She hoped it wouldn't come to that, though. She had enough to worry about; it was likely that she would be fighting all the way to Birka, for she anticipated that Thorbjorg or Katla or the seal would begin to haunt them the moment they set sail. But she'd completed the protection charm to the best of her abilities, so all she could do was put it in her pouch and hope for the best. She needed to remain strong if she was to have any hope of defending against the witches, her sudden bouts of nausea notwithstanding.

So far her illness seemed immune to both potions and spells. And she couldn't ask Oddny to make her something, because once Oddny found out Gunnhild was sick, she would do the Oddny thing and tell Eirik, and then Gunnhild would have to stay behind, and both of them would say it was for her own good. And then what would happen if the witches sent another freak storm to sink the ship? The hird had survived them before Gunnhild, but still—anything could happen, and remaining at home was a risk she wasn't willing to take.

She would push through this, no matter what.

"Don't drink too much this evening," Eirik said by way of a dismissal. "We leave tomorrow at first light."

As the men got up to leave, Oddny stayed frozen in her seat and squeezed Gunnhild's hand so hard she thought her bones would shatter. Gunnhild put a hand atop Oddny's and bade her relax, but it was hard to contain her own excitement. This was the moment they'd been waiting for ever since they'd first reunited.

"It's time, Oddny," she whispered. "We're going to find her."

PART IV

30

THE VOYAGE WENT SMOOTHLY until they rounded the southern tip of Norway and began heading east. It was sunrise and Gunnhild and Oddny were still asleep when they heard the shouts, and before they could fully rouse themselves, the ship lurched beneath them and picked up speed. The women exchanged brief looks of panic before tugging on their shoes and sea-cloaks and stumbling out of the tent—and into a fog so thick they could barely make out the mast and sail, let alone the other end of the ship.

"What's going on?" Oddny called, apprehension writhing in her belly. "Is it another storm?"

Halldor came toward them with a lantern, looking grim. "It came out of nowhere. And look."

He gestured behind him, and Oddny saw the shapes of the hirdsmen tying up the sail. But despite that, the ship was not losing speed. It was as though a giant invisible hand were moving them through the water, like little Hakon playing with his toy boat in a puddle. At the stern, the steersman fought with the rudder, which seemed to be stuck in place.

"Can't you stop the ship?" Oddny asked. "Put the oars in and—?"

"We tried, but we're going too fast. They flew out of our hands the moment they touched the water," Svein said as he came up beside Halldor. "We have spares, but not enough to try again." There was more standing water on deck than usual; some of the men were bailing it with buckets. "And we think there's a hole in the hull."

"The water is too calm." Gunnhild shuffled sideways to peer over the gunnel. "It's them. There's no other explanation."

"Well," Svein said, "at least it's not a storm."

Eirik appeared and grabbed Gunnhild by the arm, hauled her back, and called out to the rest of the hird: "Stay away from the sides. Whatever is doing this might be in the water. If anyone goes overboard, we've no hope of finding you." He turned to his wife. "Is there anything you can do?"

Gunnhild set her jaw and nodded. "Let me get my bag."

But as she turned and took a step forward, she swayed and fell to her knees, hitting the deck hard. Oddny was by her side in a moment, and Eirik at the other.

"What's wrong?" Oddny asked, and Gunnhild shoved both of them off and made for the tent. Moments later, they heard her vomit into a bucket. Oddny looked to Eirik, whose eyebrows had drawn together with worry and, if Oddny hadn't known better, annoyance, as though he suspected that his wife had been hiding something.

Gunnhild crawled back out of the tent with her witching bag over her shoulder, her staff poking out the top of it, and made to stand. Eirik took her by the elbow and helped her up.

"It's only seasickness," she said, waving him off, twisting away—only to lose her balance and nearly topple into him. He caught her before she fell.

It was Oddny's turn to take her friend's arm. "Come. You need to lie down."

"Oddny, we're trapped in a mysterious fog, being pushed toward an unknown destination," Gunnhild snapped. "I'm not going to *lie down*."

"Don't be so stubborn. If you're sick to your stomach, that poison tea of yours won't be doing you any favors."

"What else am I supposed to do?"

"Where do you think we're being taken?" Svein asked suddenly, peering out into the gloom. "When we started picking up speed, I felt like we turned to the left." He looked to the steersman, and the man nodded.

"So north," Halldor said. "Maybe they mean to run us aground. Or—"

"Or worse," Eirik said darkly. He turned once again to his wife. "Lie down. Now."

They held each other's gazes for a long, tense moment before Gunnhild said quietly, "Fine. But when we find ourselves smashed to bits against a rocky cliff, don't bother waking me. I'd rather die in my sleep than drown."

"That doesn't even make sense," Eirik said, but she'd already gone back into the tent, jostling him with her shoulder as she went. He looked to Oddny and said, "Stay with her. Make sure she doesn't . . . *go* anywhere."

Oddny had planned on doing so anyway. When she went into the tent, Gunnhild was curled up on one of the bedrolls atop the oars, facing away, sulking. Oddny dug around in her friend's witching bag until she found the leather canteen of henbane tea, made sure it was still full, and stuffed it into her healing bag for safekeeping. Peering once again into Gunnhild's bag, Oddny found that the assortment of herbs and rune sticks within indicated beyond a doubt that her friend had been lying: She'd definitely been sick when they'd left and had tried to heal herself, and worse, it seemed she'd already attempted all the cures Oddny herself would have tried.

What could be wrong with her, then? Even if she is with child, these herbs and spells should've eased her symptoms. Unless perhaps there are complications with the babe, or with her womb . . .

Oddny thought on it, but there was not much she could do if Gunnhild wouldn't tell her the truth.

After a time, Oddny poked her head out of the tent and saw that the fog had begun to clear, and the invisible hand seemed to be guiding them to land, slowing the ship as if to grant them a softer arrival. The men disembarked once the ship caught in a sand bed, and they hauled it far enough in to be secure. Oddny helped Gunnhild to the shore and they looked around at the flat, forested land around them.

"At least we're not dead," Oddny murmured.

Gunnhild was less optimistic. "Yes, but where are we?"

"We found the hole in the hull. It's big enough for something the size of a cat to get through," said Halldor to Eirik.

"Or a fox," Gunnhild said, trading a look with Oddny.

"Thank the gods we left the cats behind," Eirik muttered.

"It's a wonder we didn't sink," Halldor went on. "We *should* have sunk."

"And whatever it was got into the provisions," Svein called down from the ship, where he and some of the other men had lifted the deck boards to check on the supplies below. "The stockfish is gone, and so's the ale, and the spare ropes have been chewed through. And"—he held up the corner of a large, heavy piece of fabric riddled with holes, as though something the size of a dog had taken bites out of it—"the spare sail-cloth, too."

Eirik balled his fists and swore, stalking down to the water's edge. "Halldor. You're a man of Vestfold. Tell me where we are."

Oddny and Gunnhild watched as the two of them stood looking out over the water, their arms folded in identical poses of grim resignation as Halldor attempted to judge their position.

"We can't have gone that far off course, could we, in half a day?" said Eirik when Halldor didn't speak.

"At the rate the ship was moving, it's hard to say." Halldor pointed. "Judging by that island there—" He swallowed visibly as he realized it. "No. I know exactly where we are—I've stood on this beach before. We're north of Saeheim. The burial mounds of the ancient kings are just through the woods behind us. I used to play there as a child."

Eirik pressed the heels of his palms into his eyes and said nothing, as though this were the worst answer Halldor could have possibly given. Oddny wasn't sure why until Gunnhild reminded her, "Saeheim is Olaf's seat. We've been dragged deep into the enemy's territory." A bit of color had come back to her cheeks, but she was shivering. "And it must be exactly where Thorbjorg wants us."

Oddny racked her memory for knowledge of southeastern Norway and found she had very little. Except, "Isn't there a market near Saeheim?"

"At Tunsberg, yes, but I know better than to show my face there. It's Olaf's town," said Eirik, hands still over his eyes. He seemed to be thinking aloud: "We could row there, since the wind is gone, but even if I stay on board, my ship will be recognized."

"Are you sure?" Gunnhild asked. "It's been *how* many winters since you've been here?"

Eirik lowered his hands and gave her a look that was part incredulous, part exasperated. "Last time I was here, I killed my brother the king, sacked his hall, and looted the market. So yes, I'm sure."

"Well, excuse *me*," Gunnhild said, folding her arms.

He ignored her. "With no supplies and just over half my hird, it would be foolish to get any closer to Olaf than I am right now. If he finds out I'm here, he'll take it as provocation."

"But we need supplies," Svein said as he hopped off the ship, tossing a piece of soggy, half-eaten stockfish on the ground before him.

"Right." Eirik sighed. "Halldor, take a few men and go to Tunsberg, and bring back as much food and ale as you can carry. Svein, take a few more and work on patching the hole in the hull. Tell the rest of them to start setting up camp. Keep it light. Sleep as many to a tent as can fit. Gods willing, we won't be here long."

Svein nodded and leapt to his task.

But Halldor hesitated. "I don't think it's wise for me to go."

"Why not?" Eirik asked. "You know the way, and I take it you know the market, too. You're the best person for the job. This was your home."

"Exactly." Halldor looked uneasy. "If I'm recognized . . ."

Oddny realized at once what he was worried about—the danger he could be in if the wrong person remembered his face or, worse, called him by the name his father had given him, which Oddny didn't know and would never ask—but it took an extra moment for Eirik to come to the same realization.

"Then keep your hood up," Eirik said simply. "You're one of the best fighters I've ever met. If anyone were to remember you from—before—what's the worst they could do to you?"

Halldor opened his mouth, but Eirik clapped him on the shoulder, signaling the end of the conversation.

"I'll come, too," Oddny said, adjusting the bag slung over her shoulders. "It never hurts to have extra healing supplies."

"It's a long walk," Halldor warned her, glancing at the midday sun. "If we leave now, we won't be back until dusk."

Oddny shrugged, and Gunnhild said, "I'll come, too."

"No," said Eirik. "Once the tents are set up, you're resting."

"I've been resting all day," Gunnhild shot back.

As their conversation dissolved into bickering, Halldor and Oddny grabbed four more men and used the opportunity to slip away into the woods.

IT WAS SIMPLE ENOUGH to find what they needed at the market. Oddny had never been to such a place before and was overwhelmed by the sights and sounds of merchants and artisans hawking their wares and arguing with customers. And in the chaos, it was easy to go undetected, though she could see the massive hall of Saeheim nearby, making her feel as though she were being watched.

Oddny traded some silver she'd earned from her healing services over the winter to buy the herbs she needed. Halldor, after sending the other men off to gather the rest of the supplies, stuck close to her, carrying a sack of barley he'd bought from a farmer's wagon, the hood of his mantle pulled up to hide his face.

They were waiting for the other hirdsmen at the designated meeting place when Oddny caught a young man staring at them.

She surreptitiously tugged on Halldor's sleeve. "Don't look, but to our left—"

Halldor looked. His eyes went wide.

The man moved toward them. Oddny's heart leapt up to her throat. "Halldor. Should we run?"

"No. He won't harm us," Halldor said quietly as he lowered the barley to the ground, straightening as the stranger came to stand in front of them: He was a stocky man of roughly the same age and height as Halldor, with pale blue eyes and thick curly hair, and he was looking at Halldor as though Halldor had just risen from the dead.

"It can't be," the stranger whispered.

Halldor looked around, grabbed him by the arm, and tugged him between two market stalls. Oddny stayed in the aisle, straining to listen to their conversation as the crowd moved around her. When she turned to look at the two men out of the corner of her eye, she saw that the stranger was embracing Halldor.

"I thought you were dead," he said as he pulled away. "All this time, I thought—"

"Not here," Halldor said. "Meet me at the mound tonight. I'll tell you everything."

The man seemed to be about to argue, but then a look of panic crossed his face as he looked over Halldor's shoulder and into the market. "I'll see you there. You must go—Tryggvi is coming this way."

Halldor ducked his head and, in one swift movement, snatched up the sack of barley and threw it over his shoulder, then grabbed Oddny's arm and started moving her through the throng, not sparing a backward glance. Oddny knew better than to ask questions; now was not the time. They ran into the other hirdsmen, who were on their way to the meeting place, and regrouped, then left the market before any of them could ask why they were walking so quickly.

They were nearly halfway back to the camp before Halldor allowed them to slow their pace. By then, everyone needed a moment to rest, so they paused briefly to put down their goods and catch their breath.

"Who was that?" Oddny asked Halldor.

"Someone from my past," he said. The other men were within earshot, and Oddny figured that was all he was going to say in front of them.

She'd get the rest out of him later—she'd already decided that she was going to accompany him to his clandestine meeting tonight.

WHEN THEY RETURNED, IT was nightfall, and the camp was in a poor mood. Oddny soon gathered that it was not due just to the circumstances but also to the fact that Eirik and Gunnhild had not stopped quarreling for a single moment since they'd left.

Svein came straight up to Oddny as they approached. "Separate them. Now. Please."

So Oddny and Gunnhild ate together at the edge of the camp, Gunnhild glowering and mashing her undercooked barley with a spoon like a petulant child.

"If he thinks he can control me, he can think again," she grumbled. Then she sighed and hung her head. "This is my fault. If I'd been stronger—"

"He's only looking out for you. You're his wife."

"Whose side are you on, Oddny Coal-brow?" Gunnhild gagged suddenly and put a fist to her mouth, grimacing. "Gods. I wish this would stop."

"Are you certain you're not with child?" Oddny said, her healer's mind scrambling once again for a solution. "When's the last time your blood came?"

"My charm has held up. And my blood never came regularly anyway, so what does it matter? I dealt with this for a week before we even left. I thought the worst of it had passed."

"If you were feeling ill before we left, you should've told me."

"Right, and then you would've told Eirik and you two would've left me behind."

"And if you would've been left behind, the rest of us would be exactly where we are now, and you'd be resting in bed. Your stubbornness is only going to make you sicker."

Gunnhild stood, slammed her bowl down, and stalked away into the woods. Oddny knew that no good would come of following her.

The queen still hadn't returned when the hird began filing to their tents to sleep. Halldor, Oddny, and Eirik were the last ones awake, and when Eirik buckled on his sword, grabbed a lantern, and took his leave of them to seek out his sulking wife, Halldor turned to Oddny and said, "If anyone asks where I've gone, cover for me."

"I'm coming with you," Oddny said, slinging her healing bag over her shoulder.

"But—"

"Halldor, there's no part of your past that can scare me off. I promise." She looked away. "But if this is something you need to do alone, I respect that."

He stood and offered his hand to pull her to her feet. "Fine. But—whatever you hear tonight, just know that things aren't that way anymore."

"What do you mean?"

"You'll see," said Halldor vaguely as he led her off into the night. The moon was bright and he hadn't grabbed a lantern, seeming familiar enough with the terrain, but they could see a small light in the trees and hear snatches of Eirik and Gunnhild's arguing.

A stick cracked loudly beneath Oddny's foot. The voices stopped.

"Who's there?" Eirik asked. Oddny and Halldor held their breath, not daring to move.

"It's probably just an animal. Don't be so paranoid," Gunnhild said.

"Can you blame me, considering where we are?"

Halldor waited until the king and queen were at each other's throats again before deeming it safe to go on, still holding Oddny's hand. His own had gone clammy in her grip.

He led her to a place where the trees were spread farther apart, and between them loomed massive piles of earth covered in grass.

"Will he know which one to meet at?" Oddny asked, and Halldor pointed silently at one of the mounds. When they came around the side of it, the man from the market was standing there, alone, holding a lantern.

Halldor opened his mouth to greet him, but stopped short at the look of terror on the man's face, at the way the lantern's rope shook in his grip.

"Run," the man pleaded. "Halldor—*run!*"

Then he was shoved forward and stumbled. A slimmer man had been standing behind Halldor's acquaintance, hidden by his bulk, holding a knife at his back.

Halldor released Oddny's hand and drew his seax. "Oddny, get back."

Oddny did, as a dozen more men emerged from the darkness to corner them against the mound.

"Come, now. There's no need for that," the second man said, leering. He had the same pale eyes and curly light brown hair as the first, and was around the same age, but his face was sharper. He twirled his knife with a flourish before sticking it in the sheath at his belt.

The first man stepped in front of him and begged, "Stop. Please—"

"Get out of my way, Gudrod." The second man shoved him aside and swaggered forward, and when Gudrod made to follow him, the others stepped forward and held him back.

Halldor's hand was white-knuckled on his seax, but his tone was flat, almost bored. "You brought twelve men just to collect me, did you, Tryggvi? I'm flattered."

Tryggvi. Why is that name familiar? Oddny's sharp memory was failing her.

Tryggvi approached Halldor with a confidence that indicated that he thought the other man harmless as a mouse. That, Oddny thought, was a big mistake. She hoped that Halldor would get the chance to prove it.

"Oh, sheathe your weapon, *Halldor*," Tryggvi said, stopping a few paces in front of Oddny and Halldor, and the way he said Halldor's name—mocking, as though Halldor were a child playing pretend—made Oddny's blood boil. "You know, when Thorbjorg told me that Eirik and his party had washed up on our shore, she suggested I pay him a visit tonight. You were the last person I expected to see, but ten winters hasn't been long enough for me to forget you."

"Would that you had," Halldor said dangerously. "Let Gudrod go."

Tryggvi gave him a crooked smile. "My father has plans for you now that he knows you've been alive all this time. You'd make for a perfect marriage alliance—I wonder which foreign king he'll choose to sell you off to."

Halldor stiffened, and Oddny's vision burned red.

"How dare you?" Oddny said, stepping out from behind him. "Who do you think you are? And why do you think this father of yours has any control over Halldor's life?"

Tryggvi's eyes moved to her. "Watch your tone, woman. You speak to a king's son."

Tryggvi Olafsson. That was why his name was familiar—she'd never met him, but she'd heard of him. She turned to Halldor, confused. "But why would Olaf have any power over you? He may be a king, but kings can't just tell people who to marry, or who to *be*—"

"She doesn't know?" Tryggvi asked, smile widening as he raised an eyebrow at Halldor, who bared his teeth in a grimace.

"Know what?" Oddny demanded.

But before either Halldor or Tryggvi could respond, Eirik appeared out of the darkness from the same direction Oddny and Halldor had come, walking around the side of the mound and into the lanternlight. The dozen men Tryggvi had brought with him took a step back as though Eirik were a wolf about to bite. Tryggvi himself stood his ground.

Eirik must have seen us in the woods and followed, Oddny thought. *But where's Gunnhild?*

"Tryggvi," Eirik said by way of a greeting.

"Uncle," the other man replied pleasantly, hand resting on the hilt of the sword at his hip. "To what do we owe the honor of your visit to Vestfold? My father is offended that you haven't come to greet him."

"We were blown off course and landed here by mistake," Eirik said. "We don't want any trouble. Take your men and go. We'll be gone by morning."

"Given your history, you'll forgive me if I don't believe you."

"We don't want any trouble," Eirik repeated, but even as he said it, the rest of the hird began to emerge from the darkness behind him, all armed. Gunnhild was with them, carrying Eirik's axes. Oddny realized he must've sent her to get reinforcements.

Tryggvi backed up a few steps at last, face twisting in contempt; now confronted with twenty armed men to his dozen plus himself, he no longer had anything to smile about. He gestured at his opponents and sneered, "Ah, yes. Obviously, you've come in peace. I can see that now."

"You threatened my hirdsman first," Eirik ground out. "Walk away and this needn't come to blows."

Tryggvi's eyes widened as they moved from Halldor to Eirik, and then back to Halldor.

Then he began to laugh.

Behind him, Gudrod had stopped struggling, had gone so limp with shock that the men holding him slackened their grip. Halldor would not meet his eyes.

What is going on here? Oddny wanted to scream. From the looks on the faces of Eirik, Gunnhild, and the hird, they were wondering the same thing.

"Is that true?" Gudrod asked Halldor in a small voice. "You're in his hird?"

With one stiff movement, Halldor flipped his cloak with the blade of his seax and gestured to the arm ring at his bicep, and Gudrod's face fell.

"How could you?" he whispered. Then his eyebrows shot up. "Unless—"

"How could he what?" Eirik asked, offended. "Why shouldn't he be part of my hird? If you even knew him, you'd know that he's one of the best—"

Tryggvi stopped laughing and straightened. "If we *knew* him?" he mocked. "Uncle, do *you* know this person you've allowed into your company? Because I would know my own cousin's face any—"

Faster than Oddny would have expected, Gudrod twisted free of the men holding him and swung a meaty fist, hitting Tryggvi hard in the face. He dropped like a stone, knocked out cold, and the men grabbed Gudrod again.

But the damage had already been done.

31

COUSIN. COUSIN. COUSIN...

The word reverberated in Oddny's skull until it was all she could hear.

No one made a sound, not even Tryggvi's men. Halldor turned to face Eirik, who was staring at him as if seeing him for the first time.

"Halldor," Eirik said. "Explain."

"You knew Hallgrim wasn't my true father's name," Halldor said with a tremor in his voice, as though he was fighting to keep calm. "Hallgrim was as good as a father to me. He taught me smithing. I've told you this."

Oddny had known this, too. But she'd never asked about his birth parents, the ones he'd said were long dead. She hadn't wanted to make him dredge up the pain of the past. It seemed Eirik had been of a similar mind.

"I believe you," said Eirik, but he took a threatening step toward the other man, his pale eyes wide in the lanternlight, as if seeing something he hadn't before, "but it raises the question of who your real father is."

"Please, if you would only *listen*—"

Eirik's patience had run out. His voice rose into a roar. *"His* name, *Halldor."*

Halldor looked him dead in the eye. Took a deep breath.

And said, "Bjorn Haraldsson."

Eirik recoiled at the sound of his dead brother's name.

Oddny's feet were frozen to the spot where she stood, her hands covering her mouth. There were horrified whispers from the hirdsmen around her. Gunnhild looked ready to vomit, and this time not from her illness; she held a rawhide lantern in one hand, her husband's axes under the other arm, and looked to Oddny, a question in her eyes: *Did you know?*

Oddny shook her head. She couldn't breathe. She wanted to grab Halldor and drag him far, far away from here, but she couldn't move.

Eirik was shaking his head as well. "No."

Halldor's voice rose. "Yes. I am the eldest son of King Bjorn the Merchant, whom you killed ten winters ago at Saeheim."

"But Bjorn only had one—" Eirik gestured at Gudrod, but then closed his eyes and cringed as he remembered. "Ah. But he didn't, did he? He just didn't know you were his son." And then, to himself, "How could I not have seen it?"

"No one ever noticed me," said Halldor. "And I preferred it that way. I didn't wish to be seen back then. Not as I was, not as the person they tried to make me into. How could you have known? You and I had never met before. King Harald couldn't have cared less about me—he didn't recognize me this winter, didn't even look at me. The only one who would've known me was Olaf, and I did a fair job of avoiding him at Winternights. Had Tryggvi and Gudrod come along as well, I would've had a harder time of it."

He was talking fast, as though a dam had burst. Oddny could see his hands shaking.

"I don't understand," Eirik said. Oddny had never heard him sound so weak, so hurt. She was shocked to realize that she felt sorry for him.

"I was there. At Saeheim. I watched my father die—I watched you kill him," Halldor said through clenched teeth. "And as your men sacked his hall, I ran."

Eirik raked a hand down his face and groaned softly, disbelieving.

"I made it south to the market at Kaupang, and that's where I joined up with Kolfinna's crew," Halldor went on. "They taught me how to fight.

I raided with them for nine summers, each kill bringing me closer to being able to finally seek you out and challenge you."

"Until Oddny's farm," Eirik said.

"Yes. Until they threw me overboard. But that turned out to be fate's way of putting you in my path."

"And when you heard that my hird was passing through, you saw an opportunity to get closer to me."

"Under the guise of paying back Oddny faster, yes," said Halldor. "I would've killed you during our first fight if I could have. But if I'd ignored Arinbjorn's call and stabbed you then, you would have taken off my head without ever knowing who I was or why I was doing what I was doing—and you might not have even died. I realized then that I wasn't good enough to beat you. I had to get better."

By then the color had drained from Eirik's face. He said ruefully, "So instead, you let me train you all winter on how best to defeat me."

"At first, that was the idea. I'd hated you so much for so long. But I swear to you, things changed. I was going to let this go." Halldor gave Oddny a pleading look. "It's the truth. No one knew who my father was. No one was *going* to know, so no one would have held me to it except my own conscience. But I was willing to set that aside. I wanted to stay with the hird. I was—I was *happy*."

His voice cracked on the last word, and Oddny felt her heart break into a million pieces. She'd been happy, too. Despite herself, by the time winter ended, part of her had started to dream of what their life together would look like once Signy was safe. The three sworn sisters reunited, traveling the country with their husbands, welcomed for feasts at every hall, spending the winters together, weaving a future full of laughter and love.

That future was gone now.

How could he have kept this from me?

"Don't do this," said Eirik. "Walk away."

"I can't. Not anymore." Halldor tore his eyes from Oddny and turned back to the king, raised his chin. "Now that the truth is out, a debt is owed. And everyone here knows that I'm bound by honor to collect it or die trying, or be called a coward."

No. Oddny opened her mouth to speak, but the words wouldn't come. *No. You just said you'd set it aside. You could run. You could* live—

"No!" Gudrod tore away from his captors in one swift motion. "Halldor, *no.* I'll fight him instead. Let me be the one to die. Father wouldn't have wanted—"

"I am the elder son," said Halldor. "If you recognize me as such, you'll stay out of my way."

This can't be happening, Oddny thought.

Gudrod shrank back, cowed. Tryggvi's men didn't move to grab him again, and Halldor turned once more to Eirik.

"For what it's worth," Halldor said thickly, tears in his eyes, "this would be so much easier if I still hated you."

Eirik's voice was ragged. "Do not make me kill another kinsman."

But Halldor had already unpinned his cloak, let it drop, and slid off the thick golden arm ring that marked him as Eirik's hirdsman, tossing it to the ground between them.

"Eirik Haraldsson," he said, voice rising in strength, "I challenge you to a duel to the death to avenge my father, your brother, King Bjorn Haraldsson of Vestfold."

Eirik closed his eyes as if steeling himself. When he opened them, his face was blank as stone. "So be it."

"Get back," Svein said to Oddny, gently pulling her to the side. The hird had spread out as Tryggvi's men retreated, and now formed a semicircle around Eirik and Halldor against the burial mound. Oddny willed her body to stop shaking as the panic rose within her.

This fight was going to be close—too close.

Eirik's hirdsmen were all armed with shields, but only Svein offered up his own to Halldor, who accepted it with a grim nod of thanks. Gudrod bent and slid Tryggvi's sword out of its sheath, then presented it to Halldor, hilt first, and Halldor sheathed his seax and took the longer blade. The look that passed between the brothers was full of pain and regret and so many other things Oddny could not begin to understand—and then Gudrod averted his eyes, stepped back, and dug his fists into his hair, making no show of hiding the tears coursing down his face. Tryggvi's men dragged their unconscious leader out of the way and watched with interest.

Across the semicircle, Gunnhild approached Eirik and gave him his axes. He took them and stepped forward, swiped the back of his sleeve across his eyes, and pulled himself up to his full height, nearly a head taller than Halldor.

"Halldor Bjarnarson, I accept your challenge," said the king without inflection, taking a defensive stance. "Let's see how well I taught you."

Halldor lunged.

Eirik blocked his first blow by crossing his axes in front of him, and flung them apart to send Halldor stumbling back. Halldor tightened his grip on his sword and rushed forward again, this time trying for a hit to Eirik's flank, then his shoulder, but both were quickly deflected by the axes' shafts. His attempts became more frenzied, less deliberate. Eirik parried them all.

Oddny could barely keep track of their bodies and their weapons. Eirik was bigger, and Halldor was faster, but they seemed evenly matched.

But Oddny saw the sweat beading on Halldor's brow. He was flagging. And Eirik was only defending; he hadn't even attempted to land a blow on the other man.

Oddny's heart lodged in her throat as she realized the king's strategy. Eirik, the older and more seasoned fighter, was able to push down the hurt and the pain that had been showing so clearly on his face mere moments before. Able to lock it up and focus on the fight.

She knew at a glance that Halldor could not bring himself to do the same, and so did Eirik, who was using that to his advantage. Letting his opponent tire himself out. And Halldor was too overcome with emotion to realize.

You're no beginner! Oddny wanted to shout. *Do you not see what he's doing?*

As if hearing her thoughts, Halldor stepped back, panting. In the split second it took for him to look for another opening, Eirik made his move:

He sprang forward, hooked his axe on the rim of Halldor's shield, and ripped it from his hand. Then he feinted as if to hook Halldor's leg with the other axe, just as he'd done during their very first fight.

Halldor evaded it—but when he moved, Eirik pivoted, swung low and wide with his other arm—

And with the butt of the other axe struck Halldor in the side of the knee with enough force to shatter bone.

Halldor cried out, listed sideways as something cracked and popped audibly, causing Gudrod to let out a choked scream and Oddny to spring forward, but Svein held her back.

"Don't interfere. You'll tarnish his reputation," said the skald quietly, his eyes wet. "Let him die with his honor intact."

Halldor managed to stay on his feet and block Eirik's next swing, but lost his grip on the sword in the process. Rather than bending down to pick it up, he staggered back, slid his seax out of the horizontal sheath at his belt, and paused as if waiting to deflect the next blow.

Oddny had no idea how Halldor was still standing—but in that moment, with Eirik pulling back to strike again, Halldor made his own move, faster than his knee should have let him. He feinted right and Eirik blocked him, but then Halldor twisted and moved his seax up with a deliberate slash that caught Eirik from the middle of his cheek to his ear.

Eirik jerked backward. The cut looked shallow, but blood ran down his chin and onto his tunic like a waterfall. He reached up and touched his face, then looked astonished when his fingers came away red.

Gunnhild was by her husband's side in an instant. Oddny alone caught the flick of her hand as she slipped something into the pouch at his belt.

Eirik waved her away and she stepped back. His brows drew down in fury, and the speed with which he lunged at Halldor this time was nothing short of alarming. Halldor blocked his next blow with ferocious desperation, snagging his seax in the axe's beard and twisting it out of Eirik's hand, leaving him open—

And Oddny covered her mouth with her hands as Halldor brought the seax up to hack at Eirik's side, brutally slicing through two layers of tunic and straight into skin, just under the ribs.

Halldor ripped his blade free and Eirik stumbled back, clutching his side as if expecting his organs to spill out. Several of the hirdsmen exclaimed in horror. But opposite where Oddny and Svein stood, Gunnhild only tensed.

When Eirik pulled his hand away, this time there was no blood, for there was not even a wound beneath his torn garments. Oddny heard gasps around her, whispers. Looking down at his side, Eirik seemed temporarily disoriented, as though baffled that he was still alive—but then he looked back to Halldor, who seemed equally mystified that his blow had not landed, and the king's gaze sharpened like a predator spotting its prey.

Halldor instantly limped backward and was able to parry Eirik's next few swings, albeit with decreasing energy and speed. As he tried to dodge, he took a hit to his bicep, a hit to his thigh, the axe only slicing, thankfully not cleaving. But then a final slash into Halldor's collarbone sent him sprawling backward on the grass. The axe blade had caught him, ripped straight through his hooded mantle and the tunic beneath, and opened a wound from his shoulder to the center of his chest. It bled profusely. Oddny thought she could see bone.

All the while her mind spun and spun, repeating the moment when Halldor's blade had sunk into Eirik's side. She had seen it with her own eyes—how had that not been the hit to end the fight? Eirik's bowels should have been splattering the ground. *How* had—?

When she looked across the semicircle to where Gunnhild stood, she found her friend not watching the fight but staring right back at her, an apology in her eyes.

Oddny's gorge rose. *Gunna, what did you do?!*

But the memory of Gunnhild's winter project hit her, and suddenly Oddny *knew*.

Stop. Stop the fight. Her mouth formed the words but did not give voice to them. She stepped forward. *Stop.* Stop!

Eirik stood over Halldor now, even as the other man tried to drag himself away, but there was only the burial mound behind him. Realizing this, Halldor slumped, one hand pressed to his chest, the other shaking so badly that he couldn't get a good grip on his bloody seax.

Oddny wept. She wanted to go to him, to comfort him, to heal him—but Svein was still holding her back, though he gave her arm a squeeze as if reading her mind. Part of her still smarted from the gravity of the secret Halldor had kept from her. But that pain paled in comparison with how much she loved him.

She could not watch him die.

After throwing his remaining axe to the ground, Eirik stalked forward, drew the sword at his hip, and looked down at Halldor; his face twitched as he tried to maintain his flinty expression, but failed.

"Halldor Bjarnarson," he said hollowly, "you may tell my brother that he has gone unavenged. If there's anything else you wish to say, say it now, or save it for Valhalla."

Halldor set his jaw. Eirik raised his sword.

"Stop!" Oddny screamed, wresting herself from Svein's grip and throwing herself between the king and his nephew, facing Eirik. Beyond him, she saw Gunnhild's wild look. Saw the queen shake her head just subtly, eyes wide and pleading in the orange light of her lantern.

Oddny ignored her.

Eirik's red-rimmed eyes bored into her own. "Oddny Ketilsdottir, *get out of my way.*"

"No," she said. "She cheated."

"Step aside or I'll cut you down, too. I won't tell you again." His voice was deathly quiet. He looked as though one more thing going wrong this day would cause him to lose his very last shred of sanity.

"She cheated," Oddny repeated. "When Halldor struck your side, he should've killed you. Even you knew it—we all saw your face. Gunnhild has been working on a protection charm for herself, and she's used it on you."

"What are you talking about?"

"Look in your pouch," said Oddny, "and see for yourself."

Eirik held her gaze as he reached into the pouch at his belt—and a moment later his fingers must have brushed an unfamiliar object, because his brow furrowed in confusion.

He drew out a rune stick and stared at it.

Oddny saw the moment he realized that she was right, realized what Gunnhild had done—and what it would mean for him. And when she saw the spark of fire in his eyes as he whirled on his wife, she almost feared for her friend.

But Oddny could not bring herself to regret exposing Gunnhild's treachery.

Eirik snapped the stick in half and threw it at the queen's feet, shaking with incandescent fury. Gunnhild did not look away, eyes as intense and unblinking as her husband's as the couple stared each other down.

Whispers reached Oddny's ears, then: *Sorceress. Magic. Cheated.*

"You didn't think I could defeat him on my own?" Eirik snarled. "Do you realize how you've made me look?"

Gunnhild did not quail in the face of his rage. "I wasn't taking any chances."

"There's little honor in winning if you can't win fairly," said Oddny.

More murmurs around the circle. The rest of the hird saw the sense in her words, and when he turned back to her, Oddny saw by the look on his face that Eirik did, too. Beyond them, Tryggvi's party watched the horrible scene unfold with unabashed eagerness, while Gudrod seemed at a loss.

"I did not consent to this," Eirik said, more to his men and Tryggvi's than to his wife, and kicked the broken rune stick aside. "I didn't even know such a thing could be done."

"Halldor Bjarnarson deserves to leave here with his life," Oddny said, and Eirik spun back around to face her. "Anything less would be dishonorable of you."

Mutters of agreement from around her. She had the hird on her side; now she needed only the king.

"Besides," she said, "if the people of Vestfold find out that you slew the lost son of King Bjorn during a duel you cheated to win, they'll call you worse than kinslayer."

The semicircle was completely silent, locked on her every word as intensely as Eirik's eyes were locked on her own. She had no doubt in her mind that Tryggvi's men would tell Olaf exactly what had transpired the moment they left, and Oddny knew how things would go after that: As the story was passed around, parts of it would be conveniently altered or left out to make Eirik look worse. *He knew about the spell,* they'd say. *Cheated on purpose. Started the fight himself. Wanted to be a kinslayer for the third time.*

Eirik had realized this, too, for his face went blank as he looked past her to Halldor—still prone on the ground, close to passing out from blood loss—and sheathed his sword.

"Halldor Bjarnarson," Eirik said flatly, raising his voice so all could hear, "I sentence you to greater outlawry. You are henceforth exiled from Norway forever. Should you ever dare to return, any person may slay you with impunity."

Oddny sank to all fours as all the fight drained out of her and relief flooded in to take its place. *Halldor is going to live.*

Eirik turned and stalked toward the woods, brushing past Gunnhild without so much as a glance. The hird trickled after him and, sensing that the night's entertainment was over, Tryggvi's men hauled their leader away. Gudrod lingered, silent, unmoving.

Gunnhild remained, too, and stepped toward Oddny, lantern still held aloft. "Oddny. I . . ."

Oddny raised her body enough to sink backward onto her knees. The scar on her palm burned. Thorbjorg's insidious words from Winternights crawled out from the depths of her memory where she'd shoved them: *"You hadn't seen her for twelve winters, Oddny . . . She'll show you her true self soon enough, and then you'll regret refusing my offer for the rest of your life."*

The warning had seemed absurd at the time. Her faith in Gunnhild had barely wavered even when her friend's rituals had failed.

But Thorbjorg had been right after all.

"How could you?" Oddny whispered, raising her head to look the queen in the face.

"I wasn't thinking," Gunnhild said. When she was a few steps away from Oddny she stumbled, righted herself. She still wasn't well. "I didn't have time. I made the decision before I could fully—before it sank in that—"

"That to save your husband you'd be killing the man I love," Oddny finished. Betrayal smoldered hot and bright in her chest. When it came down to it, when the blood oaths Gunnhild had sworn with each hand had stood in direct opposition to each other, she'd picked Eirik, not Oddny. She hadn't hesitated. Not even for a moment.

"I couldn't let him die, Oddny," Gunnhild whispered. "Halldor beat him once, remember, on the practice field? And when he cut his face—when I saw the blood, I panicked—I couldn't risk—"

"Do you want to know something?" Oddny rose, fists balled, voice raw. "On your wedding night, Thorbjorg offered me a ship with a swift wind bound for Signy, and the silver to free her, in exchange for neither of us ever seeing you again."

Gunnhild looked stricken. "Why didn't you tell me about this?"

"Why should I have told you? Obviously, I refused her."

"You did the right thing—"

"Oh, did I? Now I'm not so sure."

"Oddny, please—"

"I believed in you. I was *loyal* to you. And this is how you repay me."

For a moment Oddny thought Gunnhild was going to apologize, but she knew her friend better than that. The queen's expression warped into something ugly. "I wasn't aware that your friendship had a price."

Something in Oddny snapped.

"When two people know each other as well as you girls do," Yrsa whispered in the back of her mind, *"you know the exact things to say that will cause each other the most pain."*

"You know what else Thorbjorg told me?" Oddny said before she could stop herself. "That *you* were their real target, and when they couldn't find you, they came after Signy and me instead—your *sworn sisters*. All of this—everything that's happened—is because of *you*, Gunnhild."

It was a truth that she hadn't been able to bring herself to accept until now, a truth that would cut Gunnhild to the bone, and Oddny knew it. But she didn't care. Not anymore.

"You say you married Eirik to save Signy, but it was really so you could be a queen. So you could throw it in your mother's face before she died, so you could feel powerful, so you could feel *important* for the first time in your life. All this talk about saving Signy was only to hide your own selfishness. Signy and I ruined our lives the night we took that stupid oath with you. I wish we'd never done it."

The burning feeling in her palm stopped.

By the look on Gunnhild's face, the way she stared down in horror at her right hand, Oddny knew that she had felt it, too. Their bond was broken.

"I'll find Signy on my own. I don't need you. I never did," Oddny said, looking down at her own palm, curling her fingers slowly into a fist around what was now just an ordinary scar. She looked up without raising her head. "Go home, Gunnhild."

Gunnhild looked like the wind had been knocked out of her. Mouth twitching as if she was trying to hold back a sob, she turned and fled into the darkness.

ONCE GUNNHILD WAS GONE, Oddny flew to Halldor's side, dropped to her knees, and slung her healing bag down on the grass beside her.

"Halldor," she said, turning his head to face her. "Halldor, look at me."

His eyelids fluttered and he moaned softly.

Oddny sat back on her feet. She didn't know where to begin. His breathing was shallow, there was blood everywhere, and a scream tried to claw its way out of her throat as panic enveloped her. Her vision swam.

She'd mixed herbs into teas, treated the occasional cut or broken bone, but this—this was too much.

When she was finally able to focus, she saw Gudrod kneeling on the other side of his injured brother. His face, so much like Halldor's but broader, heavier—how could she not have noticed the resemblance on sight?—was stained with dried tears. "You both need to leave. It's not safe for you here any longer."

"We can't move him," Oddny said. Her voice sounded distant to her own ears. "Not until I see to his wounds."

"What do you need for that?"

"Light. I have everything else here in my bag."

"Good." Gudrod put his lantern down next to Halldor's head. "I'll leave this here. And you need to leave the country the moment you've finished. Once my uncle finds out what happened, he'll send men here to collect you."

Red crept into the edges of Oddny's vision. "He'll do exactly what Tryggvi said he would, won't he?"

"Yes. And that would be worse for my brother than exile."

"I know," Oddny said quietly, her clarity returning. She needed to get to work. She grabbed a wad of bandages from her bag, pressed them against Halldor's thigh wound, which was bleeding heaviest, and leaned all her weight against it.

Gudrod stood. When Oddny saw the determination in his eyes, she wondered if his passivity in front of Tryggvi's men had been just a show. Perhaps he'd wanted them to underestimate him; perhaps they'd been doing so his entire life.

"With luck they haven't found my horse. They caught me on foot after I'd dismounted," Gudrod said. "I can beat them back to Saeheim. I'll get you both on a ship bound for Denmark before the sun comes up."

"Birka. We need to go to Birka."

Gudrod faltered for a moment and then nodded. "Birka it is. Just—take care of him."

"You're a good man, Gudrod Bjarnarson," Oddny said to his retreating back. "I hope you never let them take that away from you."

Gudrod paused for a brief moment before vanishing into the darkness.

"Oddny," came Halldor's sudden groan. "Oddny, I'm sorry . . ."

Oddny turned to face him, releasing her hold on the bandages, leaning over and putting a hand to the side of his face. "Hush. Save your strength."

Halldor disregarded her request. "I wanted to tell you—"

"Hush." She rummaged in her bag for a needle and sinew, but Halldor reached up with his uninjured arm and brushed his bloody fingertips along her jaw, and she turned to him again.

"—but once I'd put it aside—once I'd decided not to challenge him—once I realized things could be different—I couldn't tell you," he rasped. "I couldn't have you think—that I didn't want to avenge my father—that I was dishonorable—I couldn't have you think that of me again. I couldn't— I'm sorry—"

"There's nothing to be sorry for," Oddny said as she threaded the needle. Then she tore his bloodied pants open to expose his thigh wound. "This is going to hurt. Are you ready?"

Halldor dropped his hand and murmured in the affirmative, and she began stitching the wound closed. He barely reacted; but for the fact that he blinked occasionally and his chest was rising and falling, she might have thought him dead.

When she was done, she tied off the stitches, extracted a clay poultice jar from its wool-padded box in her sack, and smeared its contents over her work before bandaging it over his pants. Then she moved to the cut on his bicep, which wasn't bad enough to need stitches, so she smeared the poultice over it and bound it as well.

When it was time for her to address his chest wound—the worst of the three slashing hits he'd taken—she grimaced. "I'll have to rip open your tunic. I don't want to irritate the wounds by making you move to lift it over your head. Is that all right?"

Halldor still didn't look at her, but the corners of his eyes tightened in a wince. "Yes."

She found she could not rip the wool of his overtunic as easily as she could the linen layer underneath, so she cut a line from his shoulder to his belly, tearing through both layers of fabric from shoulder to navel.

"Oh no," Oddny whispered, for the clever garment he'd created to flatten his small chest was as ripped and bloodied as the rest of his clothing. It was made of wool layers and looked like the top half of a sleeveless tunic, stopping just below the ribs, with toggles that could be tightened on one side. She could see the bone of his sternum beneath the torn, bloody edges of the slash through its middle.

"I have to cut through this, too," she said. "I promise I'll repair it for you as soon as I possibly can. Is that all right?"

Halldor gave a very slight, pained nod.

Once she'd sewn up the gash and applied her poultice to it, it was time to take a look at his knee. "This next part will be the worst. I can give you something for the pain."

"No. Just do what you must."

Oddny scooted down the length of his body and unwound the leg wrap from his calf before gingerly pushing up his pant leg. His knee was swollen to three times its usual size, with a massive purple-red bruise on the side where Eirik's blow had struck true.

The sight of it made Oddny feel queasy, and no sooner had she begun to feel out the damage to his knee than Halldor made a strangled noise and passed out. That was just as well, Oddny figured as she continued her examination, her stomach lurching as she felt cartilage and bone sliding beneath the skin. Then she took out three sticks from her bag: two long ones to serve as a brace, and a small one to carve.

Once she'd set the two long sticks on either side of his knee and wrapped them in a strip of linen bandage, she took up the small one and her utility knife, and carved and sang the runes more confidently than she ever had. When she was done she took up Halldor's leg wrap and bound his knee with it atop her linen dressings, carefully placing the rune stick within the folds.

Her work finished, Oddny curled up beside him and waited for his brother to return.

32

EACH STEP FELT HEAVIER than the last as Gunnhild left the burial mounds. Part of her wished to turn around, to beg Oddny's forgiveness.

But Oddny didn't want her anymore. And in saying so, she'd confirmed Gunnhild's worst fear: that she was a curse. That her sworn sisters would be better off without her. She'd thought as much herself in her darkest moments, but to hear it from Oddny hurt more than she could put into words. So she kept walking until she reached the camp—where none of the hirdsmen acknowledged her presence, averting their eyes as she passed. Her stomach twisted.

Nearby, Svein emerged from the tent he'd been sharing with Oddny and Halldor with their bags thrown over his shoulders. He didn't get very far, for Eirik threw his sword belt down on his chest and stepped in front of the skald, blocking his way.

The empty look on her husband's face was enough to make Gunnhild's heart drop. This was not the man she loved anymore: This was the dead-eyed animal that everyone thought he was, the one he'd had to become again during the duel, the cold, calculating, brutal creature that would rather repress all emotion than face his own pain.

Tonight the man had been cut too deeply, and now the beast was back.

"What do you think you're doing, Svein?" Eirik asked.

"Bringing them their things," said the skald. "I'll only be a moment."

"If you leave now, don't bother returning."

"What? You don't mean that."

Eirik's expression didn't change.

Svein turned and went back into the tent. But instead of returning the bags to where he'd found them, he emerged moments later carrying his own ship box under one arm, the bag containing his lyre strung across his shoulders with Oddny's and Halldor's. Then he strode up to Eirik, pulled off his arm ring, shoved it at the king's chest, and kept walking.

Once he was gone, Eirik threw the ring down, turned on his heel, and stalked into the woods.

"Do not follow me," he said to no one in particular, and the rest of the hird looked away.

Gunnhild drew in a breath and ducked into her own tent, grabbed her bag of silver, and went after Svein. He must've heard the jingling of the coins and bracelets she carried, for he turned before she could call out to him.

"Take this, too," she said, thrusting the bag at him. "For Oddny. And Signy."

The skald regarded her for a long moment, as if waiting for the catch, and Gunnhild realized why at once: He mistrusted her. She remembered how Svein had stuck by Thorolf after she'd broken his heart, the looks he'd given Eirik when he thought no one was looking, like he wasn't sure what to make of him anymore. No wonder he thought little of her, too, as the catalyst for his friends' estrangement from each other.

"Please," she said, and Svein took the bag from her wordlessly, slung it over his shoulder with the rest, and carried on.

Gunnhild raised her lantern and went to find her husband. She found him pacing in a clearing, running his hands through his hair, kicking up the underbrush with each step.

"Eirik," she said as she approached him.

He didn't look at her. "Don't speak to me right now, Gunnhild. Please. Go away."

"Let me explain—"

"I said, *do not speak to me right now, Gunnhild.*"

Her voice rose in volume and pitch. "I was only doing what I thought was—"

Eirik rounded on her so sharply that she took a step back. In the light of her lantern, his bloodshot eyes were wild, his movements jerky as he lurched toward her.

"Best?" he snarled. The cut on his face had stopped bleeding, but he had not wiped the blood away. "Is that what you were going to say? What you thought was best?"

"I—"

"*You. Do. Not. Always. Know. Best.*" He was shouting now, jabbing his finger at her with each word, before throwing his hands up. "But fine. You win. You want to have this conversation right now? Let's have it."

Gunnhild retreated a few more steps. Before, the angriest she'd ever seen him was on their wedding night, when she'd been drunk and mean and he'd thrown that jug at the wall to startle her into shutting up.

This was something else.

But she'd already lost Oddny. She couldn't lose him, too. She'd tamed the beast once, and she could do it again. She had only to stand her ground.

She raised her chin. "Good. Let's."

"How many times have I asked you not to fight my battles for me?" When she made to speak, he raised a hand to silence her, and her mouth snapped shut. "This was a duel between two people. Two. Me, and him. This was *my fight*. And you dared to interfere, knowing what people would say when they found out?"

"They weren't supposed to find out," Gunnhild fired back.

"And what did you think was going to happen when I was cut and didn't bleed?"

"I wasn't thinking—"

"Yes, that much is abundantly clear. You don't understand. You're not listening to me. If dying for Halldor's vengeance was the fate the Norns had spun for me, I would have gladly met it."

"I saved your life!"

"By ruining my reputation and sullying my honor—the most important things a man has, especially if that man is a king. I would rather have died."

"Your reputation and honor were sullied before we even met. That was no fault of mine."

The words landed like a blow, and Gunnhild immediately wished she could take them back. He looked at her now as though she were a stranger. Someone he couldn't trust. And how could he? He'd let her see him in his darkest moments, had let himself be vulnerable with her—and now, knowing exactly how profoundly his past haunted him, here she was, throwing it in his face purely to win an argument.

This night had pushed him to the brink. And she was only pushing him further.

"I'm sorry," she said, pressing her hands to her eyes in an attempt to stay her tears. "I didn't mean it. I just—I couldn't lose you. The very thought—"

"You mean you couldn't lose your position," Eirik said snidely. "Don't think I've forgotten the reason you finally agreed to work with me."

She swallowed a sob. This was so close to Oddny's accusation that it threatened to break her. *Is this what they truly think of me? That all I care about is power?*

"I should have let you leave at Winternights as you wanted to." Eirik turned to walk away. "Get your things and go back to Oddny. I'm sure you'll find passage to Birka at Tunsberg. We're through."

"Oddny doesn't want to see me again."

He stopped and pivoted to face her. "What?"

"She loves Halldor, and I would've seen him die. I've lost her forever." She hung her head. "It seems that, in choosing you, I've lost you both."

She heard his footsteps approaching her, and when she raised her eyes to look at him, he stopped and lowered his hand, as though he'd been about to reach for her and reconsidered. Her heart sank until she looked him in the eyes and saw the smallest flicker of life.

"I need time, Gunnsa," he said at last, softly, turning once again to go. "We'll speak on this when we return to Hordaland."

The relief that the nickname evoked in her was short-lived, for just beyond him she saw a flash of white as a small fox darted away between the trees. Gunnhild's chest constricted. Had Thorbjorg known of Halldor's parentage when she'd brought them here, or had she merely been looking to make trouble? It didn't matter either way, she supposed.

Thorbjorg had won.

NO ONE SPOKE TO Gunnhild on the journey back to Hordaland, and she spent most of the voyage huddled in the tent with a bucket on her lap, for her nausea and vomiting had returned with a vengeance the morning they departed.

When they arrived, she learned that King Harald had gone to Avaldsnes as planned but Thora had stayed behind. In the short time Eirik and Gunnhild had been gone, little Hakon had been sent to foster with the king of England, and Thora had remained behind at Alreksstadir in protest. Arinbjorn and Runfrid still hadn't returned.

But it turned out that the estate had welcomed new visitors: Alf and Eyvind were waiting for her in the main hall.

Gunnhild nearly dropped her witching bag when she saw her brothers. They looked so *old*, though they were only ten years her senior. Alf was going bald and Eyvind's red hair was streaked with gold at the temples, and the prominent noses they'd inherited from their father had somehow become even more so—but they were *here*. And she didn't care that she hadn't seen them in more than a decade, didn't care that they'd been absent for most of her childhood, didn't care that they'd even gone so far as to trivialize Solveig's contempt for her the last time they'd seen one another.

In that moment, the sight of two friendly faces was like a ray of sunlight through dark clouds, and she ran for them and threw an arm around each of them at once. They were shorter than she remembered; she was of a height with them now.

"Little Gunna," said Alf. "You've gotten taller."

"Look at you!" said Eyvind. "*Queen* Gunnhild."

"What—what are you *doing* here?" she asked as she withdrew.

"We were traveling in the south when we received word that Father had died," said Alf, and winced at the look on her face. "You didn't know. I'm sorry."

"It was peaceful," Eyvind said gently. "Vigdis told us he went to sleep one night after Yule and never woke up."

Gunnhild blinked back tears. For all his faults, she knew that Ozur had cared for her, and now it seemed as though the last part of her old life had crumbled into the sea: Her father's hall without her father in it was incomprehensible. He'd been a fixture in the islands along the coast of Halogaland as long as anyone could remember. But Solveig had been his one and only love for almost fifty winters; it wasn't surprising that he'd taken less than a season to follow her to the grave.

"Ulfrun passed, too, not long after you left," Alf added. "Vigdis said she thanked the gods with her dying breath that she got to see you one last time."

"I see." If the news of her father's death had been a knife through her heart, that of her old nursemaid's twisted it. Gunnhild attempted to compose herself before asking, "And who is hersir now?"

"Well, one of us was supposed to be—but when we heard that not only were you alive but also married to a king, we decided that our sisters' husbands could fight over the title." Eyvind turned to Eirik, who'd been lurking a few steps behind his wife. "I'm Eyvind Ozurarson, and this is my brother, Alf. We wish to swear ourselves into your service."

Eirik considered them. "I've heard of you. I'd be glad to have two men of your reputations in my hird, once you prove to me that you can be trusted." These were the most words she'd heard out of him since Vestfold. Then he spotted someone across the hall and stiffened. "Excuse me."

He took his leave, and Gunnhild's eyes followed him to where Thorolf stood in a corner. Alf and Eyvind were saying something to her, but she barely heard it. She watched the reunion between her husband and her former lover without hearing what they were saying, both of them standing rigid as if squaring off, until Thorolf turned and gestured at the folded sailcloth behind him—a gift from his father, perhaps, as thanks for the axe, but from what Gunnhild had heard of Skallagrim she rather doubted it. At this point Eirik seemed to soften, and the conversation continued for another few moments before the two men suddenly embraced.

Gunnhild knew she should be relieved that they seemed to have patched things up, but she felt only guilt that her presence had torn them apart in the first place. Feeling ready to vomit again, she excused herself from her brothers and made her way across the crowded hall to her chamber. It seemed that every person on the estate had gathered for the hird's return, but the looks that followed her were no longer as kind as when she'd left, and the whispers were even less so:

"—she's out to ruin King Eirik—King Harald knew we couldn't trust her—"

"—I heard she's really from a Danish court, placed in Norway to spy—"

"—well, I heard she was engaged to two sorcerers in Finnmark and then had them killed so she could go seduce the king—"

Already the foul rumors had started.

Fighting down her panic, she finally swept into her chamber and closed the door behind her, leaned against it. When the cats came up to greet her, she shooed them away. She'd nearly succeeded in calming herself before she decided to cross the room and grope about in the mattress until she found her contraceptive charm. And when she pulled it out, she felt ill for an entirely different reason.

There was a line through the runes. How long had their magic been spent? When was the last time she'd checked to make sure the charm was in effect?

She sat down heavily on the bed and looked at the rune stick, then put her free hand to her belly. There was no avoiding the truth now: Oddny had been right. Gunnhild was most likely with child.

The gravity of her situation hit her so severely that it stole the breath from her lungs. The people of Hordaland, who'd been so impressed with her at Winternights, were turning against her. She'd lost Oddny and Signy. Her husband couldn't stand to look at her, and her in-laws despised her. Her brothers were here, but they'd been unreliable allies her entire life. Arinbjorn and Runfrid would never take her side against Eirik. Juoksa and Mielat wouldn't trust her after hearing she'd married a man who'd killed one of their own, and why should they? The workshop women wouldn't trust her, either, not after they heard how she'd thrown over their darling Oddny; she figured not even Ulla would speak to her again. Heid was dead. Ulfrun was dead. Her father was dead.

Worst of all, Thorbjorg had struck against her yet again, and this time Gunnhild hadn't been able to strike back. Her life had unraveled in a night.

And now she was pregnant. The very last thing she wanted at this moment was a baby, another person she'd inevitably let down.

It was too much.

She grabbed her witching bag and burst from her chamber. Thora called out her name, but Gunnhild did not heed her as she left the hall. It was raining. She kept walking, ignoring greetings from Ulla and old Hrolf the Lawspeaker as she went—she had to assume they hadn't heard about the duel, but it was only a matter of time.

It was near dark when she arrived at the birch grove, and she hadn't grabbed a shawl or the kaftan she'd commissioned Saeunn to sew for her that winter. She was soaked to the bone. The days had been steadily warming, but the nights were still bitterly cold, and the rain and the thaw had turned the ground muddy, caking her shoes and the hem of her dress.

But Gunnhild didn't feel anything. She dropped her bag beside the tree stump in the clearing, rummaged in the underbrush for dry sticks, piled them between the stump and the birch tree whose hollow held the statue of Freyja, and took out her flint and fire steel.

Once the fire was going strong, she sat facing the tree with her back against the stump, and reached into her bag—only to find her canteen of henbane tea missing. At once she realized Oddny must've swiped it when they were in the fog on the way to Vestfold—likely to prevent her from doing anything foolish, but she couldn't bring herself to be angry about it—and so instead she rooted around in the haversack until she found the nearly empty pouch of dried henbane leaves Heid had cultivated.

"Does it always have to be made into a tea?" her much younger self had asked her teacher one day in the garden. *"I heard it's poisonous."*

Heid had smiled as if that had been exactly the question she'd hoped Gunnhild would ask. *"You can burn it, too, and the smoke will send you visions without you having to leave your body. But it's hard to know whether or not they're reliable. Best to hear prophecy straight from the mouths of the dead, child, with your tea and staff, and with the warding songs to protect you. Otherwise, there's no telling who you'll invite into your head."*

But Gunnhild had her bindrune tattoo to keep out those who'd harm her. She no longer cared that she couldn't summon the spirits. She needed guidance now more than ever, and it mattered little who gave it.

She dumped a bit of the henbane into the fire and breathed in the smoke, then sat back against the stump and waited, staring up into the tree hollow. The little wooden statue of Freyja, stained with the blood of her devotees, stared back impassively, betraying nothing.

This was hopeless. Foolish, even. She slumped forward, put her elbows on her knees and her face in her hands. "I need help. I've lost nearly everything, and what remains hangs by a thread. And I—"

Gunnhild squeezed her eyes shut, tears falling into her lap.

"I am afraid."

She'd finally admitted it, but the words gave her no relief.

For a moment the only sound was the crackling of the fire, and then a woman's sweet, husky voice said, "What are you afraid of, Gunnhild Ozurardottir?"

A hand cupped her face from the side and gently turned her head, and Gunnhild's dark blue eyes met liquid gold.

The woman crouched next to her was the most beautiful she had ever seen: long hair the bright red of freshly spilled blood; a dress of the same color, trimmed with golden-threaded tablet weaving; and a gleaming necklace of polished amber at her breast, its gold filigree matching her eyes.

"Freyja was the first witch," Heid had told her a lifetime ago. *"Perhaps you'll get to meet her one day."*

"Have you *met her?"*

Heid had only smiled.

Gunnhild's eyes darted to the hollow of the tree, to the statue. Though it had been crafted with love, she found that it was a poor likeness, and Heid's own statue had been a poorer one still. But then, what mortal could hope to capture the beauty of the woman in front of her?

"Do not make me repeat myself," her goddess said.

"I'm—I'm afraid to fail," Gunnhild answered at last. "I'm afraid I'm not strong enough. I'm afraid to die. I'm afraid to lose more than I already have. I'm afraid to be nothing."

"Good," said Freyja soothingly. "How will you ever master your fear if you won't admit to feeling it in the first place? Embrace it. Wield it. Things are only going to get more difficult from here. But in the end, it shall be worth it."

"But how?" Gunnhild asked. "I don't know if I can salvage what's left. My power is gone. Oddny is gone. I'm losing Eirik. And if something happens to my child—"

"Your power was never lost," said Freyja. "You only let yourself believe it was. You lost your confidence the first time you lost a fight, the day you tried to call your teacher back, and until now you've not been able to face how deeply it frightened you to fail. It's stopped the spirits from getting through to you. But you mustn't falter, my daughter. You have so much to fight for, and when it's over—when you've sent your enemies to feast in our halls, when you've made their bodies dinner for the crows, when you've left nothing but blood and terror in your wake—all the worlds will know you for who you are. They will know your greatness. And they will know you as a mother of kings."

"As—as a what?" Gunnhild managed, for the rest of it—*blood and terror and greatness*, Heid's own words—was familiar as a lullaby.

Freyja slid her hand away and said, "You know what you must do."

"GUNNHILD. *GUNNHILD.* WAKE UP."

Her eyes snapped open and it took her a moment to realize where she was: in the grove, still sitting between the stump and the fire, sagging forward. The fire before her had burned down to nothing. It was dark, and she couldn't feel her hands or feet, and Eirik was beside her, shaking her.

She lifted her head so quickly that he reared back in surprise and relief. He set his lantern on the stump, unpinned his cloak, and bundled her up in it.

"What happened?" she asked. Her head swam with fractured memories of the vision, but her exhausted mind was unwilling to arrange them into a shape that made sense.

"I don't know. You tell me." Eirik put his hands on her shoulders. "Are you mad? What were you thinking? I was worried sick. I've been out here all night looking for you."

"You . . . were worried about me? Why?" Gunnhild put a numb hand to her forehead and it came away with a dusting of frost. Her wet clothing had frozen stiff. "How long have I been gone?"

"It'll be dawn soon. I'd planned to sleep in the armory—but when I went to our chambers to fetch a pillow, I saw you hadn't returned, so I went looking."

She held his cloak more tightly around her. Her head was clearing, but her vision was still a bit fuzzy around the edges. "Would this not be the first place you checked for me?"

"That's just it," Eirik said with a wary look at the Freyja statue. "I know the way like the back of my hand, but I couldn't find it. And just when I'd decided to go back and rouse the hird to help me search, the path just . . . appeared. Right where I remembered it."

Gunnhild looked at the statue, too. The goddess had spoken to her for what seemed like only moments, but had it taken all night?

He took her hands between his and rubbed them together. The warmth was immediate. "Can you walk?"

"I think so, if you'll help me up."

Eirik put an arm around her waist and gently eased her to standing. Her feet were numb, her legs heavy, and no sooner had he gotten her upright than she wrenched herself away, staggered forward, doubled over, and vomited next to the dead fire.

"Ah yes, my sick wife wanders into the woods in the middle of the night and doesn't come back, then wonders why I was worried about her," Eirik said when she was done.

Gunnhild wiped her mouth and straightened, wobbling, and he came forward to steady her. She waved him away. "I'm not sick. I'm pregnant."

Eirik froze for so long that she thought he might have turned to stone, but in his eyes she saw something she'd never seen before: awe and fear and hope all rolled into one. She felt it mirrored in herself.

We can be better than our parents were, she wanted to say. *We will be better than them, if you give us one more chance to be better to each other.*

"That's good news," he said at last, and her heart leapt.

"Is it?" she asked, disguising her hope with mild disinterest. "I wasn't sure how things stood between us. I thought you might choose to set me aside."

Eirik looked away, arms folded. If he wasn't ready to talk about it, she wouldn't push him, and she was surprised when he spoke.

"You made a poor choice at the duel, but I shouldn't have said those things to you." He looked to her at last. "I'm sorry."

She hesitated for a beat before throwing herself into his arms. Eirik returned the embrace and she buried her face in his neck.

"I'm sorry, too. For pushing you that night." Gunnhild pulled away to look at him. "But I won't apologize for saving your life, and I don't care what people are saying about me. I would rather be the most hated woman in Norway than be your widow."

Eirik seemed a bit affected by that; he opened his mouth, but no words came out. As if seeking an escape from having to express his feelings, he looked past her to the dead fire, then to the Freyja statue in the hollow again. "What were you *doing* out here?"

The memory of her encounter with the goddess crystallized in an instant, as though she'd been arranging broken shards of pottery without knowing what she was trying to re-create and had finally realized what shape the pieces were meant to take. She let out a sharp breath and grabbed Eirik's bicep, and he looked down at her in concern.

"There's something I must do," Gunnhild said.

THE SUN WAS FULLY up by the time they returned to the main hall. Eirik refused to let her go to the workshop as she'd wanted, instead forcing her back to their chambers to change her clothing before she caught her death. Once she was bundled up in clean, dry wools and furs to his satisfaction, Eirik slipped from the room to fetch some of the women for a ritual at her instruction. Ulla and Saeunn arrived first, rubbing sleep from their eyes, quiet and wary. Ulla had her drum, though, which was a good sign.

"Oddny is gone, and it's my fault. I'm sorry. I know you miss her. I do, too," Gunnhild said to them, her staff and steaming teacup in her hands. "But I can still find her sister. I need your help. If you would sing for me—"

The door creaked open and Queen Gyda and Hrafnhild the cook slipped inside.

"I won't be summoned like some servant," said the old queen imperiously.

"Eirik did ask you politely," Hrafnhild said.

"Yes, but he interrupted my breakfast."

"Where's Thora?" Gunnhild asked worriedly. She couldn't stomach the thought of Thora, the only member of Eirik's family who'd shown her any kindness, turning her back on her.

"Still abed. I tried to wake her, but she sleeps quite deeply, that woman," said Queen Gyda. "Now, what's this about another ritual? Why will this be any different than last time?"

Because I never should've doubted myself in the first place, Gunnhild wanted to say. *Because I take failure so seriously that I let it determine my worth.*

"It *will* be different," she asserted. "Now, will you sing for me?"

After a brief hesitation, they agreed, and Ulla drummed. Remembering Freyja's words, Gunnhild felt her confidence flare as she began to spin, and this time, when she sank under, a lone spirit waited for her. And one look at the person's face made Gunnhild burst into tears.

"Yrsa," she whispered.

Her friends' mother gave her a small, sad smile and took her hands. "Oh, Gunnhild. It's so good to see you."

"Tell me. Please. Tell me where to find her."

And Yrsa leaned forward and whispered in her ear.

33

‹───◆───›

GUDROD HAD BEEN AS good as his word: He'd returned with additional horses and with directions to where Oddny and Halldor would meet the ship before first light. He'd seemed just as surprised to see Svein waiting there with them as Oddny had been when the skald had come out of the darkness carrying their things. Halldor had been unconscious still, but Oddny had wept, relieved to be fleeing the country with more than a bag of herbs and the clothes on her back, and grateful to have her mother's Eir statue with her again; she'd packed it with her clothing instead of with her healing supplies, and had cursed herself for it until Svein had appeared.

Oddny's surprise, though, had turned into utter shock when he'd given her the bag of silver from Gunnhild—which she felt strange about accepting after all the things she'd said, but felt she had no choice but to take—and told her that in leaving the camp, he had also left the hird.

"I know she was your friend, but after everything Thorolf told me, something in me never fully trusted her," he'd explained, glancing down at where his arm ring used to be. "What she did tonight will be unforgivable in the eyes of every man who hears of it, and while I love Eirik as much as the rest of the hird, I know he won't divorce her, which makes me question his judgment."

"If they stay married, people will feel that it means he endorses what she did," Oddny had realized. "No one will believe he didn't know about the charm, or they'll think she has him under a spell. But—if you truly love him, couldn't you compose a poem about this and spread it around? Clear his name?" Poetry was power; it was why skalds were so well paid.

"I could, but not quickly enough to stop Olaf from spreading his own twisted version of the story once he hears of it. If there's one thing I know, it's that the worst rumors travel the fastest, and they're the most readily believed. People seldom listen to reason when they'd rather be angry," Svein had replied heavily. "Besides, more than anything, I only did what I felt in my heart to be right."

Oddny had never heard someone speak of what was *right* in their *heart* before, but he was, after all, a poet.

They'd made it to the ship without incident, and the crew Gudrod had enlisted seemed experienced, but it was only when the coast of Vestfold was out of sight that Oddny had been able to breathe freely. They'd sailed without stopping, for the weather had been perfect and the voyage smooth, and now, five days later, they were in Svealand, sailing through the maze of islands in the Maelar Bay until they came to the one they were looking for.

Her first glimpse of the market town of Birka astounded her. The hillfort sat on a massive rise of stone, and she could see small figures milling about atop it. Below, the town itself was made up of rows and rows of small houses and fenced-in yards, with seasonal tents and booths going up near the shore where all manner of ships were docked: small cargo vessels and warships, and other ships, from distant lands, crafted in a style she didn't recognize.

By the time they disembarked and Gudrod's crew set off to resupply for the return journey, Oddny knew that her healing runes had proven effective: Halldor could stand on his own, and could walk so long as one arm was over Oddny's shoulder. He hadn't spoken much during the voyage, which was just as well, since Oddny would've told him to save his strength. Now they made their way through the crowd at the docks, Svein at their heels, until Halldor saw someone he knew: the dockmaster. They went over to the man, and Halldor spoke with him.

Oddny barely heard what they said to each other, because she'd caught sight of a spectacle farther down the shore, and it made her stomach churn. A line of people stood in shackles, most sunburned and dressed in tattered clothing, some of them with shorn hair, all looking at their feet as potential buyers brushed by to examine them, and others haggled with the man nearby who seemed to be their keeper.

Is this where Signy was sold? she wondered, nauseated by the thought. But then Svein stepped up beside her, purposely blocking her view, and she tore her eyes away.

The dockmaster and Halldor finished up their conversation, and once the latter had retreated, Halldor said, "Kolfinna's crew hasn't sailed yet, but he wouldn't tell me why. Her cottage is this way. She usually rents it out to merchants during the summer while she's gone."

Oddny had no desire to see the woman who'd stuck an axe in her mother, but she couldn't deny that it was good news that she was still here.

They made their way to the cottage and knocked. Oddny heard rapid little footsteps inside before the door opened a crack, and she was confused when no one seemed to be there—until Halldor looked down, and Oddny followed his gaze to see the wary eye of a small child peering back at them, grubby fingers gripping the edge of the door.

Halldor smiled for the first time since Vestfold. "Hello, Steinvor."

"Ha . . . do?" The door opened enough to reveal a little girl of no more than three winters. At first the child tilted her head sideways, considering him. Then her eyes widened in recognition and she threw the door open the rest of the way. "Hado! Hado is back!"

"Could we see your mother, please?" he asked her.

Steinvor grabbed two of his fingers and led him inside. Oddny, supporting him, had no choice but to follow. Svein trailed after and set down their things once inside.

The scents of sickness and rot hit Oddny as soon as she crossed the threshold. The cottage was small, with just a table, two benches, a hearth, and a bed pallet tucked into the corner. Someone lay on the bed, head turned toward the wall, and Steinvor released Halldor and scrambled up onto the blanket. "Mama! Hado is back!"

"I heard you the first time, little one," groaned a voice that, even weakened, made Oddny's blood run cold.

"I'll give you one last chance, woman. Where are the others?"

The figure on the bed turned its head to face them—and when the light from the open door fell upon her mother's murderer, Oddny gasped. Kolfinna's face was sunken, her skin gray as ash, hair limp and greasy. Oddny had a feeling that she hadn't moved from her bed in a very long time.

"Halldor Hallgrimsson," the woman croaked, one corner of her mouth lifting in a smirk. "You looked like a drowning rat last time I saw you. Did you enjoy your swim?"

"Not particularly," Halldor said. Svein dragged over one of the benches and brought it up behind them. Halldor and Oddny sat down, and Oddny slipped her arm from beneath Halldor's shoulders and balled her fists in her lap. After giving the skald a grateful look, Halldor turned back to his former captain. "What's happened to you?"

Kolfinna looked past him to Oddny, her colorless lips curving into a wan smile. "Why don't you see for yourself?"

One gaunt hand emerged from beneath the blanket and dragged the side of it up to reveal her leg, and Oddny's stomach flipped. Kolfinna's thigh was wrapped in a bandage just above the knee, and from it a rash spread up to her torso and down her leg, the skin red and taut and swollen. Oddny knew without having to unwrap the bandages that this was the wound her mother had dealt Kolfinna moments before the other woman struck her down.

And as Oddny stared at it she heard Yrsa's last words, soft as a whisper on the wind: *"May the dragon devour you slowly in Hel."*

"Why not just take the leg?" Halldor asked. He looked a bit green.

Kolfinna put the blanket back over her leg and gave a hollow laugh. "By the time I faced the fact that this wound wasn't going to heal, it was too late. I'm done for." She closed her eyes and let out a long, rattling sigh. "Would that the valkyries would come for me, but it's Hel's hall I'll be seeing. So be it. I can only hope the wolf's sister gives everyone as warm a welcome as she did Odin's son."

Her head listed sideways, and Halldor leaned forward on the bench and grabbed her shoulder. "Kolfinna. Where did you sell Signy Ketilsdottir? Who bought her?"

The woman's brow furrowed. "Who?"

"My sister," said Oddny. "Tell us where she is, and I'll do my best to heal your leg. I swear on her life."

Kolfinna's half-lidded eyes came into focus and landed on her. "No. Let your mother have her revenge, girl. There's something else you can do for me instead."

Halldor and Oddny waited. Steinvor, bored, clambered off the bed and went over to investigate Svein. Kolfinna's gaze followed her for a moment before turning to Halldor.

"Put a knife through my heart," she said. "Make it as quick and clean as you think I deserve. And once I'm gone, take care of my girl, Halldor. You're the only one of my crew who could handle her, and she always loved you best. Swear to do these things, and I'll tell you who I sold her sister to, and where to find him."

She held up a clammy hand and offered it to Halldor, and Halldor shook it.

"She's in Courland, across the Eastern Sea," said Kolfinna. She went on to give the name of the man who'd bought Signy. He was a well-known farmer; they'd need only ask around once they arrived, and they'd find his home in no time.

When Kolfinna was done, Oddny couldn't bring herself to say thank you, so instead she said, "We appreciate your cooperation."

"What was her name?" Kolfinna asked as Oddny stood to leave. "The woman who killed me."

"Yrsa," Oddny said, the name catching in her throat.

"Yrsa." Kolfinna closed her eyes. "She was a worthy adversary."

Afterward, Kolfinna bade farewell to her daughter before Oddny bundled Steinvor out of the cottage and waited outside in the small yard, watching as the child played in the dirt of the unsown garden plot, ignorant of the fact that she'd just seen her mother alive for the last time. Svein emerged shortly after and closed the door behind him, and at Oddny's questioning look, he said, "He wants to do it alone."

Oddny looked down at her hands.

Moments later, a small, strangled sound from inside the cottage indicated that her mother's revenge was complete.

THE NEXT DAY, THE townsfolk burned Kolfinna's body and interred her remains in a mound just outside the city, where other such burials dotted the island's landscape.

By night, Steinvor grew fussy at her mother's absence and the presence of three strangers in her home, and the dockmaster's wife—who had tended to the girl last summer when Kolfinna was on the raids and who had been looking in on her several times a day since Kolfinna had taken to bed—reluctantly offered to care for her a little longer.

"Just as you and your husband get settled in," the woman said. "But only until then. I have too many children of my own."

"If you'll watch her from now until we get back from Courland," said Oddny, "it would be most appreciated."

Oddny had thought to seek passage on a ship across the Eastern Sea at once, but that night after she'd laundered Kolfinna's bed linens and aired out the cottage to clear the smell of death, she sat Halldor down to check the damage to his knee and realized it had started to swell again. And the slash on his arm, the one she'd judged too shallow to stitch, had still not healed. She ended up sewing it shut and, remembering Kolfinna's horrific wound, slathered it with extra poultice to keep it from festering.

"We're staying put until you're healed," she said firmly as she rebandaged it.

"No," Halldor said. "Take Svein and go. You've come this far—"

"And if Gudrod found himself in trouble once we left, and your uncle's men are on their way here to capture you as we speak?" Oddny said, tying off the bandage. "Absolutely not. I'm not leaving your side, Halldor Bjarnarson. And that's a threat."

Halldor hung his head, pinched the bridge of his nose. "If any harm comes to my brother, I'll never forgive myself." He looked at Oddny, then past her at the wall. "He was—the first one to call me by my name.

Hallgrim, my father's smith at Saeheim, was the second. And Kolfinna was the third, and then the rest of her crew . . ."

Oddny took his hand. She wasn't surprised that Kolfinna had known. There were few secrets on a ship, and they'd sailed together a long time. But that must've made what he'd had to do the day before even harder.

"Gudrod used to let me borrow his clothes when I'd sneak away to the smithy," Halldor continued. "He told me so many times that our father would understand if I told him my truth, but I—I never got the chance. I was too scared. In my heart, I was always his son, and once he died, it hurt that he'd never know. But I thought if I strode into Valhalla with a sword in my hand and told him that he was avenged, he'd have no choice but to accept me. So I did what a son was meant to do. Revenge consumed me, not just because I hated Eirik but because once I fought him I would finally have the validation I'd craved for so long. But now I realize—I never needed it. There's more to being a man than doing the things men are supposed to do. I think that's what Gudrod was trying to tell me. I was his brother because I said I was, and that was enough for him. And I think our father would've felt the same way."

Oddny sat down beside him on the bed and leaned her head against his shoulder, still tightly holding his hand, and she realized that she understood the meaning of his tattoo.

"The story where Loki turns himself into a salmon," she said. "To escape the gods after insulting them all at Aegir's feast, and admitting he orchestrated the death of Odin's son. I always wondered why he'd do such a thing, but I think I understand it now. He wanted to face his fate on his own terms, and take the gods down a notch on his way out."

Halldor gave her a thin smile. "I've always felt a certain kinship with Loki. But there are many different ways to interpret that story."

"You can transform yourself, but sometimes you can't escape," Oddny said. "And what you couldn't escape was being your father's son—to avenge him or die trying."

"Yes. Until I realized that I had a choice. That things didn't have to be this way," Halldor said quietly. "If Gudrod and Tryggvi's men hadn't been there, I might have tried to talk Eirik down. I didn't want to fight him, but I felt like I had to after what Tryggvi said to me. It made me feel I had something to prove again. But, Oddny—I think that if my father were here, he would tell me to let this go. I don't think the dead want us to die for them. I think a better way to honor them is to live."

"Now there's a radical thought. I think Loki would approve," Oddny said, nudging him gently with her elbow.

Halldor smiled a bit at that. This was the most she'd heard him speak in a long time, and she didn't want to push him, but there was something else on her mind.

"You know, the dockmaster's wife thought we were married. I didn't correct her." She shifted. "We could go along with it. Who would know otherwise?"

Halldor studied her. He'd not slept well since Vestfold, and the skin beneath his bloodshot eyes was a deep purple, making the pale green of his irises appear brighter.

"I don't see why not," he said. "It would be easier that way, wouldn't it?"

It would be. No bride-price or dowry would change hands; no official witnesses would be needed for the marriage. It simply *was*, because they said it was so, and in their world that was as unheard-of as a man giving up vengeance in favor of happiness, as a woman determining her own future without her family's consent.

It was, for them, perfect.

"But I still owe you ten marks of silver," said Halldor with a grin. "Right?"

"Stop that," said Oddny, and kissed him.

WEEKS PASSED BEFORE ODDNY deemed Halldor fit to travel. She'd cut new runes to hasten his healing, and before long he was able to walk with minimal assistance and had taken to doing short, light drills with Svein in the yard. When Oddny argued that he was pushing himself too far again, he said, "If I stay still, it will heal that way, won't it? It'll scar and stiffen. I need it to bend if I'm ever to fight again."

Svein had taken up lodgings at the hillfort, where he performed poems to earn some silver. He came by each day asking when they were going to set off for Courland.

"We leave first thing tomorrow," Oddny told him a little less than a moon after they'd first arrived. She and Halldor had been going down to the docks for the past several days, and the afternoon before, they'd found a ship to take them across the Eastern Sea.

Cheered by the news, Svein and Oddny went to the market for a last look around while Halldor rested. Once she'd returned from collecting the ingredients for her moon tea, Oddny found the skald speaking with two men dressed in strange garments. This was not unusual in itself—Birka was a trading hub and saw visitors from all around the known world—but she was surprised to hear Svein speaking to them in another tongue, one she'd never heard before. He gave them a small, flat parcel and some silver and parted with them before rejoining Oddny.

"I was sending word to my father of what happened at Vestfold. He's a chronicler for the caliph in Baghdad," Svein explained as they walked back to the cottage.

"Really?" Oddny asked, surprised. "But I remembered you mentioning once that your mother was Norwegian."

"She is," Svein replied. "My father met my mother on a trip through Norway when they were assigned as drinking partners at a feast. Drinking isn't part of his culture, and at first my mother was insulted that he declined to share her cup, but they ended up falling in love and he married her before he left. He came back as often as he could until she died. By then I was grown and part of the hird. I was born and raised in Norway, but spent many summers in the south as a child."

"I had no idea," Oddny said. "I've never heard you speak of this before."

"Well, we haven't gotten much of a chance to talk until recently, have we?" Svein stopped walking. "Do you have everything you need?"

"I think so." Oddny peered into the basket looped around her elbow. "Wait. I'm missing angelica for my tea. I'll be right back."

She headed back to the herbalist's stall, cursing herself as a stab of pain sliced through her abdomen, a harbinger of what was to come. Over the winter, as she and Halldor had grown close and she began to spend more time with him than anyone else, their cycles had begun shifting to coincide, so she never knew when to expect her blood. This time, with the stress of all that had happened, she'd been unprepared.

Many languages floated around her, though the main one was that of the Svear, which she could understand, although the cadence of their speech sounded more like that of singing to her ears. But as she rounded the corner to the next row of booths, she heard snatches of a conversation in Norse, and in a familiar accent at that—*Halogalanders?* Curious, she followed the voices to find two red-haired men arguing in front of a stall stocked with fine silk scarves.

"—get back as soon as possible. We don't have time for this. It doesn't matter what she looks like—we did what we were asked to do—"

"Gods, Eyvind, we need to at least get her something to cover her head. People keep asking me if she's for sale."

"But she's wearing that knife I gave her, and a *sword*, for Thor's sake. How can they not realize she's a free woman?"

"I know, but earlier a man tried to grab her—"

"The one you gave a black eye? Good. He deserved it. Vultures. Gunna will kill us if anything happens to her—"

"Alf? Eyvind?" Oddny said, and Gunnhild's brothers turned. She hadn't seen them in nearly a decade, and by the startled looks on their faces, it seemed to be taking them a moment to place her. "What are you doing here?"

At the sound of her voice, a third person pushed between the twins and then stopped in her tracks at the sight of Oddny, whose arms went limp at her sides, the basket sliding from her elbow to spill on the ground.

The woman who approached her was familiar and alien at once. The hem and cuffs of her faded copper-colored wool dress were ragged, the neckline and armpits stained, her linen underdress missing. On her feet was a pair of flimsy birch bark shoes. Her pale face with its splash of freckles was gaunt, her brown hair clumsily shorn to the scalp. Her green eyes were the same, but their mischief was gone now, replaced with something darker, something hunted, something Oddny could not begin to understand. She wore a belt with a sword and a bone-handled knife hanging from it, and the sword was familiar, too—it had belonged to their father.

And when she approached Oddny with tentative steps, Oddny remained exactly where she stood, too overcome to move, to breathe, to speak. Tears had gathered in her eyes but she was afraid to blink, afraid that the slightest movement would scare this apparition away.

Signy stopped just before her sister, face slack with disbelief.

"This is a dream," she said. She looked over her shoulder at Alf and Eyvind. "You almost had me believing it wasn't. Fate's cruelty is boundless, isn't it?" Before Oddny could speak, Signy yanked her tattered sleeve up and pinched the meat of her forearm hard enough to draw blood with her broken fingernails. "Wake up. Wake up—"

Oddny lunged forward and grabbed her wrist. "Stop that! Look at me, Signy. *Look.*"

Signy peered at the hand around her wrist, then slowly raised her head to meet her sister's eyes.

"Oddny?" she whispered, and then Oddny's arms were around her. "Could it really be . . .?"

Oddny felt the moment her sister accepted that she was truly saved, felt her whole body relax for what was probably the first time since that horrible day. Then Signy let out a keening sob and her knees buckled as she returned the embrace, dragging Oddny to the ground with her. And Oddny didn't care that the wood-planked streets were muddy from yesterday's rain, that her fallen ingredients were ruined, that her dress was dirty, that people were staring at them.

Signy was here.

And Oddny was never going to let her go again.

34

‾‾‾‾‾‾◆‾‾‾‾‾‾

THEY CONVENED IN THE cottage soon after: Alf, Svein, and Halldor sat on benches at the table, Signy and Oddny sat holding hands on the bed, and Eyvind sat on a stool and tended the stew pot over the hearth. Introductions made, Alf and Eyvind told their story first.

"Gunnhild had some sort of . . . vision." Alf gestured helplessly. "It told her where to find Signy, so she sent us to Courland with the fastest ship they had at Alreksstadir. Gunna was able to tell us every landmark in detail. It was absolutely bizarre."

"I have to admit, I didn't believe her at first," Eyvind added after taking a test sip of the stew. "I thought she was sending us on some pointless mission to see how far we'd go to please her."

"Why didn't she come herself?" Oddny asked.

"She's with child, and I guess it's making her very ill," said Alf.

I knew it, Oddny thought.

"So she sent us in her stead. We didn't even know you were here," Alf went on. "We only stopped to resupply. What are the chances?"

"Had you arrived a day later, we would've missed you," said Halldor. "We were going to leave for Courland tomorrow morning. My former captain told us Signy's whereabouts."

Signy's cropped hair was now wrapped in a bright pink silk scarf Alf had bought at the market stall, and its cheerful color stood in direct contrast to the look she was giving Halldor. Unsurprisingly, she had recognized him on sight, and Oddny could feel the hatred coming off her in waves.

"Could you explain to me what he's doing here?" she asked Oddny. "That woman tossed him overboard for *failing to capture you so she could sell you into slavery.*"

"In all fairness, Gunnhild nearly took his eye for it," Oddny said. At Signy's look of confusion, she elaborated. "She's a bird sometimes. It's hard to explain—"

Signy's eyes widened. "Yes. I *knew* it was her. Alf and Eyvind said she'd sent them, that she was alive, that she was *queen*—how did this happen? How did any of it happen? We all thought she was dead!"

"We didn't know what to tell her, because we don't exactly know, either," Alf said sheepishly to Oddny. "We got to Alreksstadir one day and left to get Signy the next. All we were told was to keep an eye out for Olaf of Vestfold's ships and steer clear of them."

"And gods, did we see them. There were so many ships heading into Vik when we passed, we skirted the coast to avoid them," Eyvind added. "When we stopped here at Birka the first time, before we crossed the Eastern Sea to Courland, we heard that Olaf was mustering a fleet. It seems he's telling everyone that Eirik came to Vestfold and killed the lost son of King Bjorn during an honor duel, and that Gunnhild cheated on his behalf—"

"So he's twisting the story after all," said Halldor with a scowl.

"Just as we suspected he would," Svein said under his breath, and Halldor gave a grim nod of agreement. Signy looked back and forth between them, her eyes narrowed.

"Wait," said Oddny to the twins. "You're telling us that a fleet is sailing to attack Alreksstadir?"

"That's what we've gathered," said Eyvind.

"Do you think Eirik knows?" Svein asked.

"If people all the way at Birka know, then I'm certain he must as well." Alf sighed. "And we're about to sail right back into the thick of it. That, Signy, is why we didn't tell you. We didn't want you to be afraid—"

"Signy isn't going anywhere," Oddny said. "Tell Gunnhild she's with me, and that we're both safe. That'll be enough for her. I know it will."

Signy turned and stared at her. "Why wouldn't we go back with them?"

How could Oddny even begin to tell her all that had transpired since the raid? The task seemed overwhelming. What had happened over the last moon or so alone—she didn't want to revisit it, because the more she did, the more she questioned her treatment of Gunnhild after the duel. Learning that Gunnhild had sent her brothers to fetch Signy, that her desire to save Signy had not wavered, even after she gave Oddny the silver to do so herself, further complicated things.

It proved that Gunnhild still cared. That Thorbjorg's warning had not been in Oddny's best interest after all, and might have influenced Oddny's reaction in that moment when she said those cruel things to Gunnhild. And that was a truth she wasn't ready to face.

Oddny stood. "I need air. Excuse me."

She went and sat on a bench in the yard, eyes closed, taking deep breaths. It wasn't long before Signy came to sit beside her, though she was quiet for a time before speaking: "Oddny. Start at the beginning."

So Oddny did. She told her everything, from the aftermath of the raid to their flight to Birka.

"But it all happened because of that oath we took, Signy," she said when she was done. "Thorbjorg planned the raid to get rid of us both, because if she couldn't find Gunnhild, she at least wanted to make sure that we would never reunite. Our oath *means* something—on Gunnhild's wedding night, Thorbjorg as good as admitted that to me. She's foreseen that only the three of us together can beat her. But . . . the opposite is also true. If we don't go back—"

"Something terrible will happen to Gunnhild," Signy finished with a glance at her own scar. When Oddny looked at her in surprise, she held up her palm and said, "This thing has been . . . *prickling* for the past moon. Almost like it's trying to warn me of something. It's never done that before."

Oddny had felt no such sensation, but she wasn't surprised. Her bond with Gunnhild had been broken, while Signy's had not.

"Everything that both of you have done has been to save me," Signy continued, and when she turned, she blinked, and Oddny realized she was crying. "Gods. I never would have thought you'd do something like this. You could've moved on and forgotten about me—"

Oddny turned on the bench and took both her hands. "How could I ever have done that?"

Tears streaked Signy's dirty cheeks. "I was so rotten to you that day."

"You were, but—you're my sister. I'd do anything for you."

Signy slipped her hands away and wiped her tears, smearing grime across her face. "I have to go back, Oddny. I owe Gunna that much. Come with me or don't, but I'm going with Alf and Eyvind. I don't have any magic, and I can't fight—but at least if I die, I'll die with Gunnhild. Yes, she betrayed you. Yes, it was terrible and dishonorable of her, and you have every right to be upset with her. But in the end, you both picked your men over each other, you realize?"

Oddny glared at her, but she couldn't exactly refute it.

"The woman who killed Mother," Signy said, looking down, picking at the dirt under her fingernails. "Halldor said she told you where I was. Why would she do that?"

"She was dying," Oddny said. "The wound Mother dealt her festered. She told us where to find you in exchange for putting her out of her misery and looking after her daughter."

Signy smiled grimly. "How poetic. And Halldor—you really do trust him?"

"I do. He's my husband. I love him."

"Enough to forsake Gunnhild, apparently. I wouldn't have thought you had it in you," Signy said with something of the old spark in her eyes, and she jabbed Oddny with her bony elbow. "Little Oddny Coal-brow, the *good* daughter, chooses a handsome warrior over her sworn sister. Shall I call you Oddny Oath-breaker now?"

Oddny hesitated, then closed her hand into a fist. There was no sensation from her scar. And that was something she now knew she must fix.

"There'll be no need for that," she said before she could change her mind. "We're going back."

THE SHIP ALF AND Eyvind had been given was small and fast, the sailors efficient and experienced. With the addition of Halldor and Svein—who refused to stay behind despite the danger—there were enough hands to take shifts instead of stopping to camp, so they were able to make haste. Oddny brewed a large batch of her tea and stored it in a jug; she sipped a little every day to soothe her worsening pain and hoped her blood would hold off until this was all over.

Halldor seemed nervous until they cleared the strait between Norway and Denmark and headed up the coast toward Hordaland. He told Oddny later in private, "I suppose if Olaf is telling people I'm dead, at least he's also telling them I was my father's son. Though of course he's only doing it because he wouldn't be able to start a war in my name otherwise."

Signy spent most of the trip obsessively sharpening their father's sword, which she wore at her hip in a sheath dangling from a borrowed belt. She told Oddny that Kolfinna had sold the sword to the same man who'd bought her, and she'd managed to convince Alf and Eyvind to buy it back along with her freedom.

She looked rather ridiculous, Oddny thought, wearing such a weapon over one of the hand-me-downs that Gunnhild had stolen from Solveig's chest, hemmed to Oddny's height and much too short for her sister. When Oddny asked why she'd bothered to bring the sword along even though she couldn't use it, Signy said, "It makes me feel better."

Oddny had little doubt of that. She wished she'd thought to make Signy a sleeping draught before they left, but she didn't have the right supplies. Her sister had awoken screaming in the night more than once and it was beginning to unsettle the sailors.

"Signy," Oddny whispered to her on the third night, stroking her sister's sweat-soaked hair. "Talk to me. Please."

"I can't." Signy hugged herself, shivering. "I can't. I can't . . ."

Oddny rubbed her back. "Tell me when you're ready, or not at all. It's your choice."

Something in her words made Signy bristle. "What's there to tell? I was enslaved for nearly a year. I was beaten. I was violated. Why would I want to talk about it?" When Oddny started to cry, Signy only looked disgusted. "Stop that. Don't make this about you. You're not the one it happened to."

Oddny left the tent and relayed the conversation to Halldor, feeling helpless and frustrated.

"Just leave her be," he told her. "She knows you're here for her."

"But this is all my fault. I shouldn't have run that day. I should have tried to save her—"

"Don't let your mind start down that path. Yes, you could've tried, but then the rest of the crew would've come and grabbed you as I tried to fight Gunnhild off. There's no use dwelling on what could've been—trust me. Signy is here now. Wait for her to tell you what she needs."

When she didn't respond except to sniffle, he hugged her, and she buried her face in his shoulder and cried until she had no more tears left.

WHEN THEY FINALLY ARRIVED at the fjord where Alreksstadir lay, they found its mouth shrouded in fog, much to the dismay of the sailors.

"It should be right there," Svein said.

Halldor sat down heavily on a thwart and stretched his bad leg, then turned his head. "Do you hear that? It sounds like—voices?"

Svein paused to listen. "There must be ships in the fog, and I'm willing to bet that they aren't Olaf's."

The wind had died abruptly, so they took to the oars and approached with caution. The deeper they went, the more the fog thickened. The disembodied voices echoed around them, making it hard to tell which direction they were coming from—and suddenly the shape of a longship materialized before them. The people aboard, whose faces Oddny could not make out, began to shout in warning.

"Port side, oars in the water!" the ship's captain bellowed. The sailors obeyed in an instant and the ship slowed and turned so that when the two vessels' sides hit each other, the impact was only a small bump.

A voice from the other ship said, incredulous, "Halldor? Svein?"

And a second, a woman's voice: "Oddny!"

"Arinbjorn! Runfrid!" Oddny cried.

Runfrid leapt over the side of the warship and into the smaller ship before sailors had finished lashing the two ships together. She nearly tackled Halldor in a hug, then did the same to Oddny before turning to Signy in surprise. "Is this your sister? You found her?"

"Gunnhild did," said Oddny.

Signy stared at Runfrid—her tunic and pants, the seax at her belt, her woman's short cape clasped at one shoulder in the masculine style—as though she were the briefest glimpse of sunlight after a long winter.

"I'm—Signy," she managed. "Signy Ketilsdottir."

Runfrid smiled wide. "Runfrid Asgeirsdottir. Oddny has told us a lot about you."

Arinbjorn followed her moments later, Thorolf Skallagrimsson just behind him. Both men embraced Svein, one after the other. Then Arinbjorn, without a moment's hesitation, turned to do the same to Halldor, who stared at Oddny in shock over Arinbjorn's shoulder.

"Aren't you supposed to be dead?" Arinbjorn asked him with more cheer than the question merited. "Or was it outlawed? Gods, the things I've been hearing."

"I suppose it depends on who you ask," said Halldor warily, as though suspecting that Arinbjorn was jesting and meant to punch him in the face on Eirik's behalf the moment he pulled away, but no blow came.

"Are we too late?" Oddny cut in, fearing the answer. Now that they were close, she could make out the ghostly shapes of many other ships stranded in the fog, but there was no telling how many.

"We don't know," Runfrid said. "What we *do* know is that there's a battle on the other side of this, and Eirik is outnumbered. We mustered ships from Fjordane, the rest of Hordaland, and some of the other districts, but we're stuck."

Arinbjorn shook his head. "We spotted Olaf's fleet and made for them. But then the wind died and they sailed right past us and this fog appeared out of nowhere. We have to wait for it to clear—"

"It won't," Oddny said. "This is the witches' doing—Signy and I saw it the day our farm was raided, and Halldor, Svein, and I saw it again on the way to Vestfold."

"Can't Gunnhild do something about it?" Runfrid asked.

"She's probably trying as we speak. Or she's tried and failed. We must get to her."

"But how?" Arinbjorn asked, more agitated than Oddny had ever seen him. "We can't move through this. We can't even see. We could smash into the cliffs. We could run aground."

Thorolf laid a bearlike paw on his shoulder. "We'll figure something out."

"What's there to figure out?" Arinbjorn shrugged him off. "*I'm* usually the one with solutions. But this time I have none."

As the sailors tried to figure out a plan, Oddny walked to the prow of the ship, contemplating. She adjusted her healing bag on her shoulder, paused at an unfamiliar slosh from inside, and reached into the bag to extract Gunnhild's leather canteen of henbane tea. It had probably gone bad by now, but maybe . . .

"Do you think you'd ever want to learn magic . . . You can see the threads . . . you've got a touch of something in you . . ."

"I have an idea," she said to no one in particular.

She hadn't realized that Signy and Runfrid had followed until Runfrid said, "You do?"

Oddny whirled on them. "I need you two to sing for me."

"Sing?" Signy echoed. "Sing what?"

"The warding songs. That's what you mean, isn't it?" Runfrid gave her a dubious look. "Oddny . . . Gunnhild spent twelve winters learning magic. I don't think it's something you can just *do*, any more than a person can pick up a lyre and call themselves a skald."

"Or pick up some herbs and call themselves a healer, or pick up a needle and call themselves a tattooist," Oddny agreed. "I know. It takes practice. But Gunnhild said I had—*something* in me. I can see the threads that bind the witches' minds to their bodies, and I memorized the chant Gunnhild used to clear the storm that hit us on the way from Halogaland. And this winter she explained a bit of what it was like to travel. And at least if I fail, we'll know we've done everything we could, right?"

"Those are the threads you two were talking about at the ritual," Signy said under her breath, and Runfrid said, "All right. Let's give it a try. But don't you need a—?"

Oddny reached into her bag and pulled out a very small distaff dressed in unspun wool, and pinched off the thread connecting it to her drop spindle.

Signy rolled her eyes. "You *would* have thought to bring your spinning along on a dangerous adventure. Mother would be proud."

"Some things never change," said Oddny without malice. She handed her bag to Signy and tucked the distaff under her arm, then turned to the men. "I'm going to try something," she said loudly, and they all stopped talking and turned to look at her.

"Oddny?" Halldor said suspiciously, standing. "What do you mean to do?"

"Something impossible. And if I succeed, we must move quickly," Oddny said. To the hirdsmen, past and present: "You remember the storm? Halfdan's witch, Katla, was the eagle causing it. I'd bet my life she's in the fog right now, too. If this works, she'll come after me. So if you see her, shoot her down."

All eyes moved to Runfrid, who said, "I won't fail if you won't."

"I can't promise that. But I have no choice but to try." Oddny squared her shoulders. "Like I said, if this works, we'll need to *move*. Our ship is the smallest here, isn't it?" When Arinbjorn nodded, she went on, "While you clash with Olaf, we'll skirt the battle, get to shore, and try to find Gunnhild. With luck, there'll be so much going on that no one will follow us."

A beat passed. Most of the men looked at Oddny as though she'd gone mad, but Arinbjorn was grinning.

"Well, you heard her," he said. "Let's get ready to cause some chaos."

Arinbjorn and Thorolf went back to the larger ship, and Svein decided to go with them, while Alf and Eyvind opted to stay with Oddny and Signy to help save their sister. Before the ships untied from each other, Runfrid gave Arinbjorn a kiss goodbye as he handed over her bow and quiver of arrows.

"If we both live through this," Arinbjorn called to Halldor as the ships broke apart, "you still owe me that rematch, Halldor Bjarnarson." He pointed to the scar across the bridge of his nose.

Halldor seemed stunned at the use of his true patronym and all it implied—solid proof that Arinbjorn *knew*, and that meant Runfrid probably knew, and neither had turned their back on him—but then he nodded, and turned to Oddny looking a bit overcome.

"Are you sure about this?" Halldor asked, hands on her shoulders.

"Not at all. Even if it does work, what if I'm not a bird? What if I'm— a narwhal, or a cat or something?" Oddny said. "I don't know if I can decide. I think it just happens."

"Then I guess it'll be a surprise." Halldor kissed her once on the forehead and then again on the lips. "Go. We'll be looking out for you down here."

Oddny went back to the prow of the ship and waited until Signy and Runfrid had joined her; then she sat down on a ship box and drank the tea. She gagged a few times—it had definitely gone bad—before finally managing to get some of it down.

Signy and Runfrid sang. Oddny closed her eyes and waited a few moments before imitating the motions of spinning, feeling a bit silly at first— and then she felt *something* under her fingers when she pinched the air near the distaff and pulled off—

A thread. *Her* thread.

Signy and Runfrid harmonized with surprising ease, and the sound enveloped Oddny like a light that warmed her down to her bones, bolstering her confidence. In the center of her sternum she felt a sensation like the jab of a hook, and just as she began to recite Gunnhild's chant, she felt something within her come loose, and then she was—

Out.

She was above them, looking down at her body on the deck: distaff in hand, eyes rolled back into her head, lips moving to form the words of the spell. Signy and Runfrid didn't falter, but cheers went up from the decks of both ships.

Halldor cupped his hands around his mouth and called, "You're a hawk!"

Oddny flew into the fog and began to circle, as she'd seen Katla's eagle do, and she felt her chant begin to shift the wind. She willed it to pick up, but then realized her flying pattern affected the direction in which it blew, so she swooped down and made for the fjord; the wind came with her, blowing the fog forward. As it cleared, she saw the ships' sails fill, and they started to move as well, with her own small ship in the lead. The sailors cheered again.

It's working, she realized in wonder. *I'm really doing it—*

Something slammed into her.

The hawk managed to evade the talons that swiped at her as she faltered, but the sudden impact didn't break Oddny's concentration. When she righted herself, she saw a one-eyed eagle, its huge beating wings dispelling the fog around them.

What do you think you're doing? Katla demanded. Before Oddny could reply, the eagle squawked in anger as an arrow whizzed past her wing.

Below, Runfrid stopped singing long enough to swear, then resumed as she nocked another arrow.

The eagle rushed Oddny—causing Runfrid to miss her target again, this time with a louder expletive punctuating her song—but Oddny dodged again and made haste toward the mouth of the fjord. Katla was right behind her.

"Shoot her down! Shoot her down!" Arinbjorn shouted, for some of the sailors had picked up their bows to help Runfrid, and the fleet was picking up speed; if Oddny didn't finish what she'd started, they'd risk slamming into the cliffs.

She flew as fast as she could, but the eagle was faster. Katla was overtaking her, had abandoned her own spell in pursuit of the hawk, and Oddny saw a flash of talons out of the corner of her eye—

But just before they reached her, one of Runfrid's arrows pierced the eagle's breast.

Oddny didn't dare look back to watch Katla fall. She'd made it to the fjord, and her ship was below her with the fleet just behind, and *she'd done it*.

She heard the splash of the eagle's body hitting the water but didn't turn around. She flew on, her wind blowing the fog into the cluster of ships anchored and lashed together in the middle of the fjord. With horror she realized that the battle was over: Tired, bloody warriors shuffled about the decks like revenants, and while some bodies floated in the water, Oddny knew others had been dragged down by Ran's net, never to resurface. At first she couldn't tell who'd won, for she spotted no familiar faces among the living or the dead, but then her bird's eyes moved to the biggest ships, each with different sails. She recognized Thorbjorg, sitting at the stern of one, staff in hand, eyes white. She was in trance.

This couldn't be good. *Where's Gunnhild?*

Oddny didn't have time to wonder, for then she spotted, on the same ship, a sight that made her stomach drop.

Eirik was on his knees, hands tied before him. In front of him stood Olaf, who seemed to have been delivering some sort of victory speech, and who now looked offended at being interrupted by the shouts of surprise from his men as Oddny's fog rolled in and surrounded them.

Satisfied that her wind was still blowing in the right direction, she swooped down to investigate.

"Well, well," Olaf was saying. "I suppose that means Thorbjorg's friend is about to sink Arinbjorn Thorisson's fleet. Would that she'd made her fog disappear altogether, but it matters little."

Eirik gave him a bland smile. Despite being covered in blood, he seemed no worse for wear. "You'd best get rid of me before Father arrives, and take care that your witches don't accidentally sink his ships as well. I sent word to Avaldsnes at the same time I did to Arinbjorn."

"I'm not going to kill you, you fool," Olaf said.

"Is that so?" Eirik flexed his fingers; his nails were bitten to the quick. "And for all these years I thought you meant to avenge Bjorn."

"I do. He was the best man I'd ever known, and he deserved better than what you did to him," Olaf said, genuine pain in his voice. But then his expression hardened, and his tone with it. "Unfortunately, I can't avenge one brother by slaying another—I'm no kinslayer. So once Thorbjorg is finished dealing with that wife of yours, she's going to be the one to put a dagger in your heart. I've promised her that much."

Eirik looked to where Thorbjorg sat, then back to Olaf. The bored smile slid off his face and he replied with a calm, cold fury that struck Oddny as deeply unnerving. "If any harm has come to Gunnhild," he said, "I will rip you limb from limb. I will destroy you so thoroughly that there will be nothing left of you to bury. I will send you to Valhalla in so many pieces that our own forefathers won't recognize you—"

"I'm not the one whose hands are tied. You may be Father's trained wolf, but I've rendered you toothless," Olaf spat. "Your threats mean nothing to me."

Oddny flew down to perch on the ship's gunnel, and Eirik turned to her.

Their eyes met. His widened in recognition.

But before he could say anything, another ship burst out of the fog and rammed into Olaf's, and Oddny took to the air again just as a figure sprinted down the gunnel of the other ship and leapt. As she rose, Oddny saw the flash of two blades being drawn midair—and moments later Arinbjorn landed hard with both feet on the back of one of Olaf's retainers, whose neck cracked against the fish mast with an audible snap as he dropped.

Thorolf came next, then Svein, then the rest. More of the ships from Fjordane attached themselves to Olaf's, reinforcements swarming them from all sides, and Eirik grinned ferociously as he leapt to his feet and clobbered the nearest man over the head with his bound fists. Arinbjorn slit his bonds with one fell swoop of his seaxes, and Thorolf kicked his axes to him across the slick deck.

Eirik bent to pick up his weapons. When he raised them, the man nearest to him soiled himself and jumped into the water. Oddny had a feeling he wouldn't be the last. The wolf had his teeth back.

As the battle began anew, Oddny spotted her ship moving through the clearing fog and she made for her body. She flew back into her chest, as she'd seen Gunnhild's swallow do, just as the ship docked. The moment she dropped the distaff and jolted awake, Signy and Runfrid both had their arms around her, and Halldor was scooping her up and swinging her around and telling her how amazing she'd been, but—

A small ship had detached from Olaf's fleet and was speeding toward them on the same wind that had brought them so swiftly to the docks. They didn't have much time.

"We have to hurry. Thorbjorg is doing something to Gunnhild," Oddny said, twisting free of Halldor. She grabbed her bag and scrambled off the ship before it was even fully secured, and Runfrid, Signy, and Halldor followed, Alf and Eyvind at their heels.

35

⊰—◆—⊱

THE ESTATE WAS UNNERVINGLY empty. Oddny made for the main hall, and the moment she threw the door open, she was greeted with a group of civilians ready to attack: all with familiar faces, armed with everything from whalebone weaving swords to pitchforks and, in the case of the cookhouse girls, several heavy frying pans. Even the thralls were there, the men armed with tools from the smithy, the women with wicked-looking wool combs and sharpened broom handles.

"Oddny Ketilsdottir," said Hrafnhild, lowering the massive kitchen knife she'd been about to swing. "Could it be? We thought you—"

"There's no time," Oddny said. "Where's Gunnhild?"

The crowd parted for Queen Gyda, who'd pushed her way to the front. "She left as the battle began. We couldn't stop her, the foolish girl. She ran for the workshop with—"

"Let's go," Oddny said at once, and her party hurried back outside—

Only to find two dozen armed men coming toward them, with Tryggvi Olafsson at their head, and more warriors exiting his ship where it had docked next to her own.

Halldor drew his seax, and Alf and Eyvind their swords. Behind them, through the still-open door of the longhouse, the Hordalanders pressed forward, their own makeshift weapons in hand.

"We meet again," Tryggvi called to his cousin.

"Go, Oddny," Halldor said without looking at her. "Find Gunnhild."

She grabbed his arm. "No. You can't. Your knee—"

He ignored her and raised his voice. "Just you and me, Tryggvi. No one else needs to get hurt."

"Ah. I'm sorry, cousin. That's not the way things are going to be." Tryggvi stopped and slid his sword lazily from its sheath. "You lot are going to go back inside and wait with the rest of them. My father will deal with you once he's done with Eirik."

"We'll see about that." Halldor turned and gave Oddny a look that said, *Go*, and before Oddny could argue with him, Signy stepped forward, unbuckling her belt and removing the sword.

"Halldor," she said, handing him the weapon, "this belonged to my father, and his father before him. As my sister's husband, you're my last living kinsman, which means it's yours."

Searching her face for signs of a jest and finding none, he sheathed his seax and took the sword. Oddny saw the gratitude in his eyes, for this meant Signy had at least accepted him as her brother-in-law, even if she hadn't completely forgiven him for his role in the raid.

"Enough games," Tryggvi said, watching the exchange through narrowed eyes.

"For once, we agree." Halldor drew Ketil's sword with one hand, its sheath in the other, and charged his cousin with a roar.

Alf and Eyvind followed, clashing with the other men as the Hordalanders poured from the longhouse and took on the rest, and Oddny grabbed Signy and Runfrid and ran.

They rounded the corner and found the door of the workshop ajar. A thin black thread trailed out of it and down to the water. Oddny frowned—this was no normal thread, but why wasn't it glowing like the others she'd seen?—and went inside.

Gunnhild was crumpled near the hearth in the middle of the floor. Her head was in Ulla's lap, and Ulla was sobbing and petting the queen's loose hair, while Saeunn and Thora sat on the edge of the platform looking crestfallen. Ulla's drum and mallet lay abandoned on the floor next to Gunnhild's staff, which was connected to the black thread that led out the door.

Oddny was at Gunnhild's side in an instant. "What happened?"

"I told her not to," Ulla said miserably. "I told her it was too dangerous—"

"She tried to dispel the fog." Saeunn shook her head sadly. "And then—something happened—she just collapsed."

Thora, red-faced and crying as well, rubbed her nose and adjusted her cloak. "She won't wake up."

Oddny looked back to Gunnhild, whose eyes were half-closed and staring dimly at nothing. "She's got a pulse. She's still breathing. But—"

"She's gone," Ulla whispered. "I've heard this can happen to our no-aidi, too. She's lost somewhere. We couldn't call her back with the songs, or with my drum—I tried—"

"Then someone has to find her," Signy said. All heads turned to her, but she was looking at her sister. "Do you have any more of what you drank on the ship? Can't you go . . . wherever she went—and bring her back?"

Oddny said, "I could try, but—"

"We'll sing for you," said Runfrid.

"And this time, I'm going, too," Signy said firmly, resting her fingers on the bone-handled knife she still wore at her belt.

Oddny took out the leather canteen. "I don't even know if I can get myself there, let alone someone else."

"We're about to do exactly what you said we needed to do, Oddny," Signy said. "You said yourself that the three of us together can beat Thorbjorg." She swiped the canteen from Oddny's hands. "So it has to be both of us who go."

Before Oddny could stop her, Signy took a swig, made a face, and passed the canteen back to her sister. Thora hurried to grab a distaff and pressed it into Signy's hands, and Signy looked more disgusted at the prospect of even *pretending* to spin than by drinking the very old poisonous tea.

Oddny had no choice but to follow suit, and she and Signy sat down on either side of Gunnhild. When the women started singing and Ulla beat her drum, Oddny again felt a hook in her chest as she began to mime spinning, Signy copying her with less elegant movements.

Down, Oddny thought as she worked. *Take me down. Lead me to her.*

The thread began to form between her fingers, but when she looked up, Signy was having no such luck. Oddny reached out and grasped her hand with the one of hers that wasn't pinching the air near the distaff—and Signy's own thread started to take shape—

Then the scar on Oddny's palm prickled and the world gave out beneath them, and they were falling. Oddny squeezed her eyes shut and braced for impact—

But it never came. And when she dared to open her eyes, she was in a dark place that went on forever, and she was alone. She could hear the warding songs and drum echoing far above her. Trembling, she took a few steps forward and called out, "Signy? Gunnhild?"

"What are *you* doing here?" Thorbjorg demanded as she strode out of the darkness. Like Oddny, she had a thin, shimmering thread stretching upward from her sternum.

Oddny's hand went to her knife. "Where is she?"

"You're not supposed to be here," Thorbjorg said, and Oddny thought she heard fear in the witch's voice.

"Too bad," said Oddny through her teeth. "What have you done with her?"

"This is all wrong." Thorbjorg fisted her hands in her pale hair, knocking her cap askew. "This was what I saw. You, here. Why is this happening? We did everything to prevent this—*you shouldn't be*—"

"Pull yourself together, girl. We're too close now for any mistakes," came a distorted voice from Oddny's right, and she turned to see a hooded figure approaching. "Gunnhild isn't coming back, but so much for standing guard against her friends. I should've known you couldn't handle this job alone when you're the one who's bungled everything from the start."

The third witch, Oddny realized. "Who are you?"

By way of a response, the witch threw off her hood—and revealed a face she knew.

"Thora?" Oddny whispered in horror. "You're—you're the seal? How is this possible? You're—up there—you're—"

The woman smiled, and it was terrible. "It's not hard to leave part of yourself behind—you've done something similar yourself, little hawk, probably without even realizing it. It's how you keep the chant going. Or in my case, the songs. And if I keep my eyes closed and my staff under my cloak, well, who would be the wiser?"

Oddny understood at once. "It wasn't Thorbjorg or Katla who ruined Gunnhild's ritual at Winternights. It was you. And you were standing right there with us. You're with us *right now*—" And she had no idea how to warn Runfrid, Ulla, and Saeunn of the traitor in their midst. "But— why? You were so kind—"

"Oh, don't look so surprised, dear," Thora said, tossing her cloak aside with a sneer so uncharacteristic of her that it made Oddny's blood run cold. "My son may be the youngest of Harald's brood, but I've foreseen that he *will* be king, and that one day Gunnhild will have a hand in his undoing. I mean to take her off the gaming board before she gets the chance. That's why I didn't stop you and your sister trying to reach her— better to do away with you all down here, where no one will ever know what happened to you. None in the waking world will be aware of my involvement. And I intend to keep it that way."

Thorbjorg, hands still fisted in her hair, gave a nervous little laugh. She said, a bit hysterically, "Why don't you just draw her a picture of our plan?"

"I said, pull yourself *together*," Thora snapped. "And this attack was *my* plan, since you're the one who started us off down the road to ruin the day you came up with the idea to kill Oddny and her sister after that *vision* you had. If we hadn't followed *your* plan, Gunnhild would still be a hermit in the woods with that old lady protecting her. She might not have even *met* Eirik if not for you! No, Thorbjorg—we're putting an end to this foolishness once and for all. It's time for you to redeem yourself."

"Where is she?" Oddny said, hand tightening on her sheathed knife. "If I have to ask you again, you won't like how I do it."

Something had changed in Thorbjorg at her companion's words. She dropped her hands to her side, giving Oddny a look that was part pity, part annoyance. "She's gone beyond your reach. And you're about to go somewhere else."

Thora chuckled. "If it's any consolation, I liked you very much, Oddny Ketilsdottir. If you'd only left well enough alone and stayed away, we would've let you live. Thorbjorg—be a dear and finish what you started at Winternights, would you?"

Thorbjorg drew her antler-handled blade and struck before Oddny could draw her own weapon. Oddny managed to dodge, but the knife ripped her sleeve—and when she stumbled back she was stunned to realize that not only was her old yellow-green dress ripped where the other witch had struck, but her arm was bleeding from the shallow cut, and it *hurt*.

"Oh, please. Don't look so surprised—you must remember this from the ritual at Winternights," Thora tittered. "What happens to you in this place also happens to you up there."

Oddny drew her knife at last. "Is that what you did to Gunnhild? Trapped and killed her down here?"

"No, no," Thora said, waving a hand. "I'm afraid the queen's fate is much worse than that. Hers is the long, slow death of the lost. Yours won't be nearly as bad."

Above them, the singing voices grew louder, the drumming faster. More urgent. Saeunn, Runfrid, and Ulla must've seen her wound. The sounds filled her chest with such hope, gave her so much courage, that she felt her own power flare. But where was Signy? Oddny didn't have time to think as Thorbjorg moved in for another strike, which Oddny barely avoided.

Oddny took a defensive stance, her own tiny blade at the ready. She tried to hide how much she was shaking, how afraid she truly was—

"Finish her, Thorbjorg," Thora commanded. "Now. Or—"

And then she made a choking noise, grappled for a moment at the tip of the blade sticking out of her chest, and crumpled.

Behind her stood Signy.

Oddny gasped. High above them, the song faltered, but the drumbeat continued on.

"I'm sorry it took me so long," said her sister as she bent to slide her bone-handled knife from the body of King Harald's latest wife. "I lost my way." Her eyes moved to Thorbjorg. "That's her, isn't it? The fox?"

Whatever confidence Thorbjorg had gained from Thora's presence was gone now. She backed away, eyes wide and fearful, dropping her knife as she sank to her knees and dug her hands into her hair. "No, no, no, no . . ."

It seems the fox, not the wolf, was toothless in the end, Oddny thought. She'd lost track of Olaf in the chaos of the ship battle, but wondered if Thorbjorg's master had any idea how badly things were going for her.

Signy started toward the witch, bloody knife raised. But Oddny got to Thorbjorg first and grabbed her by the hair, put her own knife to the woman's throat. "Where. Is. Gunnhild?"

"Below," Thorbjorg bit out. "Down. Deep, deep down. Thora severed Gunnhild's thread when she flew out over the water to dispel Katla's fog. Gunnhild is foolish and bold, and we knew she'd do exactly what she did. Thora was waiting for her in the fjord—she cast the charm, leapt right out of the water, and snapped the thread between her teeth. Don't you understand? You'll never find Gunnhild, you fools, because there's nothing *to* find. She no longer exists."

"We made short work of Thora, as you can see." But when Oddny looked over at the woman's body, it had disappeared. Not pausing to wonder about this, she turned back to Thorbjorg and pressed the knife so hard against the witch's throat that blood welled on the edge of the blade. "And Katla, too. How do we bring Gunnhild back? How do we repair her thread?"

"You're a fool if you think you can," said Thorbjorg, but it was clear that hearing of Katla's death had rattled her, for she trembled now. "Severing a person's thread separates their mind from their shape. It's one of Odin's charms. And it's a cruel one: a slow death of the mind and the body, until both are lost."

"You still haven't answered the question," Signy said from behind Oddny. "How do we get her back?"

"You don't," Thorbjorg spat. "Fools. She doesn't *exist*. Whatever made Gunnhild herself is gone. Broken apart. She is *nothing*."

"There are worse things than drowning," Gunnhild had told Oddny on the ship on the way to Hordaland, when she'd asked Oddny to pull back her thread at the first sign of trouble. *"If they manage to sever my thread, I die, and I die slowly."*

"She's not dead yet," Oddny insisted. "Her body isn't dead, so her mind can't be, either. We can still bring her back. We just have to . . . go deeper. Correct?"

Thorbjorg wrinkled her nose, but when Oddny's hand tightened in her hair and the knife bit into her neck, she snarled, "Yes. In theory. But it hasn't been done before. You're no witch, Oddny Ketilsdottir. You'll not survive this."

"You don't know the first thing about me," said Oddny.

Signy took off her belt and used it to roughly tie Thorbjorg's hands together. "And if she doesn't survive it, neither will you." She ripped the cap off Thorbjorg's head and stuffed it into the witch's mouth so she couldn't protest.

Once Thorbjorg was bound, Signy and Oddny looked at each other.

"I'm coming with you," Signy said.

"No," said Oddny. "I think, if traveling down there is the same thing as traveling down here, then I need you to sing the warding songs for me. Call her back, and I'll do the rest."

For once Signy didn't argue. Instead, she sang.

Oddny closed her eyes. The same as before, she waited for a sensation to hook her, but it didn't come from her chest: It came from the scar on her palm, a tug, bidding her come down. She imagined herself light as a feather and followed the sensation, felt herself begin to drift.

The space behind her eyelids was white, and she reached forward, groping at nothing. She knew that her mind was still in the dark place, still in the void with Signy and Thorbjorg, but she felt as though she were reaching into a mist.

"Gunnhild," she called out. "Where are you?"

A hum, a whisper in the distance: *Who?*

"It's me. It's Oddny."

The voice that replied was distinctly Gunnhild's, but she felt so very far away. *Who . . . ? Is . . . Oddny? Who . . . am I?*

I have to pull her back together, she realized. *I have to remind her who she is.*

"Your name is Gunnhild Ozurardottir," Oddny said. "You were born in Halogaland, the last daughter of Ozur and Solveig. Your brothers are Alf and Eyvind and your sisters are many."

Gunnhild, the mist whispered, and Oddny felt something start to co-alesce around her groping hand—something she couldn't quite touch, but *something.*

"Your husband is Eirik Haraldsson," Oddny said. "You're here be-cause you tried to help him win a battle. You took a big, foolish risk. And you've paid for it. Now it's time to come back."

The *something* became tangible, but not enough so that Oddny could grasp it. The scar on her palm began to thrum faintly, pulsing like a heartbeat.

Who . . . ? said the mist. *Who . . . are you . . . ?*

"Me? I told you, I'm Oddny. Oddny Ketilsdottir. Don't you re-member?"

Oddny . . . ?

"We've been friends since we were born." Oddny's voice shook. "We swore an oath to each other. That night, after the ritual. You, me, and Signy."

Oddny . . . Signy . . . ?

Oddny could almost reach the *something,* could almost close her fist around it.

"Yes. Listen—do you hear the song? That's Signy. You saved her, Gunnhild. Your brothers found her. And beyond her—that's Runfrid and Ulla and Saeunn. You remember them, don't you? All our friends?"

Friends . . . our friends . . .

Oddny's voice hitched in desperation. "Remember the game we used to play with the horns, the one that drove our fathers mad? Two bursts for hello, three for goodbye?"

She closed her fist around—nothing. Letting out a cry of rage, she squeezed her eyes shut even harder. Opened her hand, fingers splayed.

"You have always been so *frustrating*," she shouted. "I didn't even want to take that blood oath, but you and Signy outvoted me. You always did. I was the voice of reason for you two and your schemes when we were young, remember?"

No reply. Perhaps that wasn't what Gunnhild needed to hear.

Oddny whimpered. "Listen—I'm sorry for what I said to you in Vestfold. In that moment I hated you for choosing Eirik over me, and part of me still does. Part of me isn't sure I can trust you not to do the same thing again. But you never doubted that we would find Signy. You gave me that silver, but you—you sent your brothers to rescue her before I even could. You were wrong, but I was wrong, too."

The mist still seemed uncertain.

"Gunnhild—I love you. *Don't let this be goodbye.*"

Oddny's palm *burned* as her oath flared back to life, and this time when she closed her fist, she closed it around—a *thread*.

And she pulled on it as hard as she could.

When Oddny opened her eyes again, she was in the dark place, the end of a shining gossamer thread clasped in her hand. She kept pulling, and she felt Signy come up behind her and help as the thread got longer and longer, drawn out of the nothingness of the void.

But Oddny knew Gunnhild was on the other end. They needed only to keep pulling.

And finally, *finally*, with one last yank, Gunnhild appeared as if being pulled through an invisible doorway, the thread in Oddny's hand attached to the center of her chest.

36

GUNNHILD WAS NOTHING, AND then she was something
again. The last thing she remembered was flying over the water, looking
down at Eirik's ship as the men prepared for battle—and seeing a ghostly
figure waving and pointing to something in the water. And in the very
moment she'd recognized the specter as Heid, everything had gone dark.

Her fylgja had appeared to warn her after all, but too late.

And now she was falling—but two pairs of arms caught her and righted
her, and Signy held her steady as Oddny jumped up and fished around in
the air until she caught the end of a dangling gray thread. She brought it
close to the one extending from Gunnhild's chest, and the two threads
fused and began to shine as brightly as the other women's. Gunnhild's
tether was healed.

Gunnhild looked back and forth between the sisters. "Signy—?"

Signy slipped her arm from around Gunnhild's back and enveloped
her in a hug. "You did it, Gunna. Your brothers came for me. You saved
my life."

"They did? I—?" Gunnhild pulled away. "Oddny—you came back?"

Then she looked past them both, to Thorbjorg.

"*You*," she said savagely.

Thorbjorg looked at her, then at Signy and Oddny, amber eyes wide
with terror and *knowing*, as though she'd seen this happen before, as
though this was her worst nightmare coming to pass. She spat out her

gag and scooted backward awkwardly, hands still bound. "No. Wait. Please—mercy—"

Whatever she foresaw, Gunnhild realized, *whatever drove her to this, it wasn't just about Eirik or vengeance or power. Thorbjorg saw her death. And it was me, with my sisters at my back.*

Gunnhild started toward her, but Oddny grabbed her arm. "Leave her, Gunna. She's lost, and she knows it."

"Does she not deserve it, though?" Signy said, voice flat. "Let Gunna do the honors."

Oddny whirled on her sister but did not let go of Gunnhild. "Signy, killing her won't bring Mother and Vestein back. It won't—"

"Undo what happened to me?" Signy said. "I know. But watching the person responsible for it die would at least make me feel a little better."

"Thorbjorg had your mother killed, Oddny. And Heid, too. My *true* mother," Gunnhild said, her eyes not leaving the quivering little witch. "I won't leave them unavenged."

"Gunnhild," Oddny said, but her resolve was weakening, her eyes going cold. Gunnhild knew she was remembering the arrow in her brother's throat, the axe in her mother's chest, the farm burning.

"It's too dangerous to let her live," said Signy. "Gunna—do it."

Gunnhild ripped her arm away from Oddny and started forward again.

"You—you don't know what I've seen," Thorbjorg sputtered. "If you do this, it's only the beginning. You'll be a murderer. And you won't stop with me. When given the option to bargain, you'll choose to kill; when given the option for peace, you'll choose violence. And in the end, you'll be remembered as being more ruthless than even your own husband."

This gave Gunnhild pause, until she heard a whisper in the back of her mind, Freyja's voice: *You mustn't falter.*

She could almost feel the goddess's presence beside her and wondered if it was merely a hallucination—as she'd often wondered about the presence she'd encountered that night in the grove—until Freyja's voice came again: *Send my daughter home to me, Gunnhild, Mother of Kings.*

Thorbjorg seemed to think Gunnhild's brief hesitation meant she'd changed her mind, for she was much calmer when she asked, "Is that the price you're willing to pay for revenge?"

Gunnhild crouched beside her and brought her face in very close. "Yes," she said.

And then she grabbed Thorbjorg by the neck, pinned her down, and squeezed as hard as she could.

She heard Oddny's gasp of horror behind her but ignored it. All she felt was the woman's throat between her hands. All she saw was Heid's body, cold and dead on her sleeping pallet and then in her grave; the arrow piercing Vestein's neck; Yrsa crumpling.

They morphed into Thorbjorg's face, mouth open, eyes bulging. She saw flashes of whatever Thorbjorg must be witnessing in the waking world as she struggled to escape Gunnhild and return to her body. She saw snippets of her thoughts—the last moments of a ship battle; *They were never supposed to get this far*; *How is this happening?*—and felt the heartbeat beneath her fingers slowly grow weaker.

Thorbjorg's bound hands scrabbled helplessly at Gunnhild's arms and face, but Gunnhild leaned away and held firm. And suddenly the other witch stopped struggling. Her eyes stayed open. She did not move.

Gunnhild didn't let go until she felt a hand on her shoulder and heard Signy's voice say, softly, "Gunna, that's enough. She's gone."

SHE WOKE UP ON the floor of the weaving workshop with her head in Ulla's lap, and as soon as she sat up, Oddny and Signy embraced her. Ulla cried and clung to Runfrid, who sagged in relief. But Saeunn asked, "What happened down there?" and turned mournfully to the body slumped beside her.

Gunnhild made to stand with Oddny's and Signy's help, all the while staring at Thora, who'd collapsed backward on the platform. Blood seeped from beneath the body as Thora's sightless eyes stared up into the rafters, a small iron staff peeking out from beneath her cloak.

"What . . . ?" Gunnhild put a hand to her mouth. "What happened to her?"

"We don't know," Runfrid said helplessly. "She just—"

"Signy happened to her," Oddny said. "Thora was the third witch, Gunna. She was the seal. She broke your thread. She was working with them all along."

Gunnhild clenched her teeth. She had not suspected Thora for a moment; she'd been so grateful that at least one of Eirik's stepmothers seemed to like her, had been comforted by the woman's kindness in contrast to Queen Gyda's severity. Thora had made Gunnhild drop her guard. *Never again.*

Saeunn and Runfrid shifted away from the body in disgust, and Ulla drew herself to standing and spat on the floor at the dead woman's feet.

"I suppose that's why she didn't arrive until after Gunnhild collapsed." Saeunn grabbed her cane and stood as well. "King Harald is never going to believe this."

"Believe what?" said a voice from the doorway as Queen Gyda entered. The women inside were silent, so she repeated, "Believe *what*?" Then her eyes moved to Thora's body, and her back went straight as a spear shaft as she rounded on Gunnhild. "What is the meaning of this?"

"Thora was a witch," Gunnhild said.

"She said Hakon was going to be king and—and she wanted to get Eirik out of the way so there would be less competition for him," Oddny added, but in a way that made Gunnhild believe she wasn't telling the whole truth.

For a moment Gunnhild was terrified that Queen Gyda wouldn't believe them, but then, to her surprise, the older woman's eyes moved back to Thora's body—to her staff—and hardened.

"This explains some things I've long suspected." She sighed. "Saeunn is right. My husband will never believe it, and even if he does, he'll deny it—he'll blame one of you for her death before admitting to being bewitched twice, and things will not go well for that unfortunate person." This, with a pointed look at Gunnhild. "We'll move her body to the front of the longhouse with the others, and no one will be the wiser."

"With—the others?" Oddny said, eyes going wide. "Oh, gods. Halldor!" She darted away from Gunnhild and Signy, dodged Queen Gyda, and sprinted out the door. Signy grabbed Gunnhild's hand and followed.

The hillside leading down to the dock was strewn with the bodies of civilians and warriors alike, but it was clear the Hordalanders had won against Tryggvi's men. Old Hrolf was bleeding from the temple, and Saeunn flew to his side as fast as her bad knee would allow, while the cookhouse girls fussed over Hrafnhild, who had a small wound at her shoulder. Oddny wove among the survivors, frantically calling her husband's name.

Beyond, the fog in the fjord had dissipated and several ships had already come in, the battle's survivors mingling with the civilians on the hill. She saw Eirik's ship among those docked, but that was no guarantee that he was alive. With a worried look at Oddny, Gunnhild moved to help her search for Halldor, but out of the corner of her eye she saw a familiar shape at the docks and her heart leapt. Every bone in her body screamed at her to go to him, to make sure her eyes weren't deceiving her. But Oddny—

Signy squeezed her hand and said, "Gunna."

Gunnhild turned and gave her a good look. So much of her sworn sister had changed—Signy was thin enough now to be wearing a dress Gunnhild recognized as Oddny's, which was too short—but those eyes, that smile, were the same.

Signy gave her a hug. Gunnhild returned it, blinking back tears. She'd come so far, she'd done so much, and until that moment it hadn't hit her—she'd succeeded. She'd vanquished Thorbjorg. She'd saved Signy.

She'd *won*.

But not without help.

Signy pulled away and looked into her face. "I'll help Oddny look for Halldor. Go to your husband."

Gunnhild gave her one more hug and fled to the docks. She pushed her way through the crowd of bloody, haggard, exhausted warriors coming up the hill until she came to the bloodiest, most haggard, and arguably most exhausted of them all and threw her arms around him in complete disregard of the fact that it would ruin her clothing; he was splattered with blood and viscera nearly from head to toe. She had a feeling none of it was his.

Eirik held her as though they had not seen each other for a very long time. She didn't realize that she had been crying until he pulled away and wiped away one of her tears with his thumb, leaving a smear of red and grime across her cheek. She cupped his face and smoothed his beard. It was wet with blood under her fingers, but the only recent mark she saw on him was the fresh scar from his duel with Halldor.

He looked at her, then looked down. "Are you all right?"

"Yes," she said, putting a hand to the small curve of her belly. "We're both fine. You?"

"Just a few scratches. My enemies look much worse."

Gunnhild smiled, thinking again of Freyja's words. "You sent many to dine with the gods today."

Eirik jerked his head to the side. "It seems I'm not the only one."

She looked in the direction he'd indicated and saw, lying on the deck of one of the large warships, a familiar figure, pale hair hiding her face, fingers limply curled around her iron staff.

"The battle was over by then, and no one had touched her," Eirik said quietly. "She just—grasped at her throat and toppled over. As though choked by some invisible hand."

"Two, actually." Gunnhild looked down at the hands that had done the deed. Eirik hooked a finger under her chin and raised her eyes to his.

"I don't know what you were doing while I was gone, but Olaf seemed to think your death was guaranteed. He said she'd see to it. But when she fell, I knew you'd won. Especially after I saw Oddny—"

"Yes. She and Halldor came back to help us. She saved my life—"

Something caught Eirik's attention and he said, "Later," and offered his arm. She took it and followed him to where Olaf and King Harald stood.

"My father arrived shortly after Arinbjorn's fleet came through," Eirik said as they walked. "And, as you can see, he's not happy."

That was an understatement. King Harald was loudly berating Olaf while the crowd avoided them, and Gunnhild fought back a smile at the sight of a man in his fifties being reprimanded like a child. She caught Olaf's eye and waggled her fingers in a smarmy little wave.

Olaf's face purpled and he jabbed a finger at them. "You two! You started this, not me. *You* came to *my* district and started trouble in *my*—"

Before Gunnhild could argue, Eirik drawled, "Go home, Olaf. And if I ever see your face again, they'll call me a kinslayer thrice over."

"Is that a threat?" Olaf's face became, if possible, more purple.

"It is! Well done," said Gunnhild. "Perhaps you're not as foolish as you look."

"Do you hear this, Father?" Olaf raged. "Do you hear these two?"

King Harald ignored him; he was squinting at something just over Gunnhild's shoulder. "What is the meaning of this?"

Gunnhild turned.

Halldor limped toward them, battered from the battle just like the rest, but it was clear from the look on his face that his had been a different fight entirely—one much more personal. Behind him were Gunnhild's brothers, dragging a man between them: Tryggvi Olafsson, hands bound, a gag tied tightly around his mouth, eyes ablaze with shame and fury.

Halldor gestured to Alf and Eyvind and said, "Here is fine," and they shoved Tryggvi forward to land face-first on the ground in front of Olaf. Then, with a brief look at Gunnhild, the twins turned and fled rather than risk incurring the kings' wrath. Halldor, however, stood his ground.

"Tryggvi! What—" Olaf rolled his son over and looked up at Halldor. "*You?*"

"Me," Halldor said, and it seemed that was all he needed to say. He looked to King Harald without giving the slightest inclination of deference, then to Eirik and Gunnhild, and nodded. They nodded back, and Halldor turned and melted into the crowd.

King Harald scowled. "Who is that man?"

"I haven't the slightest idea," said Eirik with a perfectly straight face.

Gunnhild didn't know why he'd lied, but she followed his lead nonetheless: "Nor do I. I've never seen him before in my life."

It took all her self-control not to smile when the old king didn't argue: Not only had King Harald still not recognized his own grandson, but either Halldor had done a good enough job avoiding him all winter or

King Harald simply did not keep track of who was in his son's hird. She strongly suspected the latter.

"Liars!" Olaf had untied Tryggvi's hands and ripped the gag from his mouth, and now he hauled his son to his feet and rounded on Eirik.

"So says the biggest liar of all," Eirik shot back.

"*Boys,*" King Harald barked. "Enough. Olaf, go home. Eirik, have this mess cleaned up." He gestured to the bodies on the hillside and started to walk away.

"Respectfully," Gunnhild said, in the least respectful tone possible, "*this mess* is the bodies of the people who died defending *your* estate from *your* son's attack."

King Harald stopped and looked at her as though she'd gone mad. "I haven't the patience to deal with you right now, woman." He turned to Eirik again. "Have the thralls clean this up at once."

"There are none. I freed them all and offered them each a mark of silver if they'd stay and fight," said Eirik. Gunnhild's head swiveled to face him in surprise. When his father sputtered, Eirik shrugged. "We were outnumbered. What was I supposed to do? Let them defect to Olaf's side?"

King Harald shook his head slowly, then waved a hand and headed up the hill. The servant who'd been standing behind him, holding on to his dogs' leashes, followed. Gunnhild turned and caught a glimpse of Queen Gyda waiting near the door of the longhouse, and when the old queen caught her eye and gave the tiniest nod, Gunnhild knew that Thora's body had been placed among the rest.

It hit her then—she'd no longer have to look out for a murderous seal every time she stepped aboard a ship. And she'd be bringing her child into a world without Thorbjorg. Her relief was palpable, even as her other enemies still stood before her.

"You'll pay for this," Tryggvi spat. Then something in his face changed, and Gunnhild followed his gaze to his father's boat, where Thorbjorg's body lay. He twisted away from Olaf and said her name with such sadness that Gunnhild realized at once what the nature of his relationship with the witch must have been—and then he turned back to Eirik and Gunnhild with newly kindled rage. "You will *pay*."

Olaf grabbed his son's shoulder. "That's enough. It's over." But the look in his eyes said, *For now.*

Gunnhild raised her chin in a challenge. *Do your worst.*

"Come," Eirik said when his brother and nephew had gone. "Let's find Arinbjorn. We owe him our thanks."

Gunnhild followed him to where Arinbjorn, Svein, and Thorolf were disembarking from Arinbjorn's lead ship, all of them dirty and bloodied and grinning. Seeing Eirik covered in blood, she'd felt only relief that he was alive; seeing them all together hit her differently. She'd known that these men were capable of breathtaking amounts of violence, but it was jarring to be presented with the evidence firsthand. Everything Thorolf had told her in the tent in Finnmark suddenly made sense.

"That *leap*, Arinbjorn," Svein was saying. "Gods, I'm going to write a poem about that moment. The most incredible thing I've ever seen. You just—hopped up on the gunnel like a rabbit, and just—"

The three of them stopped and turned when they saw Eirik standing there.

"Better late than never, I suppose," said Eirik to his foster brother, but he was smiling as he stepped forward and pulled the other man into a short embrace.

"We would've never made it if not for Oddny," Arinbjorn said, turning to Gunnhild. "She cleared the fog and summoned a wind. That's how we got through. You didn't tell us she was a witch!"

Gunnhild was awestruck. That Oddny had traveled down to the void was one thing, but the rest was news to her. "She really did all that?"

"So I wasn't imagining it," Eirik said. "She *was* a hawk, wasn't she?"

Runfrid, who had finally found them in the crowd, came up behind them and said, "Eirik! Good to see you alive. Get out of my way," and no sooner had he stepped aside than she threw her arms around Arinbjorn.

Eirik turned to Svein, and a look passed between them before they clasped forearms. When they parted, Gunnhild nodded to the skald, who nodded back, and then she and Eirik turned their attention to Thorolf.

"I thought you said you weren't coming back," Eirik said with careful formality. "After you'd dropped off the sailcloth from your father and hurried back to your ship."

Gunnhild gave him a sidelong look. From what she'd observed on the day they returned from Vestfold, she'd thought he and Thorolf had reconciled. But then she noticed that Thorolf's arm ring was gone and wondered if that had something to do with her husband's guarded tone.

"I only hurried because I'd left my brother on board," Thorolf replied in kind. "Then I went to Fjordane to talk to Arinbjorn about marrying his cousin in Sogn, like I'd told you."

"Are we ever going to get to meet this brother of yours?" Eirik asked.

"I'd rather you didn't," said Thorolf, somewhat sheepishly. "He, ah . . . he takes after our father. But . . ." He looked to Eirik, then to Gunnhild, then back to the king. "You were in danger. How could I stay behind?"

Eirik shifted, and Gunnhild wrung her hands. Where moments ago she'd been victorious, now her heart was dampened by guilt. *I never apologized to him.*

When she stepped forward, he drew a deep breath as if bracing himself, but otherwise didn't move.

"I should have been better to you, Thorolf Skallagrimsson," she said. "I'm sorry. I wish to be known as someone who's good to her friends and terrible to her enemies, and my friendship is yours without question, should you desire it."

"Gunnhild speaks for both of us," said Eirik. "Whatever you decide to do now, know that you're always welcome in our company."

Thorolf looked at them. And much like what she'd felt when she had first kissed Eirik—as though she could feel the Norns spinning their fates together, as though her very fingertips were skimming the twisted thread—what Gunnhild felt now, what hung there unspoken in the space between the three of them in that moment, was also a brush with destiny.

But with it came a keen sense of foreboding, as though they were toeing too close to something better left alone, as though one too many flicks of the spindle would cause the thread binding them together to snap.

"You have my thanks," Thorolf said at last, too politely. "I'm leaving for Sogn in the morning. I'll see how things stand after I'm wed."

When he took his leave, neither Eirik nor Gunnhild followed; they stood there for a long moment, staring in the direction he'd gone, until Gunnhild said, "I'm going to find Oddny and Signy."

Eirik shook his head as if rousing himself from a trance. "Your brothers found Signy?"

"Yes, but I mean to hear the full story, and see my sisters settled in. You heard Arinbjorn—Oddny saved my life. We owe both her and Halldor our thanks. If you lift his outlawry, Oddny might even stay—"

"Gunnsa." He leaned in and lowered his voice despite the noise around them. "Halldor can't stay here. I can't declare his outlawry lifted without revealing that he's still alive."

"So? He *is* alive, which means that you didn't kill him in the duel like Olaf said, which proves Olaf is a liar. You could clear your name."

"Yes . . ." Eirik chewed this over, then shook his head. "I could, but it would be at Halldor's expense. Olaf could always deny accountability by saying he fell victim to rumor—he wasn't *there* for the duel, after all. Meanwhile, I lied to my father's face about not knowing Halldor, which would only lend Olaf credibility—and, worse, if people knew Halldor was alive, his fate would be my brother's to decide."

She blinked. "Am I missing something? What can he do to Halldor? He's a free man."

Eirik looked at her for a beat too long. "And anyway, even if Halldor has really let go of his grudge—how can things go back to the way they were between us? How can I know he's truly given up on revenge? His honor dictates that the matter isn't settled. He may feel pressured to take up arms against me again one day."

"Then settle it another way," Gunnhild said. "Compensate him. Give him the silver that Olaf refused. Have Hrolf there to mediate and name witnesses." Her eyes strayed to Thorbjorg's body, now cradled in Tryggvi's arms. "And for that matter, find someone to compensate for Rognvald as well—one of Snaefrid's other sons, perhaps? Thorbjorg was foolish, but she wasn't wrong. She was only trying to avenge her mentor. She did exactly as I would have done. What I *did* do."

"I'll think on it." He rubbed his jaw, then laid a hand on her shoulder. "Now go to Oddny."

37

A SMALL LEAN-TO TENT had been set up in Freyja's grove, and Halldor lay low there the night after the battle. After Oddny brewed her tea to combat the stabbing pain in her womb and made Halldor another for his knee, she and Gunnhild tended to the injured Hordalanders as best they could before Oddny and Signy returned to the tent at dusk. Signy was quiet, contemplative, and Oddny could tell that, despite Halldor's victory, her husband was itching to leave this place behind.

The following morning, Oddny trekked back to the estate and spent the day checking in on the wounded and providing additional treatments as necessary. Soon after she returned to the grove, Svein arrived with a small cauldron of stew and a sizable jug of ale.

"If you can't come to the feast, I'm bringing the feast to you," he said to Halldor. Then, to Oddny and Signy: "The queen wants to see you two."

So Oddny and Signy went to the main hall to join Gunnhild. They sat there drinking as Oddny told Gunnhild the tale of her first flight and Katla's death, and Gunnhild told Signy her version of the events since she'd left home. Signy listened but didn't talk, refusing to offer any details of what had happened to her between the raid and her rescue. Oddny, remembering what Halldor told her on the ship, didn't press. Gunnhild seemed to be of the same mind.

It was late in the evening and Signy had wandered off to sit next to Runfrid when Gunnhild and Oddny at last broached the topic of the duel.

"Oddny," Gunnhild began, "what happened in Vestfold . . ."

Oddny waited for her to go on. When Gunnhild's eyes met her own, there was sadness in them. Regret. But also steel.

"I'm sorry that what I did hurt you. I truly am. From the bottom of my heart. But I'm not sorry I did it. I'm not sorry I saved Eirik over Halldor. I would do it again. And if that means that our friendship is over, then I'll have to live with it."

"And I'm not sorry that I stopped the duel and told everyone you cheated," Oddny said. "Even though I knew it would hurt you—I couldn't let him die, Gunna. I love him, and you knew it."

Gunnhild shifted on her bench. "He can't stay, Oddny."

"I know. And we don't intend to."

"You don't?"

Oddny shook her head. "I'll not stay anywhere he's not welcome."

"It's not that he isn't welcome. It's that it's not safe," Gunnhild said. "Eirik won't tell me why. He says it's because they may end up feeling pressured to duel again, but I can't help but feel it's something else." She looked to Oddny as if expecting an answer, but Oddny offered none.

"Eirik means to compensate him for his father's death and call the matter settled," said Gunnhild when she didn't reply. "He offered as much to Olaf a long time ago, and Olaf refused. And *you*, Oddny—you saved my life. And you used witchcraft to do it! How can I ever thank you enough?"

"As far as I'm concerned, you don't need to. You saved Signy. And as for the witchcraft, I had no idea what I was doing," Oddny admitted. "I only remembered what you'd told me and did what I'd seen you do. I can't believe it worked."

"Oddny. Do you understand how much natural talent it takes to perform something like that with no training? Stay with me," Gunnhild said, setting her cup aside and taking Oddny's hands. "I'll teach you everything I know, and we'll learn the rest together. We'll find a way to protect Halldor. We'll work this out."

Oddny looked into her eyes and considered this. But in her heart, she knew her answer.

"I don't want to be a sorceress, Gunna. I did what I did out of sheer desperation, and I have no wish to do it again. And no matter how things stand with our husbands, you're my dearest friend. I'll always love you. But I don't know if I can completely trust you anymore, and you have reason to worry the same about me."

Gunnhild winced. "I understand. Listen—you were right when you said that saving Signy wasn't the only reason I agreed to marry Eirik. I did want to prove my mother wrong. To be important. I didn't expect to fall in love with him—but it happened, and I can't change that any more than you can change your feelings for Halldor."

"Still—I was too harsh on you in Vestfold," Oddny said. "In my heart I knew I'd gone too far, but it was only after I learned that you'd sent your brothers to rescue Signy that I could admit that to myself."

Gunnhild slid her hands away and rested both on her knees, and looked down at the scars on her open palms.

"You *were* right, though. It's just like Heid's prophecy—'One of you clouds the futures of the others. For better or worse, your fates are intertwined.' I always knew it was me. I'm sorry."

Oddny said nothing.

Across the hall, Signy sat talking with Runfrid and Arinbjorn, smiling in a way Oddny hadn't seen since they'd reunited. Though Signy had stayed in the tent the previous night, she hadn't slept well, and had woken Oddny at dawn to say she was going to meet Runfrid at the armory. After breakfast, as Oddny had walked to the main hall to care for her patients, she'd seen Signy leaning on the fence of the practice field.

Even from a distance, Oddny had noticed the hunger in her sister's eyes as she and Runfrid watched Arinbjorn and Svein spar with spears, Signy's hand gripping the hilt of her bone-handled knife. As Oddny had come up behind them, she'd heard Runfrid say, "You have to start with something smaller than a sword. I'd be surprised if you could even lift the one you gave to Halldor."

"How much smaller?" Signy had asked warily. "It has to be big enough to kill a man."

Runfrid had turned, and Oddny had seen her grin in profile. "You know, if you stick around, we could have a lot of fun together, Signy Ketilsdottir."

Oddny had stopped, stiffened, then continued on, leaving the two women standing by the fence. Signy had joined her in the longhouse later and they'd sat together in silence as Oddny did her work, but even then, Oddny had been able to tell that her sister's mind was elsewhere.

Gunnhild had followed her gaze, and her voice snapped Oddny out of her reverie: "It was our love for her that kept us bound—but now she's safe, and you and I are parting. What does that mean for Signy?"

Oddny felt a twinge of fear. Before today it hadn't occurred to her that her sister might choose to stay with Gunnhild instead of coming with her, wherever she was headed next. She'd thought it was a given that they'd remain together, but now she wasn't entirely sure.

"I suppose that's up to her," Oddny said.

THE SUN HAD BARELY risen the next morning when Oddny and Halldor arrived at the docks, but a small crowd awaited them.

Gunnhild had gifted Oddny the small ship her brothers had taken to find Signy, a small vessel with a yellow sail. It needed a minimum of six to crew it, and along with the captain and steersman, a few of the freed thralls had volunteered to accompany them despite not knowing where they were going—some in hopes of seeing home again one day, others eager to leave Norway as soon as possible. Oddny couldn't blame them.

Gunnhild, Signy, and Ulla stood near the dock. Eirik, Arinbjorn, and Runfrid were saying their farewells to Svein, who stood there with his lyre slung over his shoulder and his ship box under his arm.

"You're coming with us?" Oddny asked Svein in surprise when he came over to them.

"I mean to, if you'll have me," the skald replied. "Eirik and I have an understanding, but that doesn't mean I wish to rejoin his hird. I don't know where I'm going next any more than you two do, but it makes sense for us to stick together, yes?"

"We're going to Birka to pick up Steinvor," Oddny said. "But after that, who knows?"

Halldor said, "But we'd be honored to have you," and Svein boarded the ship.

Eirik came over to Halldor next, and the two men sized each other up just as they had on the practice field after their first match. Oddny had the distinct impression that they were going to talk about more than just the compensation Gunnhild had mentioned during the feast the night before, so she gave her husband's hand a squeeze and made to move away—but not before meeting Eirik's eyes for the briefest of moments and giving him a solemn nod, which he returned before turning back to Halldor.

Leaving them to their discussion, Oddny said farewell to Arinbjorn—who gave her a quick hug and a conspiratorial smile—and then moved to where Signy, Gunnhild, and Ulla stood, now joined by Runfrid.

"Are you ready to go?" Oddny asked Signy, fearing the answer.

Signy's throat worked, but no words came out. She reached up to adjust the pink silk scarf covering her hair. "I—I love you both so much. I never want to be parted from you again. But I . . ." She looked down at her hands, curled them into fists. "How am I supposed to choose between you after what you've done for me?"

"It's your decision," Oddny said, more calmly than she felt.

Signy raised her head to meet her sister's eyes. "I'm so proud of you, Oddny. Of how far you've come. Of everything you've done. Look at you. What would Mother say if she could see you now?"

It hadn't been intended as a barb, and Oddny knew it, but it still smarted.

"I think she'd be glad we're both alive," Oddny said. "And I don't think she'd be disappointed. You were right—everything you said that day. I did think I was special because I was trying to be everything Mother told us a woman should be. And I did feel threatened by you, because if you succeeded in breaking the mold, it would mean that Mother was wrong and I wasn't special at all. It took all of this happening for me to see the truth of things."

"And what truth is that?" Signy asked, searching her face, taking her hand.

Oddny thought, but it wasn't until she looked at Gunnhild that the words finally came to her: Gunnhild, who had appeared at Oddny's darkest time and offered her support, who had kept alive her hope that Signy would one day be found. Gunnhild, who had done her best to bring Signy home even after she and Oddny had gone their separate ways. Gunnhild, who was as determined to make her enemies pay as she was to keep her loved ones safe.

Gunnhild, indomitable.

"What truth is that, Oddny?" Signy prompted.

Oddny reached for Gunnhild's hand. The queen stepped forward and took it, along with Signy's other hand when it was offered.

And Oddny looked at them and said, echoing her sister's words from what felt like a lifetime before, "That a woman need not be defined by her men. That she can stand for herself and make her own way."

Signy began to cry, and freed her hands to wipe her tears with her sleeves. Gunnhild smiled, thin lipped, as though trying to hold her own tears back.

"That was well-spoken," Ulla said, beaming, and beside her, Runfrid grinned.

Signy shut her eyes and sniffed. When she opened them and looked at Oddny, it was with such great sadness that Oddny knew at once which way her mind had landed. Oddny looked to Halldor—who'd wrapped up his conversation with Eirik and was saying goodbye to Arinbjorn, promising him that rematch—and saw him smile in a way that made her heart light up. And she knew in that moment that whatever her sister's decision might be, Oddny was going with Halldor no matter what. And if that meant their paths would diverge, then so be it.

She turned back to Signy and said, "You've decided, haven't you?"

"Yes. I'm staying with Gunnhild," Signy said. "I want to join the hird, like Runfrid. Arinbjorn's already said he'll teach me to fight. And I want to learn. I've always wanted to, but no one ever believed I could, so I gave up even trying. But that doesn't matter. I believe I can, and I will."

"Then you'll need this," Halldor said from behind Oddny, proffering Ketil's sword.

Signy looked at it in surprise. "But I gave it to you."

"And I'm giving it back."

"It could be years before I know how to use it properly—"

"And you will. Make your father proud, Signy Ketilsdottir."

Signy hesitated briefly, took the sword, and then leapt forward to give him a hug, which Halldor returned. When they'd broken apart, Runfrid embraced him next, and he exchanged nods with Gunnhild and Ulla before heading to the ship. Oddny and Gunnhild turned back to Signy, who was taking off her belt to return the sword to its proper place.

"Are you certain about this?" Oddny asked Signy. "You've always wanted to go on adventures—"

"I did," her sister agreed. "Maybe once I can fight, once I know I can defend myself, I'll wish to explore the world, like you. But for now"— her voice was small, though her eyes blazed—"I only want to feel safe again."

Oddny understood. Though a future with Eirik and Gunnhild's retinue surely wouldn't be without peril, it would grant Signy a security Oddny couldn't promise her.

"You're truly going to stay?" Gunnhild looked more startled than pleased, and Oddny swiped a hand across her eyes, already feeling her sister's loss again like a gaping hole in her chest. But knowing Signy was alive and pursuing the destiny of her choosing would have to be enough. At least she and Gunnhild would have each other; Oddny would make her own future.

She looked to the ship, to Halldor. When he caught Oddny's eye, he smiled again, and she smiled back.

And what a future it will be.

"Father is already proud of you." Oddny turned back to Signy and nodded at the sword. "And when you see him in Valhalla a long time from now, he'll tell you so."

"Oddny," Svein called. "Captain says we've a fair wind. We should take advantage of it."

Runfrid moved forward to embrace her. "It was an honor to know you, Oddny Ketilsdottir. You will be so missed."

"Goodbye, Oddny. I hope we meet again one day." Ulla followed suit, then beckoned for Runfrid to step back with her. "We'll give you a moment."

And then it was Oddny and Signy and Gunnhild.

Signy hugged Oddny first, and Oddny held on tight, unwilling to let go, knowing that she must. Their time grew short.

"This isn't goodbye, you know," Signy whispered. "Whenever you two settle down somewhere, send word, and I'll come bother you if I can."

"I look forward to that day more than you know." Oddny released her and turned to Gunnhild. The queen shifted on her feet, mouth twitching. She was trying to put on a show of remaining calm, but Oddny knew her better than that.

"Oddny, I know I've said this already, but I'm—," she began, but she stopped when Oddny threw her arms around her and said, "I know. I'm sorry, too."

When they parted, Gunnhild's eyes were alight with mischief as she reached into her bag and pulled out two items, the sight of which made Signy gasp and stifle a sob.

"Oh, you can't be serious," Oddny said with an incredulous laugh.

"I have never been more serious." Gunnhild handed Oddny the blowing horn, its twin in her other hand. "Whenever I decide to blow it, you have until you hit the mouth of the fjord to do the same."

"Those weren't the rules," Signy protested. "It was the other way around."

"Well, I'm the queen, so I make the rules now," Gunnhild said, and turned back to Oddny with a wicked grin. "And you'd better be quick if you want to win."

AS THEY STOOD AT the stern and watched the coast of Hordaland recede into the distance, Halldor came up behind Oddny and put his arms around her. This farewell was bittersweet. She was moving forward, but she was also leaving part of her heart behind—but not for good.

I'll see them again, someday soon, she hoped. *And we'll have so much to talk about when I do.*

"Do you think Steinvor will even want to come with us?" she asked Halldor. "She's so small, and Birka is the only home she's ever known."

"She's tough. She'll be running circles around us in no time. Besides, it wouldn't be a bad thing, growing up on a ship. Just look how Runfrid turned out," he said. "But where should we go after Birka? Any ideas?"

"We can go anywhere we want. People always need healers," Oddny replied without tearing her eyes away from the verdant mountain slopes, the cluster of buildings nestled between them, and the people standing on the docks, growing smaller and smaller each moment.

Halldor said softly, "You know, I wouldn't have blamed you for staying with them."

"Are you mad?" Oddny whirled on him. "To even have a choice in this matter is more than I ever could have dreamed when I was growing up. I love you, and I love the life we're going to build together. Every day will be a new adventure."

"But you never wanted adventure. Your home is—"

She reached up and took his face in her hands. "We're free, Halldor. And we're alive, and we're together. That's all that matters. I wouldn't trade it for anything in all the Nine Worlds. My home is right here. With you."

He hugged her tightly, seeming at a loss for words, and then a horn sounded three times from the docks.

Oddny moved from her husband's embrace and blew three matching bursts, smiling through her tears. Two for hello, three for goodbye. She looked forward to the day when she would say hello to her sisters again.

But she would savor every moment of her beautiful, impossible life until then.

38

GUNNHILD LOWERED THE HORN and let it dangle from its cord over her shoulder, her other hand tightly clasping Signy's. They stood there and watched as the ship's yellow sail grew smaller in the distance.

"Thank you, Signy," she said at length. "For staying."

"Don't thank me yet," Signy replied lightly. "We haven't seen each other for half our lives. How do you know I'm not going to be terribly annoying? Besides, I mean, you married the most hated man in Norway. It seems to me you'll need all the help you can get."

"You have no idea how much I missed you," Gunnhild said with feeling.

Signy's smile remained in place, but her green eyes lost a bit of their sparkle. Gunnhild squeezed her hand tighter. For all that Signy seemed much like her old self, some wounds could not be treated with Gunnhild's spells or Oddny's tinctures. She couldn't begin to fathom what Signy had been through. Just because she'd been rescued didn't mean she'd healed. She had a long journey ahead of her, and Gunnhild intended to be there for her every step of the way.

"Signy!" Runfrid shouted, for she, Arinbjorn, and Ulla were heading back up the hill. "Come! We're going to go bother Hrafnhild for breakfast!"

"But we're not going to bother her *too* much. She's injured," said Ulla fretfully.

"Oh, Oddny patched her up well enough to boil some eggs," said Arinbjorn, and then they were out of earshot.

Signy looked to Gunnhild.

"Go," said Gunnhild, releasing her hand. "I'll see you later, trouble-maker."

Signy grinned at the old nickname and offered one of her own: "I'll see *you* later, O Future Most Powerful Woman in All of Norway." She laughed as she turned to go. "Ha! Who's the seeress now?"

Gunnhild smiled at that, but sobered when Eirik moved in beside her a few moments later. The two of them turned just in time to see Oddny's ship reach the open sea. The wind was carrying her sworn sister away, but one day it would carry her back. And maybe, by then, the two of them would have healed enough to trust each other again.

The king and queen stood there in silence, looking out over the water. At length Eirik said, "If you're well enough, I'd like to spend the rest of the summer making the royal progress, and Bard of Atloy has been asking me to visit for Winternights for a long time. He gave us the polar bear pelt for our wedding, and loyalty should always be rewarded." He grimaced. "Judging by the size of Olaf's fleet, it seems to be in short supply."

Gunnhild agreed. Thorbjorg might be gone, but their troubles were far from over—she'd seen it in Olaf's eyes, and in Tryggvi's. And that wasn't to mention Halfdan and the host of other Haraldssons who would wait to oppose Eirik until his father was in the ground or otherwise unable to stop them. News of the battle at Alreksstadir would travel just as news of the duel had, and lines would be drawn as the people of this young country of Norway chose sides. She was well aware that not all would choose theirs.

She took his hand. "Then we'll have to earn it back. Show them who we really are. We're only getting started. Now come. Let's save our worries for tomorrow."

"This peace may be brief," Eirik said as she led him up the hill.

"Then let's enjoy it while it lasts," Gunnhild replied. This had been a victory, one worthy of committing to the tapestry Queen Gyda had tasked her with creating, but she knew that there would be many more battles ahead for them.

"When it's over ... when you've left nothing but blood and terror in your wake ... all the worlds ... will know your greatness ..."

In due course they would make their enemies a sacrifice to the gods, and when their own time came, Odin and Freyja would welcome them into their halls with honor. Eirik and Gunnhild, with their loyal friends at their sides, would continue to fight until that day arrived.

But today they had each other, and the future could wait.

AUTHOR'S NOTE

IN HIS 2020 BOOK *Children of Ash and Elm*, Viking Age scholar Neil Price says that "History is . . . sometimes akin to a sort of speculative fiction of the past." I took this idea further by making *The Weaver and the Witch Queen* a work of historical fantasy instead of historical fiction, but there are a few things I want to mention in regard to what historians know versus what I filled in or created to fit my narrative.

Although the medieval Icelandic sagas that inspired this novel do a good job of making us feel like they are "real" history, minus some amusing and unbelievable supernatural occurrences, they're largely fictional accounts, though many of the characters who feature in them probably did exist. These sagas, and most other literary sources we have on the Viking Age, were written down hundreds of years after the Viking Age by the Christian descendants of the people who lived the tales, and are probably a more accurate reflection of the values and biases of the time in which they were written than of the time during which they are supposed to have taken place.

With that said, many sources detail the life of Gunnhild, Mother of Kings, and her depictions are largely negative and often contradictory. The one thing that most agree on is that she was a powerful and influential woman in her time, for better or worse. Although it's generally agreed that Gunnhild was most likely a Danish princess, for the purposes of this story I chose to follow the origin stories that describe Gunnhild as a Halogalander and a sorceress.

Since many of the sources are often in direct conflict with one another, I had to be careful in choosing which ones I would draw from. I ended up relying most heavily on two medieval Icelandic works, *Egil's Saga* and Snorri Sturluson's *Heimskringla*, although these two often contradict each other, too. However, they both corroborate the same origin story for Gunnhild, and I personally enjoy her depiction in *Egil's Saga* as the lifelong antagonist to the title character, Thorolf's brother Egil, who is mentioned in this novel (though not by name). *Heimskringla* tends to jump around in time, making it difficult to establish a chronology. Likewise, *Egil's Saga* fudges the dates of certain historical events attested more reliably elsewhere, and both diverge from mainland sources in a variety of ways, tweaking events to fit the story the author was trying to tell. I did much the same in the writing of this book. For example, I made Gunnhild's magic teacher an old woman named Heid, not the "Finnish wizards" (that is, Sámi noaidi) from *Heimskringla*. In *Heimskringla's* version of the tale, the two wizards both wish to marry her, so Gunnhild conspires to kill them with the assistance of the Norsemen who come to "rescue" her. Archaeological evidence indicates that cultural exchange and cooperation between the Sámi and the Norse peoples during this time were more prevalent than later sources like *Heimskringla* would have us believe, and some of the changes I made to the story are meant to reflect this.

From the archaeological evidence we have, it is impossible to say for certain whether Vikings were tattooed. Only the writings of Ahmad ibn Fadlan, a tenth-century travel writer from Baghdad, may have described tattoos in encounters with Rus (eastern Vikings) along the Volga River during the Viking Age. Thus, the tattoos described in this novel, along with the hairstyles, don't have a completely solid basis in history, although evidence of tattooing culture all around Europe dating back thousands of years means tattooing was not impossible among the Vikings.

The magic system in this novel, while inspired by historical sources, is largely from my own imagination. As such, I chose not to use Old Norse terms like *seiðr* and *völva/völur* to describe pre-Christian Nordic magic and its practitioners, nor terms like *goði* to refer to spiritual leaders, as they evoke a specificity I wished to avoid—both out of respect for modern-day pagans and for worry of spreading misinformation. As such, I chose to replace these words with terms like "magic," "witchcraft," "seeress," "witch," and "sorceress," which you will see used in the English translations of the sagas (except for *goði*, which also came to mean something like "chieftain" in the Icelandic Commonwealth era). Likewise, the mentions of the noaidi and their magic (*noaidevuohta*) were inspired by research and are not meant to reflect Sámi spirituality today.

The details of what the Winternights feast days entailed are almost entirely made-up except for the animal sacrifice (which is one of the most well-documented aspects of pagan rituals in the North) and the ritual sprinkling of blood, as well as the games, drinking, and the fact that weddings commonly occurred in tandem with this festival. The details of Eirik and Gunnhild's wedding and the feast that followed are also imagined.

The duck-patterned silk that Gunnhild sews into her dress is a silly little detail that has a historical basis. Fragments of such a silk were found in the Oseberg ship burial, which predates this novel by roughly a hundred years, making Gunnhild's silk an heirloom by the time it's in her hands. Other silks have been found in Viking Age graves, and they, along with a number of grave goods that originated in far-off places, indicate the vast reach of trading networks at this time. Viking Age Scandinavians were keen sailors who had contact with many other cultures even before they entered the historical record at Lindisfarne in 793 CE. Ahmad ibn Fadlan, the writer mentioned above, is actually one of our only contemporary sources on the Vikings—and he was in fact writing at approximately the same time this novel takes place, on the other side of the Viking world.

My studies of the Viking Age from textbooks, podcasts, and museums, and through my own hands-on experiences with living history, informed much of this book. "Viking" was a job title, not a race of people. Women would often travel alongside men, especially when they were settling in other lands, but would also sometimes stay home and tend to the farm, and defend it against other Vikings if necessary. Divorce was not taboo and could be initiated by either the husband or the wife. Textile work, for which women were largely responsible, was not treated as unimportant; everyone needs clothing, and the Vikings would not have gotten far without sails for their ships. And while I do believe Viking warrior women existed and should be celebrated, I also believe a woman does not have to pick up a weapon and engage in combat in order to have a story worth telling. The stubborn, clever, resourceful women of the Icelandic sagas are proof enough of this, even if their choices are sometimes questionable.

Finally, although separate gender roles are likely to have existed in the Viking Age, this isn't to say that people never crossed or blurred the boundaries between these spheres. Queerness is not a new phenomenon, and Halldor's experience as depicted in this novel is just one way that someone we would interpret as transgender could have lived. We'll never know how many people we'd recognize today as LGBTQIA+ have been omitted from history, but we have always been here, and we always will be.

INFORMATION ON FURTHER READING is available on my website. Any mistakes are my own.

APPENDIX

———◇———

I chose to anglicize all Old Norse (ON) names of people and places in this novel by removing special characters (*á, ö,* etc.) and rendering the letters *þ* and *ð* as *th* and *d,* respectively. Old Norse is an inflected language, which means that the spelling of a word can change depending on how it's used in a sentence, so I removed the case endings as well, as English does not use them. Therefore, "Eiríkr" becomes "Eirik," "Þórólfr" becomes "Thorolf," "Gunnhildr" becomes "Gunnhild," and so on. This also reflects how Old Norse names appear in English in the Penguin Classics editions of *The Sagas of Icelanders.* As in modern Icelandic, the letters *ei* together are pronounced *eyy* (as in "hey") instead of like "eye," meaning that names like Heid and Svein are pronounced *heyd* and *sveyn,* respectively (as opposed to *hide* and *svine*).

PEOPLE

Alf Ozurarson*—son of Ozur the hersir; brother of Gunnhild; twin to Eyvind

Arinbjorn Thorisson*—son of Thorir the hersir; foster brother to Eirik; close friend of Thorolf

Bjorn Haraldsson†*—son of King Harald; king of Vestfold before being murdered by Eirik; full brother of Olaf, who has sworn to avenge him; father of Gudrod

Eirik Haraldsson*—the chosen successor of his father, King Harald, and second king of Norway; later known as Eirik Blood-axe

Eyvind Ozurarson*—son of Ozur the hersir; brother of Gunnhild; twin to Alf

Gudrod Bjarnarson*—Bjorn's son; fostered by Olaf after his father is murdered by Eirik

Gunnhild Ozurardottir*—a witch; later known in history as Gunnhild, Mother of Kings

Queen Gyda*—King Harald's second wife, who oversees his estate at Alreksstadir in Hordaland; famously rejected his marriage proposal until he brought all of Norway under one rule

Hakon Haraldsson*—son of King Harald and Thora; known in history as King Hakon the Good

Halfdan Haraldsson*—son of King Harald; one of the kings of the Trondheim region

Halldor—a raider from Vestfold

Hallgrim†—a blacksmith in Vestfold who mentored Halldor

King Harald*—the first king of Norway, who united the country under one rule; father of Eirik Blood-axe, Olaf, Bjorn, Rognvald, and Halfdan, among many other children by many wives

Heid—a seeress

Hrafnhild—the head of the cooking staff at Alreksstadir

Hrolf—the Lawspeaker at the Hordaland estate; Saeunn's father

Katla—a witch in the employ of King Halfdan

Ketil†—a farmer in Halogaland; close friend of Gunnhild's father, Ozur

Kolfinna—the leader of a crew of raiders from Svealand

Juoksa—a Sámi noaidi (practitioner of magic) in Finnmark; friend of Heid and Gunnhild

Mielat—Juoksa's apprentice; friend of Heid and Gunnhild

Oddny Ketilsdottir—a farm girl from Halogaland; Signy's sister; sworn sister to Gunnhild

Olaf Haraldsson*—son of King Harald; king of the Vestfold region after the death of his brother Bjorn at Eirik's hands

Ozur the hersir*—Gunnhild's father; a hersir in Halogaland

Rognvald Haraldsson†*—son of King Harald and Snaefrid; killed by Eirik at their father's behest for practicing witchcraft

Runfrid Asgeirsdottir—a tattooist in Eirik's hird

Saeunn—head of the textile workshop at Alreksstadir

Signy Ketilsdottir—a farm girl in Halogaland; Oddny's sister; sworn sister to Gunnhild

Snaefrid Svasadottir†*—Sámi wife of King Harald; mother of Rognvald and three other sons; said to have bewitched the king for years until her death

Solveig—Gunnhild's mother; wife of Ozur

Steinvor—Kolfinna's young daughter

Svein—a skald; one of Eirik's hirdsmen

Thorir the hersir*—a friend of King Harald; foster father to Eirik; foster brother to Skallagrim (Thorolf's father)

Thorolf Skallagrimsson*—one of Eirik's hirdsmen; an Icelander whose family's interactions with Norwegian royalty are recounted in *Egil's Saga*

Thora*—mother of Hakon, King Harald's youngest son

Thorbjorg—a witch in the employ of King Olaf

Tryggvi Olafsson*—Olaf's son; cousin and foster brother to Gudrod

Ulfrun—a servant in Ozur and Solveig's household

Ulla—a Sámi woman in the textile workshop at Alreksstadir

Vestein Ketilsson—brother of Oddny and Signy

Vigdis—head of the cooking staff on Ozur and Solveig's farm

Yrsa—wife of Ketil and mother of Oddny, Signy, and Vestein

TERMS

Among these are a few terms I chose to anglicize from Old Norse because they didn't have fitting English equivalents:

disir (ON: dísir; singular: dís)—female fate spirits that were powerful enough to warrant a yearly sacrifice (disablot/ON: dísablót), though little else is known about them

fosterage—fostering in the Viking Age was different from how we think of it now, in that people would willingly send their children to be raised by others in order to build alliances and networks, and in some cases for the children to learn trades (such as the law)

fylgja (plural: fylgjur)—a female fate spirit that appears when a person is about to die or something critical is about to occur; typically runs in family lines, especially down the matriarchal line; can sometimes appear as an animal

hersir (plural: hersar)—landholder who keeps a number of armed men and is expected to muster more when the king calls upon him to fight

---

*—denotes a quasi-historical figure
†—denotes that the figure in question is deceased by the time the main action of the novel begins

hird—a king's retinue, his sworn men and bodyguards

hnefatafl (or tafl)—a strategy board game

jarls—the chieftains who governed different areas of Norway under King Harald and his sons; commonly rendered into English as "earls"

noaidi—Sámi practitioners of magic, called *noaidevuohta*

seax—a single-edged short sword

skald—sometimes rendered as "poet" or "bard"; poetry in the Viking Age was a form of currency and could make or break one's reputation, so good skalds were highly valued, especially by kings

the warding songs (ON: vardlokkur)—songs sung by women to call the spirits and protect the person communing with them

ACKNOWLEDGMENTS

The Weaver and the Witch Queen kicked my ass many, many times over the course of two years.

Thank you to the people who got me through:

To my editor, Jessica Wade: Much like *The Witch's Heart*, this would've been a completely different book without you, and not for the better. To my first agent, Rhea Lyons, for helping to shape this book in its very earliest stages. To my current agent, Brianne Johnson, for your enthusiasm for my stories and appreciation of my boundless geekery.

To Jessica Mangicaro, Yazmine Hassan, Stephanie Felty, Elisha Katz, Gabbie Pachon, Dan Walsh, and the team at Ace/Berkley. To Adam Auerbach for another lovely cover. To Daniel Carpenter and the team at Titan Books in the UK, and to Julia Lloyd for the stunning cover for the UK edition of *Weaver*. To the publishers and translators who brought *The Witch's Heart* to readers all over the world.

To Kati Felix, H. M. Long, M. J. Kuhn, Alexis Henderson, Mariah McGuire, Stephen Pollard, and Kristin Ell, for being my earliest readers; to Shannon Mullally, my one-woman hype team; to Allen Chamberlin, Emily DeTar Birt, Candyce Beal, Mirria Martin-Tesone, Angela Rodriguez, Jessica Bladek, Sarah Gunnoe, Ryann Burke, Emma Tanskanen, and Terryl Bandy; to Casey Eade, Siobhán Clark, Joshua Gillingham, Lyra Wolf and Cat Rector; and to everyone else who's had to listen to me ramble about this book for the past two years: Thank you (and sorry).

To my friends at Dog-Eared Books in Ames, Iowa, for making this author—who debuted during a pandemic with understandably little in-person fanfare—feel so special and loved.

To Allison Epstein, Greta Kelly, J. S. Dewes, Ava Reid, Hannah F. Whitten, C. L. Clark, Shelley Parker-Chan, Jaye Viner, Elizabeth Everett, Rachel Mans McKenny, and the rest of my fellow 2021 debut authors: I am so proud of all of us and so excited to see where we go next.

To my trans sensitivity readers for your insight and guidance on my portrayal of Halldor from the very first draft; to Matthew Broberg-Moffitt, whose suggestions and enthusiasm helped shape the Sámi characters in this book; to Heba Elsherief for weighing in on Svein's and Runfrid's backstories and sharing your knowledge and experience; and to Mandy Ballard and the team at Salt & Sage Books. To Eirnin Jefford-Franks for your feedback on an earlier draft, and to Villimey Sigurbjörnsdóttir for fielding my questions on characters' nicknames. Any mistakes, inconsistencies, or insensitivities are entirely my own.

To Dr. Merrill Kaplan, in whose classrooms the spark of my passion for the Viking Age was first lit, changing the course of my life forever. To Drs. John Sexton and Andy Pfrenger from *Saga Thing*, a podcast that has kindled my love of the Icelandic sagas and kept me company during long walks and even longer road trips. To Dr. Mathias Nordvig and Daniel Farrand from *The Nordic Mythology Podcast* and the amazing guests they've hosted over the years. To all the academics who have made their work accessible—there are too many of you to list here, but I do want to thank Drs. Alexander Lykke and Rolf Thiel for personally answering some questions I had. To fellow Viking Age historical fantasy author Thilde Kold Holdt for taking the time to share your experience of sailing on a Viking ship. None of the people listed above are responsible for what I did with what I learned from them, but they have my thanks.

To Daina Faulhaber, for my author photo, and for everything else. To Brittany Clay and Henry Utley; to Scot and Maggie King; and to my Viking Age living history family across the Midwestern U.S. and beyond.

To Montana, Madison, and the fam, for being my anchor during some of the most challenging years of my life. To my family, for your unwavering support. To the booksellers, librarians, podcasters, reviewers, and readers who spread the word about *The Witch's Heart*. Last, but certainly not least: Thank *you*, for reading. It truly does mean the world.

THE WEAVER AND THE WITCH QUEEN

GENEVIEVE GORNICHEC

DISCUSSION QUESTIONS

1. How much did you know about the Vikings when you started this book? Did you learn anything that surprised you?

2. In the historical sources she appears in, Gunnhild is depicted as ruthless, power hungry, and scheming. In what ways do you think the author sought to subvert those depictions, and in what ways does the Gunnhild from the book stay true to them?

3. How do Oddny's and Gunnhild's relationships with their mothers influence the decisions they make in their own lives?

4. In what ways does Oddny question and challenge the views she grew up with?

5. Who was your favorite character in the book? Who was your least favorite?

6. Were you surprised that Gunnhild ended up with Eirik and that Oddny ended up with Halldor? How do the relationship dynamics in both couples compare?

7. How do Oddny and Gunnhild make sure they have agency despite living in a strongly patriarchal society? How do the other women in the book do the same?

8. Did your opinion of Halldor change after you discovered his true relationship to Eirik? Do you think his actions were justified?

9. If you had to cast this book as a movie or a TV series, who would you choose for the main roles?

10. Eirik and the other warriors seem to be bound by a strict honor code. Even though they wield most of the power in their society, do you think they are constrained by it as well?

11. How does the relationship between Oddny and Gunnhild change over the course of the book (or from childhood to adulthood)? What do you think Gunnhild's relationship with Signy will look like moving forward?

Genevieve Gornichec earned her degree in history from the Ohio State University, where her study of Norse myths and Icelandic sagas became her writing inspiration. Her national bestselling debut novel, *The Witch's Heart*, has been translated into more than ten languages. She lives in Cleveland, Ohio. *The Weaver and the Witch Queen* is her second novel.

VISIT GENEVIEVE GORNICHEC ONLINE

GenevieveGornichec.com

🐦 GenGornichec

𝐟 GenGornichec

📷 GenGornichec